Walter Moers

The 13½ Lives
of Captain Bluebear

Being the demibiography of a seagoing bear,
with numerous illustrations
and excerpts from the
**'Encyclopedia of the Marvels, Life Forms
and Other Phenomena of Zamonia and its Environs'**
by Professor Abdullah Nightingale

Translated by
JOHN BROWNJOHN

THE OVERLOOK PRESS
Woodstock & New York

First published in the United States in 2005 by
The Overlook Press, Peter Mayer Publishers, Inc.
Woodstock & New York

WOODSTOCK:
One Overlook Drive
Woodstock, NY 12498
www.overlookpress.com
[for individual orders, bulk and special sales, contact our Woodstock office]

NEW YORK:
141 Wooster Street
New York, NY 10012

Cataloging-in-Publication Data is available from the Library of Congress

Manufactured in the United States of America
ISBN 1-58567-724-8
1 3 5 7 9 8 6 4 2

**'Life is too precious
to be left to chance.'**

Deus X. Machina

Foreword

A bluebear has twenty-seven lives. I shall recount thirteen-and-a-half of them in this book but keep quiet about the rest. A bear must have his secrets, after all; they make him seem attractive and mysterious.

People often ask me what it was like in the old days. My answer: In the old days there was a lot more of everything. Yes, there used to be mysterious islands, kingdoms and whole continents that no longer exist. They lie beneath the waves of the eternal ocean, for the waters are slowly but inexorably rising higher and higher, and one day our planet will be entirely submerged. That is why I now live in a seaworthy ship perched on a cliff high above sea level. I propose to tell you about the aforesaid submerged islands and countries and the creatures and marvels that sank below the waves with them.

I should be lying (and everyone knows I'm not a liar by nature) if I claimed that my first thirteen-and-a-half lives were uneventful. **What about the Minipirates? What about the Hobgoblins, the Spiderwitch, the Babbling Billows, the Troglotroll, the Mountain Maggot? What about the Alpine Imp, the headless Bollogg, the Bolloggless head, the nomadic Muggs, the Captive Mirage, the Yetis and Bluddums, the Eternal Tornado, the Rickshaw Demons? What about the Venomous Vampires, the Gelatine Prince from the 2364th Dimension, the Professor with Seven Brains, the Demerara Desert, Knio the Barbaric Hog, the Wolperting Whelps, the Cogitating Quicksand, the Noontide Ghouls, the Infurno, the Ship with a Thousand Funnels? What about Gourmet Island, Tornado City, the Sewer Dragon, the Duel of Lies, dimensional hiatuses, Voltigorkian Vibrobassists, rampaging Mountain Dwarfs? What about the Invisibles, the Norselanders, the Venetian Midgets, the Midgard Serpent, the revolting Kackertratts, the Valley of Discarded Ideas, the Witthogs,** the Big-Footed Bertts, the Humongous Mountains? What about Ear-spoonlets, Time-Snails, Diabolic Elves, Mandragors, Olfactils, the Upper Jurassic Current, the smell of Genff? Mine is a tale of mortal danger and eternal love, of hair's-breadth, last-minute escapes ... But I mustn't get ahead of myself!

Nostalgia overcomes me when I recall those days, but the clock of life cannot be turned back. This, although regrettable, is only fair.

Winter is following autumn in its time-honoured way. The sun, cold as the moon, is sinking into the icy grey sea below my cliff, and the wind smells of snow. But there's something else in the air as well: the scent of bonfires burning in the distance. It carries a hint of cinnamon, a whiff of adventure! I always used to follow that scent, but today I've something more important to do. My memoirs must be preserved for posterity. Frost-sprites are insinuating their clammy fingers between the floorboards of my cabin and groping for my feet. Invisible ice-witches are painting frost flowers on the windows. Hardly my favourite season of the year, but the ideal time to brew a pot of hot cocoa (with a wee dash of rum in it), fill thirteen-and-a-half pipes with tobacco, make thirteen-and-a-half slices of bread and jam, sharpen thirteen-and-a-half pencils, and begin to record my first thirteen-and-a-half lives. A bold and arduous undertaking of epic dimensions, I fear. For, as I already said, there was a lot more of everything in the old days – more adventures, too, of course.

Captain Bluebear

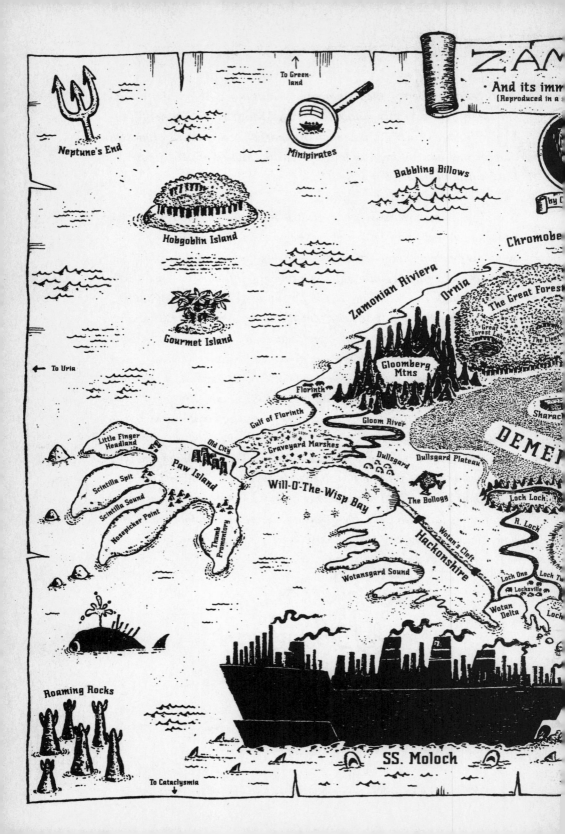

1.

My Life
as
a Minipirate

People usually start life by being born. Not me, though. That's to say, I don't know how I came into the world. Purely theoretically, I could have emerged from the foam on the crest of a wave or developed inside a seashell, like a pearl. Then again, I might have fallen from the sky like a shooting star.

The only certainty is that I was a foundling abandoned in the middle of the ocean. My earliest memory is of being afloat in rough seas, naked and alone in a walnut shell, for at first I was very, very small.

I also remember a sound – a very big sound. When you're little you tend to overestimate the size of things, but I now know that it really was the biggest sound in the world.

Its source was the loudest, most monstrous and dangerous whirlpool anywhere in the seven seas. I had no idea, of course, that my little nutshell was bobbing towards the dreaded Malmstrom. To me it was just a gigantic gurgling sound. I probably thought (if I 'thought' at all at that stage) that it was the most natural thing in the world to lie naked in a nutshell and drift across the open sea towards the origin of that deafening roar.

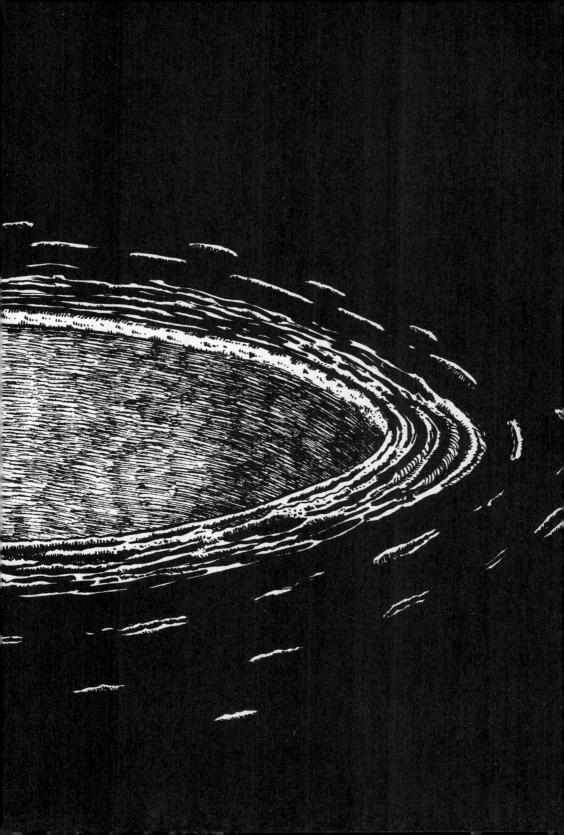

The sound grew louder and louder and the nutshell bobbed more and more violently, but I was equally unaware, of course, that I had long been in the grip of the whirlpool. My tiny boat, probably the smallest in the world, went dancing towards the roaring abyss in a miles-long spiral.

It should be borne in mind that this was just about the most hopeless predicament in which anyone at sea could find himself. Any mariner in his senses gave the Malmstrom the widest possible berth, and even if someone had come to my rescue he would have suffered the same fate: he would have been sucked down with me to the bed of the ocean, for no vessel could withstand the pull of the whirlpool.

My nutshell now began to rotate on its own axis, dancing to perdition in waltz time as it descended into the ocean's gurgling maw. As for me, I merely watched the stars spinning around over-head and listened entranced to the Malmstrom, quite free from any forebodings.

And that was when I first heard one of the Minipirates' weird songs.

The Minipirates   The Minipirates were the masters of the Zamonian Sea. Nobody knew this, however, because they were too small to be noticed. No wave was too high, no storm too tempestuous and no whirlpool too powerful for them not to defy it. The most audacious of all seafarers, they were forever seeking opportunities to demonstrate their nautical skill, even when confronted by the most potent of natural forces. Thanks to their exceptional seamanlike abilities, they alone were capable of tackling the Malmstrom.

That was how they had ended up in the whirlpool, out of pure bravado, bawling their defiant pirate songs. The masthead lookout, carefully scanning the surface for the most favourable currents and wave-tunnels, had sighted me through his tiny telescope just as I was about to be engulfed by the Malmstrom.

I was doubly fortunate to have been found by the Minipirates, of all people, because anyone of normal size would probably have failed to spot me. They hauled me aboard, wrapped me up in oilskins, and lashed me to the mast with thick ropes – a safety measure that puzzled me exceedingly at the time. Meantime, they continued to wage their heroic battle with the elements as a matter of course, scampering up and down the masts like squirrels, hoisting and reefing sails at a rate that made me dizzy just to watch. As one man, they offset the motion of the pitching, tossing vessel by hurling themselves to port or starboard, forward or aft. They manned the pumps or vanished into the bowels of the ship and reappeared with brimming buckets, leapt through hatchways, swung to and fro on the halyards. In constant motion, they wrestled with the ship's wheel, bellowed at each other, hauled on ropes, joined forces to hoist a mainsail in double-quick time, and never for one moment forgot to sing their pirate sea shanties. I even recall that one of them persisted in scrubbing the deck throughout this pandemonium.

Deluged with spray, the ship lay over on her side, reared skywards, and was actually submerged more than once, but she didn't sink. I swallowed some seawater for the first time, and am bound to say it didn't taste too bad. We glided through wave-tunnels, rode mighty mountains of foam, were tossed high into the air and carried down into the depths. The ship was hurled to and fro, buffeted, jostled and spat on by gigantic billows, but the Minipirates were undaunted. They yelled at the sea, spat back at it, and defiantly jabbed the waves with their grappling hooks. They fanned out among the masts at lightning speed, reefed sails and unfurled them a moment later. They reacted to every quirk of the sea, every puff of wind and movement of the ship, and knew at once what had to be done next. No one gave any orders, all were of equal rank. Thanks to their joint endeavours, they finally overcame the mighty ocean while I myself, securely lashed to the mast, watched their activities with the utmost amazement.

If you're as small as a Minipirate (as small as I was, too, at the time), you live in another time dimension. Anyone who has ever tried to capture a fly in his hand will know that the tiny creature is far superior in terms of speed and agility. We operate in slow motion from the fly's point of view, so it can easily outmanoeuvre and evade us. It was the same with the Minipirates. To them, what

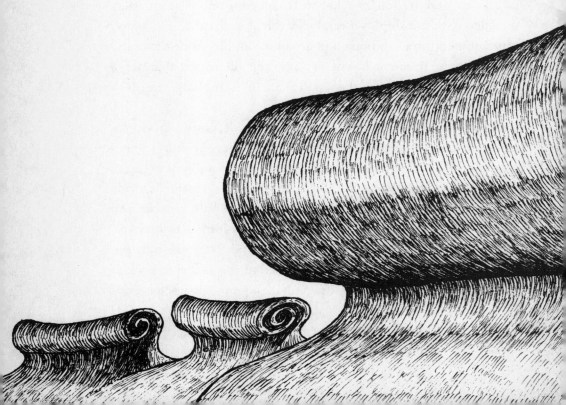

the crew of a ship of normal size would regard as a raging whirl-pool seemed a mere eddy. Every huge billow consisted of many wavelets through which they could navigate with ease. Just as a hurricane can sweep across a city and topple the tallest buildings but leave a little spider's web intact, so the monstrous whirlpool could not harm us. We were protected by our diminutive size.

So we escaped from the deadly Malmstrom. I was unaware of its true dangers, as I have said – they didn't dawn on me until much later. All I noticed was that the gurgling sound steadily faded and the Minipirates' activities became less frantic. The situation eventually eased so much that they could gather round, untie my rope, and gaze at me in wonderment.

I gazed back at them.

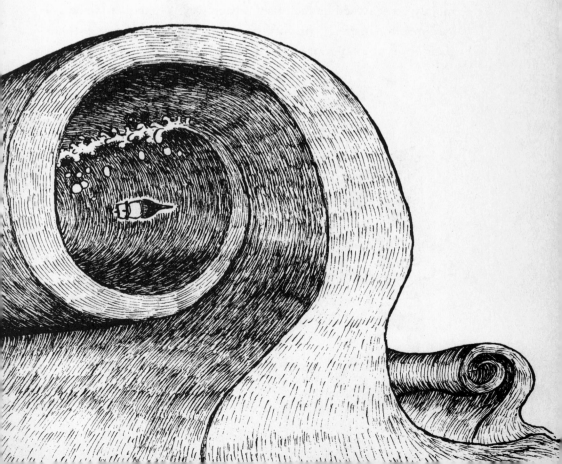

Minipirates, as their name implies, were pretty small. A Minipirate six inches tall was considered a giant by his own kind. The little creatures sailed the seas in tiny ships, ever on the lookout for a something small enough to capture. This happened very seldom – never, in fact. Truth to tell, the Minipirates had never managed to capture a single prize, not even a rowing boat, in the whole history of navigation. Sometimes, usually in desperation, they attacked bigger ships, even ocean-going giants, but their efforts passed unnoticed as a rule. The tiny buccaneers hurled their grappling hooks at the big vessels and were towed along until they gave up. Either that, or they fired their dinky little cannon, but the cannon balls always fell short and splashed harmlessly into the sea after travelling only a few yards.

Because they never captured any booty, the Minipirates lived mainly on seaweed or such fish as they were capable of tackling – sardines, for instance, or very small scampi. They didn't turn up their noses at plankton, either, if times were hard.

The Minipirates had little iron hooks instead of hands and wooden stumps instead of proper legs, nor did I ever see one without an eyepatch. At first I thought they'd been wounded during their reckless attempts to board a prize, but I later learned that they were born that way, complete with hats and moustaches.

From the
'Encyclopedia of Marvels, Life Forms
and Other Phenomena of Zamonia and its Environs'
by Professor Abdullah Nightingale

Minipirates. Despite their essential harmlessness, or possibly because of it, Minipirates affect an extremely gruff and bloodthirsty manner. They like to deliver grandiloquent speeches, preferably about successful voyages of depredation and fat prizes. The uncharitable might accuse them of a penchant for bragging. Whenever two Minipirates encounter each other [a frequent occurrence in a crowded ship], they simultaneously, with sweeping gestures and much shouting, list the merchant ships they claim to have sent to the bottom and boast of innocent seamen mercilessly keelhauled or made to walk the plank. While so doing they drink *rhumm*, a beverage compounded of seaweed juice and molasses which, although it contains no alcohol whatever, stimulates their imagination and quickly slurs their speech. Minipirates have rather weak heads.

I have often witnessed such encounters and listened to the Minipirates' grandiose rodomontades. I must, however, admit to having been influenced by their richly embroidered tales and extravagant flights of fancy. They taught me that a good white lie is often considerably more exciting than the truth. Telling one is like dressing up reality in its Sunday best.

To a Minipirate, nothing was worse than boredom. As soon as one of them grew even the slightest bit bored he betrayed such agony of mind that it wrung your heart. He would sigh and groan and shake his hook at the sky, ruffle his hair, and sometimes even tear his clothes. This only made matters worse, because he would then bemoan the rents in his outfit and accuse fate of heaping him with misfortune. Boredom being a frequent guest aboard every ship at sea, the Minipirates were forever moaning and groaning. If they weren't moaning they were boasting. And if they were neither moaning nor boasting they were belting out pirate songs. Such was the atmosphere in which I grew up.

I became the central feature of the Minipirates' life. During the five years I spent with them, their activities revolved around me to the exclusion of almost everything else. It was as if I had at last lent some meaning to their ludicrous existence. They made touching efforts to teach me all they knew about buccaneering and the piratical way of life. They devoted entire days to singing me gruesome pirate songs, uttering oaths, hoisting the Jolly Roger, drawing maps that purported to show the location of buried treasure. Once they even tried, for my benefit, to capture a vessel at least a thousand times bigger than their own. That was a day that taught me the meaning of abject failure.

The seaman's trade, from raising anchor to caulking seams and bracing the shrouds, I learned simply by watching and lending a hand.

I began by scrubbing the deck. It can be a real art to scrub a deck clean of every voracious bacterium, but not so smooth as to render it slippery underfoot (a particularly important consideration in the case of the Minipirates, with their spindly peg-legs). Soft soap with a small admixture of sand is the ideal substance for scouring decks: the soap for cleanliness and the sand for grip. I learned how to sail close-hauled and how to lie to in a lull, how to make the most of a following breeze, how to wear ship, how to go about in a heavy sea, and how to stop dead (a trick mastered only by the Mini-pirates, who used it to avoid dangerous collisions with sizeable fish – in their case, anything bigger than a cod).

Knots are one of the most important aspects of a seaman's life. I don't mean the speed of a ship, which is also measured in knots, but the many ways of tying a hempen rope. I learned 723 different methods of tying a knot, and I know them all by heart to this day. I can (of course) tie an ordinary reef knot, but also a Minipirate's Double Skirtlet, a Storm Cravat, a Goose Gallows, a Hobgoblin Hitch – even a Double Gordian.

Seaman's knots

I mastered the Hempen Twist and the eight-strand Octopus Noose, the Manilla Maze and the Rio Rope-Yarn, the Buccaneer's Bowline and the Captain's Clinch. Blindfolded, I could tie two eels in a knot so complex that it would have taken them longer than a lifetime to disentangle themselves. Aboard the Minipirates' ship I became something in the nature of a senior knotmaster. Whenever a knot was needed, they came to me. I could tie a knot in a fish. I could even, in a dire emergency, tie a knot in a knot.

Knowing your waves

Navigation, of course, is especially important at sea. The Minipirates, who had very few technical aids, were unfamiliar even with the magnetic compass. They steered in accordance with a system based on observation of the motion of the waves. People say that one wave resembles another, but they're mistaken. Watch waves for long enough, and you'll realize that every one is different. Each wave undulates in its own particular way. Some are pointed and precipitous, others rounded and flat. Waves can be thick or thin, green or blue, black or brown, turbid or transparent, large or small, broad or long, cold or warm, salty or sweet, noisy or silent, fast or slow, harmless or lethal.

Every wave has a stature of its own, so to speak. It possesses not only a face of its own but an individual hairstyle in the shape of the foam on its crest. Waves are differentiated by their mode of

22

progression. Those in southern waters favour a nonchalant, rolling gait; those in northern seas stride briskly along because of the cold and the danger of congealing into ice floes. Caribbean waves dance in calypso time, Scottish waves form line abreast and march along to the strains of inaudible bagpipes. Anyone who makes a detailed study of the subject will know which waves like to be where. Small green ones with funny little cow-licks of foam are found in shallow tropical waters, dark and muddy ones near the coast and particularly in estuaries, big blue ones in cold, deep seas, and so forth. You can also tell precisely where you are from their appearance: whether you're sailing in shallow waters or above invisible sand banks and coral reefs, whether you're near land or on the high seas, whether the current is treacherous – even whether the water contains sharks or merely herrings. If sharks are around, the waves develop a slight tremor.

I also learned all I needed to know about daily shipboard maintenance: how to repair planks, how to remove sea-snails from the hull (and cook them in a seaweed bouillon), how to keep my feet in a heavy sea, how to lower a boat, throw a lifebelt, stand my turn as masthead lookout. Within a year I was a fully trained, able-bodied seabear and no longer threw up in rough weather.

Seaweed cuisine The Minipirates gave me plenty to eat, mainly seaweed and skinny little fish. They knew over four hundred ways of preparing these dishes, which ranged from 'seaweed *natur*' to a highly sophisticated soufflé, and I was privileged to sample every one of them. My present aversion to seaweed may possibly have stemmed from the Minipirates' dietary habits.

Say what you like about seaweed: it contains all the important vitamins and proteins a little bluebear needs in order to grow – too many of them, perhaps, because I grew at a speed that began to make me – and, more particularly, the Minipirates – uneasy. Having at first been smaller than my rescuers, I was the same size as them after a year. After the second year I was twice as big, and after four years my height was five times theirs.

It can well be imagined that my rapid growth made a very unpleasant impression on sea rovers whose small stature endowed them with a natural mistrust of all things big. After five years on board I had become so large and heavy that I threatened to sink their ship.

Although I failed to appreciate it at the time, the Minipirates did the only right thing by marooning me on an island one day. I'm sure they didn't find it easy. They gave me a bottle of seaweed juice and a loaf of home-baked seaweed bread to see me on my way. Then, moaning and groaning, they sailed off into the sunset. They knew that life without me would be considerably more tedious.

As I sat there, naked and forlorn on the shores of a lonely island, I thought about my predicament for the first time. It was, in fact, the first time I'd ever *thought* at all, because I'd never managed to form a clear idea about anything in the eternally noisy atmosphere of the Minipirates' ship.

Marooned

I'm bound to admit that my first attempts at cogitation were far from unfathomably profound. The first thought that came into my head was of hunger, the second of thirst, so I greedily wolfed the seaweed bread and hurriedly drained my bottle of seaweed juice. My tummy was promptly pervaded by a pleasant glow, as if someone had lit a little camp fire inside me. Accompanying this sensation was a certain self-assurance that encouraged me to take the bull by the horns and explore the island's vast palm forest. This early experience may be said to have become a maxim that has governed all my future lives. However great the challenge, it's easier to overcome with a decent meal inside you.

Then came nightfall and, with it, darkness.

Darkness...Until then I hadn't known what that was. It had always been light with the Minipirates, even at night. Their ship was brilliantly illuminated as soon as dusk closed in. Any Minipirates' vessel is a miniature sensation at night. It looks like a tiny floating funfair, sound effects included, because Minipirates are terribly frightened of the dark. They believe that night is the time when Hobgoblins come to feed on sailors' souls, and that those evil spirits can be kept at bay only by lavish lighting and the maximum possible output of noise. So my former shipmates not only illuminated their vessel with lanterns, flaming torches, strings of coloured fairy lights and small fires, but let off one signal rocket after another and created such a hellish din by singing, shouting and hammering on iron saucepans that no one could get a wink of sleep. Sleeping was done in the daytime. As for Hobgoblins, we were never troubled by them.

So it was dark for the first time. And with the darkness came a novel sensation, one that had never afflicted me before: fear!

It was a very unpleasant feeling, as if the darkness had infiltrated my body and were flowing through my veins. Having swayed so soothingly in the wind only minutes before, the lush green palm trees had now become black figures lurching towards me with their huge paws raised in menace.

Floating in the sky was a thin crescent moon, the sight of which surprised me because I had never noticed it in the permanent blaze of light on board ship. The wind rustled in the fronds of the palm trees and transformed them into a throng of whispering

ghouls that hemmed me in, ever closer, and groped for me with
skeletal fingers. Despite myself, I suddenly thought of the Hobgoblins.

I strove to suppress the thought, but it was no good. I missed the
Minipirates' hysterical hubbub, their raucous voices and, above all,
their extravagant lighting – the lighting that kept Hobgoblins
away. I had reached the absolute nadir of my young life: naked and
alone, I was marooned in the midst of a dark, unfamiliar forest and
beside myself with fear. All at once I sighted a very alarming
phenomenon among the palm trees: serpentine threads of green
light, quite far off at first but quickly drawing nearer. I also heard a
nasty, high-pitched electric hum and an occasional hollow,
mocking laugh of the kind uttered by the horned creatures that live
down well shafts. This, so the Minipirates had told me, was how
Hobgoblins advertised their presence.

From the
'Encyclopedia of Marvels, Life Forms and Other Phenomena of Zamonia and its Environs'
by Professor Abdullah Nightingale

Hobgoblins. These beings fall into the category known as Universally Reviled Life Forms [see also →*Spiderwitch, The*, →*Troglotroll, The*, and →*Bollogg, The*]. This includes those creatures resident in Zamonia and its environs whose deliberate policy it is to spread panic among their contemporaries and, in other respects, to indulge in antisocial, disruptive and killjoy behaviour of every description. Of repulsive or even terrifying appearance, Hobgoblins usually operate in packs, making frightful noises and singing horrific songs. They delight in alarming utterly defenceless creatures.

My first tears   It was all too much for me. I felt a hot liquid well up inside my head. My eyes, my mouth and nose became filled with it, and my only recourse was to yield to this internal pressure: I *wept*. I wept for the first time in my life! Fat, salty tears plopped on to my fur, my nose ran like a tap, my whole body shook in time to my sobs. Everything else was secondary now. The encircling Hobgoblins, the darkness, the fear – all were subordinate to this mighty outburst of emotion. I wept and sobbed, stamped my little hind paws, bawled at the top of my voice. Like two miniature cataracts, the tears continued to stream down my fur until I resembled a wet floorcloth. I broke down completely.

Then calm descended. My tears dried up, my sobs subsided. A reassuring sensation of warmth and weariness overcame me. My fear had vanished. I even plucked up enough courage to raise my head and look the Hobgoblins in the face. They were hovering around me in a semicircle, six or seven flickering figures outlined in ghostly light, their arms and legs dangling limply like uninflated inner tubes. They stared at me in silence for a while, almost touched. Then they started to applaud.

I won't mince matters: the Hobgoblins were a thoroughly unpleasant bunch. Their slithery movements, the slight electric shock you received when they touched you, their high-pitched, sing-song voices, and, above all, the dubious pleasure they derived from terrorizing helpless fellow creatures – all these attributes were utterly repulsive. There was also the smell of rotting wood they gave off (it was associated with their sleeping habits) and, more particularly, their disgusting form of nourishment. But more of that later.

Yes, the Hobgoblins really were the end, but I went with them notwithstanding. After all, what choice did I have?

I didn't understand a word they said – or sang, whichever – but I quickly gathered that they wanted me to accompany them. In view of my predicament I felt it was the wisest policy, though heaven alone knew what they would do to me.

They glided ahead through the forest, gracefully flowing around every obstacle like water snakes composed of green light. If their path was barred by something too big or solid – a boulder, for example, or a fallen mammoth tree – they simply slipped straight through it as if it were no more substantial than mist.

I found it quite difficult to keep up with them, but they politely paused every now and then and waited for me to catch them up. They spent these intervals singing some rather awful songs. The tunes themselves sounded so sinister, I was glad I couldn't understand the words.

The forest graveyard I was utterly exhausted, my fur full of leaves, thorns and little twigs, when we finally reached our destination: a large clearing in the middle of the forest. Rotting away in this clearing were the hollow trunks of hundreds of huge trees inhabited by hundreds or possibly thousands of Hobgoblins. For the time being, this graveyard for forest giants was to be my home.

2.

My Life
with
the Hobgoblins

It very soon became apparent that the Hobgoblins had not taken me in out of the goodness of their hearts. That same night they indicated in sign language what they expected of me: I was to weep for them.

From the
'Encyclopedia of Marvels, Life Forms and Other Phenomena of Zamonia and its Environs' by Professor Abdullah Nightingale

Hobgoblins [cont.]. Hobgoblins originate when a will-o'-the-wisp *[Lux Dementiae]* comes into contact with a pocket of Zamonian grave-yard gas. Graveyard gas is an evil-smelling vapour that rises from decaying coffins when the soil above them has not been tamped down sufficiently to render it gasproof. Will-o'-the-wisps come into being when glow-worms are struck by lightning and go fluttering on in an electrically charged condition. When a will-o'-the-wisp encounters some graveyard gas - as it usually does, for obvious reasons, above a public burial place - the gas molecules and light particles combine to form that ill-starred invertebrate commonly termed the Hobgoblin.

It's clear that nothing good can come of such a combination. If you don't have a spine you don't need a nervous system, and anyone devoid of nerves is devoid of feelings as well – hence the Hob-goblins' overpowering interest in the emotions of other living creatures. People always covet what they themselves do not possess. Once you know how Hobgoblins come into being, you aren't surprised that they should take such an inordinate interest in unpleasant emotions like fear, despair, and sorrow. To a Hob-goblin, a crying fit – in other words, something in which all these emotions are present at the same time – is the greatest thing since sliced bread.

The Hobgoblins   The Hobgoblins ushered me over to a huge, mouldering tree trunk that lay there like a toppled factory chimney and thrust a few leaves under me so that I could sit down on it in comfort.

The clearing was steadily filling up with Hobgoblins. Humming to themselves, they glided through the trees in search of their seats.

It was weird to see so many hundreds of them lighting up the arboreal graveyard. Together they generated a dome of green light that overarched the scene in a ghostly manner. Nervous whispers and giggles filled the air until the last of the Hobgoblins had found seats and focused their gaze on me. Then silence fell.

I sensed what was expected of me, but somehow I wasn't in the mood. I was feeling thoroughly uneasy, but not uneasy enough to cry. I felt I hadn't a drop of liquid left inside me, and my mouth and throat had never been more parched. I did my best, though. I pulled all kinds of faces and tried to squeeze out a tear, but to no avail.

I tried sobbing, but all that emerged was a hoarse croak. The Hobgoblins were becoming restive. Some of them broke into a low, ominous sing-song, and the air crackled with little electrical discharges. I rocked to and fro for a bit, as if racked with sobs, and rubbed my eyes to start the tears flowing, but my movements remained wooden and contrived, and still the tears refused to come.

Several of my audience rose from their seats. There was a universal hiss like the sound of gas escaping from a fractured pipe. One or two Hobgoblins glided from their tree trunks and came slowly snaking towards me, clearly with evil intent. I tried self-pity. I reminded myself that I was a little, naked, abandoned, very hungry bluebear, that I had no parents, no home, no friends. I thought of my happy times with the Minipirates and of the fact that those days were gone for evermore. I felt I was by far the most pitiful, forlorn, hungry little blubear in the whole world, the most pathetic creature that ever… And at long last the tears started flowing!

And how they flowed! They poured down my cheeks in veritable cascades, inundating them with salt water. They spurted from my eyes, ran down my nose and trickled over my lips. I emitted heart-rending sobs, threw myself on my tummy and hammered the hollow tree trunk with my little forepaws, so hard that the forest rang with the sound. I lashed out with my hind paws and tore at my short fur. I crouched on all fours and howled at the moon like a little, homesick puppy. It was a first-class crying fit, far better and more prolonged than the first.

And then, quite suddenly, it was over. I sat up, sniffing, and wiped away the last of my tears. Seen through the moisture that veiled my eyes, the Hobgoblins looked weirder than ever. They were sitting quite still, staring at me.

Utter silence.

I gave a final sniff, ready for anything. Whatever they did now – eat me, or whatever – I felt strangely indifferent. A Hobgoblin seated on a tree trunk at the back began to applaud, half-heartedly. The others continued to sit there without moving. A second joined in the applause, then a third and a fourth, and suddenly, as if in response to a secret word of command, they all stood up and applauded till the forest shook. They uttered shrill cries of delight and whistled on their thin, ghostly fingers. Many picked up branches and beat a rhythmical tattoo on the hollow tree trunks. An incredible din arose. Flowers were thrown in my direction. Here and there a Hobgoblin shot high into the air like a green flare. All in all, those habitually unemotional creatures gave an amazing demonstration of delight. It rather moved me, I must confess.

There's no other way of putting it: I had literally become a star overnight. Although I wasn't paid any money (I didn't even know that such a thing existed), the Hobgoblins remunerated me for my lachrymose performances with food. Nothing special, mainly nuts, berries, bananas, and an occasional fresh coconut washed down with spring water, but more than that I didn't need in those days. My hosts had very soon grasped – Neptune be praised! – that I wasn't their peculiar form of food. The fact was, they lived on fear. I knew from the Minipirates that Hobgoblins glide across the sea at night in search of ships whose crews they can terrify with their weird singing. Once they've succeeded, they suck in the fear like milk through a straw.

My fur used to stand on end when I saw those diaphanous spirits return from their nocturnal raids glutted with fear, plump and bloated like deep-sea sponges. At first they wanted to take me with them on their gourmet excursions, but they dropped the idea when they saw I couldn't walk on water.

Despite my initial abhorrence of the Hobgoblins, I have to admit I enjoyed my evening performances more and more as time went by. The stage fright beforehand, my steadily improving technique, the thunderous applause at the end – I became positively addicted to it all. I found it ever easier to burst into tears (and I can still do so today, on the few occasions when tears become necessary for histrionic purposes).

I had only to think of something sad, and I was off. I enriched my programme with dramatic crescendos and pauses for effect. I could run the whole gamut from faint sighs to despairing sobs and frenzied paroxysms of weeping. I learned to synchronize the rhythm of my sobs with the melody of my pathetic cries so perfectly that miniature symphonies resulted. I could turn up the volume of my screams until they attained pinnacles of hysteria, to relapse a moment later into deep valleys of snuffling lamentation. Sometimes I would subject my audience to intolerable suspense by blubbering almost silently to myself for minutes on end, then suddenly howl like a homeless seal pup.

The Hobgoblins were putty in my hands. Their ovations grew louder, longer and more enthusiastic every night. They almost smothered me with flowers, wove wreaths for my brow, showered me with berries and other fruit. No wonder I began to enjoy my role more and more. It was an intoxicating sensation to stand behind the footlights and be applauded (even when the only applause was the Hobgoblins' eerie wails and the only light their faint green glow). The reader should not, however, forget that I was still very young – this was only my second life.

I soon became notorious for my star performer's airs and could sometimes be as temperamental as a prima donna. If my audience failed to applaud frenetically enough, I turned sulky and left the stage without giving them an encore. Many were the nights I tormented the Hobgoblins by feigning a headache and refusing to appear at all. I became rather loathsome – almost as loathsome as the Hobgoblins themselves. I grew more and more like them, in fact. I started to imitate their eerie voices and hum their songs. Having at first insisted on sleeping by myself in the open, I later joined them for the night in their hollow tree trunks. I snuggled down among the humming spirits and dreamed their gruesome dreams. Before long I began to smell, like them, of rotting wood. Sometimes I also glowed a little in the dark because their luminous gas had lodged in my fur. I even made several vain attempts to walk on water, so as to be able to accompany them on their forays. On one occasion I almost drowned in a forest pool.

I myself was completely unaware of how hard I was trying to become a Hobgoblin. It's quite natural for a young person to want to be like other people. The worst of it was, I'd clearly reconciled myself to spending the rest of my days on the Hobgoblins' island.

A horrific reflection

One evening, when I was making yet another attempt to walk on water (I had taken to using very shallow pools for experimental purposes), I saw my own reflection in a big puddle. I not only caught myself aping the Hobgoblins' slithery movements but uttered one of their frightful, bleating laughs. The ripples on the puddle made my limbs undulate like a Hobgoblin's. I was appalled.

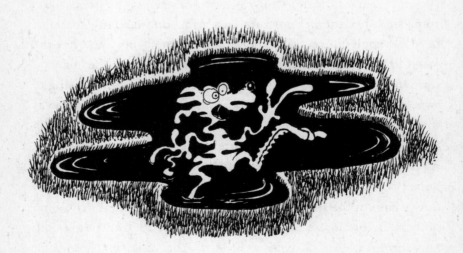

What, it suddenly occurred to me, would the Minipirates think if they could see me like this? I felt deeply ashamed. My cheeks burn, even today, when I recall that spectacle.

It was then that I resolved to escape from the Hobgoblins' island. When bad habits become a habit, you have to turn over a new leaf.

3.

My Life on the Run

At dawn one day, when early morning mist was drifting sluggishly across the clearing, I stole out of the forest. The Hobgoblins were still fast asleep in their hollow tree trunks. They had returned from a successful raid during the night, bloated and humming with contentment. Now, snoring and squeaking in their sleep like gorged opossums, they were digesting the fear they had absorbed. I gave them a last, distasteful glance, then set off for the beach.

I escape by sea

In the days beforehand I had dragged some small fallen trees from the edge of the forest to the shore and lashed them together with creeper. As the sail of my raft I used a big, fat palm leaf. I had scooped out a few coconuts, filled them with water, sealed them up again, and tied them to the mast with thin lianas, together with the unopened coconuts that were to serve as food. That was the sum total of my supplies.

I pushed my raft out into the breakers. The tide was just turning, so I was quickly carried out to sea. Where would the wind and waves take me? I had dispensed with a rudder on the principle that fate must be given a chance.

I was feeling wonderful. It seemed that the wind in my fur and the wild sea beneath me existed solely to transport me into a world of adventure. Could anything be more exciting than a journey into the unknown, a voyage of discovery across the great, wide ocean?

Becalmed

Three hours later my raft lay becalmed, bobbing in the midst of a vast expanse of motionless water. Could anything be more tedious than a sea voyage? The sea? Pooh! Just a salt-water desert, smooth

47

and featureless as an enormous mirror. Any pool in the Hob-goblins' forest had more to offer. Nothing happened, not even a seagull flew past.

I had been hoping for unknown continents and mysterious islands, or at least for a Minipirates' ship, but not even a message-in-a-bottle floated by. After a considerable time, a rotten plank came my way. It took hours to drift past. That was the most interesting sight I'd encountered on my voyage to date. I cracked open a coconut and began to feel bored.

The younger you are, the more excruciating boredom becomes. Seconds crawl by like minutes, minutes like hours. You feel you're being stretched on the rack – a time-rack, as it were – and very slowly torn apart. An infinite succession of wavelets splashes past, the sky is a bright blue vault of infinite extent. If you're a relatively inexperienced seafarer and watch the horizon, you feel it must disclose something breathtaking at any moment. But all that awaits you beyond it is another horizon. I would have welcomed any diversion – a storm, a seaquake, a terrible sea monster – but all I saw for weeks on end were waves, sky, and horizons.

I was beginning to yearn for the Hobgoblins' nauseating company when the situation changed dramatically. Although there was little wind, the sea had been unusually agitated for some days. The calm green water had transformed itself into a turmoil of grey foam, the air was filled with soot and the smell of rusty metal. Hopping excitedly to and fro on my raft, I vainly strove to discover the cause of it all. Then came a sound like never-ending thunder. It drew nearer and nearer, and the sky grew darker by the minute. I had my longed-for storm at last.

The SS Moloch   Or so I thought until a huge, black, iron ship appeared in the distance.

She had at least a thousand funnels, so tall that their tops were hidden by the smoke that rose from them. Soot entirely obscured the sky and turned the sea the colour of Indian ink, thanks to the smuts that kept raining down on it like black snow.

At first I thought the ship had come straight from hell to crush me, she seemed to be bearing down on me so purposefully. Then I was lifted by the bow wave and swept aside like a cork. I could now observe the iron colossus from a safe distance as it glided by like a dark mountain of metal. The screws that propelled it must have been bigger than windmills.

I don't know how long the ship took to sail right past and disappear from view, but it must have been about a day and a night. Not that I knew it at the time, she was the *SS Moloch*, the largest ship that ever sailed the seas.

From the
'Encyclopedia of Marvels, Life Forms
and Other Phenomena of Zamonia and its Environs'
by Professor Abdullah Nightingale

SS Moloch, The. With 1214 funnels and a gross registered tonnage of 936,589 tons, the *Moloch* is held to be the biggest ship in the world. No precise specifications are available, or none that can be scientifically validated, because no one who has set foot in the *Moloch* has ever returned. Thousands of tales are told about this vessel, needless to say, but none that has any recognizable claim to credibility.

At night, thousands of portholes – the windows of that floating metropolis – shone brighter than the stars. The pounding of the engines was deafening. They sounded like an ironclad army tramping across the ocean.

During the daytime I tried to spot some of the crew, but the deck was so far above me I could scarcely make out a thing. Whenever distant figures came to the rail and threw garbage over the side, as they did from time to time, I set up a tremendous hullabaloo. I yelled and gesticulated, jumped up and down on the raft and waved my palm-leaf sail, but my efforts were as futile as the Minipirates' attempts to board a merchantman.

They weren't without their dangers, too. On more than one occasion I was almost sucked into the wash of the gigantic propellers, and swarms of sharks crowded around the hull to fight for the scraps of food that were forever being thrown overboard. At times the creatures were so numerous that I could have walked to the ship's side across their backs.

But the most astonishing feature was something else. In spite of the huge vessel's monstrous ugliness, it held a mysterious fascination for me. There was no discernible reason for this. Although the ship was repulsive in every way, my dearest wish was to sail the seas in her. This desire had taken root in me when the *Moloch* first appeared on the horizon, a tiny speck growing bigger the nearer she came. While she was passing my raft it became positively overpowering.

'Come!' said a voice in my head.
'Come aboard the Moloch!'

The words had an unearthly ring, as if uttered by some dis-embodied being in the world hereafter.

'Come!' it said. *'Come aboard the Moloch!'*

I should have liked nothing better than to obey its summons. I now know it was my good fortune that the sharks formed an in-surmountable barrier between me and the ship, but at the time it nearly broke my little heart to watch the *Moloch* sail away.

'Come! Come aboard the Moloch!'

The gigantic ship eventually disappeared from view, but the sky remained dark for a long time to come, like the aftermath of a receding storm.
The voice in my head grew ever fainter.

'Come!' it said, very softly. *'Come aboard the Moloch!'*

Then they were gone, both the ship and the voice. It saddened me somehow to think I would never see the *Moloch* again. I wasn't to know what an important part she would play in one of my lives.

The sea had been calm and silvery again for days, the sky clear except when an occasional little fair-weather cloud came drifting over the horizon. Having seen the *Moloch*, I had lost all respect for my own craft. There couldn't have been a more cogent demonstration of the difference between a ship and a raft.
I was just debating whether to jump overboard and strike out for land when I heard two voices, loud and clear.
'I did, take it from me!' said one.
'No, you didn't!' snapped the other.
I peered in all directions. There was nothing to be seen.
'I did, so!' the first voice insisted.
'Pull the other one!' said the second.
I stood on tiptoe. Still nothing in sight far and wide.
Nothing but waves.

'But I told you only the other day, don't pretend I didn't!'

Was madness knocking at my door? Many a doughty mariner had been driven insane by the monotony of life at sea. All I could see were waves: little ones, middling ones, and two quite sizeable specimens heading straight for me. The nearer they got, the more audible the voices became.

'Who do you think you are, giving me orders? If anyone gives the orders around here, it's me!'

The two waves were having an argument.

From the
'Encyclopedia of Marvels, Life Forms and Other Phenomena of Zamonia and its Environs'
by Professor Abdullah Nightingale

Babbling Billows, The. Such waves almost always come into being in very remote and uneventful sea areas seldom frequented by ships, usually during prolonged spells of calm weather. No detailed scientific study or analysis of their origins has yet been

undertaken because Babbling Billows have a tendency to drive their victims insane. The few scientists who have ventured to study them are now confined under guard in padded cells or lying on the ocean floor in the form of skeletons with tropical fish swimming in and out of them.

Babbling Billows normally appear only to shipwrecked sailors. They circle their helpless victims for days or weeks on end, bombarding them with tasteless jokes and cynical comments on the hopelessness of their predicament until the unfortunate seafarers, already weakened by thirst and exposure to the sun, completely lose their reason. An ancient Zamonian myth constitutes the basis of the popular fallacy that Babbling Billows are the material manifestations of oceanic boredom.

More shipwrecked sailors have, in fact, been killed by Babbling Billows than by thirst, but that I didn't know at the time. To me they seemed no more than a welcome distraction from the tedium of the doldrums.

The two waves were quite close by now. When they saw me on my ramshackle raft, naked and bleached by the scorching sun, they had a fit of the giggles.

'Good heavens!' cried one. 'What have we *here*?'

'A luxury liner,' cackled the other. 'Complete with sun deck!'

They sloshed to and fro with laughter. Although I wasn't sure what they meant, I thought it wise to establish contact with them by laughing too.

They circled the raft like a brace of sharks.

'I expect you think you've gone mad, don't you?' asked one.

'Babbling Billows are the first symptom of sunstroke, did you know that?' asked the other.

'Yes, and after that come singing fish. Why not make it easier on yourself? Just jump in!'

They sloshed to and fro, pulling frightful faces.

'Hoo-oo-oo!' cried one wave.

'Woo-oo-oo!' cried the other.

'We are the Waves of Terror!'

'Go on, jump! Put yourself out of your misery!'

I had no intention of jumping. On the contrary, I was delighted that someone was making an effort to entertain me at last. I sat on the edge of the raft and watched the waves' performance with amusement.

'But seriously, youngster,' said one of them, aware that they were getting nowhere, 'who are you? Where are you from?'

It was the first time in my life anyone had ever asked me a question. I wanted to answer it, but I had no idea how to.

'What's the matter, boy?' the other wave demanded brusquely. 'Swallowed your tongue? Can't you speak?'

I shook my head. I could listen but not speak. Neither the Minipirates nor the Hobgoblins had thought it worth my while to learn how to speak. I myself had never thought it so until that minute.

The two waves looked first at me, then at each other, with a lingering expression of profound dismay.

'But this is awful!' exclaimed one. 'He can't speak – have you ever heard of anything so frightful?'

'Never!' cried the other. 'I imagine it must be even worse than *evaporating*!'

They circled me with a solicitous air.

'The poor little creature! Fancy being condemned to perpetual silence! How pathetic!'

'Honestly, it's the most distressing thing I've ever seen in my life!'

'Distressing is a pale description of my reaction to such a fate. It's a tragedy!'

'A classical tragedy!'

And they both began to weep bitterly.

From one moment to the next they calmed down, put their crests together, and went into a huddle.

'I don't feel like tormenting him.'

'Neither do I, I'm too upset. It's strange, but…well, somehow I feel like *helping* him.'

The other wave shook itself a little. 'Yes, me too! An odd sensation, isn't it?'

'Very odd, but interesting too, somehow. Crazy and novel and quite unprecedented!'

'Crazy and novel and quite unprecedented!' the other wave repeated enthusiastically.

'Yes, but *how* can we help him? What on earth can we do?'

They continued to circle my raft, deep in thought.

'I've got it!' cried the first wave. 'We'll *teach* him to speak!'

'You think we could?' the second wave said doubtfully. 'He looks a bit retarded to me.'

One of them sloshed right up to me. 'Say "Ah",' it commanded, looking deep into my eyes and extending a seawater tongue.

'Ah,' I said.

'You see!' it cried. 'Anyone who can say "Ah" can learn to say "binomial coefficient" in no time at all!'

I am taught to speak

In the weeks that followed, the Babbling Billows tirelessly circled my raft and taught me to speak. First I learned simple words like 'sun' and 'sea', then harder ones like 'longitude' and 'circumnavigation'. I learned big words and little words, nouns and verbs, adjectives and adverbs, conjunctions and prepositions, nice words and swearwords you should never say at all. I learned how to spell and pronounce, decline and conjugate, substantivize and genitivize, accusativize and dativize. Then we got on to clauses – principal clauses and subordinate clauses, pendant clauses and relative clauses – and, finally, whole sentences.

To avoid any misapprehension, I must add that the Babbling Billows didn't teach me to write, only to speak. The written word is redundant on the high seas. Why? Because paper gets wet too easily.

But the Babbling Billows were not content merely to teach me to speak; they wanted me to master all forms of speaking perfectly.

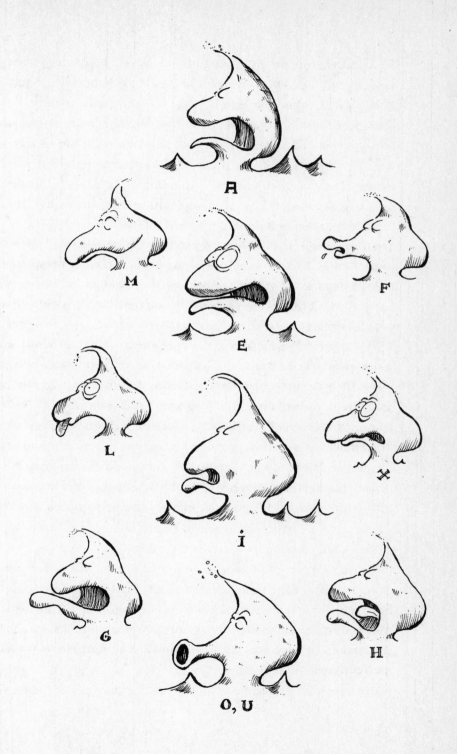

They taught me to murmur and maunder, gabble and prattle, whisper and bellow, converse and confabulate, and – of course – to babble like themselves. They also taught me how to deliver a speech or a soliloquy and initiated me into the art of persuasion; not only how to talk someone else to a standstill, but to talk my way out of a life or death situation. I learned to hold forth under extremely difficult conditions – standing on one leg, for instance, or doing a pawstand, or speaking with a coconut in my mouth while the Babbling Billows showered me with seawater.

Their spitefulness had long ceased to be perceptible, probably because they had never before been engaged in such a responsible and interesting activity. They became utterly engrossed in it, and I have to admit they were genuinely good teachers. Where babbling was concerned, they knew their onions.

I myself became a master of the spoken word. My progress after five weeks was such that the waves couldn't teach me any more – indeed, I'd almost surpassed them. I could utter any given phrase at any required volume, both forwards and backwards. 'tneiciffeoc laimoniB' (binomial coefficient) was among the simpler ones.

I could deliver a speech, propose a toast, swear an oath (and break it), declaim a monologue, compose a verse, oil a compliment, talk drivel, blather incomprehensibly. I could speak my mind, wax indignant, sound off, wag my tongue, run people down, fire off a tirade, give a lecture, deliver a sermon, and – from now on, of course – spin a seaman's yarn of my own.

Now that I'd learned to speak I could at last hold a conversation, though only, for the time being, with the Babbling Billows. I didn't have much to tell them because my experience of life was so meagre, but they had plenty to impart. Anyone who had traversed the oceans for centuries, as they claimed to have done, was bound to have seen a few things in his time. They told of mighty hurricanes that drilled holes in the sea, of giant sea serpents that fought each other with jets of liquid fire, of transparent red whales that swallowed ships whole, of octopuses with miles-long tentacles capable of crushing whole islands, of water sprites that danced on the crests of waves and caught flying fish with their bare hands, of blazing meteors that made the sea boil, of continents that sank and surfaced again, of underwater volcanoes, ghost ships, foam-witches, sea-gods, wave-dwarfs, and earthquakes in the depths of the ocean. What they liked best of all, however, was to run each other down. Whenever one of them got separated from the raft, the other promptly cast aspersions on its character and urged me not to believe a word it said, et cetera. The worst of it was, I couldn't tell them apart. They were, in fact, identical twins. For once, and in this particular case, the preconceived notion that one wave resembles another proved to be correct.

I had long become used to the two of them. You make friends quickly when you're young, and you think things will remain the same for evermore. But a day came when the Babbling Billows' lighthearted manner underwent a change. They had been circling the raft for several hours without uttering a word. This was unusual, and I wondered if I had done something wrong. At last they came sloshing over to the raft and proceeded to hum and haw.

'Well, I suppose we ought to...' said one.

'The law of the sea, et cetera...' snivelled the other.

Then they both began to weep.

Once they had pulled themselves together, they explained the situation to me. It seemed that a strong current had been running for some days, and the Babbling Billows knew they must follow it. If they remained in the same spot for too long, they evaporated. That was why they were doomed to roam the seas in perpetuity.

'Many thanks for everything,' I said, for I could speak now, of course.

'Oh, don't mention it,' said one of the waves, and I could tell it was fighting back the tears.

'I'm lost for words for the very first time,' it went on.

I am named for life

'We've got something for you,' said the other wave. 'A name!'

'Yes,' said the first wave, 'we're calling you Bluebear.'

The Babbling Billows obviously didn't have much in the way of imagination, but still, I'd never had a name before. They each gave me a damp hug and sloshed off, sobbing as they went. I felt like crying myself.

I watched them making for the horizon, their silhouettes outlined against the orb of the slowly setting sun. But they perked up after only a few yards and started babbling again.

'Now listen to *me*...'

'There's nothing *you* can tell me *I* don't know already!'

'That's what *you* think!'

And they went on babbling. Even when darkness had fallen and they'd been out of sight for hours, I could still hear them squabbling in the distance.

My supply of coconuts was gradually running out, and my arduous language lessons had almost completely exhausted my reserves of liquid. What was more, a merciless sun had been beating down on my unprotected head for quite a while, for I was drifting ever further south.

After three days my brain was so dehydrated that I simply sat there, torpidly contemplating the surface of the sea. If you stare at seawater for long enough, you start seeing the strangest things in the foam: wild beasts, dragons, hordes of sea monsters locked in battle, dancing water sprites, leaping mermaids, weird grey shapes equipped with horns and tails. I soon got the feeling I could see the bottom of the ocean. I glimpsed translucent palaces floating beneath me like glass submarines. I saw a kraken with a thousand tentacles, a pirate ship manned by clattering skeletons singing frightful songs. And then I saw the most terrible sight of all: a huge gargoyle of a face, ten times bigger than my raft, with a single eye the size of a house rolling around in its socket until only the white showed.

The huge eye

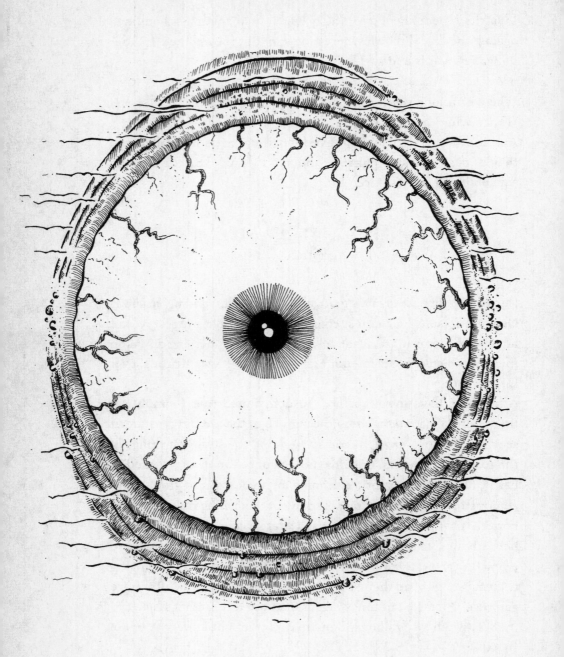

Beneath it was a mouth big enough to swallow any ship, the massive lower jaw studded with countless long, pointed teeth. The creature's throat was gaping greedily, and looking down it was like looking into a watery grave. The face was covered with scales and horny wrinkles, small craters and deep scars. I went on staring into the water in a daze.

But I wasn't scared by the sight. After all, it was only a figment of my desiccated imagination.

Or so I thought. But it wasn't. It was a Tyrannomobyus Rex.

From the
'Encyclopedia of Marvels, Life Forms
and Other Phenomena of Zamonia and its Environs'
by Professor Abdullah Nightingale

Tyrannomobyus Rex, The. A plagiostome belonging to the selachian order of fishes and related to the killer whale, the giant moray eel, the shark, the carnivorous saurian, and the cyclops. It derives its size from the whale, the conformation of its lower jaw from the moray eel, its urge to devour anything its maw can encompass from the shark, its instinctive habit of chasing anything that moves from the saurian, and its single eye from the cyclops. Over 140 feet long, the Tyrannomobyus Rex may readily be numbered among the largest predators in the world. Its skin is studded with knobs of cartilage and black as pitch, which is why it is also called the Black Whale. The head consists of a single large slab of bone that enables it to ram quite sizeable merchantmen and send them to the bottom. Fortunately, the Tyrannomobyus Rex is almost extinct. According to many experts, the specimen that has been rendering Zamonian waters unsafe for decades is the only one still in existence. Numerous whalers have tried to kill it, but none has succeeded and many have never been seen again.

I didn't awake from my daydream until the Black Whale surfaced right in front of me. It was as if the sea had given birth to an island. Towering over my raft was a mountain of black blubber sprinkled with warts the size of boulders. Water streamed down the fatty furrows in the monster's back and cascaded into the sea. Sucked into one of the whirlpools created around it by these waterfalls, my raft began to rotate.

The air was filled with a throat-catching stench.

I clung tightly to the mast and tried to breathe as little as possible. The whirlpools subsided, but the whale blew a gigantic fountain of water into the air, possibly as much as 300 feet high, through the vent in its head. I was so fascinated by this spectacle that I never stopped to think what its consequences might be from my own point of view.

For a moment it seemed as if the fountain had turned to ice. It hung there in front of the sun like a transparent, frozen waterfall. I could see thousands of fish in it, large and small, whole schools of cod and porpoises, a few sharks, a largish octopus, and a ship's wheel.

Then the fountain fell back into the sea. The water descended on me like a ton of bricks. It smashed my raft to pieces and carried me down, further and further, into the depths. Fortunately, although I was surrounded by sharks, they were far too dazed to snap at me.

The pressure eased at last and I shot to the surface like a cork. Scarcely had I drawn a breath and got my bearings (I was right in front of the monster's cyclopean eye) when it opened its mouth to gulp some more water.

In the whale's jaws

I was brutally sucked into the whale's jaws. I feel sure that this wasn't directed specifically at me – indeed, I doubt if the monster had noticed me at all, not being the kind of prey that would have justified the effort. The whale was simply breathing in.

Suspended from its upper lip were innumerable whiskers, the yard-long, lianalike tentacles with which it filtered its food. I managed to catch hold of one as I was swept along and clung to it while the water rushed beneath me into the creature's maw. It wasn't easy, for the whiskers were slippery and gave off a disgusting stench of rotting fish, but I hung on with all my might.

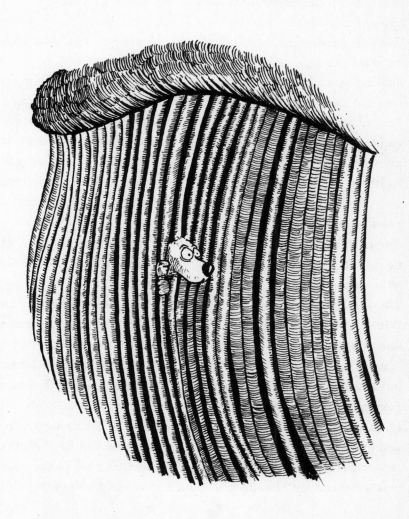

Having finished taking in water, the whale began to shut its mouth again. My next task was to avoid being swallowed. To achieve this I started swinging back and forth on the whisker. It would be my bad luck if the mouth closed while I was on the inside.

The lips were closing very slowly.

I swung in.

The lower lip emerged from the sea, big as a sand bank.

I swung out.

With a gurgle, the last of the water disappeared down the monster's throat.

I swung in.

I would have done better not to venture a glance at the whale's dark maw. Yawning beneath me was a chasm coated with dark green slime, a hissing hole filled with gastric juices. I was so scared, my strength wellnigh deserted me. Momentarily relaxing my grip, I slithered a little way down the whisker, then tightened it in the nick of time.

I swung out.

The monster's lips shut with a snap. I had managed to finish my final swing on the outside and was now perched on the whale's glutinous lower lip.

The cyclopean eye was rolling overhead but failed to notice me. Without giving the matter much thought, I reached for the nearest knob of gristle on the upper lip and began my ascent.

It wasn't easy to clamber up the huge creature's warty epidermis, but I was urged on by a courage born of despair. I climbed right past the eye, from one gristly protuberance to the next, scaled the forehead, which was a miniature mountain of black, horny skin, and made my way down into the deep wrinkles that furrowed the monster's brow. Thereafter the going became easier. The slope was less steep, and I soon reached the foothills of the back.

There is no polite way to describe the whale's stench. Proliferating on its back were whole coral reefs, forests of seaweed, colonies of clams. Stranded fish were flapping everywhere, crabs and lobsters scuttling excitedly to and fro.

I continued to toil across the viscous surface until I came to a cluster of harpoons protruding from the whale's gristly back. There must have been hundreds of them. Many were old and rusty, with rotting wooden shafts, but the gleaming steel barbs and brightly polished handles of others indicated that they hadn't been there long. The harpoons were of all sizes. They ranged from normal ones that I myself could have thrown to big ones as much as fifteen feet long, which had clearly been hurled by giants, and tiny ones no bigger than a toothpick, which had probably belonged to Minipirates. Dangling from one of them, entangled in his own line, was the skeleton of a luckless whaler.

The harpoon forest

The whale was absolutely motionless now – motionless as a ship that has run aground. I took advantage of this lull to reflect on my predicament. My raft was now being digested somewhere in the Tyrannomobyus's innards. Sooner or later the monster would dive once more, either carrying me down with it or leaving me floundering in the sea with nothing to cling to. I decided to improvise a new raft out of harpoon shafts. They were largely of wood, and still attached to many of them were corks for buoyancy and lines with which I could tie them together. My first step was to extract a brand-new harpoon some nine feet long.

A slight tremor ran through the whale's back as I pulled it out. Not an alarming reaction, it was accompanied by a faint grunt and followed by a huge, pleasurable sigh that rang out far across the sea. The same thing happened when I extracted the next harpoon, except that the sigh was even more prolonged and pleasurable, perhaps because the harpoon was more deeply embedded.

The whale evidently liked what I was doing. I guessed I would be

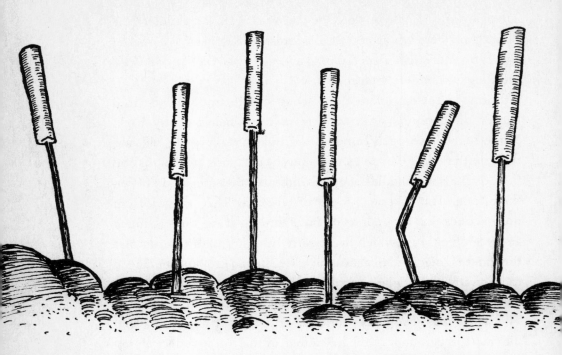

safe for as long as I went on removing harpoons, so I extracted one
after another from the huge creature's back, proceeding as gently
and carefully as possible so as not to madden it by yanking out a
barb too quickly. Within a very short time I was an expert at
extracting harpoons. You have to begin by levering the shaft back
and forth to loosen the barb in the gristle, and then, with a gentle,
oscillating movement, pull it out.

The more carefully and skilfully I extracted the barbs from the
whale's flesh, the more pleasurable its grunts became. One huge,
contented sigh after another went whooshing across the sea – an
audible manifestation of the monster's relief. I was so engrossed in
my work, I never even noticed that it had got under way again. A
refreshing breeze was my first indication it was very slowly
propelling itself along with gentle movements of its tail. It showed
no signs of being about to dive.

Removing the harpoons was hard work. Many of the barbs were so firmly embedded that it was a real struggle to get them out. The very long harpoons were lodged in the gristle more deeply and stubbornly than most, having been hurled by powerful arms. I sweated and slaved, but it made a welcome change from lolling around in idleness on the raft.

I doubt if anyone apart from me has ever heard a Tyrannomobyus Rex sigh. It's a sound unlike any other, a sort of groan of gratitude for deliverance from years or even centuries of torment. Assemble ten thousand sea cows at the bottom of a mine shaft, persuade them to utter a simultaneous sigh of love and add the wingbeats of a million bumblebees drunk on honey, and you might produce something akin to that penetrating, contented hum.

After half a day or so my work was nearly done. I had extracted hundreds of harpoons. Only one remained, and that I removed with a certain ceremony. A final sigh of relief rang out over the sea. Tyrannomobyus Rex was harpoon-free.

I realized my mistake a moment later. By removing the last harpoon I had also disposed of the whale's only reason for tolerating my presence on its back. It prepared to dive, as I realized when it drew a deep breath. In my eagerness I had completely lost sight of the need to build another raft. I had thoughtlessly tossed the harpoons into the sea.

Yes, the Tyrannomobyus Rex dived, but so slowly, almost gently, that I wasn't directly endangered by its submersion. It went down by degrees, like a very big ship with a tiny leak. I slid off its back into the mirror-smooth water while the last knobs of gristle were silently engulfed. Then it disappeared altogether. A few huge bubbles rose to the surface, presumably a final farewell from its air hole.

The water was warm. I doggy-paddled around for a bit, trying to get my bearings. A few cork floats could be seen here and there. Perhaps I could collect enough of them to fashion a makeshift lifebelt. As I was swimming towards one I spotted a seagull overhead, the first I'd seen for a long time. It was flying westwards, into the setting sun.

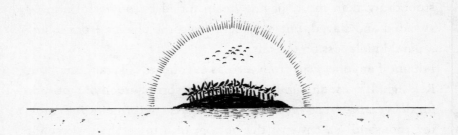

A cloud of screaming seabirds was circling above a point on the horizon with the sun melting into the sea beyond them. A ship, or had the whale surfaced in another place? I swam towards the place. The nearer I got, the more clearly I seemed to discern a small palm forest beneath the birds. Soon I could make out a coastal strip: an immaculately white sandy beach and, beyond it, some luxuriant vegetation.

Whether by chance or by design, the whale had dumped me near an island. Alluring scents came drifting across the sea towards me. Appetizing aromas I'd never encountered before, they included vanilla, grated nutmeg, wild garlic, and roast beef. The island smelt good. Having discovered the place, I resolved to take possession of it by right.

The sun had almost disappeared by the time I crawled ashore. I was so exhausted I simply lay down on the sand and dozed off at once. Before I finally drifted into dreamland I heard a chorus of inane giggles coming from behind the curtain of forest nearby. But I didn't care, I had nothing to fear. Whoever they might be, those people, they were my subjects.

4.

My Life on Gourmet Island

The next morning I was roused from my dreams of discovery by a choir of songbirds. A gigantic, breathtakingly beautiful butterfly had perched on my nose and was fanning me with cool air. A coconut plopped into the sand from a nearby palm tree and split in half with such precision that not a drop of the precious milk was spilt. The milk was delicious, cool and refreshing, and the flesh melted on my tongue like cream. A flock of humming-birds hovered above me for a moment, then formed line ahead and went whirring off into the palm forest. The island seemed to want to welcome its discoverer in person. It was time to inspect my new domain. I brushed the sand from my fur and set off into the interior.

I still can't find the words to do justice to the paradisal splendour of Bluebear Island (as I provisionally christened it). Clouds of colourful butterflies fluttered through serried ranks of huge, shady palm trees with golden fronds and snow-white trunks. Some of these butterflies were as big as seagulls and had wings that shimmered like mother of pearl. Growing beneath the trees were flowers such as I had never seen before, with silver petals and leaves of glass.

Other flowers, which had cups that seemed to consist of blue light, could sing in low, subdued, sing-song voices like tiny, industrious elves. I passed tall plants that smelt of vanilla and could unfurl their gorgeous, multicoloured leaves like peacocks displaying their plumage. Other, tuliplike flowers with thin yellow stems were forever changing colour. If you looked at them for too long, they turned puce and giggled. That was the sound I'd heard on the threshold of sleep.

I came to a clearing in which some pale green orchids were phosphorescing in the deep shade of the palm trees that fringed it. They were blowing iridescent soap bubbles. Other orchids stood among them, bursting the bubbles with their long, tonguelike stamens. The humming-birds had assembled above the clearing and were amusing themselves by doing some formation flying.

Potato fritters But the most amazing thing of all was situated in the middle of the clearing, where a small pool of cooking oil was bubbling away in an appetizing fashion. The hissing and spitting seemed to grow louder as I approached. At the edge of the pool were some plants whose long stems terminated in potatolike excrescences. As I drew near the stems bent and dipped these in the sizzling oil. I could only gaze at this process in amazement. The stems eventually straightened up and dropped a few potato fritters at my feet. I picked one up and sampled it. Ah, what bliss! I had never tasted

anything more delectable. Greedily, I gobbled up the rest of the potatoes as well.

The further I ventured into the interior of the island, the more unusual the vegetation became. Tinkling among the trees was a dense network of brooks and rivulets. On examining these more closely, I discovered them to be of different colours. Many looked like ordinary water, but others were white as milk or yellow as orange juice. I bent and drank from one of the yellow streams. It really was orange juice.

The white streams consisted of pure, cold milk. Overhanging them were large plants with thick, dark brown seed pods. When I accidentally brushed against one of these plants, dozens of pods fell into the milk, dissolved, and temporarily turned the stream pale brown. I quickly stooped and lapped up some of this delicious drinking chocolate.

Cocoa on tap

Growing on the banks of the rivers were fruit and vegetables such as I had never seen before, including blue cauliflowers that smelt and tasted like roast pork with crackling. The flowers brimmed with honey, and you could even eat their leaves, which tasted like white toast. Lengths of thin creeper dangling from the trees smelt faintly of garlic and could be eaten like spaghetti. The trees themselves excreted delicious sauces and gravies from their knotholes when the bark was tapped. Mushrooms the size of pumpkins stewed in their own juice below ground. You had only to break off a piece to see it grow back again within minutes.

The island seemed completely devoid of horrors. There were no cannibals lurking anywhere, no treacherous quagmires, no evil spirits, no dangerous wild beasts. There weren't even any of the usual unpleasantnesses like spiders or earwigs, snakes or bats, only creatures that were either beautiful or, if not beautiful, cute: butterflies and songbirds, hares and squirrels, hamsters and flamingos, humming-birds and dainty little cats. They were all very trusting and showed no sign of fear, which indicated that the denizens of the island lived in peace. There was plenty of food for all, so they had no need to prey on each other.

I had discovered an earthly paradise.

The climate was temperate, neither too hot nor too cold, with an average shade temperature of 75 degrees Fahrenheit and a steady, refreshing breeze. It never got very cold, even at night, because the forest floor gave off a pleasant warmth and purred like a contented cat when you stretched out on it.

I really hadn't expected such splendour, in fact I found it slightly embarrassing to have hit the jackpot on my very first voyage of exploration. After all my hardships and tribulations, I felt as if I'd finally come home.

For the first few days I toured the island in a kind of dream. I hardly dared to touch its treasures for fear they would dissolve into thin air like a mirage. But they were real enough. After a while I plucked up the courage to sample them all, taking a morsel here, a sip there. Many things were an acquired taste – after all, my diet hitherto had consisted exclusively of seaweed, berries, nuts, and water – but many others I took to at once, like the drinking chocolate from the river of milk and the honey from the flower cups.

It was a while before I learnt what to do with the island's unfamiliar flora, but I learnt very quickly. The long, noodlelike creepers tasted delicious when dipped in the warm pulp of the giant tomatoes that grew everywhere. All the grass on the island was edible. Slightly nutty and bitter in flavour, it went well with potato fritters.

The fruit was sensational in its variety. In addition to ordinary coconuts, bananas, oranges, apples, nuts and grapes there were exotic plants tasting like vanilla and cinnamon that exuded sweet milk or were crunchy as crispbread. One red, banana-shaped fruit tasted of marzipan, while the leaves of a fat, comfortable-looking tree had a gingerbread flavour.

I eventually became acquainted with all the island's delicacies.

My daily routine In the mornings, immediately after waking up, I would totter over to the river of milk, shake the cocoa plants, and slurp up great mouthfuls of drinking chocolate. Then I paid the honey-flowers a visit and picked myself a slice of toast. After that I usually retired to a clearing and munched my breakfast while watching the humming-birds daringly loop the loop for my entertainment. The little cats would come running up and rub themselves against my fur, purring, or romp around in the morning sun.

After breakfast I made a regular habit of touring my domain. The island was not very big, only a few hundred yards in diameter, perhaps, but chock-full of minor sensations. The singing flowers learned a new song every day, and I spent hours listening to their silvery voices and watching the butterflies perform their flirtatious aerial ballets. The squirrels, too, were fond of showing off their acrobatic skills. Most of the time one of them sat perched on my head or shoulder and let me carry it around.

My favourite feasting-place at lunchtime was the pool of oil. I generally ate my potato fritters with rocket, or sometimes a morsel of blue cauliflower.

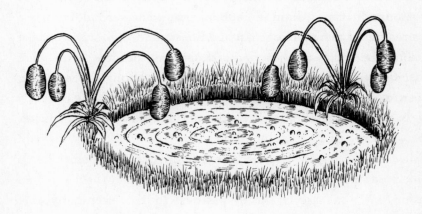

After lunch I liked to take a nap. In the afternoons I often went for a swim in the warm sea. The water around the island was calm and clearly uninhabited by any dangerous sea creatures. I lay floating on my back for hours or sat in the gentle surf, which continually washed up thousands of tiny shellfish between my legs.

I liked to spend the end of the day on the beach, watching the sun go down with the little cats for company. At dusk I went back into the forest, curled up on the warm, purring, mossy ground, and dreamed of being the skipper of the big iron ship I'd seen.

My diet was extremely well balanced at first. I ate at long intervals, took plenty of exercise, and was satisfied with the range of food on offer. After a month or two, however, I began to eat snacks between meals. Nothing elaborate, just a potato fritter here, a slice of toast there, and now and then one of the fat chocolate drops from the cocoa plants. It sometimes irked me that the cuisine was so limited. After six months I introduced a second breakfast consisting of two slices of toast and honey, a teatime snack of cake (from the cake tree), a sundowner (mushrooms with blue cauliflower), and a selection of fruit before retiring for the night. Instead of long walks I took siestas. As time went by the intervals between my meals became steadily shorter. I inserted extra courses between my first and second breakfasts (in-between breakfasts, I called them), regaled myself with an appetizer just before lunch (marzipan fruits, chocolate drops, dollops of honey) and followed it up with an assortment of pastries. In the afternoon came potatoes and liana-spaghetti in tomato sauce plus more pastries and fruit. I divided supper into several courses to spin it out until bedtime. I generally began by wolfing a whole mushroom, then a blue cauliflower. Then, after a brief interval for digestion, some milk. Then potato fritters with rocket and pastries to follow. Just before going to sleep, a few more slices of toast and honey.

In the end I even got up to eat in the middle of the night. I would stagger blearily through the forest and plunge my snout in the river of milk, stuff myself with chocolate drops, or slurp wild honey straight from a flower cup. I was often haunted by nightmares, most of them to do with food.

The island's vegetation underwent an amazing change. Whenever I had eaten too much of a particular food, kindly Nature saw to it that some new and even more exquisite delicacy sprouted elsewhere. Fat, strong-scented truffles had lately been flourishing beneath the forest floor. I took a while to get used to their intense flavour, but once I had I couldn't leave them alone. They went especially well with liana-spaghetti. Ceps now grew where ordinary field mushrooms had grown before. The height of a man, they made an elegant dish when combined with fresh rocket. Vast quantities of oysters were being washed up on the beach. Although it had never before occurred to me to eat a raw, slippery oyster, my gums had become steadily more sensitive, my taste buds more fastidious, my palate more refined. I was soon slurping down two dozen oysters between each course. Huge lobsters came waddling out of the sea and committed suicide in the pool of seething oil. I discovered, once I had learned how to crack their massive shells, that the flesh inside was absolutely delicious.

I had become accustomed to dividing the day into meals. I couldn't sleep properly any more, my stomach was always too full. I merely dozed a little, half asleep and dreaming of my next meal. Completely unused to physical exertion, I simply crawled or rolled from one course to the next.

Varied vegetation

By the time a year had gone by I was as fat as bacon rind and as *A year later* round as a football. I weighed many times what I had weighed when I first set foot on the island and proudly claimed it as my own. I hadn't seen the sea for months. I was thick with grease and stank like a snack bar. I exuded cooking oil from every pore. I had ceased to wash and brush my fur – I hadn't even risen on my hind legs for weeks. Every movement was a terrible effort and made me stream with sweat. My breathing rattled and whistled in my chest. I could no longer see my hind paws because they were obscured by my bulging tummy. Even my eyelids had grown fatter, so I found it increasingly difficult to keep them open. My thoughts were of nothing but food. I spent the whole time planning new menus, lusting after new taste sensations, envisioning ever more daring combinations of ever more exotic foods.

One day – I was just between my thirteenth and fourteenth meals and already wondering anxiously whether a whole man-sized mushroom would be enough for supper – the wind suddenly changed and I smelt something I'd never before smelt on the island. It was the sort of unpleasant stench that might have been given off by a thousand aquatic plants rotting away in a stagnant pond. For some reason I felt ripe, as overripe as autumn fruit – or, rather, like a fattened hog being led to the slaughter.

And then the island began to shudder beneath me. I tried to stand *The island awakes* up, but no sooner had I succeeded than my head swam and I collapsed. I had literally forgotten how to stand.

Within seconds the palm trees around me seemed to wilt, shrivelling up into ugly little withered plants resembling skinny black hands. All the other plants withered too, and the lush grass became transformed into a black carpet like a field of scorched stubble. Ugly little holes appeared all over the place, opening and shutting like fishes' mouths. I even thought I spotted teeth inside them. My paradise was turning into a hell.

Birds and butterflies fell to earth as if shot, crumbled away to dust, and seeped into the quaking soil. The air was filled with a loud, horrific sound like a hundred wild boars smacking their lips and belching. I made another attempt to get up and stagger off, but I was rooted to the spot: one of the withered plants – it had once been a singing flower – grabbed me by the ankle and hung on tight. Then it started to grow, very, very quickly.

I was hoisted into the air and suspended upside down at a height of eighty or ninety feet. Absolutely terrified, I looked down and saw that the island, now completely devoid of vegetation, had split in two. An immense cleft ran straight through the middle of it, gaping like the jaws of a shark. I found myself gazing into a huge, stinking mouth studded with thousands of rotting teeth.

From the
'Encyclopedia of Marvels, Life Forms
and Other Phenomena of Zamonia and its Environs'
by Professor Abdullah Nightingale

Gourmetica insularis, The. The Gourmetica insularis is a heterotrophic carnivorous plant, that is to say, one of the very rare family of plants that feeds on organic rather than inorganic matter, like most flora. The Gourmetica is among the Zamonian life forms that attract their quarry in an unsportsmanlike manner, being distantly related to the much smaller Venus flytrap and the equally rare →*Spiderwitch*. It is capable of transforming itself into a kind of floating paradise in order to lure and fatten its prey in the most ingenious way. A mature Gourmetica can attain a circumference of several miles but needs only 300 pounds (live weight) of fresh meat, or thereabouts, to feed itself for a year. This must be provided by one of the more highly developed mammals, however, because fish or birds will not do. The Gourmetica is firmly anchored to the seabed - a blessing on Nature's part, when one considers what havoc a mobile carnivorous plant of this order could wreak in a heavily populated seaside town.

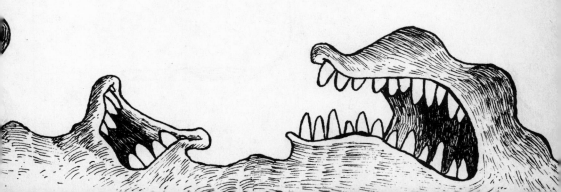

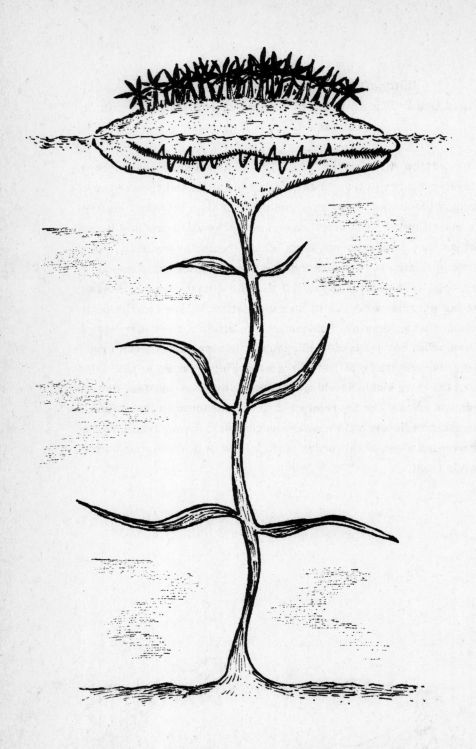

So there I hung, high in the air, the black claws holding me poised above the huge mouth just as I myself had prepared to drop a grape into my own mouth only minutes earlier. Looking down into the plant's gaping maw, I could see cascades of saliva gathering within it. A tongue like a huge green snake came writhing up towards me from the depths, accompanied by a blast of air so foul that it almost robbed me of my senses. Then the grip on my ankle relaxed. Finally released altogether, I fell head over heels into the gullet of the treacherous aquatic plant.

They say people see the whole of their lives replayed like a film before they die. In my case it was a very short film: the Minipirates, the Hobgoblins, the Babbling Billows, Gourmet Island. Was that all? Evidently it was, for I was plummeting in free fall into the jaws of a huge, merciless plant that showed absolutely no sign of relenting.

It's amazing how vividly you perceive things in a situation of this kind. I noticed, for example, that the Gourmetica's teeth were in a shockingly neglected condition, some of them being overgrown with seaweed and colonies of shellfish, others suppurating and coated with a thick, vile-smelling film of slime. Lodged between them were the skeletons of sharks and small whales and the bones of seals and sea lions that had presumably strayed in by mistake. At the back of the throat I even sighted the splintered remains of a rowing boat with two human skeletons on board. The gullet opened, ready to engulf me and convey me into the digestive tract. I actually had time to analyse the differences between my current predicament and my very similar encounter with the Tyrannomobyus Rex. They were as follows: (a) The whale had not tried to swallow me with evil intent; the Gourmetica was not only doing so deliberately but had planned and elaborately staged the whole thing well in advance. (b) I had been washed into the whale's mouth, whereas now I was in free fall. (c) The Gourmetica had no whiskers I could have clung to.

I shut my eyes.

At that moment something very strong grasped my right wrist and checked my descent. For a second I hung above the abyss, then I was yanked into the air. I shut my eyes and looked down: I was being plucked from the vegetable monster's gaping jaws.

It began to close them in hopes of thwarting my escape, but just before the mighty teeth slammed shut I was towed through the narrow gap that remained. Onwards and upwards I soared while the Gourmetica writhed in fury below me. It reared up, opened its vast mouth once more, and snapped at me, but I had gained too much height. The rotting teeth crashed together in vain. It shook its huge head and emitted a frightful howl of rage that went echoing far across the sea.

Only now did I venture to look up.

A strange bird   A sizeable creature – I hesitate to call it a bird – was holding me in its talons. I was suspended beneath it like a mailbag about to be jettisoned at any moment.

'In luck again, weren't we?' said the strange bird.

I was speechless. It released me once more and I fell like a stone, straight towards the Gourmetica's gaping, bellowing mouth. The bird performed a daring loop-the-loop, and I landed with a thud on its back. Laboriously, I struggled into a sitting position.

'Er … Many thanks for saving my life,' I heard myself say in a daze. The strange bird slowly turned its head and contemplated me with wide, watery eyes.

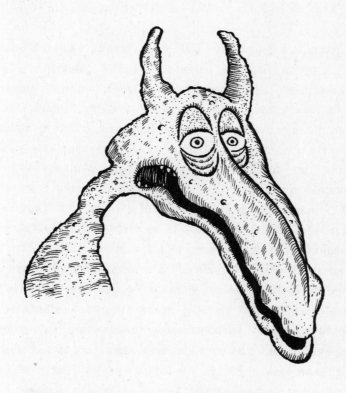

'That's all right,' said the bird. 'It was all in a day's work.'
'You mean it's your job, saving lives?' I was flabbergasted.
'Saving lives *in the nick of time*!' the bird replied rather smugly. '*That's* my job.'
It preserved a brief silence, presumably to let that information sink in. Then it introduced itself: 'Deus X. Machina, at your service. That's my professional name, to be honest. You may call me Mac – everyone does.'
'Pleased to meet you,' I said. 'My name's Bluebear.'

From the
'Encyclopedia of Marvels, Life Forms
and Other Phenomena of Zamonia and its Environs'
by Professor Abdullah Nightingale

Pterodactylus Salvator, The. The Pterodactylus Salvator or Roving Reptilian Rescuer belongs, like the Zamonian →*Sewer Dragon* and the →*Tyrannomobyus Rex*, to a family of dinosaurs close to extinction. The world's surviving population of pterodactyls is estimated at several thousand, but their numbers are steadily diminishing. Although they possess a few birdlike attributes, for instance horny beaks and wings capable of aerodynamic propulsion, they lay no eggs and behave in a very unbirdlike manner from other points of view as well. They eat no earthworms or fieldmice, adhere to an exclusively vegetarian diet for reasons of physical fitness, and are linguistically gifted to a high degree. Common to them all is a propensity for preserving other life forms from danger. Pterodactyls pursue that goal with thoroughly professional alacrity, operating in accordance with a strict code of conduct. They endeavour to make their operations as exciting and dramatic as possible, even competing to see which of them can wait longest before effecting a rescue. That is why they spend so long circling above their prospective customers and refrain from coming to their assistance until the very last moment. There is no satisfactory scientific explanation for the altruistic conduct of these flying lizards. Taciturn and uncommunicative on principle, pterodactyls make no attempt to account for their behaviour. It is, however, presumed to be associated with their imminent extinction. Since dinosaurs have made no noteworthy contribution to history apart from eating and being eaten, pterodactyls are trying to leave their mark on the memory of man by being helpful.

94

Where I was concerned, Mac had been circling the island for days, knowing precisely what lay in store for me. He could easily have rescued me before, but no – he had to wait until the very last moment.

'You're nice and plump,' said Mac, not looking at me. 'You really tucked in down there, eh?'

I blushed.

'Those damned aquatic plants!' he exclaimed in disgust, and spat into the sea. 'I hate them, the beasts. I've already had to rescue a whole bunch of people this year. There are always a few fools ready to fall for their cheap tricks.'

I blushed still more.

'Let this be a lesson to you,' Mac went on. 'Nothing in life is free, not even the food you eat.'

I deigned to make a note of this.

On the skyline was an island with a lofty pinnacle of rock projecting from it. Mac headed straight towards it.

'This planet is full of dangers,' Mac shouted into the headwind. 'You have to take good care to avoid them – keep your eyes skinned all the time.' He continued to make for the crag, vigorously flapping his wings.

'Er...' I started to say.

But Mac wasn't listening. 'Always on the *qui vive*, that's my motto. Drop your guard for an instant, and you've had it!'

We were still racing towards the crag. Another two wingbeats, and we would crash right into it.

'Look out!' I shouted. 'A rock!'

Mac screwed up his eyes, then opened them wide.

'Ouch!' he yelled, and went into an almost vertical climb. We missed the tip of the rock by inches.

An awkward silence reigned for some minutes. Then Mac cleared his throat.

'That was, er...' He broke off. 'Well done, my boy! You've got sharp eyes.'

He cleared his throat again.

A proposition

'I'm going to let you in on a secret,' he went on, 'but you must swear by all that's holy you'll never tell anyone.'

I would have done anything for him. He'd saved my life.

'You see, my eyes aren't as sharp as they used to be. I'm getting a bit, er, short-sighted these days. I'm three thousand years old, after all.'

I still don't know if that was really true. Roving Reptilian Rescuers tend to exaggerate.

'But for heaven's sake keep it to yourself! If my colleagues get to hear of it I'll be finished, professionally speaking.'

He sighed.

'The thing is, I've only got another year before I retire. I'll have to keep going till then, but it's getting harder and harder. I only saw you because you're so exceptionally fat and blue.'

Mac turned his head so that I was looking straight into his dim eyes.

'Listen, youngster, I've a proposition for you. Stay with me for a year – be my navigator, my helmsman. Tell me where the action is, and I'll provide you with free board and lodging. What's more, you'll get to see something of the world. Dramatic, last – minute rescues, beautiful damsels in dire peril – things like that. What do you say?'

5.

My Life
as
a Navigator

Before I took up my duties as a navigator, Mac kitted me out with some working clothes. We normally operated at altitudes where the air was very thin and painfully cold, even for someone in a bearskin.

My navigator's outfit

Mac set me down on a mountain top, disappeared for a couple of hours, and returned with two articles of clothing, a thick red sweater and a pair of dark blue trousers.

'I got them from a farm,' he explained. 'They were hanging on the line to dry. I wouldn't call it stealing. Who knows, maybe we'll save the original owner's life some day.'

You see things in their true perspective, looking at them from overhead. In my year as Mac's navigator I learned much that proved useful in my subsequent lives as a seabear. I had always imagined, for example, that the world resembled a bowl of water with a few islands floating in it. From my vantage point on Mac's back I perceived that it was an immense sphere, some of it covered with water and some with extensive continents. I had never thought it possible that such agglomerations of dry land could exist. We sometimes sailed over broad plains for weeks without sighting the sea. For the first time I saw mighty mountain ranges, big rivers, lakes, and forests. Mac flew me over the poles, and I marvelled at their mountains of pure ice. I saw the jungle, an endless green sea of gigantic trees from whose canopy of foliage the heads of fire-breathing dragons occasionally peered forth. We circled active volcanoes and warmed ourselves in the waves of heat given off by their mighty pillars of fire.

Mac showed me deserts, many of sand, others of multicoloured rocks, and never tired of explaining geological conformations. He enlightened me on alpine glaciers and peat bogs, quicksands, mud flats, and geological faults. Mac's view of the world was mainly of a professional nature; as he saw it, danger lurked everywhere. A person could drown in marshes and quagmires, be

Lurking dangers

swallowed up by crevasses, be overwhelmed by avalanches, meet a watery end in mud flats. If we flew over a forest, Mac automatically scanned it for dangerous species of animals and demons and gauged the risk of fire because of drought. Rivers we checked for piranhas (we simply dropped a dead fish into them and erected a warning sign if the water seethed), seas for the presence of sharks, and lakes for water snakes, lethal salamanders, and giant crocodiles.

To Mac, an iceberg drifting in the rays of the setting sun was a hazard to shipping, not a breathtaking spectacle; a forest waterfall a threat to inexperienced boatmen, not a welcome source of refreshment; a cloudcastle hovering over a Caribbean island the precursor of a tropical typhoon, not one of Nature's paintings. Even empty desert could turn out, under Mac's stern gaze, to be a death trap replete with dangers: venomous gila monsters, giant spiders, electric scorpions loitering under stones, mirages that led the credulous astray, heat capable of driving a person insane with sunstroke.

A windless sea could be just as dangerous as one that was lashed by the most violent of storms; more sailors died of thirst in the doldrums than drowned in hurricanes. Mac's glum manner was the product of his daily misgivings about everything and everyone. Each of them, large or small, had etched another furrow in his skin and turned him into a living map of anxiety.

The Roving Reptilian Rescuers kept tabs on the world in accordance with a complicated shift system I never entirely fathomed. They had divided the whole planet into grid squares, each of which was watched over by one pterodactyl. These grid squares were reallocated after a certain length of time to prevent boredom from setting in.

The shift system

101

Mac would occasionally meet some other pterodactyl on a bare mountain top. I generally preserved a discreet distance while they exchanged professional tips, dinosaur gossip, information about the distribution of grid squares, and a few dry quips. All Roving Reptilian Rescuers were inveterate loners. Social intercourse wasn't their scene, and none of them ever made an exception to that rule.

Meantime, I had lost a lot of weight. During our long-haul flights I performed exercises on Mac's back: press-ups, knees-bends, et cetera. Now and then I would hang from his talons and do chin-ups. Mac saw to it that I was properly fed. He would set me down on a treetop or a mountain peak, fly off, and return with a beakful of fruit and vegetables, after which we would munch away in silence and enjoy the view. I had soon regained my former weight and acquired a few muscles into the bargain.

I never quite discovered how Mac knew when someone was in danger. It was instinctive, I guess. As a rule we flew along at random until Mac suddenly cocked his head and stopped flapping his wings. Then he said 'Work to be done!' and altered course. Once we reached the target area I did the precision

work, piloting Mac to our customer with pinpoint accuracy. I could steer him like an aircraft by using his horns as joysticks. Either that, or I simply told him where to go: 'Further to the right, left a bit, down a bit, up a bit, now grab him!' – that sort of thing.

We rescued explorers from the clutches of forest demons before they were devoured; we caught mountaineers just as they were tumbling into deep ravines; we hoisted shipwrecked sailors off ice floes and out of shark-infested waters; we extricated lost children

Last-minute rescues

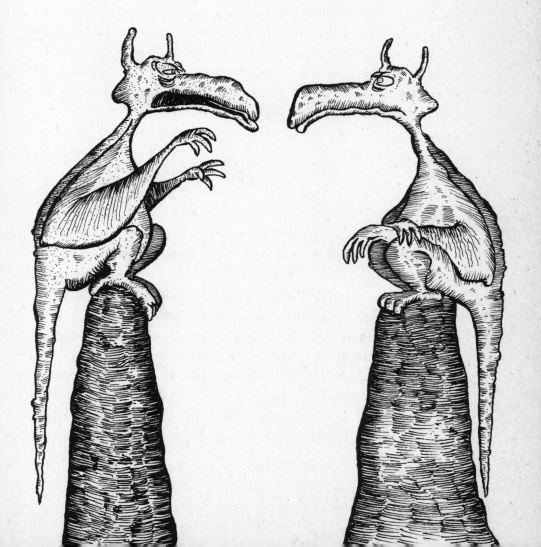

from gloomy forests before moss sprites could drive them mad; we preserved fanatical vulcanologists from death in boiling lava; we hauled foolhardy people out of swamps and quicksands; and, of course, we often saved gluttonous idiots who had fallen for the wiles of a Gourmetica insularis and bore them out of the danger zone.

And – needless to say – we always waited until the very last moment.

Having completed a mission, we usually transported the customer to safety and flew off at once. Mac found gratitude intolerable. Many customers wanted to entertain us, make a fuss of us, shower us with gifts, adopt us, marry us, and so on. I wouldn't have objected to a little fuss, but not Mac. 'That's all right, it's my job,' he told them. 'Be a bit more careful and avoid eating meat in future.'

Then we soared off.

The greatest source of danger was recklessness. Although many of our customers had got into difficulty through sheer bad luck, our clientele included a hard core of incorrigibles who positively sought danger and, for unidentifiable reasons, wanted to pit themselves against the elements. Mountains had to be climbed, rapids negotiated, spooky swamps traversed after dark. Some blithely sang as they strode through benighted forests notorious for their population of werewolves, others insisted on watching volcanic eruptions from the crater's edge or tornadoes from the eye of the storm.

I recall an incident at Demon Rocks (we were already operating in Zamonia by this time) which could hardly have been surpassed for stupidity. We had spent the whole day watching from afar as a man clambered around in that ill-famed mountainous region. He was obviously an inexperienced climber. His shoes were far too light, and he had set off in a slight drizzle. 'There'll be trouble,' was all Mac said, and I strove to keep the man in sight as Mac circled at a considerable distance to prevent our being spotted.

At the foot of Demon Rocks lay a dense crystal forest whose yards-long daggers of glass bristled close to the rock face. The bleached skeletons of incautious climbers hung, clattering, on many of those lethal spikes. Responsible mountaineers shunned the area just as seamen steered clear of the Malmstrom.

Despite this, the man succeeded in climbing Demon Rocks. But the ascent tends to be the simpler, less dangerous part of a climb; the descent is riskier and more complicated. We resigned ourselves to a long afternoon's wait, at the end of which we would probably have to pluck the numskull out of some crevice into which he had fallen.

Far from it, however.

Having ascended the highest peak, the climber spread his arms.

'He's holding his arms out,' I told Mac, who couldn't see him at that range.

'Is he?' said Mac. 'Then he's going to jump.'

'Jump?'

The climber launched himself into space.

'He's jumped!' I cried.

'I told you so,' growled Mac.

The madman fell like a stone. Demon Rocks were several miles high, and awaiting him below were the crystal daggers.

'Let's go!' I cried.

'No,' said Mac.

'What!'

'It's his own fault. He needs to be taught a lesson.'

The man had now fallen a mile. We might just make it if we set off right away.

'You can't do this, Mac! Come on, move!'

'No,' said Mac, and flew another leisurely circuit.

Fifteen hundred feet to impact...

'But Mac, we can't just watch like this.'

'I'm not watching. I can't see him in any case.'

Nine hundred feet... The drizzle had given way to a heavy downpour, and visibility was steadily deteriorating.

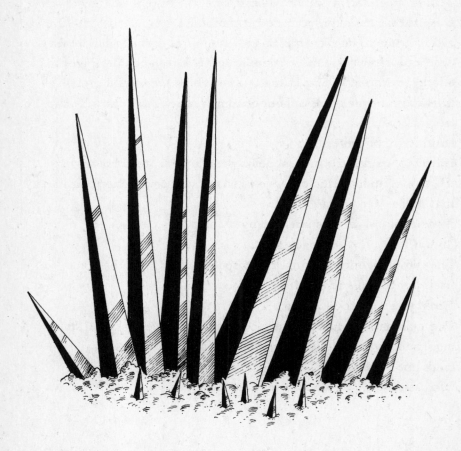

'Mac! I order you get going at once!'

'I don't take orders from you.'

Six hundred feet...

I couldn't understand why Mac was doing nothing. By now the situation was wellnigh hopeless.

Three hundred feet...

'Mac! I can't bear to watch!'

'Don't look, then. I'm not.'

A hundred and fifty feet.

'Now!' squawked Mac, and flapped his wings harder than I'd ever known. The slipstream almost tore me off his back.

He was flying fast, but in the wrong direction. I twisted his horns to the right to bring us back on course.

'Now!' Mac cried again, and flapped his wings even more fiercely. We shot forwards a good three hundred feet.

Another sixty feet to impact...

'Now!' Mac cried for the third time. His wings clove the air with such force that the sound hurt my ears.

Another thirty feet and the climber would be skewered by one of the crystal daggers, but we ourselves were still a good six hundred feet away. I applied slight pressure to Mac's horns, putting him into an even steeper nosedive.

'Now!'

Fifteen feet... Six hundred to go...

'Now!'

Six feet... Still another three hundred...

'Now!'

Only an inch separated the falling climber from the tips of the glass daggers.

'Grab him!' I shouted.

Mac caught hold of the man's left leg and yanked him upwards.

We deposited the mountaineer on a plateau. Mac gave him a tongue-lashing and demanded to know what he'd been thinking of. 'Nothing much,' the man replied. 'I just wanted to see how good you Roving Reptilian Rescuers really are.'

'I told you he deserved to be taught a lesson!' growled Mac as we flew off to find ourselves some supper.

I was a talented navigator. Although I never received a word of praise or appreciation from Mac's beak (he was incapable of that), I could tell from his little ways that he respected my work. Whenever we completed a successful salvage operation, for instance, he would emit a self-satisfied hum like an unmusical cat attempting to sing. That hum told me I'd done a good job. I, too, began to develop a nose for danger as the weeks went by. Sometimes I sensed at the same moment as Mac that there was work ahead. I knew it from a sudden smell borne on the wind – the scent of distant woodsmoke mingled with a whiff of cinnamon. My knowledge of the earth increased, grid square by grid square. We flew over Africa and the Antarctic, Borneo and the Black Forest, Tasmania and the Himalayas, Siberia and Kathmandu, Heligoland and Death Valley, the Grand Canyon and Easter Island, and eventually over the continents of Cataclysmia, Zombia and Yhôll, which no longer exist. Yes, I soon came to know the earth like a vast mosaic in which only one piece was still missing: Zamonia.

Zamonia

Zamonia was recognizable from a great height by an offshore island in the shape of a bear's paw, hence its name, Paw Island. On the way to our new grid square we approached Zamonia from the north-east, where it was traversed by mountain ranges. We flew over the mainland for weeks on end, steering a zigzag course because Mac wanted me to acquire a general overview of the continent. Zamonia possessed the most diverse scenery. In addition to desert plateaux I saw pinnacles of ice, mangrove swamps, vast wheat fields, stony wastes, and mixed forests. In the far west were some mountains known as the Gloombergs, whose peaks were considerably higher than the others. One prominent feature in the middle of the continent was a desert, the biggest I had ever seen. But what interested me most of all was the capital of Zamonia. This was Atlantis, at that time the biggest city in the world.

From the
'Encyclopedia of Marvels, Life Forms
and Other Phenomena of Zamonia and its Environs'
by Professor Abdullah Nightingale

Atlantis. Capital and seat of government of the continent of Zamonia. Classified as a megalopolis, Atlantis is divided into five administrative districts, each of which really constitutes a kingdom in its own right: Naltatis, Sitnalta, Titalans, Tatilans, and Lisnatat. These urban districts are, in their turn, divided into subdistricts: NALTATIS into Santalit, Tisalant, Satalint, Sitaltan, Tintasal, Tansalit, and Anstlati; SITNALTA into Stalinta, Satintal, Stanilat, Talnatis, Nastilat, Titanlas, and Tinsalat; TITALANS into Alastint, Lisatant, Aslitant, and Santatil. As for LISNATAT, whose inhabitants voted against subdivision, it is merely divided into North Lisnatat, South Lisnatat, East Lisnatat, West Lisnatat, and Central Lisnatat. All the above subdistricts are divided into subsubdistricts whose enumeration would transcend the scope of this publication. At the time of writing, each of the five administrative districts is inhabited by approximately 25 million living creatures, so the total population of Atlantis may be put at roughly 125 million, or, if one includes all the anonymous, unregistered creatures resident in the sewers, at almost 200 million.

From the air Atlantis looked like the toy collection of a demented giant. Quaint little houses with red, green and golden roofs stood cheek by jowl with white minarets and black factories with belching chimneys. Some buildings were constructed of stone, timber, and iron, others of silver, gold, and crystal. Corkscrew towers jutted into the sky for miles, so high that I had to steer Mac round them on a slalom course. I saw pagodas and shanty towns, palaces and tenements, onion domes, marble mansions, and gigantic cathedrals. The city was threaded with innumerable rivers and canals spanned by bridges of complex design. There was movement everywhere. Steamships, sailing boats and canoes plied the rivers, massive captive balloons hovered among the towers and skyscrapers. But what fascinated me most of all about Atlantis were the bustling streets, which were alive with pedestrians and vehicles. I would dearly have liked to land there, but Mac was against it.

'Cities are the end,' was his verdict. 'They're madhouses.'

I simply couldn't persuade him to land, however much I begged and pleaded. I had no choice but to promise myself that I would visit Atlantis some day.

The last grid square we surveyed included the South Zamonian Sea between Wotansgard Sound and Three-Quarters Island, on which stood the Impic Alps. We had already flown around for three days without spotting anything of note apart from a chamois, which we rescued from the clutches of a mountain demon, so I was delighted when, early on the evening of the third day, Mac suddenly raised his head and sniffed the air. It was filled with a scent he recognized. He altered course to the south-west and I took up my navigator's position just behind his head with one forepaw on one of his horns and the other over my eyes to shield them from the rays of the setting sun. There was something afoot that differed from our routine rescue operations. Even the air around us was unnaturally turbulent, swirling violently as if something very large had just passed through it.

CRASH!

A menacing sound like distant thunder.
We flew low over Harvest Home Plain. Nothing to be seen but scattered farmhouses, endless fields of wheat, and an occasional small village. It would have been pretty hard to come to grief there. There were no treacherous swamps, no precipitous cliffs, not even a lake in which to get cramp while swimming.

CRRASH!!

The ground was vibrating violently as if rocked by small, rhythmical earthquakes. The wheat fields had been flattened at intervals of half a mile. The flattened areas, all of which were the same shape, resembled giant footprints.

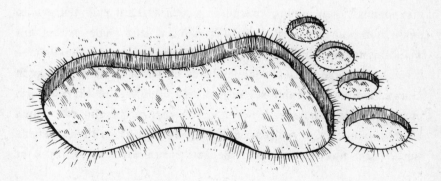

CRRRASH!!!

'A Bollogg,' said Mac, as if that explained everything.

From the
'**Encyclopedia of Marvels, Life Forms
and Other Phenomena of Zamonia and its Environs**'
by Professor Abdullah Nightingale

Bollogg, The. The Bollogg [Cyclops stupidus] belongs to the Giant Cyclops family, which includes all one-eyed, outsize life forms over 75 feet in height. Although Giant Cyclopses do not exceed 500 feet as a rule, a Bollogg can grow to a height of two miles and is thus the only living creature to be classified among Zamonia's exceptional natural disasters [→*Eternal Tornado, The*, or →*Sharach-il-Allah, The*]. It has even been inferred from skeletal remains that Bolloggs existing in very ancient times could attain a height of twelve miles. Fortunately, very few Bolloggs still survive in Zamonia. They are currently estimated to number no more than half a dozen.

Bolloggs possess the unique ability to survive without a head. Although born with heads, they lose all forms of social awareness and communicative instinct the bigger they get. When they reach a height of 150 feet, if not before, their capacity for human contact disappears. Their ability to speak, which is only rudimentary to begin with, becomes completely atrophied, and their brains are scarcely needed any more. From 5000 feet onwards the Bollogg attains that rare state of independence in which sense organs such as eyes and ears become superfluous. At 6000 feet or thereabouts, most Bolloggs discard their heads, which are, in any case, only loosely connected to the rest of their biosystem. From then onwards they take in nourishment through their pores, which are so big that birds, mice, and even piglets and lambs can be ingested and fed into the circulation. A Bollogg has only to roll around in a field of wheat to satisfy its hunger for months to come. The discarded head is usually left behind [an average Bollogg head can exceed 1200 feet in diameter] while the rest of the body continues on its way, presumably in search of its missing cranium.

CRRRRASH!!!!

And then we saw it: a Bollogg all of two miles high was steadily tramping through the South Zamonian wheat fields. Its fur was dark, almost black, like a gorilla's. It resembled that animal in other ways, too, with its long, dangling arms and apelike feet, except that gorillas grow no bigger than a wardrobe and keep their heads on their shoulders.

The Bollogg

CRRRRRASH!!!!!

Although it had already trampled a few farmhouses underfoot, it probably hadn't harmed any of their occupants. People can usually hear and sense the approach of a Bollogg in time to get out of its way.

One or two countryfolk had already emerged from their boltholes and were mourning their ravaged fields and farmyards. We soared over them, resolutely making for the Bollogg, which was only a few miles ahead and had now come to a halt. Mac must have sensed something long before, and even I had registered the growing intensity of the danger in the air. I could now make out a building at the Bollogg's feet and see, as we drew nearer, that its barred windows were crowded with dozens of little dogs, all howling in the most pathetic manner.

'Wolperting Whelps,' said Mac.

From the
'Encyclopedia of Marvels, Life Forms
and Other Phenomena of Zamonia and its Environs'
by Professor Abdullah Nightingale

Wolperting Whelps. One of South Zamonian agriculturalists' chief sources of income is the breeding of Wolperting Whelps. This industry is based in the town of Wolperting and the countryside that surrounds it. Highly prized as pets throughout Zamonia, Wolperting Whelps are regarded as the acme of cuteness, even surpassing Hackonian Cuddlebunnies and Zamonian Dormice in that respect.

The building was one of the typical local dog farms, and its owners had presumably fled hell for leather, leaving their captive, defenceless charges to their fate. I shook my head at such irresponsibility. If there were such a thing as a popularity scale for life forms, Bolloggs would come right at the bottom and Wolperting Whelps in first place. They are the cutest creatures in the world. They serve no particular purpose; they exist merely to delight the eye and gladden the heart. Wolperting Whelps live on affection, so the saying goes.

Wolperting Whelps [cont.]. There is a theory, as yet un-supported by scientific evidence, that Wolperting Whelps live on affection when very young. One cannot exclude the possibility that they possess telepathic powers that enable them to assimilate the affection they are shown and convert it into calories. Despite their relatively cute appearance, it should be added that these quaint little puppies grow up into Wolpertingers of impressive size. At puberty they measure as much as ten feet from nose to tail, have three rows of fangs, walk on their hind legs, and tend to be pugnacious. They take only six months to reach maturity, so inexperienced Whelp-owners can be traumatized by their lapdogs' rapid development.

CRRRRRRASH!!!!!!

The Bollogg came to a halt.
'We don't have much time,' Mac observed. 'The Bollogg's about to sit down.'

'Where a Bollogg sits down,' runs an old Zamonian proverb, 'no Gloomberg Moss will grow for a thousand years.' On the very rare occasions when a Bollogg sits down, it does so with a vengeance, and this one was about to park itself on a building filled with Wolperting Whelps.

Fortunately, these giants are slow movers – *very* slow movers. So slow that it's almost agonizing to watch them in action. Our specimen was now going into a crouch, but it would be some time before its posterior came into contact with the roof of the dog farm. Its sluggishness was our only hope. Some thirty Wolperting Whelps were scrabbling at the windows and whining. Before the Bollogg's backside crushed the building, therefore, we would have to extract every last Whelp and fly it out of the danger zone. There wasn't room for more than three or four of them on Mac's back in addition to myself. The great rump was descending at around 300 feet a minute, which meant roughly ten return trips in ten minutes – on the face of it, a sheer impossibility.

I had never seen Mac work so fast. This time every last second counted, so histrionic tricks would have been out of order. We flew over to one of the windows, where I wrenched the thin grille out of its seating and extracted four puppies. Then we zoomed off as fast as possible, hurriedly dumped the little animals out of range of the Bollogg's backside, and flew back again.

Meantime the Bollogg was steadily hunkering down. The huge black creature had already shrouded the canine prison in shadow. We carried a second load of puppies to safety. On the third run one of them fell off, so we had to go back and retrieve it.

That wasted precious seconds.

On the fourth run, one of the puppies – I still vividly recall the red fleck on its forehead – behaved in a thoroughly foolish way. The panic-stricken little creature couldn't manage the leap from the window into my arms, so I had to do something foolhardy: holding on to one of Mac's horns, I leaned right over and grabbed it by the scruff of the neck. It rewarded me for my pains by biting me on the paw.

By the time we had flown to and fro five times, the Bollogg's backside had reached the top of the house and was starting to crush the chimney. Bricks went tumbling into the interior and terrified the puppies still more. The roof timbers were creaking ominously. By the seventh trip the roof was already caving in under the pressure. Shingles snapped off the battens and whistled around our ears like bullets. One of them hit Mac smack between the eyes, but he displayed total indifference (pterodactyls being covered in an inch-thick layer of horny skin).

The first roof timbers cracked, piercing the walls of the upper storey and sending plaster and mortar flying in all directions. It was as if the building had opened fire on us. The puppies howled and whimpered fit to melt a heart of stone. On the eighth run the upper storey collapsed in a shower of bricks, beams, and iron pipes. A batten snapped off and came whizzing towards us like a javelin. It would have made a shish kebab of the four puppies behind me if Mac hadn't evaded it by performing a graceful dive.

On the ninth run, only the ground floor remained intact. The upper floor had been emptied of puppies and crushed soon afterwards. The last of them had taken refuge in the cellar and were whimpering through the cellar window. The foundation walls exploded with a roar, bricks disintegrated into a red sawdust that almost robbed us of visibility. We dumped our penultimate consignment.

On our last flight the Bollogg's behind had subsided to such an extent that Mac and I could only just squeeze through the narrow gap between it and the ground. We hauled the remaining puppies out of the cellar window and set off on the return journey.

Flying was out of the question, now that the Bollogg was only three feet from the ground. Each with two puppies on our backs, we endeavoured to crawl out of the danger zone on our bellies. We almost passed out, the Bollogg gave off such a stench. Behind us, the cellar ceiling caved in with a crash. I suddenly found myself enveloped in a maze of greasy strands: my view was being obscured by the long, slimy hair that dangled from the Bollogg's backside. Was I crawling in the right direction?

'This way!' I heard Mac croak. 'I'm out already!'

I crawled in the direction of his voice.

'This way! Come on, quick!'

At last the hairy curtain parted: I was in the open! Mac was already shepherding his passengers out of the danger zone.

I was about to remove the puppies from my back when I noticed that there was only one of them. I tossed it to Mac, who caught it in his beak, and crawled back into the forest of Bollogg hair.

The other little creature, beside itself with fear, was hanging from a sticky strand like an insect stuck to flypaper. I plucked it off, hugged it to my chest, and wormed my way, panting, into the open air. Behind me, the Bollogg's posterior came to rest with a sound like thunder. The ground shook so violently that miles-long cracks appeared in the surface.

Then peace returned and the dust settled. I scrambled to my feet and looked for Mac. He was lying on his back, bathed in sweat and breathing heavily, while the rescued puppies romped around him and nipped his wings.

Once a Bollogg has sat down it ceases to be a danger, at least for some considerable time. The colossal creature can remain motionless for as long as two years before getting up again. While Mac was flying around in search of other Reptilian Rescuers who could help us to find the puppies a home, I looked after the quaint little animals. We recovered from our frightening experience in the shade of the gigantic Bollogg. Each of the puppies wanted me to fondle it. They were probably famished and eager to feast on my affection.

Once the puppies had been found good homes and Mac had given the dog farmer a severe dressing-down, we flew off. I was mightily proud of our rescue operation. Mac made no comment, of course, but he purred like a cat beside a warm stove.

The remainder of my year with Mac literally flew by. I felt so much at home in my new life that I could well have imagined going on like that for ever. I never contemplated a change – not, at any rate, until Mac announced at supper one night that we must soon go our separate ways.

'I've got a chance of a room at "North End", the Roving Reptilian Rescuers' Retirement Home on the Worm Peninsula,' he told me, avoiding my eye. 'Full board, congenial company, a good view of the icebergs in Shivering Sound. Sea serpents are reputed to mate there in the autumn. It's a breathtaking spectacle, by all accounts.' I didn't know what to say.

'All right,' he went, 'I can also think of pleasanter ways to end my days than playing chess in a home for superannuated pterodactyls, but that's the way of the world. My eyesight isn't getting any better. Besides, it's time you mingled with people and got to know the serious side of life.'

'I can do without the serious side of life,' I replied.

Mac ignored this. 'I'll take you to a place where they teach the really important aspects of existence: darknessology, arcane sciences,

Zamonian poetry, Grailsundian Demonism, and so on. I'm going to enrol you in Professor Nightingale's Nocturnal Academy.'

'A school, you mean?'

'A special school for special individuals like you. You must have the finest education there is, and that you can only get at the Nocturnal Academy.'

'But I couldn't afford it!" I protested rather feebly. 'I'm completely penniless!'

Mac's big, bloodshot eyes fixed me with a lingering gaze.

'That doesn't matter,' he said. 'Professor Nightingale owes me. I saved his life once – in the nick of time, what's more.'

Farewell to Mac   There were no big speeches when Mac and I said goodbye. After a flight lasting five days he set me down in the Gloombergs, a mountain range in north-west Zamonia. It seemed that the highest educational qualifications were obtainable only in the continent's highest region. We landed outside an unprepossessing cave, doorless, dark, and forbidding. There was an 'N' carved into the rock face above the mouth of the cave, and a black arrow on the wall pointed into the interior.

'The entrance to the Nocturnal Academy,' Mac explained.

I shook his talons, bereft of speech. For a whole year he had been my moral support and his back the ground beneath my feet.

'Always keep your eyes skinned,' he croaked, rather falteringly, 'and avoid eating meat as far as possible.'

He gave my forepaw another firm squeeze, then soared into the air. It was a majestic sight, marred only by the fact that he was flying straight for a wall of rock.

'Climb!' I yelled.

He did so at the very last moment – as usual – and skimmed over the crag. Then he disappeared into the lee of the mountains.

Dark and sinister-looking, the entrance to the Nocturnal Academy gaped like a mouth in the iron rock face. Another of my lives lay behind me; the next loomed ahead, fraught with menace and uncertainty. I was about to exchange a wild, emancipated, adventurous existence for a classroom in a gloomy cavern. It wasn't a very alluring prospect.

For one brief, defiant moment I thought of simply turning around and running away – no matter where to – but beneath me yawned the chasms of the Gloomberg Mountains. The slopes were steep and offered few footholds. I drew three deep breaths and made my way into the dark tunnel.

6.

My Life in the Gloomberg Mountains

'**K**nowledge,' Professor Nightingale bellowed in the classroom, opening his eyes until they were as big as saucers, 'knowledge is night!' This was a maxim derived from Nocturnomathic philosophysics, a subject taught exclusively at the Nocturnal Academy.

Professor Nightingale often said such things, probably in order to disconcert us. There was method in these seemingly nonsensical statements: by the time we'd grasped their total idiocy, our thoughts had strayed in every conceivable direction. This was precisely what the professor wanted: to steer our thoughts in as many different directions as possible.

In this particular case, however, there was a grain of truth in what he'd said, for Professor Nightingale was a Nocturnomath. Nocturnomaths are the most intelligent beings in Zamonia (and probably in the entire world, if not the universe). In normal lighting they have an IQ of 4000, but when darkness falls it attains astronomical heights. That is why Nocturnomaths favour the darkest conditions possible, and why Nightingale's Nocturnal Academy was housed in a dark complex of caves in the Gloomberg Mountains. In his spare time the professor was working on a system whereby darkness could be rendered darker still. To this end he had installed a darkroom which he alone was permitted to enter. We ourselves had no great desire to enter it in any case, for the noises we heard when we listened at the door were far from inviting.

A run-of-the-mill Nocturnomath has three brains, a gifted Nocturnomath four, a Nocturnomath of genius five. Professor Nightingale had seven. One was in his head, four grew out of his skull, and a sixth was located where the spleen normally resides. As for the seventh, that was an object of eternal speculation among his pupils.

To the superficial eye he looked rather small and frail. His spindly little arms dangled – superfluously, it seemed – at the sides of his

bent body, which was precariously supported by two wobbly legs resembling lengths of garden hose encased in trousers. He was slightly humpbacked, and his head, with its four external brains, was tremulously balanced on a long, scraggy neck. His big, bright eyes protruded so far from their sockets, we were always afraid they'd pop out of his head, especially when he became agitated.

Yes, Nightingale made an extremely frail impression, but appearances were deceptive. He simply preferred to solve problems by dint of mental exertion. I was actually present one day when the professor opened a can of sardines merely by applying his mind to the task. After witnessing that feat, I never flicked another paper pellet at him behind his back.

'You're very *special*!' he would bellow at us, so loudly that we all gave a jump. He was forever reminding us that every graduate of his Nocturnal Academy was unique in his or her own way. He had a point, too: we really were rather out of the ordinary.

The Nocturnal Academy had precisely three pupils at this time: Fredda the Alpine Imp, Qwerty Uiop, the gelatine prince from the 2364th Dimension, and yours truly, the bluebear. Professor Nightingale made it a rule only to accept life forms of which it could be proved that only one example existed on earth, so the Nocturnal Academy was very much an elite establishment. Perhaps I should give a slightly more detailed description of my classmates and the teaching staff before proceeding with my story, because they really merit some explanation.

Fredda:

Fredda, the only female creature at the Nocturnal Academy, was madly in love with me. So much for the good news. The bad news: Fredda was an Alpine Imp, and Alpine Imps may well be the ugliest creatures imaginable. No, let's not beat about the bush: Alpine Imps are *far and away* the ugliest creatures imaginable.

The Alpine Imp

From the
'Encyclopedia of Marvels, Life Forms
and Other Phenomena of Zamonia and its Environs'
by Professor Abdullah Nightingale

Alpine Imp, The. An inhabitant of the Impic Alps in southern Zamonia, the common Alpine Imp may generally be numbered, like the Gulch Troll and the Glacier Gorgon but unlike the Troglotroll or Avalanche Ogress, among the so-called guileless mountain demons, in other words, mountain-dwelling sprites devoid of evil intent.

Although innocuous in manner, the Alpine Imp is condemned to relative solitude by its repulsive appearance. Yet the true extent of its ugliness cannot be detected. Providence has been kind enough to conceal Alpine Imps in a growth of matted hair so dense that their physical characteristics can only be guessed at. The sight of a clean-shaven specimen would be more than the eye could endure. Alpine Imps usually vegetate among the highest peaks of the Impic Alps and can climb like chamois equipped with the arms of a chimpanzee. There is a popular belief that they can even walk on clouds, but this unscientific conjecture may safely be consigned to the realm of legend.

Alpine Imps are trusting and affectionate by nature, but their feelings are seldom returned - a circumstance that has led to their gradual extinction. They make a habit of landing on mountaineers' rucksacks from a great height. Having done so, they give full vent to their affection by letting out a blood-curdling scream. This behaviour accounts for the fact that any climber who has ever encountered an Alpine Imp never scales another mountain and becomes a deep-sea diver or a mine superintendent.

Fredda was startlingly immature and silly for her 400 years. She continually interrupted our lessons by making peculiar noises and bombarding me with paper pellets on which she'd scrawled hearts and arrows or declarations of love. She used to trip me up during break, sit on my back, and stick her pencil in my ear until I promised to marry her. I was powerless to resist these attentions, for Fredda possessed the strength of ten mountain gorillas, the reflexes of a puma, and the stamina of a dolphin. No one in school was a match for her except Professor Nightingale himself.

Fredda couldn't speak, only scream, but Nightingale had begun by teaching her to write and presented her with a pen and a thick memo pad. This she took everywhere with her. She communicated with us by means of these slips of paper, on which she wrote in copperplate. A conversation with her looked something like this:

I: 'Hello, Fredda.'

Fredda:

> *'Good morning, Bluebear.'*

I: 'Sleep well?'

Fredda:

> '*So-so. I've got a nestful of Gloomberg bats in my hair. They squeaked all night long.*'

I: 'Ugh!'

I couldn't return Fredda's feelings, as I've already said, but I was very fond of her. If somebody loves you, you always love them a little in return, even when they're an Alpine Imp.

Qwerty:

The gelatine prince

A gelatine prince from the 2364th Dimension, Qwerty was as transparent as a jelly and the best friend I made during my schooldays. We were all exceptional, but Qwerty was the most exceptional of us all. His place of origin, the 2364th Dimension, is a world that cannot be conceived of by anyone possessing fewer than four brains.

Qwerty was not only a prince of the 2364th Dimension. He was really its king, because he had been on the way to his coronation when he tripped over a fold in the red carpet and fell head first into a dimensional hiatus. The 2364th Dimension is dotted with such holes. If you fall into one, you go tumbling through the entire universe into some other galaxy. Making your way back is extremely difficult. First you have to locate a dimensional hiatus, which is hard enough in itself. It must also be the right one, of course, so that you find your way back into the right dimension. But more of that later. Qwerty was a prisoner in our world, therefore, but he bore his fate with remarkable composure. He liked to act tough and was always cracking jokes. He also devoted a great deal of thought to other people's cares and concerns, but being his best friend I knew that, when he was alone, he shed gelatinous tears and yearned for his home.

Everything there was quite different from our own world. For instance, Qwerty was accustomed to feeding on music, but even our most highbrow music struck him as crude and primitive. It should be explained that in the 2364th Dimension music is played on instruments made of milk. Professor Nightingale had devised a method of keeping Qwerty fed. Using sophisticated underwater

Milk music

133

microphones, he recorded the song of the sea horse, mixed it with the rhythm of thunderclaps, the baying of Baskerville hounds, the inaudible squeaks of bats, the groans of graveyard worms, and a few highly original noises of his own. He then played the whole thing backwards at twice the original speed. Qwerty confirmed that this bore quite a resemblance to the music of his homeland. The rest of us always left the room when he had his musical meals.

Professor Abdullah Nightingale:

Over and above his educational activities, the professor enjoyed an awesome reputation in contemporary Zamonia as a world-class scientist, explorer, and inventor. He had invented the ant motor, a form of propulsion based solely on the industriousness of Zamonian glow-ants. These produced heat and, thus, sufficient energy, when necessary, to drive a steamroller at a speed approaching that of sound. Fuel consumption was limited to a cup of honey poured into the machine from above.

Professor Nightingale's inventions

The professor had also invented the volcanic suit, an all-enveloping garment of woven quicksilver galvanized with un-meltable ice (another of his inventions) in which you could not only immerse yourself in molten lava but, if you removed the hood, cut a dash at cocktail parties.

During one of his dives in Krakatoa's still active crater Nightingale discovered the lava-breathing fire-fish, a species he not only caught and tamed but contrived to use as the basis of a new invention, the fire-fish-powered cave-heating system. If fire-fish were deprived of lava and placed in ordinary drinking water, they automatically changed their cellular structure and transformed themselves into a kind of living lava. These aquatic creatures breathed water like normal fish and thus made it boil. Fire-fish could also be used for brewing coffee, although they left a slightly fishy aftertaste. They were only really suitable, in the gastronomic domain, for making bouillabaisse.

In the chlorophyllaceous circulation of the Gloomberg alga Nightingale had localized the so-called supercalorie. A single one of these was sufficient to sustain an adult for a whole week. The professor endeavoured to make Giant's Teeth algae the Nocturnal Academy's official school meal, but was thwarted by his pupils' aversion to them.

His aquashoes, which enabled one to walk on water by solidifying it with the aid of H_2O rays, remained in vogue only until it was found that the water, which had congealed into a jelly, could not be restored to its original consistency. Because every body of water in and around Zamonia would eventually have been rendered undrinkable and unnavigable, aquashoes were banned throughout the continent. But Nightingale tried to make a profit even out of this setback. Having collected the solidified water, he diluted it with aromatic substances, cut it into slices, and sold it as edible water in an assortment of flavours. This product he named 'Professor Nightingale's Solid Soup'. It didn't sell, however, because no one felt like eating soup on which people had tramped around in his peculiar shoes.

Nightingale was also the inventor of the scintilla shower, a small plywood cubicle surmounted by a hopper in which, he believed, scintillas would accumulate if the occupant pondered on major problems. According to Nightingale's celebrated scintilla theory, scintillas were the basic material of the ideas, or invisible electroparamagnetic aerial worms, which pullulated throughout the atmosphere. Because good ideas always crop up when least expected, Nightingale had advanced the theory that this phenomenon depended on the density of the scintillas in the surrounding air. He also believed that scintillas had a special predilection for dark, confined spaces smelling of pinewood. If a person sat in a dark, confined space smelling of pinewood and thought big thoughts, therefore, the scintillas would stream out of the hopper into the scintilla shower and come rattling down on the seated thinker's head. Although the existence of scintillas and the effectiveness of the scintilla shower could never be scientifically proved, we pupils happily retired to the cubicle to smoke home-rolled cigarettes of Gloomberg algae.

The Chamber of Unperfected Patents

Another of the professor's inventions was a gold extractor that filtered the gold out of the most worthless pebbles, compressed it, and minted it into beautiful coins. He also devised the handy diamond press, with which a lump of anthracite could be compressed into a diamond in one second flat. (The last two inventions had rendered Nightingale financially independent.) He had taken out patents on self-cleansing toilet paper, magnetic paint, a flying carpet, chameleon wallpaper, the Diabolic Elf microscope (with which Qwerty and I examined specimens in our spare time), cyclopean spectacles, and a chisel so tiny it would split an atom – if your fingers were small enough to hold it. More romantic than useful was the furiometer, which could convert paroxysms of rage into harp sonatas.

Nightingale was famous for the suicidal courage he displayed in the interests of scientific progress. One of his most daring experiments was a personal trial of the vibrogirdle. This belt was capable of causing the atoms in a body to vibrate so violently that the wearer could pulsate his way through any given object or someone else's body. Armed with a vibrogirdle, one could pass through a wall or a tree, the door of a safe or a pane of glass, without harming them (or oneself). After several small-scale experiments with solid brick walls and sheets of metal, the professor decided to vibrate his way through the Gloombergs. The experiment was very successful at first. Nightingale swiftly penetrated the atomic structure of the ferruginous mountains and had reached their midpoint when the vibrogirdle simply cut out: he was imprisoned in the mountains' densest concentration of molecules and could neither advance nor retreat. Anyone else would have found this a nightmarish experience, but to Nightingale it was the best thing that had ever happened. Why? Because he had discovered absolute darkness for the very first time. It is said that the basic ideas for all his subsequent scientific feats occurred to him in this state of utter darkness. After this incident, which transformed his life, he devoted himself almost exclusively to the study of lightlessness. This, of course, was possible only because his vibrogirdle was reactivated after a moment or two by a mild earthquake registering two on the Richter scale. He kept the vibrogirdle and other unsuccessful inventions in a room at the Nocturnal Academy. This was secured with an airlock (a Nightingale device consisting of oxygen concentrate) and bore the following inscription:

Unperfected Patents Chamber

The contents of the room included a square-wheeled bicycle for climbing stairs, a type of vacuum cleaner for sucking up lightning, a pair of so-called quicksand trousers, and – of course – some aquashoes. Nightingale had an interesting anecdote to tell about each of these objects. Deus X. Machina featured in the one about the quicksand trousers. Years before, Mac had rescued the professor from a swamp into which he had waded to test the efficacy of his quicksand trousers. The latter were based on an inversion of the vibrogirdle principle and suffered from similar defects. Grains of sand got between the contacts of the sparking plugs of the crude motor that propelled the trousers, which cut out and left Professor Nightingale sinking in the quicksand. If Mac hadn't rescued him – at the very last moment, needless to say – there would have been no Nocturnal Academy.

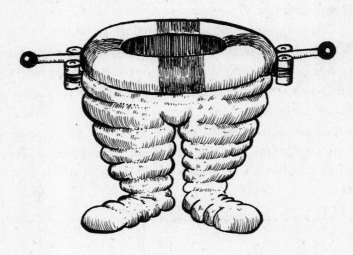

In the classroom   Although I really can't pretend I went to school willingly, the professor's lessons did possess a unique quality. Once he started teaching, you forgot about everything else. When he finally tottered into the classroom (he was nearly always late) and removed his four mortarboards (which he wore partly out of vanity and partly to keep his external brains warm), he got down to it right away.

He also, at that moment, lost his tremulous movements and frail appearance. Prancing up and down in front of the class, lightfooted as a ballerina, he presented his subject matter with a gift for mime and vocal acrobatics that would have enabled any actor, dancer or singer to gain international stardom. Whatever the subject he was teaching, he had the knack of putting it over physically.

With the aid of a few grimaces or contortions, nothing more, he turned before our marvelling eyes into a zebra or a bluebell, a piece of rock crystal or a microbe, an atom or a Pythagorean theorem. Professor Nightingale had taken the teaching profession into the realm of art, and in art, as in all the other disciplines he had mastered, he was a genius.

We were taught no lessons, no single subject, in the traditional manner. Instead, every day was devoted to a long, nonstop lecture by Nightingale in which he jumped from subject to subject, seemingly at random, holding forth sometimes on wind power, sometimes on poodle-breeding or vegetable drugs, and pausing occasionally to scrawl a formula, foreign word or diagram on the blackboard.

Whenever he changed subjects one could see him switch from one brain to another. This he did by inserting his little finger in his left ear and turning it fractionally, screwdriver fashion. There was a faint click like a dislocated finger springing back into place. Sometimes, when he crashed his gears, it sounded as if a crowbar was being crushed between two cogs. It always set my teeth on edge, and Fredda's bristly hair stood on end in any case, but Qwerty liked the sound because it reminded him of a pop song from the 2364th Dimension.

These abrupt changes of subject were far from arbitrary, however, but that I didn't realize until much later. Listening to Nightingale was like reading a very long novel with a complicated plot whose threads don't converge until the end, or like spending years watching a painter at work on an enormous mural. I did, in fact, spend years at the Nocturnal Academy, but they passed so quickly and eventfully that I never got around to counting them.

Having become acquainted with the world from above in Mac's company, I now explored it from within. I began to grasp how everything was connected, from the cellular structure of a dandelion seed to an exploding star in the Horsehead Nebula. I learned all there was to know about the origins and population of Zamonia. I knew the names of all the kings, tsars, princes, sheriffs, presidents, caliphs, popes, tyrants, sultans and strongmen who had ever ruled the continent. I learned about their background, their boyhood, their eating habits, and the exalted or scatter-brained ideas that had prompted them to favour a particular form of government or driven them insane. I learned of the existence of such contrasting monarchs as Polpap Peth the Altruistic, who conducted affairs of state from a bed of nails, and Kivdul II, a megalomaniac who, purely for his personal delectation, erected a full-sized artificial volcano whose crater he used for staging operas based on the narrative poems of Wilfred the Wordsmith.

We heard of Zamonia's emergence from the sea a million years ago, of its original population of dinosaurs, megadragons, huge insects, Bolloggs and protodemons, of their gradual extinction and the continent's colonization by other life forms from all over the world. Nightingale told us of the Cyclopses' Two Thousand Years' War, of the great Waterkin rebellion, of the building of Atlantis, and countless other events in Zamonian history.

From history Nightingale made an instantaneous transition to physics. He mimed every element that goes to make up our planet, starting with the basic ones: fire, water, earth, and air. As fire he writhed and undulated like the tongues of flame from a flambeau, producing such a genuine hiss and crackle that we began to feel quite warm and thought we could smell smoke. As water he began by rolling leisurely back and forth on the floor to illustrate the unhurried ebb and flow of the tides, then drew himself up into a tidal wave and rushed at us with such a convincing roar that we were all seized with a momentary fear of death by drowning. As earth he first crumpled up like an ordinary clod and then, delving ever further below the surface, mimed one rock formation after another until, having assumed the form of lava, he vented himself in an impressive volcanic eruption. I still recall how Fredda shielded her face with her hands.

As air he also began quite innocuously as a mere puff of wind. He frisked across the classroom, blew gently into Fredda's unkempt hair, and fanned cool, agreeable breezes in our direction with his hands. By flapping them harder he generated stronger winds that abruptly developed into squalls and then into a tornado, which he mimed by rotating on his own axis like a demented Ventisprite, spinning across the classroom, sending papers flying, and

sweeping the pencils off our desks. Meantime, he bellowed like a whole herd of panic-stricken buffalo. We gripped the desks and held on tight.

After that came subsidiary elements such as sulphur and iron, tin and iodine, cobalt and copper, zinc and arsenic, all of them perfectly illustrated in mime. Arsenic, for example, he portrayed by grabbing his throat and emitting a death rattle to show what happens if you swallow that element by mistake; mercury by twisting his arms and legs into such contortions that they almost looked like butter melting on a hotplate; sulphur by emitting loathsome farting sounds and disgusting smells that gave us a foretaste of hell.

Lastly, he introduced us to elements that are now extinct but then possessed attributes that strike us today as magical. Known as cemolium, rronkium, and perpenium or unzium, they were the subject of the wildest myths, and there were adventurers throughout Zamonia who still went prospecting for them.

Zamonium

But the rarest and most legendary element of all was zamonium. I pricked up my ears when Nightingale came to speak of it, possibly alerted by the strange undertone his voice had suddenly acquired. The professor seemed ill at ease with his subject for the very first time. He disposed of it in conspicuous haste, merely informing us that zamonium is the only element capable of thought, that only a small quantity of it existed, and that this had mysteriously vanished. Then he stuck his finger in his ear and quickly switched to another brain and a different subject.

In class Fredda kept passing me her little memo slips, most of them bearing poems that dealt with her two favourite subjects: her homesickness for the Impic Alps and her romantic obsession with me. They weren't great literature, but at least they rhymed. For instance:

Impic Alps, so far away,
listen to my sad refrain!
Will there ever come a day
when I see you all again?

Or:

Blue must my beloved be,
blue as billows in the sea,
blue as bluebirds on the wing,
blue as sapphires in a ring.
Yellow? Thank you very much!
Green I wouldn't even touch.
As for red, it leaves me cold,
but I'll love Bluebear till I'm old.

I preserve an especially vivid memory of the lesson in which Professor Nightingale portrayed the gradual emergence of life on our planet, from the unicellular organism to the highest life forms in existence.

He began by personifying a void, curling up into a ball and asserting in a faint, almost inaudible voice that he wasn't there. This one could well believe, he looked so small and inconspicuous at that moment – indeed, had he told us he genuinely wasn't there, we should probably have gone looking for him in the passage outside. Then he started to develop, at first into a cell, a tiny, sinuous creature that nervously wriggled through the warm primeval seas. Shoulders twitching, Nightingale imitated a cell lurching through the prehistoric ocean until, by degrees, he calmed down and transformed himself into a jellyfish. He inflated his body, extended both arms, rotated very slowly on his own axis, and seemed to be sinking, elegant as an open sun umbrella, into the depths. Next he became transmuted into a primeval fish, a predator equipped with huge jaws and projecting teeth. In search of prey, Nightingale dived under the desks and actually vanished for a while before suddenly rising to the surface with his eyes rolling wildly – a sight that frightened Qwerty almost to death.

Thereafter he blew out his cheeks and turned into a plump toad. This waddled along on dry land, croaking loudly, until it abruptly transformed itself into a huge, vicious, hissing alligator. Nightingale himself was so pleased with this performance that he slithered across the classroom on his belly a couple of times, teeth bared, and snapped at our ankles until we all climbed on our desks, squealing in terror. Highly delighted by this little joke, he proceeded to turn into a dinosaur.

To begin with he portrayed a leisurely herbivore, the huge but harmless brontosaurus. He lumbered ponderously to and fro, extended his long neck, and browsed on the pot of geraniums on his desk. To our amusement, he plucked a few of the flowers with his lips and munched them with relish. Eventually – and this sight has etched itself into my memory for ever – he presented an impressively authentic personification of Tyrannosaurus Rex, the most dangerous carnivorous predator of its day.

Getting up off all fours and standing erect, he peered around the classroom, ran his tongue over his teeth in a slow, sinister fashion, and scratched himself behind the ear with one little claw-tipped foreleg. Then he raised his head, screwed up his big, round, scientist's eyes into narrow, menacing slits, and sniffed the air in all directions.

We all suddenly felt like dinosaur food.

Nightingale, or rather, the Tyrannosaurus Nightingalius, threw back its head and let out an ear-splitting roar. It was the most frightening sound I'd ever heard, the bellow of the Gourmetica insularis included. Fredda leapt from her chair, jumped on to my back, and clung there, trembling. Qwerty adopted a defensive stance, to the extent that a gelatinous creature from the 2364th Dimension can stand up at all. I myself prepared to bid the world farewell.

The dinosaur turned its head back and forth as if unable to decide which of us to devour first. Then, with lizardlike gait, it slowly waddled towards us. I could have sworn the ground shook with every step it took. Saliva dripped from its jaws, and I felt quite sure that this time Professor Nightingale had lost his reason – that each of his seven brains had malfunctioned simultaneously, and that he would act out his Tyrannosaurus Rex role to the bitter, bloody end. We had all crawled under my desk and were clinging to each other in terror. Saliva dripped on to the classroom floor as the Tyrannosaurus bent over us with parted lips and treated us to its craftiest grin. Then it suddenly stopped short and looked up as if it could hear an alarming sound in the distance. With a grunt of surprise, it took a crumpled piece of paper from the desk and tossed it into the air. The ball of paper landed on its head. As if fatally injured, it staggered dramatically towards us, let out another spine-chilling roar, and finally collapsed only inches away. The professor had just demonstrated what caused the dinosaurs to become extinct: a shower of enormous meteorites.

'Once the dinosaurs had disappeared,' Professor Nightingale's lecture concluded, 'there was really only one more interesting stage in the development of life.' He spread his arms wide and grinned.

'It's right here in front of you: A Nocturnomath – the zenith of Creation.'

We were given no homework, no classroom projects, no marks, no oral tests. Nightingale asked no questions, never checked our state of knowledge, and never urged us to pay attention. He simply spoke and we listened.

Asking questions was completely taboo. Nightingale alone decided what subjects to tackle and when, what syllabus to study, or when it was time to move on to something else. He was like a radio whose knobs were being twiddled by a madman. He jumped from molecular biology to petrology, from petrology to ancient Egyptian architecture, from that to the study of putrescent gases on other planets, and from that to entomology with a detour that embraced the portrayal of the three-winged Zamonian bee in Atlantic encaustic paintings of the 14th century. We were taught what mattered most about Florinthian cheese sculptures, the caryatid culture of the sacred buildings of Grailsund, the therapeutic properties of the Peruvian ratanhia root, the mating dance of the Midgard Serpent, the leading lights of Zamonian speleology (of whom Nightingale was one), and the 250 principles governing the Aphavillean Declaration of Independence – all in a single afternoon.

Between classes we loitered in the gloomy tunnels or killed time in our bleak, windowless rooms. Occasionally we ventured out on to the ledge in front of the entrance to the Nocturnal Academy, where Mac had dropped me. We never lingered, however, because conditions at that altitude were extremely cold and windy even in summer. We simply stood there drawing in deep draughts of air until we developed hallucinations. Once we had satisfied our need for oxygen we retired to the gloomy maze of tunnels. We took no physical exercise, which Professor Nightingale thought absolutely pointless. He held that all forms of sport killed off essential brain cells. 'Every overdeveloped muscle has a major intellectual achievement on its conscience,' was his considered opinion.

Our spare time

There were no forms of entertainment, no games or books or anything else that might have distracted our attention from the professor's lessons. When one lesson ended he would promptly retire to the darkroom to pursue his darkness experiments while we hung around, ate canned sardines, or dozed until he emerged and embarked on the next. Lessons were our only source of interest in the Gloombergs. That, no doubt, was another reason why Professor Nightingale had chosen to establish his Nocturnal Academy there.

I whiled away many an afternoon by persuading Qwerty to tell me about the 2364th Dimension. He didn't like to do so because it aggravated his homesickness, but once he started there was no stopping him.

For some reason, there were a lot of carpets in his native dimension. One might even say that it consisted almost entirely of carpets, any gaps between them being occupied as a rule by dimensional hiatuses. In the 2364th Dimension a carpet denoted safety and stability; miss one, and you went hurtling into space. This was why carpet-weaving was the art that enjoyed the highest local esteem.

Great efforts were made to turn every inhabitant of 2364 (as I must call Qwerty's homeland for want of a proper name) into an efficient carpet-weaver. All other activities were held to be forms of idleness. Try as he genuinely did to convey some idea of 2364's carpets, even Qwerty found it impossible to describe their manifold patterns and weaves, shapes and colours, sizes and materials.

Wall-to-wall carpeting was frowned on, of course. Although there were broadloom carpets of vast dimensions, they never ran right up to the walls because there weren't any walls in 2364. Qwerty told me of lovingly hand-woven runners made of pure gold thread, and of others consisting of several layers of cobwebs for durability's sake. The inhabitants of 2364 had raised the art of weaving and knotting to a level that defies our comprehension. They could produce a carpet out of any conceivable material. According to Qwerty, 2364 boasted carpets made of glass, wood, sheet metal, and marble – even tea.

Everything was expressed in carpet form. Qwerty reported enthusiastically that poems and whole novels and epics were woven on looms, as were newspapers for adults and long, coloured runners with plenty of pictures and not much text for children. Very small, wafer-thin rugs served as banknotes, and for transportation the inhabitants used flying carpets of medium size or the larger carpet buses for which bus stops were installed throughout the 2364th Dimension.

For entertainment purposes one visited the carpet museum. Displayed there were carpets from bygone eras made of obsolete materials and bearing mysterious inscriptions in the runes of long extinct languages – ancient specimens rendered so threadbare by years of constant use that one could look through them into space. Contemporary artists vied with one another in devising new shapes and colours. There were circular and triangular carpets, star-shaped and corrugated ones, incredibly wide ones and some whose pile was so deep you had to fight your way through it like someone wading through a field of wheat.

In addition, every inhabitant of 2364 wove an autobiographical carpet, a sort of diary, retirement home and shroud all in one. All the memories, information, scenes and events people deemed important were woven into their carpet as time went by. Their latter years, during which it became steadily more dangerous to walk on other people's carpets, they spent largely on their own, passing the time by looking at the scenes and memories they had recorded. When they died they were rolled up in their carpet and thrown down a dimensional hiatus. Personally, in view of all their efforts to avoid these pitfalls during their lifetime, I found this a rather barbaric practice.

As for Qwerty, it greatly saddened him that he no longer possessed an autobiographical carpet of his own.

Canned sardines Meals at the Nocturnal Academy were as follows. Professor Nightingale never ate at all, or so it was said (he was rumoured to live on darkness). For everyone else – discounting Qwerty – there were canned sardines. Since Professor Nightingale attached no importance to food, he wasn't too concerned about his pupils' diet. 'I don't care what they eat as long as it's always the same thing,' was his motto.

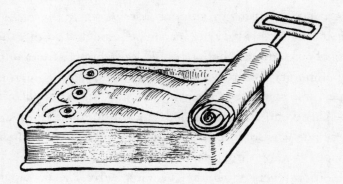

Foodstuffs appealed to him only if they were very long-lasting, easy to prepare, extremely filling, and sold in stackable containers. Canned sardines perfectly fulfilled those requirements. The Nocturnal Academy's pupils made a virtue of necessity and devised the most ingenious ways of preparing them. There was nothing to wash them down with except pure spring water, which came straight from the rock.

We were set no homework or exams, as I have already said, and there was nothing that might have assured Professor Nightingale that we were listening to him at all, let alone retaining what we heard. Even so, I had the feeling that I was becoming steadily brainier, and I could tell that the others were too.

The thing was, we'd taken to discussing and, if possible, cracking problems after school which the professor had only broached in class and left unresolved. Our standard of conversation rose day by day. Having begun by working out simple sums or correcting our spelling mistakes, we compiled our own logarithmic tables and deciphered some early Zamonian hieroglyphs unaided. After a few months we tackled the doctrines of Manu Kantimel, the founder of Grailsundian Demonism, and not only disproved them all but demonstrated that he had based them on an 11th-century message-in-a-bottle from Yhôll.

Whenever Fredda wasn't actually clinging to my back and inserting writing implements in my facial orifices (she had recently started on my nostrils), we sat in the dining room and wrangled over Hackonian xenoplexy or the fluctuations of elf-wing atoms when exposed to magnetism.

One discussion between Fredda, Qwerty and myself ran more or less as follows:

A philosophical debate

I: 'I'm just working on the foundations of South Zamonian Yobbism.'

Qwerty: 'Oh, you mean the philosophical school of thought which assumes that no one object implies the existence of any other provided they're viewed with the requisite insensitivity?'

I: 'Precisely.'

Qwerty: 'A most interesting intellectual approach. I infer from it that experience is the sum of ignorance plus militant stupidity.'

Fredda:

I entirely disagree. That's far too crude a theory for my taste – it's what happens when barbarians devote themselves to philosophy. The founder of Yobbism grew up in a swamp and hits his critics on the head with a club, everyone knows that. Let's talk about astronomy instead. I've lately come to the conclusion that the universe isn't expanding at all. But it isn't contracting, either. It's simply vacillating.

Qwerty: 'Are you talking about a self-contained model of the world with the curvature symbol k = +1, in which phases of expansion and contraction periodically alternate?'

I: 'Now *that's* too crude for *my* taste!'

And so it went on...

I became incredibly well-read, although there wasn't a single book in the whole academy. In one of his lectures Professor Nightingale made a passing reference to *The Cyclopean Crown*, the epic poem by Wilfred the Wordsmith. Within a few hours I could recite it from start to finish, word for word, knew the forename of every early Zamonian deity, and could have turned out some flawless hexameters of my own. Nightingale also said something about Yohan Zafritter's *The Black Whale*, a 4000-page novel describing the hunt for a Tyrannomobyus Rex, and before long I had not only memorized the entire text but knew how attach a line to a harpoon and coil it round a bollard in the stern. I also knew what 'whale' was in Latin, Greek, Icelandic, Polynesian, and Yhôllian, to wit, *cetus, κητοζ, hvalur, piki-nui-nui*, and *trôm*.

At the risk of being suspected of bragging, I was a walking encyclopedia of general knowledge. I had mastered all the languages in the known world, both dead and in current use, including all the Zamonian dialects – and they alone numbered over 20,000.

I knew whole sonnets of Zamonian baroque poetry by heart, was an expert on Atlantean air-painting, Dullsgardian minnesinging, and the analysis of comets' tails. I could calculate the hourly

A sound education

153

expansion of the universe by observing the oscillations of the Gloomberg algal cell, replace a dislodged auditory ossicle with pincers, determine the blood group of a fossil insect by means of ommateal diagnosis, and gauge the number of animalcules in a glass of water from their weight – with my eyes shut. Grailsund Library, Zamonia's largest collection of specialized works on demonology, did not list as many titles in its inventory as I myself carried in my head. Although I detested mathematics, the squaring of circles, the cubing of ellipses and the solving of problems of all kinds were child's play to me.

My knowledge was far from confined to literature, the sciences, philosophy, and art. I was also versed in every conceivable sphere of daily life. I knew how to repair a church clock and cut a camshaft, how to calculate the statics of a dam, trepan a skull and construct a time bomb, how to put up a solid bell frame and clear a blocked toilet, how to tune a cello and palpate a liver. I could draw the ground plan of a cathedral, conduct a symphony orchestra, and calculate the trajectory of a cannon ball in a crosswind. I could, in no time at all, have fashioned an elegant lady's shoe out of a piece of untanned leather and a stout thatched roof out of reeds. I knew how to grind a lens and brew tasty wheat beer. I knew the names of every star in the sky and every micro-organism in the ocean.

The one thing I didn't know was the source of all this knowledge.

Fredda's farewell

Then came the day when Fredda left us and was sent out into the world, her schooldays having ended. I should really have been relieved to be rid of such a pest, but I wasn't. Fredda was my first love, after all, even if she was only an ugly Alpine Imp and our relationship was pretty one-sided. I'd grown accustomed to her, that's all, and she was simply irreplaceable when it came to bringing our intellectual flights of fancy down to earth. I failed to understand how Nightingale could be heartless enough to kick her out, for that was just what he did. Alpine Imps have a congenital inability to cry, fortunately, or she would doubtless have kicked up a terrible fuss.

Her leavetaking was an extremely subdued occasion. Fredda was given no party, no diploma or school-leaver's certificate. She simply said goodbye to us all (to me with a hoarse croak and an overly wet kiss) and was then conducted by Professor Nightingale to a fork in the tunnel. With a last sad wave in my direction, she hesitantly disappeared through the Nocturnal Academy's official exit, which was rumoured by its pupils to lead into the labyrinth of passages that threaded the interior of the Gloomberg Mountains.

On returning to the classroom we found Fredda's desk occupied by a newcomer, a timid unicorn named Flowergrazer.

Flowergrazer was as unlike Fredda as anyone could possibly imagine. A quiet, attentive pupil, he spoke in a low, inaudible voice and was boring in the extreme. He devoted his spare time to

Flowergrazer

writing poems, all of which dealt with unicorns who were lonely, deeply distressed by their solitude, and called Flowergrazer.

A change sets in Professor Nightingale's lessons had undergone a change of some kind, and I'd recently found it difficult to follow him. Although the subjects were no harder and his lectures as fascinating as ever, I simply couldn't take them in any more. No sooner was school over for the day than I lost all recollection of what I'd been taught.

I sometimes caught myself not listening at all and allowing my thoughts to stray. On such occasions, when subjected to a keen glance from Professor Nightingale, I would feel guilty. Although I still solved differential equations in my head after school, it seemed to me that I was growing steadily more dim-witted.

Knio and Weeny After a short time the Nocturnal Academy acquired some more new pupils, two rather uncongenial individuals named Knio and Weeny.

Knio was the last surviving representative of a species known as the Barbaric Hog, which really says it all. He had more muscles than a plough horse and incredibly bad manners. When you were talking to him he either kept punching you or slapped you on the back with one of his fat trotters. He had short, greasy hair, foul breath, and – although he was only eight years old – a bad case of five o'clock shadow. He was continually uttering oaths in which prominent roles were played by all manner of gods, giants, or other legendary creatures. 'By the Midgard Serpent!' he would cry, or,

'May the Megadragon devour me if it isn't true!' When we were in bed at night he used to torment us with his prodigious flatulence, of which, to crown everything, he appeared to be proud. 'Watch out,' was the customary prelude to one of his phenomenal farts, 'here comes Wotan's revenge!' The rest of us would pull the covers over our heads and hold our breath until the worst was over. It would have been pointless to remonstrate with Knio because he was stronger than any of us now that Fredda had gone.

Weeny was a Gnomelet, the last of that family of miniature cyclopses. Gnomelets were a rather degenerate form of cyclops, neither strong nor awe-inspiring nor possessed of any other notable cyclopean attributes, but disagreeably pushy, sneaky, cowardly, lazy, arrogant, covetous, and greedy. Weeny was also short-sighted, not that he could help that. He kept fixing people with his single, piercing eye, which didn't exactly add to his charms.

It was amazing how many obnoxious qualities could be accommodated in such a small body. Weeny always insisted on talking big although he had little to say, for his intellect was barely more developed than Knio's. He was the kind of miniature cyclops that picks a quarrel, then hides behind someone bigger and stronger and incites him to violence. Looked at from that angle, Knio and Weeny were the worst possible combination.

I lose my one remaining friend

When Qwerty finally had to quit the Nocturnal Academy, my world almost collapsed. From then on I became a stranger among strangers.

'It's an absolute certainty that we'll never see each other again,' said Qwerty, when bidding me farewell. 'I intend to throw myself into the first dimensional hiatus I can find, and the odds against our meeting again will be 460 billion to 1!' – 'No,' I replied, having swiftly worked out this statistical problem in my head, '463 billion to 1.' It really was extremely unlikely; the chances of winning the lottery 15,000 times in succession (with tickets bought at the same counter) were, in fact, greater. I silently shook Qwerty's gelatinous hand. Then Professor Nightingale conducted him to the exit tunnel. After that, my sojourn at the Nocturnal Academy became steadily more unendurable. Even the lessons had become a torment. It no longer interested me to hear what Professor Nightingale had to say about the crystalline structure of snowflakes, the habits of the Andean lama, or the brushwork of the calligraphers of the Eastern Incisors. His pearls of wisdom ran off me like water off a duck's back. I had reached the stage where I no longer understood what he was talking about – in fact I sometimes felt he was speaking an entirely unknown language.

Still more of a trial, however, were the evenings I spent with my new classmates. Their standard of education was shockingly low. They were just getting to grips with multiplication and capitals or lower-case letters, whereas I was debating major problems of astrophysics in my head. One night, Knio and I had an argument about the nature of the universe. He had an appallingly crude conception of the physical world.

Another philosophical debate

'The earth is a bun floating in a bucket of water,' he asserted defiantly.

'And what is the bucket standing on?' I demanded, trying to floor him.

'The bucket stands on the back of the Great Cleaner who polishes the universe to all eternity,' Knio replied self-confidently.

'This universe she polishes so assiduously,' I said, 'what in the world does *that* stand on?'

'The universe doesn't stand on anything, it lies,' Weeny put in. 'The universe is as flat as a slice of sausage, you see.'

'And what, pray, does the slice of sausage lie on?' I had him now!

'On the bun, of course,' replied Knio.

You simply couldn't have a rational argument with such barbarians.

To take my mind off Knio's farts, Flowergrazer's lamentations and Weeny's bragging I had developed the habit of solving philosophical riddles that had never been solved before. One night, when sleep had eluded me yet again because a philosophical problem was preying on my mind (I was reflecting that I was bigger than Weeny, so I was big; at the same time, however, I was smaller that Knio, so I was small; but how could I be big and small at the same time?), I passed Professor Nightingale's darkroom on my way to the canned sardine store.

The professor's darkroom

A terrible splintering sound penetrated the heavy door and went echoing along the passage. Whenever the professor was pondering an especially ticklish problem, he made a noise like a nutcracker demolishing a large walnut. This noise issued straight from his brains, a fact that impressed me on the one hand but gave me the shivers on the other. I was about to tiptoe on when a loud 'Come in!' made me freeze in mid movement.

No pupil had ever been privileged to set foot in the professor's mysterious domain. I was beginning to think I'd made a mistake when I heard Nightingale's voice a second time.

'Come in, but don't let any light in!'

On opening the door I felt as if the darkness were flowing over me like molasses. 'Come in and shut the door!' Nightingale commanded, so I obediently tiptoed inside.

The gloom that enveloped me when I shut the door behind me was so absolute that I got the wind up. It was a darkness I could feel on my skin, the way I'd felt it on Hobgoblin Island when, for the very first time, I spent a night without any lights on. But this darkness was audible as well. It gripped me like an icy fist, making a humming sound so faint and despairing that my fur stood momentarily on end.

I hadn't been in the chamber for more than a few seconds when I got the feeling I'd been blind since birth and had no idea what light was. I groped for the doorknob, but I didn't even know where ahead or behind were, still less up or down. I felt I was floating in starless space, weightless and utterly alone.

'Don't go!' Professor Nightingale said sharply. 'One gets used to it.'

I hadn't the slightest notion where he was. My dearest wish was to run for it, screaming in terror, but I strove to remain polite. 'It's, er, very dark in here,' I understated.

'Poppycock!' barked the professor. 'The ambient lighting registers four hundred nightingales.'

The 'nightingale', I knew from my lessons, was a unit of luminosity invented by the professor himself (modesty wasn't his long suit). A nightingale corresponds roughly to the light prevailing on a starless night during a lunar eclipse. To take a more down-to-earth example, the interior of an airtight refrigerator registers (when the door is shut and the light has gone out) precisely one nightingale. Thus, a luminosity of four hundred nightingales was equivalent to the darkness prevailing in four hundred closed refrigerators. It was correspondingly cold as well.

'The nightingalator is running at only half speed. I've even blindfolded myself because I find the light too bright.'

Nightingale removed the blindfold. I could tell this because his eyes glowed in the dark like a pair of searchlights. A Nocturnomath's eyes always glow, even in daylight, but the effect was far more impressive in absolute darkness, perhaps because of the brains revving away behind them. Caught in their beams, I somehow felt guilty.

'Why creep around in the middle of the night, eh?' the professor demanded, playing the twin beams over my face.

'I, er, couldn't get to sleep because I, er, couldn't get a philosophical problem out of my head. I was turning it over in my –'

'Nonsense!' Nightingale brusquely cut me short. 'You couldn't get to sleep because Knio, that antediluvian idiot, pollutes the air with his barbarous expulsions of wind! You couldn't get to sleep because you can't take any more of your classmates' childish chatter. You couldn't get to sleep because you miss your conversations with Qwerty and Fredda.'

The old man knew simply everything. He shook his head, and the beams from his eyes roamed the room like those of a lighthouse.

'You've been here too long... Now your time is up. One moment, I'll switch off the nightingalator...'

I heard a series of faint, mysterious clicks and it slowly grew lighter. Although the lighting that now prevailed would undoubtedly have been described as dim under normal circumstances, I found it quite bright after the darkness that had preceded it. I could at least distinguish the outlines of the curious apparatus Nightingale was tinkering with.

It looked like a factory in miniature, or rather, like several little interconnected factories with countless tiny smokestacks and boilers, cables and cogwheels, pumps and engines. There were bellows rising and falling, pistons sliding in and out, little chimneys that emitted occasional jets of flame, and air shafts with black

steam issuing from them. (The reader may, perhaps, object that black steam doesn't exist, and that I'm confusing it with black smoke. I must nonetheless insist that the odourless water vapour issuing from the nightingalator was black as night itself, not white.)

I even thought I discerned some shadowy little figures flitting around on the iron stairways and catwalks, miniature factory workers carrying tiny spanners, but that, I'm sure, was just my imagination. The mechanical pounding gradually slowed but never ceased entirely.

'What exactly is a nightingalator?' I ventured to ask.

'A nightingalator,' the professor proudly and promptly declared, as if I'd pressed a button in his chest, 'is a darkness-manufacturing machine invented by myself. With the aid of the so-called nightingalasers generated by this wonderful contraption, exceptionally dark, starless patches of night sky can be cut out and transported straight to this chamber, where the nightingalator stores and refines them. This enables me to bottle the darkness like wine from a cask. I can also condense or dilute it as required. A triumph of darkness research – or nightingalology, as it is termed by experts in this scientific field.'

The sole expert in this field, of course, was Nightingale himself. It was only then that I spotted the big telescopic tube projecting from the nightingalator to the ceiling. Unlike a normal telescope, this one had a kind of knot in the middle. In the ceiling I made out an aperture that could be closed like a camera's diaphragm. It must have led to a shaft through which the night sky was visible.

'The darkness in here,' I said for something to say, 'does it come from outer space?'

'It does indeed, my boy. You won't find denser darkness any-where – it's the eternal blackness of the universe! Did you know that ninety per cent of the universe consists of dark matter? No one has ever been able to observe it until now. Its existence could only be inferred from its gravitational effects, but I, with my nightingaloscope, have discovered and isolated it!'

He gestured grandly at the telescope.

'Whenever you look up at the stars, you're seeing the past. The light of the stars you see in the firmament is millions or even billions of years old. People are always talking about the light of the stars, but the darkness between them is just as old – indeed, much older as a rule, and there's far more of it! Darkness ages like wine: the older it is, the better. The darkness in this room is nearly five billion years old – an exceptionally fine vintage.'

He sniffed and smacked his lips like a connoisseur sampling an expensive bottle of claret.

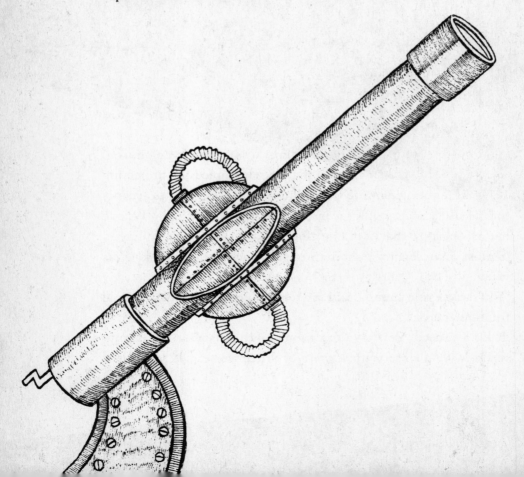

'I won't overtax your brain with details, my boy – besides, it's a top secret matter. All I can tell you is that I've invented a sophisticated system of prisms, lenses and mirrors that enables me to *bend my nightingalasers in space* and send them through a wormhole!'

He sat back complacently, fitted his fingertips together, and twiddled his thumbs like a barrister who has just presented the judge with a cast-iron alibi.

A wormhole, to quote a standard item of knowledge in the Nocturnal Academy's syllabus, was a kind of short cut through space, a secret tunnel in the space-time continuum through which very distant points in the cosmos could be reached more quickly than usual. If I had understood him correctly, Nightingale was saying that he'd sent his lasers on a sort of time-warp journey through space.

'And that's not all!'

He indicated another part of the nightingalator – one that resembled a mechanical hedgehog.

'My rays are capable of cutting out sizeable chunks of cosmic darkness. Then, with the aid of this retromagnetic particle vacuum cleaner (the Nightingale 3000, patent pending) I can suck the said material straight out of the universe! Imagine, darkness direct from the furthest corner of the cosmos, vacuum-packed for millions of years, here on this very table! Darkness can get no darker!'

The professor emitted a grunt of triumph.

'All the cutting process leaves behind in the sky are holes so abysmally dark that they annihilate light itself. Future generations of scientists will rack their brains over the source of those black holes, tee-hee!'

Black holes

He said no more for a while, just grunted to himself in an absent-minded way.

165

'But I still haven't found a way of putting this dark material to good use,' he growled. 'It's here, but it has no practical applications – it's so damned *negative!*'

He lapsed into a brooding silence.

I felt I ought to say something encouraging.

'Perhaps the material must first get used to its new environment. I well remember my first week in the Gloombergs. I myself felt –'

'Pooh!' the professor cut in brusquely. 'What do *you* know about the mysteries of the universe?'

He was right – what did I know about them? My brain really was feeling rather overburdened with details. Having made enough of a fool of myself already, I thought I'd better bow out as gracefully as possible.

'Well,' I said as I edged towards the exit, or what I took to be the exit, 'it's getting late. I won't intrude on you any longer...'

'The door's in the opposite direction,' Nightingale murmured vaguely. Then a sudden thought seemed to strike him.

'No, don't go! Stay here – please,' he said in an uncharacteristically polite and gentle tone. 'We could have a bit of a chat.'

This was a novelty. Nightingale had never conversed with me before – he never conversed with anyone on principle. To him, a conversation meant that he held forth while others greedily absorbed his pearls of wisdom. He welcomed the occasional timid question because it gave him a chance to deliver another lengthy monologue, but he disliked empty chatter. Nocturnomaths hate conversations.

'You've probably been wondering how you've managed to learn so much in so short a time,' Nightingale began.

'Perhaps I'm exceptionally gifted?' I hazarded rather incautiously.

'Gifted? Pooh, nonsense!' he barked, so loudly that I retreated a step.

'Forgive me...' He lowered his voice again. He was simply unused to holding a normal conversation, but he was doing his best. 'Does Knio strike you as gifted? That porcine blockhead has a brain the size of an atomic nucleus. When the lights go out he thinks the world around him ceases to exist, but by the time I'm through with him he'll be knowledgeable enough to construct a submarine blindfolded or discover a cure for the common cold. It's nothing to do with brains, it's bacteria.'

'Bacteria?' I knew, of course, that bacteria were minute organisms capable of transmitting diseases.

'Precisely. You must simply conceive of knowledge as a disease – a disease we Nocturnomaths transmit. The closer a person comes to a Nocturnomath, the more knowledge he becomes infected with. Take a step towards me.'

I did so, although I was far from reassured by the thought that he was a source of infection. I had never been as near him before, not even in class.

'Closer!' Nightingale commanded.

I took another step, and suddenly a tide of information surged through my brain. It was all to do with darkness research, a subject I had never studied in any detail. All at once, I felt I was an expert in that field.

'So tell me,' the professor demanded, 'what do you now know about darkness?'

'Oh, it's all quite simple once you rid yourself of the preconceived idea that darkness is merely the absence of light,' I was astonished to hear myself say. 'You have to learn to treat light and darkness as energy sources of equal status.'

'That's just the trouble,' Nightingale put in. 'The thing is, darkness has such a bad reputation. People always associate it with unpleasant things, but it's simply another – albeit darker – form of luminosity. We need it quite as much as we need light. Without darkness everything would wither and die. There would be no sleep, no relaxation, no energy, no growth. Night gives us the strength to withstand the rigours of the day. Haven't you ever wondered why we feel so refreshed and full of energy after a good night's sleep?'

'To be honest, no...' I felt ashamed. I was so concerned with the ultimate problems of philosophy that I'd never asked myself that simple question.

'It's because of the darkness we've taken on board. A nap during the day is no good at all – you tend to feel more lethargic than ever, am I right? Darkness is pure energy. Your reserves become depleted during the day. You burn them up, grow weary, and have to sleep some more. In the dark you accumulate fresh strength, and so on... I'm convinced that a person who only lives at night need never die.'

I was tempted to conclude that Professor Nightingale was speaking of himself. He was intensely agitated. His glowing eyes protruded from their sockets like red-hot cannon balls, his voice rose still higher.

'On the contrary!' he declared. 'That person would accumulate more and more strength until he developed into something surpassing our present powers of comprehension: highly distilled intelligence coupled with immortality! Eternal life! Eternal night! Eternal intelligence!'

All at once it sounded as if a spanner had fallen into the works: the professor had changed gear again. He thumped one of his external brains with the heel of his hand.

'Er... but I digress. Where had I got to?'

'The bacteriological transmission of knowledge.'

'Right! The nearer you are to me, the smarter you'll become – it's as simple as that. But the problem is, your grey cells can only absorb so much. Not everyone can have seven brains, can they? Your capacity for absorption is now exhausted, that's why you can't concentrate on your lessons any more.'

I blushed. So he'd noticed!

'That's all right. It simply means your time is up.' I was already familiar with that sudden, husky tone of voice and knew that it heralded a change. I'd heard it from the Babbling Billows and from Mac, from Fredda and Qwerty. It signified that a departure was imminent.

'There's nothing more I can teach you,' the professor went on. 'You now know as much as a hundred universal scientists, world chess champions and brain surgeons rolled into one. That ought to be enough to launch you on a suitable career. I'm short of space here, so a new pupil will be taking your place. Your schooldays are over, my lad. Tomorrow I shall conduct you to the exit tunnel. It's a long trek through the mountains, but a bluebear with your brains will find the way out. Good night.'

Our conversation, which had again become rather one-sided, was at an end. I groped around until I found the doorknob.

'Oh yes, my boy,' Nightingale called after me, 'about that philosophical problem of yours...'

'Yes?'

'You're neither big nor small.'

'What am I, then?'

'Medium-sized.'

So Professor Nightingale really was a mind-reader.

When I walked into the classroom the next morning, I might have been entering it for the first time, it seemed so unfamiliar. A new pupil was sitting at my desk: a dodo – an albino dodo, to be precise, because it had bright red eyes and snow-white plumage.

I said goodbye to Flowergrazer, Knio, Weeny and the dodo, whose name was Odod. They meant nothing to me, those classmates of mine, so I didn't feel the least bit sad. A strange mixture of fear and eagerness overcame me as I followed Professor Nightingale to the exit.

The encyclopedia   Once there, he did something I found genuinely surprising because it was so unlike him: he gave me a hug. I had never been as close to him before, not even the previous night. His brief embrace sent another mass of knowledge surging through my brain. Millions of letters whirled around in my mind's eye, then formed themselves into words, scientific facts, whole treatises, and, finally, into a book whose title flared up for a moment, clearly legible, and then vanished.

Professor
Nightingale's

ENCYCLO-
PEDIA

of Marvels, Life Forms and Other Phenomena
of Zamonia and its Environs

A-Z

It was Professor Nightingale's standard work on Zamonia, his accumulated store of knowledge about that continent and its environs. He had etched it – telepathically, as it were – on to the hard disk of my brain.

'Another thing,' he said in a subdued voice. 'Two rules: if you get hungry or thirsty, simply lick the walls of the tunnel. Your thirst will be assuaged by the condensation that always adheres to them, your hunger by the spongy fungus whose slight fluorescence provides a modicum of lighting. This contains Gloomberg algae and is thus a major source of vitamins, minerals, carbohydrates, and roughage.'

'And the second rule?'

'Never trust a Troglotroll!'

'A Troglotroll?' I said. 'What's that?' But the professor had already thrust me into the darker of two tunnels and hurried off with his coat tails flapping.

Uninviting though it was, the maze of tunnels in the Gloomberg Mountains, I entered it with a feeling of relief. My schooldays were over. Real life awaited me with open arms!

My eyes soon became accustomed to the dim light, and I strode along in a highly optimistic mood. No more stupid, piggish Knios or sneaky little Gnomelets, no more suicidal unicorns, no more canned sardines and boredom. The dank, dark tunnel seemed a place of beauty because it was taking me to freedom.

I had my first misgivings after walking for about an hour. What was I doing in this cheerless labyrinth? Where was the exit? Besides, I was hungry.

A can of sardines wouldn't have gone amiss. Why hadn't I simply stayed at the Nocturnal Academy? Why couldn't you remain at school after completing your education? Was there a law against it?

I could become an assistant teacher at the Nocturnal Academy – or a janitor, for that matter. I would take on the humblest cleaning jobs unpaid. Anything would be better than roaming around in this clammy labyrinth, at the mercy of an uncertain fate. What did I know of the world that awaited me outside? It was a vast and incalculable place alive with hardships, dangers, and ill-disposed creatures – that much Mac had taught me only too well. On the back of a Reptilian Rescuer I'd been safe, but now I had to fend for myself.

I decided to go back to Professor Nightingale and ask him to keep me on. Why hadn't I thought of that during our conversation last night?

I turned on my heel and walked back to the Nocturnal Academy. *A futile decision* Yes, I could already picture myself pursuing a comfortable, desk-bound career. At the professor's side I would hand the torch of wisdom to a never-ending stream of grateful students, and in our spare time we would devote ourselves to darknessology. Perhaps Nightingale really was on the track of the secret of eternal life. I could assist him with his experiments and might even give him the hint that helped to achieve the vital breakthrough. We would share the official honours and awards. I wasn't greedy, after all.

An intersection? I couldn't recall coming to one earlier. Forks, yes; intersections, no. Thoroughly perplexed, I stopped short and peered in all directions. A drop of condensation fell from the roof and landed plumb on my nose.

I had obviously gone astray.

Every bend seemed to offer the prospect of salvation, of light at the end of the tunnel, but all I encountered each time was yet another fork or some even more complex ramifications. I thought it wise to favour tunnels that led downhill because the exit must be at the foot of the mountains, but there were times when they led uphill for hours on end. The downhill tunnels had to be somewhere else entirely. I climbed higher and higher.

I felt an occasional puff of wind on my cheek. At first I thought it was fresh mountain air blowing into the cave mouth I longed to reach. But then I realized that it was always the same puff of wind. A prisoner like myself, it had been desperately roaming this labyrinth in search of a way out, perhaps for many thousands of years.

I tried to assume that my schooldays weren't over at all – that this was Professor Nightingale's idea of a final examination, and that those who managed to extricate themselves from the labyrinth had passed it. All I had to do was think laterally – turn my thoughts in every possible direction.

I debated which field of knowledge would be most helpful to me. Mathematics? Philosophy? Biology? Geology? Astronomy? Zamonian poetry? I came to the conclusion that, to begin with, my legs would be the greatest help of all. Unfortunately, they couldn't have been in worse condition, thanks to my persistent lack of exercise and unbalanced diet.

I walked on. Sometimes I broke into a slow trot, sometimes I shuffled along, but I kept going, on and on, without a break, until exhaustion overcame me. Then I sank to the ground and slept for a minute or two before struggling up and plodding onwards for hours and days on end.

From time to time I licked a tunnel wall and sampled the rusty mildew and salty condensation that had been clinging to it for millions of years – at least, it tasted like that. I took one mechanical step after another. You couldn't call it walking any more. I tottered along between the tunnel walls like a drunk, head sagging, shoulders drooping and arms dangling, a picture of misery, a lost, despairing bluebear with cramp in the calves. At some stage my strength finally gave out. I lay down, firmly resolved never to get up again.

For several hours I remained lying on my back, spreadeagled with my gaze fixed on the roof of the tunnel. I had made up my mind to dematerialize, vanish without trace, rust away like a piece of old iron, and thus become an integral part of the Gloomberg Mountains. It seems that rusty tunnel walls have an unwholesome effect on overtaxed brains. I would never have entertained such an idea under normal circumstances, but anyone who has brooded on it for hours will feel, in a truly physical sense, what it's like to rust

I rust away

175

away. It's a strange but far from unpleasant sensation. You surrender to the forces of nature, utterly serene, then slowly turn metallic. Your body becomes coated by degrees with fine, rust-red fur and starts to crumble. The rust eats into you, ever deeper. Layer after layer flakes off, and before long you're just a little mound of red dust to be blown away by a captive puff of wind and scattered along the endless tunnels of the Gloomberg Mountains. That was as far as my dire imaginings had progressed when my shoulder was nudged by something soft and slimy but not unfamiliar. It was Qwerty Uiop.

An old friend

'What are you doing here?' he inquired anxiously.

'Rusting away,' I replied.

It was a while before I could more or less sit up, and it genuinely surprised me that I didn't crumble away like an old ship's biscuit. Grunting and groaning, I got up off the floor of the tunnel while Qwerty waited impatiently. On my hind paws at last, I felt life seeping back into my bones. Qwerty's presence gave grounds for optimism. Having jointly solved astronomical problems of the greatest magnitude, we would surely locate the exit together.

The dimensional hiatus

'I've found a dimensional hiatus,' Qwerty announced.

'A dimensional hiatus?' I replied. 'Why, that's wonderful!' I sounded rather unconvincing, no doubt, because it meant that we would soon be going our separate ways again.

'It was quite simple. I stumbled on it, so to speak – in fact I nearly fell into it the way I did on the way to my coronation. Come, I'll show you.'

The dimensional hiatus was in a parallel tunnel just around the corner.

However, I'd always had a rather more glamorous mental picture of the entrance to another dimension. To be honest, I couldn't see a thing.

'You can't see it,' Qwerty explained. 'You can only smell it.'

I sniffed. A faint, entirely unfamiliar smell hung in the air.

'It's definitely a dimensional hiatus, it smells of genff,' said Qwerty. I had no idea what genff was, nor did I wish to be enlightened. Having found the dimensional hiatus some days earlier, Qwerty had been wondering whether to jump into it ever since. The odds against his landing in his home dimension were several billion to one.

'I may end up in a dimension teeming with monsters whose staple diet consists of gelatine princes from the 2364th Dimension. It's a terrible risk.'

'Perhaps you'll be lucky.'

'I never am. I'm the kind of prince that falls down a dimensional hiatus just before his coronation.'

I had never seen Qwerty so irresolute. Even though it ran counter to my own wishes, I simply had to encourage him to take the plunge – it was my duty as a friend. If he didn't risk it now he would never bring himself to do so, and that would leave him roaming our dimension for ever in a state of profound unhappiness. I tried to find the right words – words that were simultaneously motivating, sympathetic, heartening, comforting, and irresistibly persuasive.

'Go on, jump!' I said.

'I can't!' he wailed. 'What if I land in a sea of boiling tar or the jaws of a dinosaur? The cosmos contains innumerable places that are harmful to the health of gelatine princes. Some dimensions are reputed to consist of nothing at all. There are billions of situations less favourable than my present predicament.'

'You think too much, that's your problem. You may land in the arms of a pretty gelatine princess from the 2364th Dimension.'

'Gelatine princesses don't have any arms.'

'Are you absolutely positive it's a genuine dimensional hiatus?'

Qwerty sniffed. 'It *is* a dimensional hiatus, I can smell it!'

'Try again. Maybe you're wrong.'

He took another sniff.

'Genff,' he said. 'Genff without a doubt.'

And that was when I pushed him in. 'Aaargh!' was all he got out before he disappeared into the void.

Pushing people into dimensional hiatuses is the sort of thing you do in a fit of youthful impulsiveness, without giving much thought to the consequences. But it's not like pushing someone off the edge of a swimming pool; the effects of falling into a cosmic aperture are rather different. An adult would have thought the idea over carefully and decided against it. It wasn't until some minutes after Qwerty had melted into the tunnel's rusty floor that I had my first misgivings. What if his fears had been justified? He might even now be expiring in the fangs of a primeval dinosaur or stewing in a sea of boiling tar. I had probably murdered my best friend.

There was only one way to find out: jump in after him. If Qwerty had landed in a dinosaur's jaws, I myself deserved no other fate. I got ready to jump.

On the other hand, if Qwerty really had landed back in his 2364th Dimension there would be no point in my jumping at all. Besides, I would very probably emerge at some utterly outlandish spot in the universe. Even if I did land in the 2364th Dimension, it was absolutely inconceivable that I would be able to live on a diet of music produced by instruments made of milk. I drew back.

But was this the act of a true friend? What had I got to lose? After all, Qwerty's dimensional hiatus seemed to be the only way out of this diabolical labyrinth. I held my nose like a diver and prepared to leap into the unknown.

'Jumping off the edge of the pool is strictly prohibited!' growled a stern voice.

I spun round. A peculiar figure emerged from beyond a bend in the tunnel. Short and thickset, it was precisely half my height and entirely covered with warts and scattered tufts of hair. It looked like an old beetroot afflicted with some frightful skin disease.

'Who... who are you?' I asked uncertainly.

'I'm a Troglotroll,' the figure blurted out. 'No, wait, that's *The Troglotroll* wrong! I'm a swimming pool superintendent disguised, just for fun, as a Troglotroll. I may bear a superficial resemblance to a Troglotroll, but I'm really a swimming pool superintendent, ak-ak-ak!'

Even the gnome's laughter was peculiar.

From the
'Encyclopedia of Marvels, Life Forms and Other Phenomena of Zamonia and its Environs' by Professor Abdullah Nightingale

Troglotroll, The. Distantly related to the Common Gnomelet, the Troglotroll can claim to be the most despised creature in Zamonia, more so even than the →*Bollogg*. Whereas other malignant life forms are at least distinguished by their audacity or demand respect on account of their physical superiority, the Troglotroll possesses no laudable attributes at all; worse still, it doesn't even pretend to any and rejoices in its obnoxiousness. In certain administrative districts in Zamonia, 'Troglotroll!' is considered a personal insult carrying a heavy fine. It has been known to spark off barroom brawls, duels, family feuds - even minor civil wars.

The Troglotroll is a semihumanoid shadow-parasite of the lowest order. In other words, it favours dim, dank surroundings, shuns daylight, and lives in other creatures' homes [→*Mountain Maggot, The*] - without, of course, asking their permission or paying them rent.

'To be quite honest, I'm not really a swimming pool super-intendent,' the figure said very quickly. 'I'm a mines inspector. I inspect mines.'

He gave the tunnel wall an experimental tap.

'Yes...very nice...excellent tunnelling technique,' it muttered approvingly, and continued to tap the wall with its knuckles.

'What the hell,' it cried suddenly, flinging its arms wide in a theatrical gesture. 'Why tell a lie? I'm not a mines inspector at all, I'm the Emperor of Zamonia on a secret mission! Travelling incognito, hence my disguise! I may bear a superficial resemblance to a common Troglotroll, but underneath I'm an all-powerful monarch! That explains the absence of a sumptuous coronation and my rather shabby get-up. It's camouflage, that's all.'

Very slowly, I edged along the wall of the tunnel, ready to take to my heels at any moment. I was obviously dealing with a madman.

'All right, I admit it,' said the creature, withdrawing its former assertion unasked. 'I'm not the Emperor of Zamonia, I'm a Pelp. Although we Pelps bear a superficial resemblance to Troglotrolls, we're far more noble-minded. That's what I am: a Pelp in

Troglotroll's clothing. Does that sound convincing?'

'Yes, very convincing,' I said in a faltering voice, still edging slowly backwards. I had almost reached the bend. Once there, I would run for it.

'All right, all right, I *am* a Troglotroll!' the creature suddenly yelled. 'The bane of the Gloombergs! A repulsive, warty, hairy creature with evil intentions! An object of universal loathing! A social outcast!' The Troglotroll subsided on to his hands and knees and crawled around in front of me, sobbing bitterly. The situation was becoming more and more unpleasant.

'You may kick me a bit if you like,' he whimpered, looking up at me with tear-filled eyes. 'Everyone else does.'

I cautiously approached the Troglotroll and gave him an encouraging pat on the back.

'Now, now, things could be worse,' I said consolingly. I promptly regretted having touched him because my palm was smeared with his greasy sweat, which gave off a rancid smell.

'How would you know?' he snapped – so brusquely that I shrank back like someone recoiling from a dog that had suddenly displayed signs of rabies.

'Do you think I *chose* this life?' The Troglotroll got to his feet and glared at me. 'This filthy fur, these warts, this eternal vegetating in dark tunnels devoid of fresh air, deprived of light, destitute of hope? Do you think *that's* the career I had in mind for myself?'

It wasn't easy to devise an encouraging, inoffensive response. I made a surreptitious attempt to wipe my paw on the wall of the tunnel.

'I'd much rather be a butterfly!' His voice took on an airy, dainty note. 'A thing of beauty, fluttering without a care in the sunlight.' He gave a rather unsuccessful imitation of the fluttering of a butterfly's wings. I was beginning to feel sorry for him.

'To exist simply to gladden people's hearts, to give pleasure – to exist *to be good*...' The Troglotroll performed a few clumsy pirouettes, then stopped short and stared gloomily at the ground. 'Is that such a reprehensible ambition?'

He wasn't such a bad fellow after all. The rudiments of self-improvement and the intention to achieve it were definitely present.

'But I'm just a Troglotroll!' His voice sounded once more as if it came from the depths of a well shaft. 'The most despicable creature in the history of creation, that's me! I'm the bitter end!'

He banged his head against the wall. It made a hollow, disagreeable sound.

'I'd sooner be a cockroach!' he whimpered. 'Or a tick. Even bacteria have a better reputation.'

I tried to buck him up. 'Outward appearances don't matter. True beauty comes from within.' I blush, even today, at the banality of my attempt to console him.

'But that's just it!' sobbed the Troglotroll. 'I'm utterly depraved on the inside as well. Lying and cheating? Acting malicious for no reason and taking pride in it? That's my forte – that I'm first-class at! Looking for an unscrupulous rogue? I'm your man! But a single good deed? Impossible!'

And then I had an idea which might justly be described as brilliant. I was reminded of the Babbling Billows. They had converged on me with evil intent but turned over a new leaf by teaching me to speak.

'I've had an idea: we'll kill two birds with one stone. You simply show me the way out! Like that, I'll escape from this labyrinth and you'll perform a good deed. It's the answer to all our problems. Do you *know* the way out?'

The Troglotroll eyed me mistrustfully.

'Of course, often been there. Not a nice place, though – too much fresh air, too much light. But I can take you there all right. Sure it'll help?'

'A hundred per cent sure. I know people whose lives have been transformed by a good deed.'

I was at least certain that the Troglotroll's good deed would change my own life for the better.

'I'm unconvinced,' he said. 'But we may as well give it a try.'

I could see a change take place in the Troglotroll as he walked on ahead. Having at first shuffled morosely along in front of me, he progressively straightened up. His gait became light and springy, almost balletic.

'Ak-ak-ak!' he chuckled. 'It's incredible! The nearer we get to the exit, the better I feel. I'm in great form. I feel... how can I put it?'

'Good?'

'Good! That's just the word for it! I feel *good*!'

'That's the reward for your good deed,' I explained, 'a clear conscience. It really perks you up.'

'I think I'm going to change my entire way of life,' the Troglotroll cried eagerly. 'I could do so much good. I could come with you – leave the Gloomberg Mountains, go to some impoverished country and help the needy, perform a good deed every day, ak-ak-ak!'

'That's a very laudable intention,' I told him encouragingly. 'Once you know how the system works, you just can't stop. It's like an addiction.' I was feeling rather proud of myself, I can't deny. It's nice to be able to help someone, especially in such a practical way.

'Absolutely! I can hardly wait to perform my next good deed. I'd never have thought myself capable of such a thing!'

'You never know till you try.'

'And you'd really take me with you?' asked the Troglotroll. 'On your adventures, I mean.'

'What gave you that idea?'

'Well, I thought we might… the two of us together… I mean, out there…' He broke off.

'You really want to leave the Gloombergs?'

'I'd never dare to on my own, but with someone like you – well, that would be another matter.'

I studied the Troglotroll in profile. I was beginning to regret my helpfulness. It certainly wouldn't be any easier to make my way in real life burdened with a creature like that, but I had to finish what I'd begun.

'Naturally,' I said. 'Of course I'll take you along.'

The Troglotroll performed a touching little dance of joy in front of me and gave me his hand. I clasped it. It was even more moist and sticky than his back.

We walked for several hours, but still no cave mouth came in sight.

'Is it very far now?' I asked.

'I should say so, ak-ak-ak!' tittered the Troglotroll, and he darted down a side tunnel.

'What are you doing?' I called after him.

'Leaving you in the lurch!' he called back out of the darkness.

'*What!* Why are you doing this?'

His reply came from very far off. 'Hard to say. I'm a Troglotroll, that's all. I can't help myself.'

He was so far away by now, I could barely hear him. 'I've led you much deeper into the maze. You were quite close to the exit when we met, ak-ak! Ak-ak-ak-ak-ak-ak-aaaak!'

The last I heard of him was his mocking laughter. Then I was alone again. I sat down on the tunnel floor and started laughing too. It wasn't a very nice laugh – in fact the very sound of it gave me the creeps. If there's one piece of advice I can give the readers of my autobiography, it's this: Never trust a Troglotroll!

I'd reached the end of the road, that much was certain. I was utterly exhausted and bereft of hope. All my faith in others (especially Troglotrolls) had been destroyed. I felt at least a hundred lives old. I lay down at an intersection, one that seemed very familiar to me, and promptly fell asleep.

Bad news from a puff of wind
I was roused by a gentle current of air in my ear. I sat up.

'Hello,' said a faint voice.

There was no one to be seen.

'Where are you?' I asked.

'Here, right in front of you,' whispered the voice.

'I can't see you.'

'Nobody can. I'm a puff of wind.'

It was the puff of wind I'd felt several times. I'd never conversed with one before, but I decided to give it a try.

'Do you know the way out of the Gloombergs?' I asked.

'I'd hardly be flitting around in these stuffy caves if I did,' the puff of wind replied. 'I'd be wafting over the mountains and seas with my brothers and sisters. I'd be propelling the clouds across the sky or brewing up a tremendous storm. I'd be doing something useful, like blowing a ship across the ocean or driving a windmill – anything rather than going to seed in this crazy labyrinth.'

'How did you get in here?'

'It was the most disastrous moment in my life, believe me. I curse it to this day! I was sailing over the Gloombergs in glorious, sunny autumn weather, free as air...'

The puff of wind sighed.

'Then I passed this mountainside here. It was full of caves. I wafted over to them and peered in, wondering what they were like inside... I looked around for a bit, and there you have it – the whole sad story. I've been searching for the exit ever since. How did *you* get in?'

'My teacher sent me.'

'Nightingale?' asked the puff of wind.

'Yes! How come you know his name?'

'I've come across a lot of people in here who curse his name. Their bones lie scattered everywhere in this labyrinth.'

My blood ran cold.

'Perhaps we should join forces,' I said. 'Two might find the exit quicker than one.'

The puff of wind gave a contemptuous whistle. 'I doubt it, you're far too slow. By the time you'd groped your way along a stretch of tunnel, I'd have searched it a hundred times – and I've been in this labyrinth for over four thousand years. That'll give you some idea of your chances, ak-ak-ak!' The puff of wind's malicious laughter sounded strangely familiar.

Still cackling, it materialized before my eyes and assumed the shape of a Troglotroll.

'You must be thinking I'm a Troglotroll,' it said, 'but I'm not one at all. I'm just a puff of wind that has temporarily taken on the guise of a Troglotroll. That sounds convincing, doesn't it?'

I had tensed every muscle, poised to spring at the little gnome and throttle him until he showed me the exit, when the ground started to vibrate.

'Oh, a tunnelquake,' remarked the Troglotroll. 'You'd better dissolve into thin air like me. If you don't, I can't vouch for your survival, ak-ak-ak!'

Still cackling, he vanished.

And I woke up.

One thing I hadn't dreamed: the ground really was shaking badly. I could also hear a frightening noise, a loud, savage, ominous din, an audible threat. It sounded as if something was deliberately and inexorably heading straight for me through the iron mountain. There were sounds of grating and grinding like icebergs colliding, and sometimes I thought I heard a sort of belch, as loud and hollow as if it had been emitted by a dragon at the bottom of a well. Then came a fiery hiss and crackle, and the air became unbearably hot. The wall of the tunnel started to glow like a hotplate, red at first, then yellow and finally white, until it dissolved into a pool of molten iron.

I had to leap aside to prevent my paws being burnt by the stream of metal. The noises died away, and a dense cloud of greasy black vapour came gushing through the hole in the wall. My fear was overridden by my eagerness to know what had caused this spectacle. When the smoke slowly drifted away down the tunnels and became less dense, I was able to make out a figure on the other side of the hole. It was roughly three times my height and made of gleaming metal.

From the
**'Encyclopedia of Marvels, Life Forms
and Other Phenomena of Zamonia and its Environs'
by Professor Abdullah Nightingale**

Mountain Maggot, The. Although its outward appearance renders this hard to believe, the Mountain or Iron Maggot [Vermis montanus] belongs to the same family as the common earthworm, but is much more highly developed. The Mountain Maggot bears a biological resemblance, on the one hand, to the primitive whipworm [Trichocephalus dispar], especially as regards its digestive organs; and, on the other, to the structurally far more complex tube-dwelling worm [Hermella complexiensis]. At a mature stage of development,

Mountain Maggots attain roughly the size of a Cloven-Hoofed Steppe Unicorn and are thus Zamonia's third largest species of worm, surpassed only by the →*Lower Zamonian Chalk Leech* and the →*Midgard Serpent*. They live by gnawing their way through the mineral deposits in the Gloomberg Mountains [their only habitat], filtering all the nutrients out of the metal they devour, and digesting them. For this purpose they are equipped with masticatory organs so exceptional that any saurian predator would covet them. The mature Mountain Maggot is also capable of spitting fire like the Firework Dragon of the Brazilian rain forest, to which it is not, however, related, for dragons belong to the nodulodermal family, whereas the Mountain Maggot's epidermis is so smooth that it looks polished. Its entire body does, in fact, consist of gleaming stainless steel. Its lower jaw is shaped like an excavator shovel edged with sawteeth coated in diamond dust. It has pincers in lieu of hands and steel claws in lieu of feet, and its body terminates in a huge, tapering metal file. The mechanical appearance of the Mountain Maggot has given rise to the belief that it may be of manmade origin and hail from another planet or another dimension. It is more probable that nature has found its own way of defying the hostile environment of the Gloomberg Mountains by countering it with a metallic life form. The Mountain Maggot is probably the strongest creature on our continent relative to its size. In outward appearance, it is one of the most impressive sights Zamonia has to offer, and its potential dangers can only be likened to those of an omnivorous Sabre-Toothed Saurian when robbed of its young.

Professor Nightingale is exaggerating here. The creature that stood before me in a pool of molten iron without even noticing it looked truly fearsome, I grant you. It would be easy for me to embroider a bloodthirsty legend still further and tell how I waged a death-defying battle with the monster, but my lives have been so rich in breathtaking experiences that I've no need to contribute to the Zamonian public's mistaken image of the Mountain Maggot. There is enough 'literature' of that sort, books entitled *How I Mastered the Mountain Maggot* or *The Stainless Steel Satan*, in which self-styled experts on the Mountain Maggot describe their alleged duels with the creature. The fact is that none of these authors has ever set foot in the Gloombergs, and that all their information about this peaceable creature was acquired at second or third hand, largely from legends passed on by word of mouth or from other, equally worthless books on the subject.

Mountain Maggot, The [cont.]. The origins of the Mountain Maggot are lost in time and cannot be determined with any scientific exactitude. According to one ancient Zamonian legend, the first Mountain Maggots crawled out of the dung excreted by Giant Cyclopses; according to another, they evolved from the tears of the Storm Gods [→ *Gloomberg Tempest, The*]. What is certain, given the present porous condition of the Gloomberg Mountains, is that the earliest Mountain Maggots must have begun to gnaw their way through them hundreds of thousands of years ago. Although no scientific proof of this has yet been adduced, it is surmised that, in addition to its vermicular relationship, the Mountain Maggot has an affinity to the termite. This is suggested by the perforations in the Gloombergs, which are reminiscent of a termites' nest.

Mountain Maggots are solitary creatures. When two of them meet, as they occasionally do, they tend to ignore each other. One of biology's great unsolved riddles is how Mountain Maggots reproduce in view of their lack of contact with others of their kind. The answer may lie in another Zamonian legend that tells of 'the Great Queen,' a maggot that lives in the interior of the Gloombergs and lays steel eggs from which the infant grubs emerge. There is, however, no scientific confirmation of this.

The Mountain Maggot didn't notice me at all – or, if it did, no more so than I would have noticed a fly on the wall. It simply went on with its work, marched over to the next tunnel wall, opened its stainless steel jaws, and blew out a jet of flame the thickness of my forepaw. Then it tore off some big chunks of half-molten metal with its pincers, tossed them into its mouth, and noisily swallowed them. Having swiftly made a new hole, the creature climbed through it. I am one of the few to have witnessed the fascinating process whereby a Mountain Maggot makes its way through the Gloomberg Mountains.

The wall of metal melts, and there
a hole comes into sight.
I feel a gentle breath of air
and through the gap streams light.

What was that?

'Mountain Maggot, The' [poem]. This seventy-eight-stanza poem by Wilfred the Wordsmith is regarded as the acme of Zamonian organic verse.

Organic verse? Wasn't that the highest form of Zamonian poetry – one at which so many mediocre poets had failed? Yes, but what did it have to do with the Mountain Maggot?

Organic Verse. In this, the supreme manifestation of Zamonian lyricism, the poet adopts the perspective of an organism which is so rarely found as to escape notice in the normal course of events, e.g. →Reptilian Rescuer, The or →Mountain Maggot, The. Widely regarded as the finest example of organic poetry is the poem →'Mountain Maggot, The' by →Wilfred the Wordsmith.

I remembered now: I knew all of Wilfred the Wordsmith's sonnets by heart, but I'd shirked learning 'The Mountain Maggot' because of its immense length.

'Mountain Maggot, The' [poem] [cont.]. Wilfred puts himself in the place of a Mountain Maggot and gives a highly detailed account of its laborious journey through ferruginous rock. In the final verse he makes the Maggot find its way out into the open air and thereby lends meaning to its seemingly pointless endeavours. This suggests that the poet intended his rhyming quatrains to be a hymn to a hard-working life and its underlying purpose.

Of course! If anyone could find a way out of the Gloomberg labyrinth, it was a Mountain Maggot. I had only to follow at its stainless steel heels until it melted a wall that led to the open air. Gingerly, I climbed through the hole, which had cooled, and into the next tunnel. By now already one passage further on, the Maggot was burning a hole in the tunnel wall with its blowtorch breath. At last I had a definite chance of escaping from the labyrinth. You can't beat a good education!

Following the Maggot was fairly simple. It took no notice of me even when I came within eyeshot, and once, when I lost sight of it for a short time, I could tell which way it had gone by the freshly melted holes and metallic, crunching sounds.

The Mountain Maggot

I amused myself en route by mentally dipping into Nightingale's encyclopedia, which for some reason kept quoting 'The Mountain Maggot', over and over again. I know it by heart to this day:

Give way it must, that iron wall,
and let me through it climb.
I cannot stop to eat it all,
I never have the time.

I bore holes with my fiery breath,
digest the iron with ease
and chew it with my stainless teeth
as if it were but cheese.

Away, you Troglotrolls! You'd best
steer clear of me. Begone!
Although I never pause to rest
my work is never done.

To give the poet his due, Wilfred the Wordsmith certainly had what it takes to turn oneself into a Mountain Maggot. I particularly liked the verse about the Troglotrolls.

My only problem was the Maggot's stamina, which seemed to be inexhaustible. It never stopped to rest and didn't appear to sleep either – not, at least, while I was following it.

Mountain Maggot, The [cont.]. The Mountain Maggot belongs to the unisomnolent genus, i.e. it sleeps only once in its life. This it does shortly after attaining its two-hundredth birthday, but for fourteen years at a stretch. During this time it subsists on its accumulated mineral reserves and breathes only once a month.

I myself was running out of stamina after following hard on the creature's heels for three days. The speed and diligence with which it worked were colossal. More and more often I had to sit down and take a breather – I even dozed off from time to time. On one occasion I awoke to find the Mountain Maggot gone. The nearest hole had cooled off long ago, and I couldn't hear it at work. Ahead of me lay a fork in the tunnel. If I took the wrong turning, all my efforts would have been in vain.

First right and second left - hurray,
it's easy to remember.
If only I can find the way
I'll get out by December.

The last hole in the wall had led to the right, so I now followed the poem's instructions and turned left. There was no guarantee that Wildred's suggestion was correct, of course. It might simply have been poetic licence.

But it was my only hope. Sure enough, in the next passage I found a relatively fresh maggot-hole. I climbed over hissing pools of molten iron, stopped to listen in the passage after that – and was relieved to hear the familiar sounds of the Mountain Maggot at work. I hurried in their direction. Strangely enough, I got the impression that the darkness was becoming less intense. I turned a corner and ran full tilt into a wall of light.

The wall of metal melts, and there
a hole comes into sight.
I feel a gentle breath of air
and through the gap streams light.

My eyes gradually accustomed themselves to the glare. Fanned by a cool breeze, I saw the Mountain Maggot standing with its back to me in the circular hole that led to the outside world. I drew nearer, quite unafraid, and walked right up to it. Even now it took no notice of me. Perhaps, like me, it was simply too

The hole in the mountain

overcome by the panorama that presented itself to our gaze. Beneath us, the crests of the Gloombergs stretched away into the far distance, and the clouds beyond them formed a flat expanse as white as cotton wool. It seemed we were on one of the highest pinnacles of rock in the entire mountain range, and the view below was obscured by mist. The sunlight warmed my stiff limbs, my hopes revived.

Then a fat black storm cloud thrust itself in front of the sun and the temperature dropped in an instant. I leaned out and peered over the edge: the peak was several miles high and the surface of the Gloombergs as smooth as polished marble – not even the most experienced climber could have found a foothold. All my hopes vanished in a flash. The Mountain Maggot made some sniffing, lip-smacking noises, nervously shuffled from foot to foot and emitted exclamations that sounded like 'Eeee!' and 'Oooh!' Then it turned abruptly and went back into the tunnel. I hesitated for only a moment, then followed. What use was an exit at this altitude? I had no choice but to remain with the creature and hope that it would sometime make an opening lower down.

Swiftly but aimlessly, or so it seemed, the Mountain Maggot burrowed ever deeper into the mountain, and I went with it.

BOOOOOONNNNNGGGGG!

What was that? A bellnote in the bowels of a mountain? The Maggot stopped short.

BOOOOONNNNNG!

There it was again, a little fainter and further away.

BOOOOOOOOOOOONNNNNNNNNNNNGGGGGG!

A third bellnote, louder and nearer than the first two. 'Eee! Oooh!' said the Mountain Maggot.

**BONGBONGBONGBONGBONGBONGBONG
BONGBONGBONGBONGBONGBONGBONG
BONGBONGBONGBONG!!!!!!!!**

I had yet to learn what a thunderstorm in the Gloombergs entailed. It seldom if ever rained in those mountains, but when it did, it did so with a vengeance.

From the
'Encyclopedia of Marvels, Life Forms
and Other Phenomena of Zamonia and its Environs'
by Professor Abdullah Nightingale

Gloomberg Tempest, The. Because of their iron content, the atmosphere above the Gloomberg Mountains always carries a heavy electrical charge. Thunderstorms are a very rare natural phenomenon there. When they do occur, however, the consequence is something that need not fear comparison with any other natural disaster and is known as 'The Gloomberg Tempest' or 'The Tantrum of the Gods'. Within minutes, gigantic black rain clouds accumulate above the mountains, miles high, and dispense raindrops as big and heavy as kitchen stoves. A single one of these raindrops can fill a bathtub or slay an elk. Millions of flashes of lightning per second turn night into day, darting in directions from which normal electrical discharges are debarred. Long, thin thunderbolts go hissing into valleys and send up cascades of white sparks; others, wide as streets, cleave whole mountain peaks in half. Bolts of globe lightning fall to earth like spinning comets. Huge explosions at their point of impact create smoking craters filled with molten iron. The flashes of lightning take a wide variety of forms. Some undulate through the mountains like giant serpents, others are short and sharp like spears - they even quiver for a moment after piercing the ground. As for the accompanying thunder, it sounds as if demented giants are beating the iron mountains like a gong.

What we were hearing were the first immense raindrops striking the hollow mountains and making them ring. Then the thunder started, amplified a thousandfold by the reverberating tunnel walls. I had never been exposed to such a din in all my life.

For the first time, I was glad to be inside the Gloombergs. The elements were welcome to rage outside – I couldn't have wished for better protection than the mountains' miles-thick layers of iron. The Mountain Maggot was looking worried, however. It turned on the spot, emitting whimpering sounds, and seemed to be looking for something.

'Eee! Oooh! Eee! Oooh! Oooh! Eee! Eee!'

That such an immensely strong, almost invulnerable creature should be anxious made me anxious too. Why should it be scared of a thunderstorm when we were in the middle of a mountain?

Gloomberg Tempest, The [cont.]. The Gloomberg Mountains are porous in structure, being perforated like a termites' nest [→*Mountain Maggot, The*] by countless passages. Because many of these lead to the open air, the mountainsides afford the masses of water teeming down during a Gloomberg Tempest numerous apertures through which to penetrate the tunnels and wash them out. This is hygienically beneficial to the mountains but life-threatening to the creatures that inhabit them. Natural denizens of the Gloombergs like →*Mountain Maggots* and →*Troglotrolls* do, however, possess innate skills that enable them to survive under such conditions. A Mountain Maggot, for example, can hold its breath for as long as two hours.

I was anything but a natural denizen of the Gloombergs, nor did I possess any innate skills that would have enabled me to survive under water. The fat, heavy raindrops began by collecting into rivulets, developed into streams as they ran downhill along the tunnels, and finally became raging torrents. At some points they filled whole passages like water rushing down a drainpipe. Not that I realized it yet, I was in mortal danger.

I face death by drowning

The Mountain Maggot had found a projection in the tunnel wall and driven its steel claws into the rock. It clenched its powerful jaws and hugged the wall. This was a Mountain Maggot's customary method of coping with a Gloomberg Tempest: it clung to the rock and held its breath until the flood subsided.

The thundering masses of water propelled the air in the tunnels ahead of them, creating a shock wave that heralded the cataclysm to follow. It wasn't until I felt the wind in my fur that I sensed that something very unpleasant was coming my way. Then, with the roar of a subway train entering a station, the flood came racing around the bend.

Preceded by a circular plug of foam, it sped towards me, washed over the Mountain Maggot and thundered on in my direction. I took to my heels, but the water closed over my head almost immediately.

I'm good at holding my breath, but I can't manage two hours. With the requisite preparation – a little meditation and some deep breathing exercises – I can hold my breath for up to twenty minutes. At sea you're sometimes submerged by sizeable waves, or sucked under by a sinking ship, or swallowed by a whale, or carried down into the depths by a kraken. In short, good lung capacity is part of every seabear's basic equipment. On this occasion, however, I'd had no opportunity to meditate – indeed, I didn't even get a chance to draw a decent breath. *Under water*

From one moment to the next I was completely engulfed in liquid, a doubly shocking experience when you've long been living in extremely dry conditions. The flood propelled me through the maze of tunnels like a rifle bullet. A roaring sound filled my ears, and all I could see was an explosion of white sparks occasioned by the pressure of the water on my eyeballs. Then, because I wisely and instinctively shut my eyes, I couldn't see anything at all. I sped through the darkness, blind and weightless, spinning round and round as I went. The air in my lungs slowly began to make its presence felt. When you breathe under normal circumstances, air is a welcome guest that keeps coming and going. Breathe in, and it enters the bronchial elevator, rides it down to the lungs, and takes a quick look round; breathe out, and it exits by the same route. In this instance the air remained imprisoned. After a while it seemed to expand, pressing against the walls of my lungs like a small, captive beast desperately seeking a way out. To take my mind off this unpleasant sensation I decided to open my eyes briefly. The water was surprisingly clear, being irradiated by the phosphorescence on the tunnel walls, and I could even see minute air bubbles dancing around my body in a frenzied ballet. Air bubbles! If each bubble contained some oxygen, several might contain a whole breath – and there were thousands of them! They might even be the remains of the puff of wind I'd encountered in the maze of tunnels. I had only to reach them and suck in the life-giving oxygen, so I puckered my lips into a short straw and performed a few contortions, manoeuvring my head into the vicinity of a string of whirling air bubbles.

I had just reached the nearest of these life-saving globules of oxygen when the whole bunch put on speed. I followed them, swimming strongly, and closed with them once more. Only three strokes separated me from the nearest bubble. One... two... and... An eddy overtook me, captured the serpentine string of bubbles, and bore them off down a dark side tunnel.

I yelled with disappointment, thereby expelling the last of the oxygen from my lungs. A submarine constricted by water pressure must experience the same sensation.

Then I saw the Troglotroll. Or rather, I *thought* I saw the Troglotroll, because it was likelier to have been a hallucination conjured up in my brain by lack of oxygen. The creature drifted

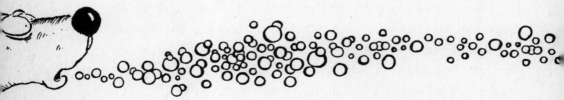

past me lying on its back with its hands clasped behind its head. It overtook me provokingly slowly, gave me an amiable smile, and waved before it vanished round a bend in the tunnel. No doubt about it: this was the end. My internal organs seemed to be inflated to bursting point. My eyes were bulging from their sockets, my ears roared as if I were standing at the foot of the Niagara Falls. I felt as if boiling water were flowing through my veins and collecting in my lungs. A violent fit of coughing assailed me.

I was ready to give up. I would simply open my mouth and let the water in – anything was preferable to this torment. I opened my mouth and breathed in, prepared to die by drowning.

But it wasn't lethal water that filled my agonized lungs; it was clear, life – giving mountain air.

The rainwater had found its own way out and sluiced me out as well – through the last hole the Mountain Maggot had made.

I was free at last.

But at what a price! My exit was situated at an altitude of roughly *The exit* five miles. I went plunging down like a fish trapped in a waterfall – a thin but very long waterfall. The view of Zamonia must have been magnificent, but I had no time to enjoy it. Such was the abrupt end of my life in the Gloombergs.

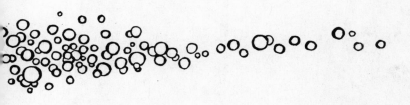

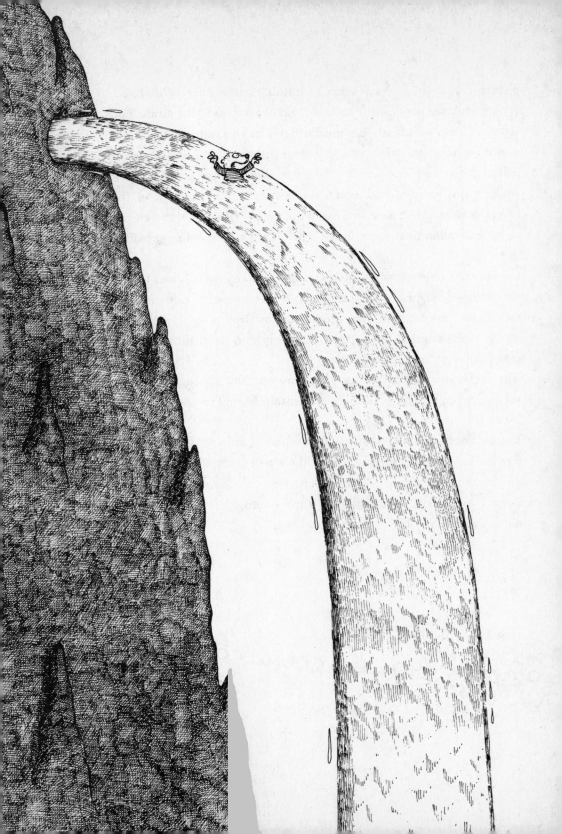

So the transition from my sixth life to my seventh was a watery one. I continued my downward progress until there were only two miles to impact. This was a predicament that called for exceptionally careful coordination between my mental faculties and physical abilities.

'Canned sardines,' said a voice in my head.

What?

'Canned sardines.'

It sounded like Professor Nightingale, but what was all this nonsense about canned sardines?

'Knowledge is night,' said Nightingale's voice.

Only a mile and a half to go. I could see that the waterfall ended in a lake. However, when you fall from such a height it makes no difference whether the surface you hit is concrete or water. It was a perfect opportunity for a Reptilian Rescuer, but there wasn't one in sight. Perhaps I was in the grid square that had been left unsupervised by Mac's retirement.

'Tyrannosaurus Rex.'

The encyclopedia in my brain seemed to be quoting headwords purely at random.

'Knowledge is night!'

Only a mile left.

The professor had always used this aphorism as a way of steering our thoughts in every possible direction. What else had he said?

'Canned sardines.'

True, canned sardines. Canned sardines were very filling. They came in cans. The cans had to be opened. Nightingale had applied his intellect to that problem.

'Bacteria.'

Nightingale had infected me with his intellectual bacteria. Was he hinting that I myself was capable of similar mental feats?
Another two thousand feet, at a rough guess.

'Tyrannosaurus Rex.'

The professor had turned into a dinosaur. Ergo, it was possible to transform oneself by the power of thought. Was I meant to turn into a dinosaur? Where was the sense in that? I would only become heavier and hit the water even harder.
Eighteen hundred feet...

'Canned sardines.'

He meant me to turn into a sardine! *A fish trapped in a waterfall...*
That made more sense. As a sardine I would be bound to survive the fall. But how had Nightingale done it? He had seven brains, I had only one.

'Knowledge is night!'

Darkness. Of course. Darkness enhances one's intelligence. I shut my eyes.

Fifteen hundred feet...

I thought of sardines. A shoal of them appeared in my mind's eye, gliding through the waterfall with me as we plummeted into the depths.

Twelve hundred feet...

I metamorphosed, but not into a sardine. I became a primordial *The sardine trick* cell, just as Nightingale had done in the course of our lesson. I grew bigger, developed into a multicellular organism, a tiny, glassy fish. Scales sprouted from my translucent skin, gills and powerful fins appeared. I felt myself filling up with bones. I inhaled the water like fresh air. I had turned into a sardine at last.

The water gave a sort of jolt and a hurricane of air bubbles seethed around me. I had dived into the lake almost without noticing it. Eager to reach the surface, I struck out with my fins, but they weren't fins any longer, they were my legs and paws. I surfaced and took a deep breath. I'd ceased to be a sardine, that was quite obvious, because my clothes and fur were sodden by the time I'd laboriously swum ashore.

I wrung out my clothes and shook the water out of my fur. Naked and rather stiff but alive and contented, I sat down at the water's edge and surveyed my surroundings. The lake was fringed with huge fir trees, and I greedily inhaled the fresh, resin-scented forest air. Fat rain clouds were still chasing each other across the sky, but the storm was over – indeed, the setting sun was blazing down through scattered rents in the clouds. I had every reason to feel pleased. Not only had I escaped from the maze of tunnels; I had cheated death twice over: death by drowning and by multiple injuries. What had happened?

Had I really turned into a fish? Or had Nightingale used the encyclopedia to hypnotize me into behaving like one?

Whichever, he had helped me to embark on a new life.

7.

My Life
in
the Great Forest

From the
'Encyclopedia of Marvels, Life Forms
and Other Phenomena of Zamonia and its Environs'
by Professor Abdullah Nightingale

Great Forest, The. The Great Forest owes its somewhat unimaginative name to the fact that no one wants anything to do with it, even in theory. It is simply avoided on principle. Everyone gives it a wide berth and advises everyone else not to set foot in it. The few people who have entered the forest in defiance of this advice have never been seen again. Many assert that the forest is inhabited by plant-sprites and leaf-witches; others surmise that it is a single evil being whose roots reach down to Hell and are watered by the Great Goat himself. Where these legends come from and on what factual circumstance they are based is unknown. The inhabitants of Zamonia have simply and tacitly agreed never to enter the Great Forest.

Darkness was falling when I wandered into the forest. Old wives' tales don't impress me. I'm not scared of forests and haven't been so ever since I lived on Hobgoblin Island. An experience like that inures you to such things. On the contrary, I relished the silence and, more particularly, the fresh air. After all the time I'd spent in that airless maze of tunnels, fresh air seemed an incredible luxury. The storm had receded as quickly as it had come. The treetops were bending in the gentle breeze which was all that remained of it, and beneath them reigned a cool, cathedral hush. Looking up through the canopy of foliage I could sometimes glimpse the dark depths of the cosmos strewn with twinkling stars. So much space above me! The trees became denser the further I went, but I walked on briskly. If a plant-sprite or leaf-witch really did live here, I wouldn't have objected to a little company.

All that aroused my misgivings was the absolute silence. Even in Hobgoblin Forest there had been noises, owls hooting, birds twittering, squirrels scampering, woodpeckers' Morse, the omnipresent rustle of insects foraging on the forest floor. Here I heard nothing of the kind, just my muffled tread on the soft carpet of leaves and the occasional snap of a rotten branch under my hind paws. So bad was the Great Forest's reputation that even worms and ants avoided it.

At length, tired out with walking and fresh air, I simply curled up on the forest floor, covered myself with leaves, and went to sleep. It was the most refreshing night's rest I'd had for ages, totally dreamless and as peaceful as the Great Forest itself.

It was late the next morning – almost noon – when I awoke. I gathered a few berries, nuts and chestnuts, munched a handful of dandelion leaves, and washed the whole meal down with some cool water from a spring. Then I set off, meaning to leave the forest behind me as soon as possible and get to the nearest outpost of civilization. I pictured a little village on the edge of the forest, a place in which to practise a profession with the knowledge I'd acquired at the Nocturnal Academy, at least for a limited period. I could work as a teacher, give lessons in astronomy and fossilology, nightingalology, Zamonian archae- ology and ferromagnetic deep-sea botany. Name an occupation and I would pursue it. Lacemaker wanted? At your service! I could have worked with equal facility as a sponge diver or violin maker, wine grower, piano tuner or dentist. I could have translated books from all languages into Zamonian or vice versa. Perhaps there was an opening for a grinder of telescope lenses, or an expert on

I make plans

geodetic oscillations between the poles. I might even be able to open a small private school of my own and pass on Nightingale's store of wisdom to my pupils. Thanks to the excellent education I'd received at the Nocturnal Academy, my professional opportunities were positively limitless.

Quite contrary to its evil reputation, the forest was a wonderful place. The best thing about it was its absolute normality. It wasn't a creeper-infested, almost impassable jungle like the forest on Hobgoblin Island, or a treacherous tropical paradise with singing flowers and glass vegetation like the Gourmetica insularis; it was just a healthy forest of the kind that grows in temperate climatic zones, with tall firs and sturdy oaks, slender poplars and an exceptional number of silver birches, the latter arrayed at such regular intervals that they might have been individually planted by hand. Berry-laden bushes grew here and there, and every few steps one came across sun-dappled clearings sprinkled with daisies and toadstools or crystal-clear streams and pools.

It was a genuine delight to roam the forest. I came across no obstacles at all, not even a fallen tree. My chronic headache, the eternal dry cough occasioned by particles of iron, the backache I'd got from bending double – all these were things of the past. I walked all day long, almost without a break, it was such a joy to be out of that rabbit warren. Then darkness descended on the forest once more. I would soon have to find a place to sleep. The possibilities were legion, and it was hard to settle on one of the many picturesque sleeping quarters that presented themselves. I had just come to a clearing when my nose picked up a feeling I'd never experienced before.

Although the reader will rightly object that you don't detect emotions with your nose, that was just what happened here.

I smelt the feeling of being at home.

It was a strange but far from alarming sensation. And then I was transfixed by the most beautiful melody I'd ever heard. Someone was humming in such a sweet, true voice that tears sprang to my eyes. I tiptoed to the edge of the clearing, hid behind a big oak tree, and looked for the source of the song.

There, seated amid a sea of daisies and illumined by the last, slanting rays of the setting sun, like a saint in an old painting, was a girl. But not just any girl: she was a girl bear, and her fur was as blue as my own.

From the
'Encyclopedia of Marvels, Life Forms
and Other Phenomena of Zamonia and its Environs'
by Professor Abdullah Nightingale

Great Forest, The [cont.]. According to one legend, the Great Forest used many years ago, in its inhabited days, to be the haunt of a special kind of bear with coloured fur [→*Ursus polychromus*]. These animals are said to have been good-natured, sedentary creatures with a talent for bee-keeping. The legend further states that they vanished from the forest one day, but nobody knows why or where they went to.

No wonder I felt at home here. Perhaps this was the forest of my primeval ancestors. There had to be something in the legend, instinct told me so, and the existence of the girl bear proved this beyond doubt.

Although I thought, in my initial transport of emotion, that the girl

214

bear's fur was the same colour as mine, this wasn't entirely true. Mine is more of a dark navy with a touch of ultramarine, like the deep, turbulent sea, whereas hers was a much paler blue like that of the sky, the cornflower or the forget-me-not.

I had never seen a more fascinating creature. From now on and for all eternity, this girl bluebear would be the focal point of my existence. The sole purpose of my life was to love her. I yearned to defend her from any danger that dared to contest our happiness, fight it off with tooth and claw, and I would have ripped the heart out of that danger – if it had one – and devoured it raw. I felt capable of boiling away the ocean to a bowl of fish soup, just with the flames of my passion. I could have stopped the world rotating, then reversed and restarted it, just for one more glimpse of the gesture with which she stuck a daisy behind her ear.

Only one thing, of that I felt quite certain, was beyond me: I could never accost the girl.

The reader will now assume, with some justification, that my very next move was to introduce myself to this wonderful creature and win her heart. She was, after all, in addition to all her other merits, the only other bluebear that had ever come my way. I felt an almost agonizing urge to speak to her. The conditions for a first encounter could hardly have been more favourable: sunset, my restored appearance, the romantic glade. Fate had destined us for one another (of that I was convinced). But at that moment I was overcome by an emotion I'd never before experienced in that particular form: timidity. I instinctively sought an even better hiding place behind a big clump of stinging nettles.

Agonized shyness

The very thought of emerging from the undergrowth and introducing myself to the girl brought me out in a cold sweat. What if I tripped and fell flat on my face? What if she laughed me to scorn? Or took fright? First impressions, they say, are always the most important. Would she think me ugly? What state was my fur in? Did my breath smell? Were my flies buttoned? Had I washed my ears? Those and other equally absurd ideas flashed through my mind, although in my existing state I found them perfectly reasonable. To begin with, therefore, I continued to crouch in the undergrowth as though paralysed and confined myself to marvelling at the girl bluebear from afar.

And that was really all I did for the next few days: remain in hiding and feast my eyes on the beautiful stranger. The forest and its dense undergrowth, the corpulent oaks with their tracery of branches, the tall grass, the stinging nettles, ferns and blackberry bushes – all offered plenty of cover.

The cottage in the clearing

The girl bluebear lived in a little cottage on the edge of the clearing where I'd first seen her. The house was built entirely of timber and faced with split logs. It was a rendezvous for all the animals I'd missed elsewhere in the forest. All sought shelter there, and all had made their homes either in the clearing itself or nearby. Birds had built their nests in the leafy canopy, squirrels and voles scurried in and out of the doors and windows as if it were the most natural thing in the world. Brimstone butterflies fluttered across the glade, portly bumblebees hummed with contentment as they went in

search of honey, and a family of nine ducks swam in the little stream that flowed through the centre of the clearing. In front of the cottage was a small garden expertly divided into functional and ornamental sections. In the former, plump cauliflowers and pumpkins proliferated, fat tomatoes gleamed, and big rhubarb leaves shielded a double row of radishes from the sun. Rosemary, parsley and chives grew alongside bright red poppies and wild roses. A funny little potato patch, a row or two of carrots and onions, a miniature forest of watercress, clumps of marjoram, mint, and sage – it was clear that the gardener not only displayed an unerring aesthetic sense but had a firm grasp of dietarily essential foodstuffs and the Zamonian and international herbs that went with them. Also growing there were thyme and dill, angelica and arrowroot, rocket and chervil, eggwort and coriander, rabbit's delight and elfweed, borage and mustard and cress, monkshood and camomile, basil and curly-leafed petroselinum, saxifrage and slipperwort.

Saxifrage and slipperwort

In the ornamental section, the loveliest of Zamonian flowers grew peaceably alongside other, exotic varieties. Witches' pride and golden primrose, calendula and campanula, asphodel and mandragora, columbine and angel's eye, hydroganja and ruggerball, ranuncula and Atlantean rose, begonia and parsley orchid, seahorse grass and sassafras blossom, Gloomberg moss and coconut-scented cowslip, black-eyed Susan and paradise lily – all were as admirably arranged as the colours on a master painter's canvas. What a wonderful place to live in!

The girl bluebear spent her days feeding the animals and tending her garden. Sometimes, too, she took a basket and disappeared into the forest, to return at dusk laden with freshly gathered fruit, berries and mushrooms. When supper was in preparation, tempting aromas issued from the cottage and drifted across the clearing.

I observed the girl at all her activities: not only hoeing in the garden and feeding the animals but seated on the grass, reading. So she was well educated on top of everything else! I was delighted to note her choice of reading matter: not just any old book but Professor Nightingale's *Encyclopedia of Marvels, Life Forms and Other Phenomena of Zamonia and its Environs*!

She actually owned a hardback edition of that work. What a sound basis for endless conversations of an intellectual nature! Could she possibly be, like me, a graduate of the Nocturnal Academy? I drew up a mental balance sheet: she was beautiful, intelligent, and kind to animals; she could cook and sing; she was a bear and had blue fur. All these items went down on the assets side.

In the end I took to following her on her walks through the forest. I did so at a due distance, flitting from tree to tree like a timid, demented woodland sprite. Numerous animals converged on her and suffered her to fondle them. They emerged from their hiding places wherever the girl went. Squirrels hopped in time to her singing and squeaked the tune, a white stag sometimes hung her basket on its antlers and carried it awhile. She was obviously popular with all the creatures of the forest and adept at communing with them. Even savage wild boars became playful pets in her presence.

I now spied on her at every opportunity and on every occasion, from her morning yawn and stretch in the cottage doorway to her nightly blowing out of the candle on her windowsill. I also – I blush with shame as I pen these words – watched her at her morning ablutions in the stream.

I had never derived such an inexplicable feeling of happiness purely from looking at someone, or, more surprising still, just from thinking about them. And this feeling became more intense with every hour, every day I spent in the proximity of the girl bluebear. So, in turn, did my abhorrence of myself and my craven failure to reveal my presence. Morning after morning I vowed I would wait for a favourable moment to emerge from the forest, politely introduce myself, and make her a proposal of marriage. Instead, I continued to cower among the rhubarb leaves like a frightened rabbit.

One morning, when I awoke rather later than usual, the girl bluebear had already disappeared into the forest. For a while I cursed myself for oversleeping. Then, plumbing the very depths of infamy, I decided that this would be an excellent opportunity to sneak into the girl's private domain. I stole across the clearing and started up the veranda steps. The first step gave under my unaccustomed weight, and an agonized groan went echoing through the forest. I promptly recoiled and paused to listen. Was she coming back? No, not a sound.

So I crept across the veranda and through the door into the little kitchen-living room. Heavens, what a dear little place! Ranged on the shelves were teacups designed for dainty little paws, and beside them tiny plates just big enough to accommodate a mouthful. Yes indeed, everything in the cottage seemed specially designed for someone at least three sizes smaller than me. I went over to the miniature stove and lifted the lid of an equally diminutive saucepan. What joy! It contained five dear little dumplings floating in creamy brown gravy, and before I knew it I'd wolfed one of them.

It tasted sensational, a potato-flour dumpling simmered to a turn, perfectly seasoned and enriched with saffron, velvety on the outside and soft as a pear within. At its heart was a preternaturally light dough consisting of breadcrumbs, raisins and dried plums. This gave off an aroma of onions, nutmeg and black pepper that tickled the gums before the dumpling melted on the tongue like butter. I had never dreamed that the culinary art could elevate such a simple dish to such heights. However, the dumpling wasn't a patch on the gravy or sauce that went with it. In this nectar, which had doubtless been carefully simmered for days over a low heat, reducing it to an essence, hand-picked mushrooms had dissolved into pure flavour. An entire forest, complete with the scent of resin and pine needles, the freshness of morning dew and the wholesome juices of berries and herbs, enveloped my tongue. All my conjectures about the girl bluebear's culinary skill were surpassed. I wriggled in ecstasy as the dumpling slid down my throat.

Then I came to my senses. Had I left an indication of my presence? Did the girl bluebear count her dumplings before she left the house?

There were four left. What a cold, uncongenial, rectangular number! Wouldn't three dumplings look considerably more aesthetically pleasing and be less likely to arouse suspicion than four?

All good things come in threes, as everyone knows, so down went the offending dumpling. I wouldn't have thought it possible that this one could have excelled its predecessor in refinement, but it was true. It had a heart of apricot and cinnamon seasoned with ground white pepper. Exquisite! I emitted a jubilant, blissful growl, half tempted to roll around on the floor in ecstasy. I had never tasted anything more delicious. What surprises did the three remaining dumplings conceal beneath their velvety white coats? Would it make a perceptible difference if the girl bluebear found only two dumplings left instead of three? I doubted it. The next dumpling had a rhubarb and cottage cheese filling flavoured with honey. Supremely delectable! It's common knowledge that honey holds a special attraction for bears. Right in the middle of the dumpling, doubly protected by the dough and the cottage cheese filling, was a hazelnut-sized blob of pure acacia honey. This, when it took my tongue by surprise, sent me into such a gustatory frenzy that I actually shook a leg. I broke into a kind of dumpling-worship dance, so to speak, hopping in a circle like a native American and growling rhythmically as I did so. In passing I rather casually wolfed the two remaining dumplings (one filled with plum jam, the other with cranberries and cream cheese). Then I proceeded to lick the saucepan clean. Bending over the stove, I lapped up the mushroom sauce like a husky dying of thirst.

'Hello,' said a voice behind me.

I straightened with a jerk and turned round.

I've seen only two spectacles during my various lives that impressed me as being flawlessly beautiful. One was a view from Mac's back of the ice mountains in the Antarctic Circle illuminated by the aurora australis. The other, for all the embarrassment of the moment, was the sight of the girl bluebear standing in the doorway with a basketful of berries, smiling at me.

'I, er... ah... er...' I stammered, completely at a loss.

She looked at me, and there was no surprise or fear in her gaze, still less annoyance or anger. On the contrary, she wore an expression entirely consistent with the emotions churning around in my own breast. It was the look of a girl bluebear hopelessly in love.

The whole distressing game of hide and seek had been quite unnecessary. We were destined for one another, we would live together for evermore, here in this forest glade or aboard a ship on the high seas – wheresoever fate chose to take us. I had found my niche in life. My everlasting quest was at an end. Only three paces separated me from my future happiness. Throwing off all my timidity, I strode boldly over and folded her in my arms.

She felt exceedingly thin and sticky, like a length of ship's rope smeared with tar – indeed, she suddenly looked like a tarry rope as well. More precisely, the girl bluebear had vanished, and in her place was a taut, sticky rope. The cottage, too, had disappeared into thin air. The clearing was still there, but it was empty save for some thin black ropes stretched across it in a skilful, systematic way, like a spider's web. And I was stuck fast to one of those ropes.

From the
'Encyclopedia of Marvels, Life Forms
and Other Phenomena of Zamonia and its Environs'
by Professor Abdullah Nightingale

Spiderwitch, The. The Common Spiderwitch or Witch Spider [Tarantula valkyria] belongs to the family of four-lunged

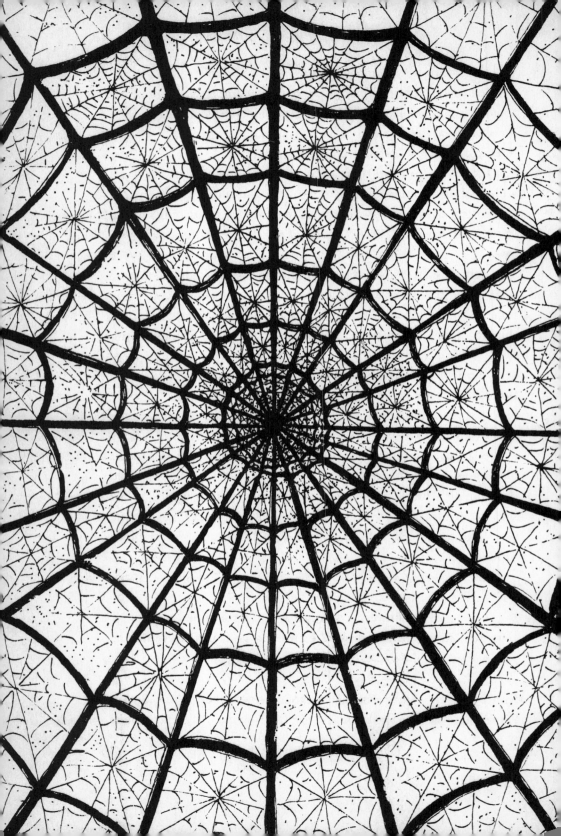

megaspiders, e.g. the bird-eating spider, but attains a considerably larger size. Its predatory techniques have never been fully investigated because no researcher has ever got near enough and lived to report his findings. The Spiderwitch is classified among those Zamonian life forms which employ unfair methods of luring their quarry, e.g. →*Carnivorous Oyster, The,* →*Gourmetica insularis, The,* and the venomous →*Frog Prince.* The Spiderwitch is usually black, with dense, shaggy, reddish brown or fox-red hair and coppery fur on the flattened extremities of its legs and palps. It is held in low esteem by other creatures because of its bad manners and malicious nature, one exception being the Tarantula Tick, a parasite that lives in its fur. Its bite [depending on the victim's size] can be innocuous, injurious to health, or absolutely fatal. An adult Bollogg, for example, will scarcely notice its bite, whereas a 200-foot-long water snail can suffer for several weeks from inflammation of the jaw area accompanied by dizzy spells and breathlessness. In creatures less than 50 feet long the bite is not only lethal but inevitably causes the victim to dissolve entirely into a viscous, readily digestible liquid, similar in appearance to white of egg, which the Spiderwitch sucks up with its mandibles. It can attain a height of 25 feet, has four to eight legs depending on its age [it is born with four legs and acquires another pair every hundred years], twelve eyes, four beaklike mouths, and, on the top of its head, a funnel-shaped, sharply tapering horn which vaguely remembles a witch's hat and has given it its name. It probably uses this horn to skewer its victims and transport them to its storage net. The Spiderwitch can excrete a sticky solution that induces delusions of a wish-fulfilling kind; in other words, hallucinations that conjure up a vision of what the victim most ardently desires. The Spiderwitch coats its webs in this secretion. Because it cannot be fitted into any evolutionary pattern, the creature is assumed to have entered Zamonia by way of a comet strike or a dimensional hiatus. It nests exclusively in the Great Forest. That is why the reader is here advised, most strongly, to give the place a wide berth.

Many thanks, Professor Nightingale! I had learned all about the Great Forest at the Nocturnal Academy. I knew that it covered 17,000 square miles and was a densely wooded tract of land whose luxuriant forms of vegetation ranged from evergreen trees to mosses and subterranean truffles. I could cite the Latin names of every plant in the forest and ascertain the age of every tree by means of bark analysis, but I did not learn that it was inhabited by an omnivorous Spiderwitch until I awoke in its web.

I was probably the last person to grasp this fact, as many readers will have guessed, but love – as everyone knows – is blind. The beautiful girl bluebear wasn't what she seemed. Not only was she no girl bluebear; she wasn't even a girl or anything at all. She was merely an illusion, a figment of my imagination generated by the hypnotic vapours emanating from the fluid to which I was adhering. I thought I'd spent whole days in the clearing, whereas everything had occurred within the space of a few minutes, or only seconds. I had probably hurled myself at the spider's sticky web with open arms, and now I was caught fast in it like a common house fly.

I began by endeavouring to free my paws. The adhesive substance was viscous; I could move my paws a good inch to and fro, but I couldn't, however hard I tried, detach them from the web. I mobilized my reserves of optimism. Perhaps there wasn't any Spiderwitch in this area; perhaps it had merely spun a web and moved to another part of the forest. That was possible, after all, wasn't it? Who was to say it would definitely return?

Spiderwitch, The [cont.]. Once the Spiderwitch has spun a web it leaves it and goes off to spin more webs in other places. Thereafter the creature checks its skilfully constructed traps for prey at regular intervals. It may be days or weeks before it returns to a web, but return it will, on that you may safely stake your last cent, your sanity, and the health of your entire family.

So I was hopelessly stuck, and the Spiderwitch would *beyond a doubt* be coming back to liquidize me with its bodily fluids. What use was the encyclopedia in my head if it never supplied me with vital information until too late? Why hadn't Nightingale told us anything in class about Spiderwitches and their hypnotic secretions? I was beginning to have considerable doubts about the Nocturnal Academy's educational system.

I submitted the cobweb to detailed scrutiny for the first time. To give the Spiderwitch its due, it was a masterpiece of the weaver's craft. The creature had not only stretched ropes taut between the trees and attached them to each other, but filled every interstice with smaller cobwebs spun from threads of steadily diminishing thickness. If one looked very closely, one could see that these smaller cobwebs were themselves filled with even smaller ones in which, if I'd had a magnifying glass, I would doubtless have discovered smaller ones still. Any living creature, be it never so microscopically small, would have been trapped by this diabolical snare.

The cobweb to end all cobwebs

It wasn't just a cobweb, it was a work of genius. Had a cup been awarded for insidious trapping techniques, it would have gone to that treacherous snare. The spider appeared to devote all its energies and intelligence to constructing these masterly examples of the predator's art, of which there were probably thousands in the Great Forest. No wonder these woods were now destitute of animals. The last surviving deer and bird, the last surviving beetle, butterfly and mayfly must ultimately have become entangled in one of the Spiderwitch's webs.

It is doubtful if there is a more horrible way to die than in the mandibles of a Spiderwitch. It very carefully coats its victim in an acidic, nauseating fluid that begins by eating away the skin and then, with excruciating lentitude, turns the flesh into porridgelike, readily digestible sludge. The victim experiences unendurable pain as his bones are...

Thanks very much, but I'd sooner not know all the gory details! It might be nice if the encyclopedia could give me a few practical tips from time to time. For instance, on how to extricate oneself from a Spiderwitch's web.

Once a living creature has become entangled in a Spiderwitch's web, only the spider itself can free it. This it does by means of the liquefactive process described in detail above. Where research into the relevant field is concerned, the Spiderwitch's secretion is considered to be the undisputed king of liquid adhesives. There is no chemical, vegetable or other compound that can dissolve the said secretion.

That was nice to know. Not only was I trapped in the web of the Zamonian continent's most bestial life form, which would sooner or later pass by and turn me into porridge – no, it had also been scientifically demonstrated beyond a doubt that the adhesive imprisoning me was indissoluble.

Except by water.

What?

Except by water. Remarkably enough, only ordinary spring, rain or tap water is capable of neutralizing the adhesive properties of the Spiderwitch's secretion.

Aha, water. There was water, certainly, a whole streamful of it, but all of fifty feet away. How could I get to it? Could the encyclopedia suggest some answer to this problem? Hello? Come in, encyclopedia! The forest remained silent.

Perhaps the spider had only just spun its web and wouldn't return for a week or two at least. It might well rain in the interim. Then I could free myself with ease and quit the forest in a hurry.

Great Forest, The [cont.]. The Great Forest gets most of its water from the numerous underground streams that permeate the soil. It very seldom rains in the Great Forest - only, in fact, on the occasion of one of the rare Gloomberg Tempests. If a Gloomberg Tempest has just occurred it may be months, if not years, before the next rain can be expected.

Information of this kind was enough to blight anyone's hopes. My optimism was gradually yielding to more realistic considerations. Perhaps the spider had spun the web a long time ago and was coming to collect its prey at this moment. It might even have been lurking in the undergrowth all this time, feasting its eyes on the sight of its helpless victim.

What was that? Had I just heard a rustle in the bushes?

No, of course not. I was well on the way to losing my mind from fear. It was only some branches stirring in the wind.

There it was again! That wasn't the wind: some leaves in the undergrowth across the way were waving to and fro in an unnatural manner. There was something alive in there! What sort of creature could it be? The Great Forest was deserted save for the Spiderwitch and me.

Another rustling sound, louder and more prolonged than before. The undergrowth parted, and an incredibly hideous, repulsive-looking creature slunk slowly towards me.

It was no Spiderwitch; it was the Troglotroll.

'Ak-ak-ak!' he cackled. 'I may look like a Troglotroll, but don't be misled. I'm really a forester – the Great Forest's forester-in-chief. Incognito, of course, hence my deceptively genuine-looking Troglotroll disguise. Does that sound relatively convincing, at least, or should I admit right away that I'm a Troglotroll?'

'Cut it out!' I snapped. 'I'm in an extremely unpleasant predicament. There's some water over there. If you'd be good enough to –'

'One moment,' the Troglotroll broke in, lounging comfortably on the grass. 'How did you get into that mess? I mean, you've got to be pretty stupid to get caught in one of those things. I've seen them all over the forest, but I'd never have taken it into my head to try and kiss one. Ugh, looks like a huge spider's web. Anyone who isn't absolutely cuckoo would give it a wide berth.'

'It's a long story.'

'I'm listening.'

'Er, this liquid here makes you think the web is the loveliest thing imaginable, not a web at all... It positively hypnotizes you and, er... it's very hard to explain... How come you weren't taken in by one?'

The Troglotroll sniffed a bit, then shrugged his shoulders. 'No idea. Perhaps because I can't imagine anything lovely, just horrid, nasty things. Ak-ak!'

230

'It doesn't matter anyway, not now. Would you be kind enough to scoop some water out of the stream and sprinkle it over my hands? It's the only thing that'll release me.'

'Is that all? Just some water from the stream?'

'Precisely. I'd be most grateful.'

'All right.' The gnome wagged his head and waddled over to the stream. Kneeling down, he cupped some water in his hands and carried it carefully over to me like a waiter with a trayful of champagne glasses.

Just before reaching the web he stopped short.

'Hurry up!' I called impatiently. 'What's wrong?'

'I came within an ace of forgetting I'm a Troglotroll. I'm behaving like a Boy Scout!'

'That's neither here nor there,' I said, trying to sound as casual as possible, because I already guessed which way the wind was blowing. 'Just bring the stuff here.'

The Troglotroll let the water trickle slowly through his fingers into the grass. 'Phew!' he said. 'Only just stopped myself in the nick of time. I very nearly performed a good deed.' He wiped some imaginary sweat from his brow with the back of his hand.

'Hey! Would you please fetch some more water and release me at last? The spider may turn up at any moment. This is no joke.'

'I'm not being funny, I'm a Troglotroll. Don't tell me you've forgotten our little adventure in the mountains?'

'No, I haven't forgotten it, but I forgive you. Leading someone astray is rather different from leaving them to be devoured by a giant spider. You wouldn't do a thing like that.'

'Yes, I would. It's my job.'

'You wouldn't!'

'Now listen, my boy!' said the Troglotroll, very serious all of a sudden, and there was a look of genuine regret in his eyes. 'You don't seem to grasp what a fix you're in. I'm a *Troglotroll*, the most abominable creature in Zamonia. I couldn't help you even if I wanted to – which I don't! It's simply not in my nature. All I want, and all I *can* do, is *not* to help you! In present circumstances, I'm the most treacherous person you could possibly have met. I mean, it would be only too easy for me to help you – child's play, in fact – but I won't. Lurking back there in the forest is a giant spider as big as a house, and all I'd have to do to save you is fetch a little water. But I'd sooner leave you to your uncertain – no, your absolutely certain fate. Only a Troglotroll could do that. You've got a greater chance of being released by the spider itself than by a Troglotroll. Put that in your pipe and smoke it!'

And the Troglotroll disappeared into the undergrowth.

'I'm really sorry!' he called. 'That's to say, I'm not even that, ak-ak-ak!'

I flew into a rage I'd never have thought myself capable of. Shrieking and vituperating, I tore at the spider's web and yelled curses so vile that not even as hated a creature as the Troglotroll had heard them before (neither had I). Seemingly endowed by my maniacal fury with colossal strength, I wrenched at the sticky rope until the anchor trees shook, tugged at the cobweb until the blood pounded in my temples. It did, in fact, stretch a little and became steadily thinner. I tugged still harder, emitting noises like a weightlifter on the verge of rupturing himself. The spider's rope became as thin as a silken thread, expanded until it was almost invisible – but it didn't snap.

My strength eventually deserted me, and the thread contracted into a thick rope once more. I roared and raved, hurled imprecations after the troll, assured him that I would pursue him to all eternity and described what I would do to him. I kicked up what was probably the loudest din the Great Forest had heard in its many thousand years of existence. Until it suddenly dawned on me what I was really doing, in other words, personally ringing the Spiderwitch's dinner bell.

Nowhere does a noise sound louder than in a forest where no other noises can be heard. It might be thought that a mountain valley or a cathedral would produce the loudest echoes, but they sound far more impressive in deserted woods. Undiluted by the hooting of owls or the rustle of insects or other noises, they rebound from tree to tree, leaf to leaf, pine needle to pine needle, until they combine to produce a monster of a sound far louder than their original cause. That is frightening enough in itself, but in this case there wasn't just a monster of a sound: there was the sound of a monster.

Spiders move silently as a rule, but that applies only to the lightweights. I was here dealing with a three-ton spider, and I could already hear it in the distance as it drove its yards-long legs into the forest floor like a piledriver. At first the ground just vibrated gently, but then my ears detected an eightfold tread that seemed to be making for me fast and purposefully.

Boom! (one) **Boom!** (two) **Boom!** (three) **Boom!** (four) **Boom!** (five) **Boom!** (six) **Boom!** (seven) **Boom!** (eight). Eight booms. Eight legs. So the spider was fully mature.

Sailing over the clearing at an altitude of several miles was a tiny rain cloud, probably a belated leftover from the Gloomberg Tempest. I stared at this cloud. Perhaps I could persuade it to shed a few drops by telekinesis. I stared until my eyes almost popped out of my head. I commanded it, again and again, to rain on the spot. For a moment it seemed to pause immediately overhead, perhaps because the wind had dropped, but then it sailed blithely on until it disappeared behind the canopy of foliage, leaving nothing behind but clear blue sky. That was probably the last chance of rain for months to come, if not years.

BOOM! (Water!) **BOOM!** (Water!) **BOOM!** (Water!) **BOOM!** (Water!) **BOOM!** (Water!) **BOOM!** (Water!) **BOOM!** (Water!) **BOOM!** (Water!)

'Water! Water! Water!' Like a man dying of thirst, I could think of nothing else.

From the
'Encyclopedia of Marvels, Life Forms
and Other Phenomena of Zamonia and its Environs'
by Professor Abdullah Nightingale

Water, Zamonian. In Zamonia, water occurs in many very different forms, not only as a liquid, but also as a solid [ice] or a vapour [mist]. Solidified water, a rarer variety, is a byproduct of aquashoes [→*Professor Nightingale's Solid Soup*]. The largest reservoir in Zamonia is the Zamonian Sea, which surrounds the continent, though this is hard to render drinkable and must be desalinated at great expense.

**BOOM! BOOM! BOOM! BOOM!
BOOM! BOOM! BOOM! BOOM!**

For this reason, drinking water is extracted mainly from rivers, lakes, and underground watercourses. Sweet water is found exclusively in the subterranean caverns of the →*Demerara Desert*, red and green water in the caves beneath the Muchwater Marshes, where it is a product of the discoloration caused by Slipper Animalcules during the mating season.

**BOOM! BOOM! BOOM! BOOM!
BOOM! BOOM! BOOM! BOOM!**

Magnetic spring water, which can flow uphill, is sometimes found on the slopes of the Gloomberg Mountains, which have a substantial iron content. The Trappist monks of the Church of the Chastened Chestnut used this water to make their so-called Uphill Beer, intending to revolutionize the brewing industry and facilitate consumption [it was hoped that a tankard need only be put to the drinker's lips, not tilted]. Their experiment was an abysmal failure, however, because the beer rose into the air of its own accord and floated off into the blue.

BOOM! BOOM! BOOM! BOOM! BOOM! BOOM! BOOM! BOOM!

The encyclopedia's useless items of information were only making my situation worse. I would have given anything to be able to switch it off.

Birolanian Birchwater, which is sometimes excreted during heatwaves by the Birolanian Turf Birch, is regarded in certain circles as a sacred liquid endowed with a miraculous ability to cure incurable diseases. Other natural sources of liquid for use in an emergency include rain clouds, the morning dew on vegetable foliage, pressed cacti, camedar humps [→Camedar, The], and human tears and saliva, which are 90 per cent water.

Tears! Saliva! My own body consisted largely of water! All I needed to do was spit! Incredible how slowly one's mind works, especially in situations of the utmost urgency.
So I collected some saliva in my mouth.
That is to say, I *tried* to collect some but failed: my throat was absolutely parched. Terror had transformed my mouth into a drought area, my tongue was as dry and rough as a sheet of emery

paper, my gums were parchmentlike. The saliva seemed to have hidden away in my pores for fear of the Spiderwitch. I found it quite impossible to coax so much as a droplet to the surface.

BOOM! BOOM! BOOM! BOOM! BOOM! BOOM! BOOM! BOOM!

But tears! All I had to do was cry! I had not only learned to weep to order but promoted weeping to the status of an art form. I was a champion – no, the *world* champion at that form of activity! Except that I hadn't engaged in it for a long time, and the situation in which I found myself made concentration difficult. From the sound of its footsteps, the Spiderwitch had almost reached the clearing.

BOOM! BOOM! BOOM! BOOM! BOOM! BOOM! BOOM! BOOM!

So I mentally squeezed my tear ducts as hard as I could. I pictured scenes of almost unimaginable grief, incidents of a profoundly tragic nature, the funerals of my best friends – even my own. But I was quite simply out of practice. Or was it that I was older? A youngster weeps at the drop of a hat; when you're older, the tears flow rather less easily. Was I still *capable* of weeping?

BOOM!
BOOM!
BOOM!
BOOM!
BOOM!
BOOM!
BOOM!
BOOM!

BOOM!

The final 'Boom!' dispelled my last remaining doubt that the Spiderwitch had reached the clearing. I couldn't see the whole of it yet, just one of its eight eyes peering through the foliage, probably to see what was struggling in its web. Then it squeezed the upper part of its body through the treetops. Pus-yellow spittle was oozing from a spout in its belly, presumably the deadly secretion that would dissolve me.

And then, for the first time, I heard the Spiderwitch's voice. A sound that deprived me of hope, it might have been made by all the dangerous representatives of the animal kingdom at once. It combined the menacing growl of a tiger with the venomous hiss of a cobra, the derisive cackle of an evil spirit with the hoarse laugh of a hyena and the sound of a vampire bat greedily drinking. It sent shivers down my spine and brought tears of terror to my eyes.

I started to weep – not deliberately or in simulated sorrow, but from genuine, hopeless, mortal fear! The tears spurted from my eyes in two thin streams, and I still had just enough presence of mind to aim them at my imprisoned hands. But for whatever reason, whether I was squinting from sheer terror or sobbing so hard that my body was shaking, the jet missed them by a good six inches.

There are times in life when you become convinced that the entire universe has assembled in some gloomy back room and resolved to conspire against you. This was one of those times. But there are also times that restore your faith in Lady Luck. The two or three seconds it took for my tears, having shot past their target, to rebound off the petals of an orange lily on to the branch of a birch tree, which bent and released a captive fern frond, which sprang erect and projected my tears at a canopy of chestnut leaves laden with raindrops from the recent Gloomberg Tempest, which in turn sent them pattering down on me like a cold morning shower

– those seconds were one such fortunate moment in time. It was the moment when fate released my hands from the spider's web and signalled the start of my marathon run through the Great Forest.

My marathon escape from the Great Forest

I had never run in my life, if the truth be told. The Minipirates' ship was too cramped and Hobgoblin Island too cluttered with fallen trees; running was out of the question on my raft; the most I ever did on Gourmet Island was take a leisurely stroll (in the end on all fours); my time with Mac was spent entirely in the air; and the Nocturnal Academy's curriculum did not include athletics.

The first hour

So I was obliged to run for the first time in my life, and not only run, but – no half measures! – run for my life. I got into a long-distance frame of mind, knowing that the key to success was either greater speed or greater stamina. I realized at the same time that the dice were loaded against me. Being a bear, not an antelope, I had two short, relatively unathletic hind legs. The spider's legs were not only very long but eight in number.

Off I ran, fast enough to put a safe distance between me and the spider but not *too* fast, for fear of getting out of breath. My main advantage was my size, because I could slip between trees and under branches, whereas the spider had to forge a laborious path through all that barred its path – dense foliage, forked branches, close-set tree trunks – by trampling them underfoot or wrenching them apart. The creature's strength was prodigious – its body weight alone was sufficient to bend aside full-grown spruce like a reed – but its progress was forever being obstructed: it had to barge its way through the forest in a zigzag fashion, whereas I

241

had a clear run. Things would have been different in open countryside, where its long legs would soon have decided the issue.

The secret of running is breathing. Breathe in, two strides, breathe out, two strides … Arms slightly bent, hands clenched in front of the chest, push off the ball of each foot in turn. The first hour was no problem. I ran steadily, lithely through the trees with the strength of youth in my heels and fear – a great incentive – at my back. I obviously had a natural talent for running. My lead

increased minute by minute, the spider lost ground yard by yard. Sooner or later, I felt sure, it would fall behind completely and abandon the chase. After half an hour of this endurance run its footsteps rang more faintly in my ears:

**BOOM! BOOM! BOOM! BOOM!
BOOM! BOOM! BOOM! BOOM!**

The second hour was easier still. I felt is if my body were manufacturing renewed energy out of fresh air and pumping it straight into my legs through my veins. I became positively intoxicated. My stride steadily lengthened, my confidence grew. The longer I ran, the greater my reserves of energy seemed to become: the more energy I consumed, the more I acquired. Stopping to rest was pointless, it only made you wearier, prevented you from getting back into your stride again. I even put on speed. The Spiderwitch fell further and further behind.

BOOM! BOOM! BOOM! BOOM!
BOOM! BOOM! BOOM! BOOM!

The third hour wasn't quite as easy. I began to sweat more profusely than I'd ever done, even in the most tropical heat. The salty fluid streamed down me but didn't fall to the ground; it remained lodged in my fur, because I had no chance to pause for a few moments and shake it off. This increased my body weight considerably, making me feel as if I were swathed in wet hand towels. The sweat sometimes obscured my view for seconds at a time, and I had to be careful not to collide with a tree. But I still felt confident of winning the race, even though the spider had made up some ground. Its footsteps were unmistakably louder again.

BOOM! BOOM! BOOM! BOOM!
BOOM! BOOM! BOOM! BOOM!

The fourth hour was a definite improvement, perhaps because I *The fourth hour* had ceased to feel my body. I'd become no more than a soaring, incorporeal spirit that glided over the forest floor like a hovercraft. There were two possibilities: either my body had triumphed over pain and exhaustion or – the likelier alternative, I suspected – it had come to a halt at some stage and sat down, because I couldn't feel it any more. But I continued to run on in spirit, and my spirit was swift as the wind. The spider was now almost out of earshot.

BOOM! BOOM! BOOM! BOOM!
BOOM! BOOM! BOOM! BOOM!

By the fifth hour I didn't know who I was or what I was doing. *The fifth hour* There were times when I almost stopped running from sheer bewilderment, only to be preserved from disaster by my intellect, which fortunately took over just in time. My mind was in the strangest state. I suffered from increasing delusions of grandeur – I actually believed at times that the forest existed solely to provide me with a marathon course. My weightless body soared higher and higher, and before long I could survey the entire forest. I felt sure I was monitoring its every movement, determining the direction of every root, the growth and destiny of every stalk of grass, every leaf and branch throughout its extent. Then I rose still higher until, as if looking down through a giant magnifying glass, I could see the whole of Zamonia and make out each of the living creatures that inhabited it, all of whose names I knew and whose destinies I sagely directed. Eventually I soared into space and looked down on the entire planet, expertly superintending its rotation and gravitational pull and sending a hurricane or two across the oceans.

From the
'Encyclopedia of Marvels, Life Forms
and Other Phenomena of Zamonia and its Environs'
by Professor Abdullah Nightingale

Marathon Fever. A rare condition observable only in Zamonian marathon runners. After some five hours of strenuous marathon running in the atmosphere prevailing in Zamonian mixed forests, with its extremely high oxygen content, the body temperature rises to 113 degrees Fahrenheit. In a person in a standing or recumbent position, this would be fatal; in someone engaged in running, it merely releases so-called bazirs into the blood, in other words, bacillumlike corpuscles productive of temporary delusions when they reach the brain. Far from putting marathon runners at a disadvantage, however, these help to desensitize them against their natural exhaustion and spur them on to further feats of athleticism. The said hallucinations are all of a pleasant nature, being associated with rapid progress. Those who have them tend to imagine that they are creatures noted for their speed, e.g. gazelles, cheetahs, or swallows.

In my case I probably imagined myself to be a winged forest deity, but what did that matter as long as the delusion made me run faster? By now the Spiderwitch had become a matter of complete indifference to me. Was it still within earshot?

BOOM! BOOM! BOOM! BOOM!
BOOM! BOOM! BOOM! BOOM!

246

In the sixth hour I regained possession of my mind and my body, the former being clearer and the latter heavier than ever before. I felt I was toting a sack of cement, my legs seemed to be filled with lead, and the sweat clinging to my fur weighed me down. I stumbled along, half dazed and bereft of all my former self-confidence. The marathon fever had evaporated, and my delusions of grandeur had yielded to a more realistic appraisal of the situation. This told me that my strength was giving out, and that the spider had definitely made up some ground.

BOOM! BOOM! BOOM! BOOM! BOOM! BOOM! BOOM! BOOM!

During the seventh hour the light began to fade and the forest was traversed by a refreshing breeze that dried my sweat and restored my energies.

With nightfall came darkness. My eyesight has always been good, even in poor light, as I'd demonstrated in the Gloomberg Mountains. Moreover, a seaman's innate bump of direction and an exceedingly keen sense of smell enable me to move as confidently as a bat in almost total darkness. I smell trees before I collide with them, and my internal compass always steers me in the most favourable direction – instincts which only a bluebear possesses. Furthermore, I could clearly hear the Spiderwitch and gauge its distance from me when it crashed through the forest like a giant on stilts, especially as it couldn't suppress its furious snarls and greedy slobbering sounds. I mustered all my strength for a final spurt. I would either shake off the Spiderwitch once and for all or be devoured by it. I was staking everything on a single throw of the dice.

My education at the Nocturnal Academy, and particularly my lessons in biology, now paid off. I twisted and turned like a rabbit, dived down holes like a fox, sprinted like a zebra in flight. I flitted across the forest floor, zigzagging like a lizard, or disappeared completely into dense foliage and wriggled through it like a grass snake.

But the spider's eight eyes enabled it to find its way in the dark at least as well as I could. Its greatest advantage, however, was despair, which spurred it on to unprecedented feats. It was ages since anyone apart from me had strayed into the Great Forest, so the creature's last meal lay far in the past. Spiders can survive on their accumulated food for immense periods of time, but sooner or later the last calorie is consumed. If I escaped the Spiderwitch's clutches now, it would not have the strength to lure and ensnare another victim, least of all after expending so much energy on this marathon. It would have to crawl back into the forest empty-handed and starve to death there.

I could clearly hear it trying to put on a spurt.

BOOM! BOOM! BOOM! BOOM! BOOM! BOOM! BOOM! BOOM!

Meantime, I was no longer capable of switching, just like that, from one escape technique to another. I wasn't a weasel or a gazelle; I was a bear, and bears are essentially slow-moving creatures that like to take things easy. My legs were dragging me down like ships' anchors, and every muscle in my body hurt in its own particular way. Worst of all, though, was the voice inside me, which kept urging me to let everything go hang and take a nap. The Spiderwitch had long ago sensed my weakness and summoned up its remaining strength. This quickly reduced my lead. The creature felled whole rows of trees with a single scything blow from its claw-tipped feet, ripped bushes out of the ground with its pincerlike jaws, and hurled imprecations into the darkness in Spiderwitch. It made up a lot of ground while I cursed my plan to stake everything on a single throw, because my strength was really giving out at last.

BOOM! BOOM! BOOM! BOOM! BOOM! BOOM! BOOM! BOOM!

I continued to drag myself along, though exhaustion was depriving me of my natural instincts. I bumped into trees, tripped over roots, and got tangled up in undergrowth. I made little headway, whereas the Spiderwitch was steadily reducing the distance between us.

BOOM!
BOOM!
BOOM!
BOOM!
BOOM!
BOOM!
BOOM!
BOOM!

BOOM!

The Spiderwitch was right behind me now, only a single arachnidan stride from its coveted prey. The whole marathon run had been a futile waste of energy. I was debating whether to simply stand my ground and face up to the creature – I might with luck achieve something in a straight fight if it was even more exhausted than I – when I detected a strange but familiar scent. 'That's odd,' I thought. 'There's a smell of genff!'

Where, I wondered, had I heard that peculiar word? Just as I remembered, I fell head first into a dimensional hiatus.

8.

My Life in the Dimensional Hiatus

When you stumble into a dimensional hiatus you fall in every direction at once: down and up, right and left, north and south, east and west. You also fall through time, not only in reverse but at twice the speed of light, following a trajectory known as the Nightingalian octaval loop. Professor Nightingale was the first – as usual – to describe this phenomenon. The Nightingalian octaval loop should be conceived of as a double loop in the shape of an eightfold figure of eight of which one-eighth is situated in space, one-eighth in time, and the remaining six-eighths in the other six dimensions. This means that, while falling, you're everywhere in the universe at every point in time.

This process is very confusing at first, and the reader would be well advised not to try to form a mental picture of multidimensional space. It has been estimated that even a Nocturnomath would take an entire lifetime to picture even one square yard of it.

From the
'Encyclopedia of Marvels, Life Forms
and Other Phenomena of Zamonia and its Environs'
by Professor Abdullah Nightingale

Multidimensional Space. It is really quite easy to picture a square yard of multidimensional space - provided you have seven brains.

Simply picture a train travelling through a black hole with a candle on its roof while you yourself, with a candle on your head, are standing on Mars and winding a clock precisely one yard in diameter, and while an owl, which also has a candle on its head and is travelling in the opposite direction to the train at the speed of light, is flying through a tunnel in the process of being swallowed by another black hole which likewise has a candle on its head [if you can imagine a black hole with a candle on its head, though for that you will require at least four brains]. Join up the four points at which the candles are burning, using a coloured pencil, and you'll have one square yard of multidimensional space. You will also, coincidentally, be able to tell the time on Mars by the clock, even in the dark, because - of course - you've got a candle on your head.

So you're *everywhere in the world at once*: in the Alps and on the Atlantic Ocean, at the North Pole and in the Gobi Desert, on the Nile and in the Brazilian rain forest. You're also, as already mentioned, present at every point in time. To cite a few alternatives: one million years ago and the day after tomorrow at half-past three; in the autumn; in springtime; in summertime; at Christmas; and a hundred or a hundred thousand years from now.

But you're not only on earth; you're also on the moon and on Saturn, in the Horsehead Nebula and on Cassiopeia's starry throne, on the far side of Betelgeuse and beneath the wings of Pegasus, on the left horn of Taurus, in the constellation of Cancer, and everywhere else in the known universe. *And,* just to make matters even more puzzling, you're in every other *unknown* universe as well! So anyone falling down a dimensional hiatus really goes places – everywhere, to be exact.

This deluge of optical stimuli would normally drive a person insane, but the brain's response to a fall down a dimensional hiatus is remarkably self-protective: it lapses into a state of mild dementia, or as Professor Nightingale has termed it, 'carefree catalepsy'.

From the
'Encyclopedia of Marvels, Life Forms
and Other Phenomena of Zamonia and its Environs'
by Professor Abdullah Nightingale

Carefree Catalepsy. The muscular and cerebral paralysis into which one's mind and body subside when confined to a dimensional hiatus for a considerable length of time. This state of almost complete physical and mental torpor renders one unimpressed by anything, even a plunge down a dimensional hiatus. The body is pervaded by an agreeable feeling of lassitude, the ears become abnormally hot, and the face takes on a broad, fatuous grin. This condition is very distantly related to the state of helpless ecstasy engendered by two 360° loops on a roller coaster.

Such was my condition when I encountered Qwerty. I was roaming the constellation of Orion and Qwerty was clearly still in free fall in the dimensional hiatus into which I had pushed him. Either that, or he'd fallen down another one.

Since anyone in a dimensional hiatus is everywhere at the same time, as I have already said, it was really only a matter of time before we met up again. Qwerty came sailing weightlessly towards me in slow motion, revolving on his own axis, and gave me a foolish grin as he sailed past. Like me, he was obviously in a state of carefree catalepsy, hence our remarkably blasé reaction to this incredible coincidence.

'Hi, Qwerty!' I called.

'Hi, Bluebear!' he called back with a casual wave.

Then he sailed on towards the Rigel Nebula while I zoomed off in the opposite direction. Now that it had taken place, this fantastic incident completely banished the possibility that our paths might cross again somewhere, at least according to the general laws of probability.

The condition known as carefree catalepsy even enables a person to sleep while falling through a dimensional hiatus – indeed, it's positively soporific. I became more and more sleepy as I plummeted through endless, universal space.

My eyelids drooped and I sank into a sleep filled with dreams of just about everyone who'd played a role, however minor, in my life to date. Minipirates bellowed pirate sea shanties, Babbling Billows sloshed past, Hobgoblins whispered requests for encores, I plunged again and again into the jaws of the Gourmetica and was rescued from them each time by Mac, Fredda bombarded me with meteorites, Professor Nightingale rode past on his Nightingalator, brains clicking furiously, a Mountain Maggot nibbled an iron moon, and – needless to say – the Troglotroll also sailed past, waving amiably. But there were also creatures and things I'd not yet encountered: black-clad figures riding beasts like camels, a floating city, a head the size of a mountain, and an endless stream of fantastic, simultaneously frightening and fascinating life forms: giants, dwarfs and demons, monstrous worms

and huge avian predators. At the time I took this to be an inco-
herent phantasmagoria, but I realize now that I was dreaming of
my future.

Then I was jolted awake by an earsplitting blast on a horn. No, in
reality I was still dreaming, because now it was the *Moloch* I encountered for a second time. The ship seemed very real – I could
even see the underside of her vast hull, which was overgrown
with coral reefs, shellfish cities, and forests of seaweed. Escorting
her through the universe were thousands of sharks, jellyfish, and
moray eels.

That is how you soar through time and space, in a state midway
between dreaming and carefree catalepsy, until you suddenly
tumble through one of an unimaginable number of dimensional
hiatuses and emerge at some point in the cosmos. I wondered
where that point would be. Not, I hoped, in another dimension.

**From the
'Encyclopedia of Marvels, Life Forms
and Other Phenomena of Zamonia and its Environs'
by Professor Abdullah Nightingale**

Dimensional Hiatuses. Anyone venturing into a dimensional hiatus
should realize in advance that everything in an alien dimension can
be fundamentally different. It may lack something important - air,
for example - or the atmosphere may consist of water, or lead, or
concrete. The laws of nature that prevail there may be quite
different from our own. There may be no gravity, no time, or no

space. Another dimension could, for instance, consist of congealed boredom or musical frigidity, of lethal poison gas or a solar temperature registering many thousands of degrees, of high-voltage electricity or unfulfilled wishes.

There are said to be dimensions in which sorrow is the staple food of creatures that vegetate in little pools of grief. Many dimensions are so tiny - minidimensions with very, very small natural laws - that our planet would be compressed to the size of a pinhead on entering them. Others, again, are so big that even their atoms are bigger than our native planet. There are some dimensions in which only thoughts can survive and others inhabited exclusively by unpleasant sensations like hunger or envy in the form of little red pretzels that can sing. Anything is possible!

Land in a two-dimensional dimension and you're squashed as flat as a pancake. A one-dimensional dimension will stretch you like an endless rubber band, a five-dimensional one will transform you into a radio wave with a headache. As for an eight-dimensional dimension, its appearance cannot be conveyed in our language. Only one thing is certain: those who enter another dimension must change their way of life, possibly in the most drastic manner.

When I came tumbling out of the dimensional hiatus I felt as if a hand had reached down my throat into my stomach and turned me inside out like a wet sock (I can't think of a less distasteful simile). I turned a few somersaults, first through the air and then across the ground, before I came to rest.

I sat on my backside, trying hard not to be sick, and looked down at the surface I'd landed on to see what it was made of.

It's extremely important to know what material the surface of an alien dimension consists of when you land on it. If it's concrete, for example, you can expect relatively stable natural conditions; if

In another dimension

261

it's lava or cometary gas, you're done for. The ground beneath me was not only soft but strewn with artistic designs.

It was a carpet.

Very long and some hundred yards wide, it was flanked by yawning expanses of outer space. Other strips of carpet criss-crossed the dimension like intergalactic motorways covered with pretty patterns, and flying carpets were zooming around all over the place.

About a hundred yards from me stood a magnificent throne. Still rather dazed, I got up and tried to adjust my clothing. Then someone nudged me from behind and I turned round. It was Qwerty Uiop.

Actually, it wasn't Qwerty Uiop – it was someone who looked very like him. But so did the two hundred thousand-odd other creatures arrayed on the strip of carpet behind me. These endless rows of gelatinous, Qwertylike figures pulled me back, ever further into their wobbly ranks. It seemed that I had been blocking their view of the throne, which they considered very important for some reason. That apart, they didn't take umbrage at my presence. A group right next to me struck up a kind of tune. Not only did it sound awful but – this is the gospel truth – they played it on instruments made of milk.

Then a great commotion arose, and thrusting its way through the restless crowd came a little procession. At its head – and this time I was sure of it – marched Qwerty. You can recognize your very best friend when you see him, even in the midst of two hundred thousand look-alikes. I called his name, but my voice was

drowned by the general tumult and I was pushed back still further. Qwerty oozed majestically along, then detached himself from the crowd and slowly and deliberately approached the throne. The music took on a dramatic flavour, which made it sound even more frightful than before. Qwerty couldn't possibly have heard me above the din, so I wormed my way forwards and went up to him.

How it had happened I couldn't tell, but I'd obviously landed in his dimension just as he was about to be crowned. I had to get to him before he fell into the dimensional hiatus.

An angry murmur ran through the crowd as I hurried towards him, but Qwerty didn't hear that either – the music was too loud. Tremendously excited, no doubt, he continued to make for the throne. I was just behind him, so close that I could almost have grabbed him, when my foot caught in a fold in the carpet. I stumbled, nearly lost my balance, and blundered into Qwerty from behind. Propelled by me, he rolled to the edge of the carpet, toppled off it into space, and vanished into thin air. The crowd froze, the music died away. I went to the edge of the carpet and stared helplessly into the void.

There was a faint smell of genff.

It wasn't Qwerty who had tripped, as he had always believed, it was me. *I* was responsible for his having landed in our dimension – in purely mathematical terms, the most improbable happening in the universe and one that no one would credit. By now the crowd was wobbling angrily towards me. Without a moment's hesitation, I launched myself into space.

From the
'Encyclopedia of Marvels, Life Forms
and Other Phenomena of Zamonia and its Environs'
by Professor Abdullah Nightingale

Equitemporal Tunnelling of Dimensions, The. The time known to us is divided into EARLIER and LATER, NOW and IMMEDIATELY, SHORTLY and PREVIOUSLY, YESTERDAY and TODAY, TOMORROW, SOON, EVENTUALLY, AT ONE TIME, FINALLY, ULTIMATELY, FORMERLY, HITHERTO, and MEANWHILE. But all of these junctures once occurred in the PRESENT and will sometime be in the PAST, and, after a considerable period, IN THE OLD DAYS - or, to use somewhat more old-fashioned terminology, IN DAYS OF YORE. How can this be? It's hard to say. The only certainty is that dimensions are connected by tunnels whose entrances and exits are dimensional hiatuses, and that time flows back and forth through these tunnels from one dimension to another. This may provide an answer to the major question of how time can vanish while remaining omnipresent.

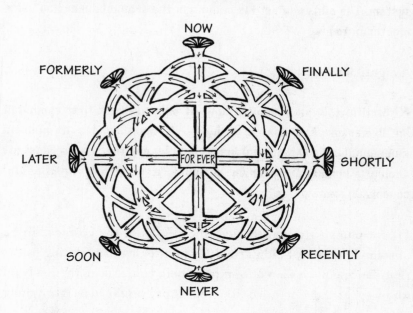

I hope this affords the reader a reasonably satisfactory explanation of how I was able to participate in a future event that had taken place not only in the past but in another dimension. I myself was temporarily less preoccupied with this problem than interested in knowing where I would land this time. After the incredible coincidence that had landed me in Qwerty's dimension, my chances of emerging in my own, native dimension were very slim – indeed, absolutely nil.

From the
'Encyclopedia of Marvels, Life Forms
and Other Phenomena of Zamonia and its Environs'
by Professor Abdullah Nightingale

Dimensional Hiatuses [cont.]. Once a person has travelled from one dimension to another, returning by the same route is the unlikeliest thing that could happen to him in the known dimensional system. The odds against his landing in the original dimension are a nightillion to one.

A nightillion?

Nightillion. A mathematical unit of measurement first computed by Professor Abdullah Nightingale. A nightillion is a quantity unimaginable by the normal brain, only by one that has at least six ancillary brains. In common parlance, a nightillion signifies 'inconceivably many'.

I went plunging down through the depths of the cosmos. To be absolutely honest, I didn't find this journey half as exciting as the first. Once you've seen one spiral nebula you've seen them all and know what they look like, so a repeat performance isn't anything like as thrilling. Like an old space-flight pro, I was preparing myself for a longish bout of carefree catalepsy when my descent was abruptly cut short and I tumbled out into another dimension.

I realize that I'm running the risk of losing my last well-disposed reader, but I have a duty to tell the truth and can only report what actually happened: I popped out of the very same dimensional hiatus into which I'd originally fallen. This was not only the most improbable of all the possibilities in the universe, but the most unpleasant. Why? Because the Spiderwitch would be waiting for me beside the hole, and the odds against my escaping it had been drastically shortened, not lengthened, by my fall. Already exhausted by my marathon run, I had since been subjected to the stress of falling through a dimensional hiatus.

In any case, my existence between the dimensions was at an end. Had it been the longest or the shortest of my lives to date? Hard to say. Both, perhaps.

But there was no Spiderwitch in sight.

Nor was it night-time, as it had been when I fell down the hole, but broad daylight.

Same place, different time

It would, after all, have been a *truly* impossible coincidence had I tumbled out of the dimensional hiatus at the very same moment in time. That simple fact accounted for the spider's absence: I had emerged on another occasion. It was another day, perhaps. Another week. Another month. A year or a century later. Or a million years earlier. Any juncture in history was possible.

The spider had gone, that was the main thing. Perhaps it had crawled back into the forest to die of starvation. Perhaps it had yet to be born. Perhaps it had tumbled into the dimensional hiatus after me and was sailing through outer space. Best of all, perhaps it was even now cooking in a primeval lake of boiling pitch or would in the future be devoured by monsters still more frightful than itself.

But one shouldn't bear a grudge. It was conceivable, though not very probable, that the creature had found its way back into the dimension from which, according to Professor Nightingale's theory, its ancestors had come. The universe abounds in possibilities.

For all that, I hurriedly proceeded to quit the sinister forest. The trees became steadily sparser, and within an hour I had reached the edge. A curtain seemed to part, disclosing a view of a new world. I was looking down at a pale brown, apparently endless plain whose extremities melted indistinguishably into the sky. There wasn't a single tree or mountain for as far as the eye could see. This was quite all right with me, after all the dire experiences I'd previously undergone in mountainous or wooded areas.

I was completely dehydrated, so I replenished my reserves at a forest spring and drank, greedily and noisily, for minutes on end. Then I made my way down a hill and across some withered grass until I reached the edge of the great plain. The surface consisted of very fine brown, sticky sand that smelt of vanilla. I stuck a paw in it and tasted some: it was pleasantly sweet. This had to be the Demerara Desert of which Nightingale had told us in class. Somewhere over there, at the far end of that desert, Atlantis must lie. I wanted to go there.

Before I could set out on such a hazardous trek, with all its predictable hardships, I needed a whole capful of sleep. I simply stretched out on the soft, sugary sand. The sun was high, but I was too exhausted for that to matter. While slowly drifting off, I reflected on my somewhat unusual situation and tried to gauge whether it should be deemed good or bad.

I didn't even know if I was in the future, the past, or the present. There were only two certainties: first that I was in my home dimension, and secondly that I was in Zamonia. That, at least, was encouraging. Furthermore, I hadn't arranged to meet anyone. My past lay behind me, my future ahead, and I had no commitments either way, so it didn't really matter what the date was.

Consoled by that thought, I fell asleep.

9.

My Life in the Demerara Desert

From the
'Encyclopedia of Marvels, Life Forms
and Other Phenomena of Zamonia and its Environs'
by Professor Abdullah Nightingale

Demerara Desert, The. Most deserts are wide, flat tracts of land rendered largely deficient in vegetation by lack of water except in places where underground springs favour the development of oases.

Deserts are divided according to their nature into rocky, sandy, salty, or sweet deserts. The Demerara Desert, a mixed desert of the latter category, consists of Precambrian shell limestone, Early Zamonian lava flour, and prehistoric sugar with a thermal value of 55,000 calories per cubic yard. The sugar derives from an expanse of wild sugar cane which thousands of years of exposure to sunlight has concentrated into pure, crystalline cane sugar. The basic constituent of the Demerara Desert is a sweetish-tasting carbohydrate, soluble in water and alcohol but not in ether, which forms osazones when mixed with phenylhydrazine. These, depending on the number of carbon atoms in the molecule, may be trioses, tetroses, pentoses, hexoses, heptoses, octoses, or nonoses.

Because of the baking properties of their staple material, the Demerara Desert's surface formations are far more diverse and bizarre than those of other deserts. The wind, which both accumulates sugar dust and disperses it, makes a major contribution to the Demerara Desert's sculptural appearance. It can pick up sugar, transport it through the air for many miles, and add it to an existing sugar sculpture, only to erode parts of the formation a few hours later. Thus the outward appearance of the Demerara Desert changes continuously and far more dramatically than that of other deserts. If the air is moist enough and the wind strong enough, they can produce works of art that would turn any sculptor green with envy.

The fanciful appearance of this expanse of desert has always attracted adventurers, gamblers and other rootless individuals who prefer disorder to order. Many have gone off into the Demerara Desert to seek their fortune, but very few have ever returned, and many of those that did were in a state of mental derangement.

A rude awakening

I was awakened by the Spiderwitch – it was standing right over me when I opened my eyes. All I saw at first, being dazzled by the sunlight, was its long, thin, hairy legs. With relish, the creature dribbled some of its secretion right on to my face. The corrosive process was already under way, because I couldn't move so much as a finger. Perhaps my body had already been destroyed or was at least half dissolved. I tried to scream, but even that was too much for me.

Then I woke up properly. A friendly camedary was standing over me on its thin, rickety legs, licking my face.

From the
'Encyclopedia of Marvels, Life Forms and Other Phenomena of Zamonia and its Environs'
by Professor Abdullah Nightingale

Camedary, The. Hoofed mammal belonging to the suborder known as Tylopoda. The hybrid offspring of a camel and a dromedary, the camedary possesses all the attributes of both animals and thus has three humps. Some ten feet long from muzzle to tail, it is sensationally unintelligent but capable of carrying heavy loads in extreme desert temperatures. Its three humps enable it to store immense quantities of water, and it can, if need be, work flat out for as long as three weeks without taking a drink.

Situated on the humps are specially bred teats from which, with a modicum of skill, drinking water can be extracted. Camedaries vary in appearance between plug ugly and plain stupid. Although they seem far from ideal mounts, what with their matted coats, shambling gait, half-closed eyes, and irksome, bleating voices, they are faithful and amiable by nature, can easily be ridden with the aid of a crude bridle, and have no dietary fads. What is more, their dung makes excellent fuel. Camedaries are bred by the →*Muggs*, a nomadic tribe that has roamed the Demerara Desert from time immemorial, reputedly in search of a legendary city named →*Anagrom Ataf*.

The next thing I saw, once I had rubbed the sleep out of my eyes, was a trio of figures attired from head to foot in dark blue robes. Protruding from the eyeholes in each robe were two little telescopes.

One of the figures bent over me.

'A bluebear!' he said, more to his companions than to me. 'How muggly!'

I got to my feet at last and brushed the sugar-dust from my fur. Not far away I saw more such figures in dark blue robes – five hundred of them, perhaps, and at least as many camedaries.

'Who are you, if I may make so bold?' I murmured with the fearless torpor of someone just roused from his slumbers.

'That would be telling,' said the one who had bent over me. He took me by the arm and assumed a confidential tone. 'Can bluebears keep a secret?'

The tallest of the three broke in impatiently.

'We're Muggs – I'm sure you must have heard of us. We're on our way to Anagrom Ataf. Would you care to come with us?'

From the
'Encyclopedia of Marvels, Life Forms
and Other Phenomena of Zamonia and its Environs'
by Professor Abdullah Nightingale

Muggs, The. Nomadic desert tribe resident in the →*Demerara Desert* of Zamonia. Thrown together by chance, this is an ad hoc community of social dropouts and outcasts who sought salvation in solitude but failed to find it and formed a nomadic tribal association whose numbers are still growing. If the Muggs find persons lost or suffering from hardship in the desert, they take them under their wing and into their tribe regardless of status, wealth, gender, or the dimension from which they come. Avowedly unwilling to lead a conventional, orderly, middle-class existence, the Muggs pursue their own ideals of freedom, leisure, and independence, preferably in extreme temperatures.

The Muggs are sociable, hospitable, fond of animals, and firmly opposed to altercations of any kind. They readily espouse muddled sociopolitical ideas and have a predilection for bizarre names. They are expert camedary breeders [→*Camedary, The*] and have for some years been roaming the Demerara Desert in quest of a legendary city named →*Anagrom Ataf.*

The Muggs' clothing consists of a length of dark blue muggwool [a wool obtained from a blue edible mushroom which also plays a predominant role in the Muggs' diet [→*Muggroom, The*]. Several yards long, this cloth is wound several times around the body and head until no ray of sunlight can reach the skin. Two miniature periscopes are always worn at eye level because the Muggs make a habit of burying themselves when sandstorms are imminent and like to keep a lookout.

It may have been because I was sleepy, or because I was still eager to put as much distance as possible between me and the Great Forest, but I accepted the Muggs' invitation without a second thought. Another incentive was the casual, friendly way in which they treated me. At least none of *them* wanted to dissolve my body with some purulent secretion and devour me. That betokened something of an improvement on my recent company.

My admission to the Mugg tribe was gratifyingly informal and unbureaucratic. I was swathed in a length of dark blue cloth (I politely declined the periscopes) and someone loudly called out 'Anagrom Ataf!', whereupon all the other Muggs bellowed the same two words. Then the caravan set off and I simply trotted along with it.

After a while I was approached by one of the Muggs, who asked if I was hungry and would like some muggroom to eat.

From the
'Encyclopedia of Marvels, Life Forms
and Other Phenomena of Zamonia and its Environs'
by Professor Abdullah Nightingale

Muggroom, The. Biologically speaking, a rather inadequate description of the Lower Zamonian cactoid mushroom, which thrives exclusively in certain areas of the →*Demerara Desert*. The Lower Zamonian cactoid mushroom grows only in layers of soil that are situated far below sea level, exposed to strong solar radiation, and provided with an adequate sugar content. This hybrid plant possesses very great nutritional value, together with other qualities particularly prized by the →*Muggs*.

The Muggs lived almost entirely on this blue cactoid mushroom, and so, now that I was by way of being an honorary Mugg, did I. We were in a desert, after all, and there was little else to eat unless you fancied sugar or knew how to catch and cook venomous electric adders or hydrascorpions.

Muggrooms grew under almost every sizeable stone in the Demerara Desert, never went out of season, and were easy to pick and preserve. When you've eaten a lot of muggrooms (and the Muggs ate them all the time), you get into a stupidly emotional frame of mind. For one thing, you attribute far greater importance to all you see and all that happens than it merits; for another, everything strikes you as funny in some way. Most of the Muggs were in a permanent state of ecstatic hilarity, and we often had to halt the entire caravan because some member of the tribe was so tickled by the sight of a cactus leaf or a fold in the dunes that he couldn't be persuaded to move on.

The Muggs were forever laughing and chuckling, and someone was always having a fit of the giggles. The caravan made it a rule to halt during these paroxysms of mirth. A Mugg in that condition was known to be quite helpless and could not be left in the desert on his own – it might happen to anyone, after all. Many such paroxysms went on for hours, and the victims had to be tied to a camedary's hump to enable the caravan to proceed. Other spasms were so infectious that the whole caravan was gradually overcome and ended up rolling around on the ground. In consequence, our progress was rather slow.

On the other hand, it was the muggroom which ensured that the Muggs made any progress at all. Its effects were such that the simple act of walking acquired a dreamlike quality. You could march for hours without getting tired and remained in the best of spirits. It felt as if you were traversing the moon on ten-foot legs made of chewing gum, even when trudging up a sand dune in murderous temperatures.

Muggrooms tasted delicious, I might add, having a flavour midway *Versatile mushrooms* between tuna and roast pork with a faint, appetizing hint of sage. They were tastiest and most effective when eaten raw and least effective when roasted or boiled. They could also be grilled or steamed, puréed or fried in oil and preserved. When dried and packed in airtight containers they kept almost indefinitely, though concentrated muggroom lasted even longer when pounded with a mixture of salt and ant oil and compressed into little balls that could be chewed for hours. When boiled up with desert sugar and vanilla, then cooled and broken into squares, they made delicious muggroom toffee. Finely ground muggrooms were used to season muggroom dishes, though this struck me as nonsensical as seasoning lemons with lemon juice. All you had to avoid were the thorns, which contained a lethal poison. Prick yourself on one, and you were dead before you hit the ground. Without its thorns, however, the muggroom was quite harmless. You had only to remove the bones, so to speak.

Travelling by camedary gave me a certain amount of trouble at first. Riding that desert beast isn't exactly comfortable and takes a lot of getting used to.

On horseback you feel as if you're moving in time to classical music; a camedary seems to progress to the beat of a drum played by a drunk. It puts its feet down in a wholly arbitrary order, sometimes favouring a forefoot, sometimes a hind foot, and is forever tripping itself up. It sways first right, then left, falls to its knees and struggles up again. If I have ever in my lives suffered from anything akin to seasickness, it was on a camedary in the middle of the desert, not aboard some ship on the high seas.

*The Muggs'
secret*

I would dearly have liked to know what the Muggs looked like under their dark blue robes, but they made a great secret of this. As I discovered in the course of time, they travelled, slept, and even bathed with their bodies entirely shrouded in those peculiar lengths of cloth. What a Mugg looked like in the nude was one of the great mysteries of the Demerara Desert. According to an anthropologist who had specialized in the subject and written a dozen or more books about it, Muggs were one-time Alpine Imps who had suffered from total hair loss and were so ashamed of this that they swathed themselves in dark blue robes and took refuge in the desert. I myself do not subscribe to this theory. It is based solely on three Alpine Imp hairs which the aforesaid anthropologist found in a crevice halfway between the Impic Alps and the Demerara Desert.

Life in the caravan was exceptionally harmonious. Disputes, altercations, problems, et cetera, were wholly repugnant to the Muggs, who always sought the most acceptable solution. Even when they disagreed on which way to go, as they sometimes did, they didn't take a vote on the matter because a vote would have betokened a conflict; they compromised by adopting a zigzag course.

The Muggs were fond of music, but only of home-made music produced by home-made instruments, which they liked to play round their camp fires at night. It wasn't particularly good music, in my opinion. It was more a way of making a soothing noise that would lull everyone to sleep. Most of the instruments, into which the Muggs hummed in a melodious way, consisted of dried cactus stalks hollowed out and stripped of their thorns. Others had drumskins made from camedary udders and were beaten very slowly. Those Muggs who didn't play instruments simply swayed to the beat and conveyed their appreciation of the musicians' efforts by uttering an occasional, encouraging 'Muggly!' Finally, tired out after the long day's march and sedated by the music, we would all subside into the dust of the desert floor and fall asleep.

We must have presented an astonishing sight as we trekked across the desert like a procession of dark blue, giggling mummies. Despite their uniform outward appearance, Muggs were staunch individualists. This made us something of a walking paradox, a community of lone wolves welded into a pack by force of circumstance. The Muggs had rules like every community, but they were so refreshingly different from traditional rules and regulations that it was almost a pleasure to obey them. Twelve in number, they had been discovered by the Muggs in a so-called desert message-in-a-bottle.

These messages-in-a-bottle are always turning up in the Demerara Desert. They are often, especially in an emergency, the only means of sending an SOS. You cork up your messages in glass bottles and insert them in a drifting dune in the often illusory hope that it will forward them fast. Sadly, drifting dunes are thoroughly unpredictable where speed and direction are concerned, so the chances of their ending up in the right hands are very slim. The message the Muggs found must have been in transit for a very long time, because the paper was yellow with age and the writing on it faded and in an old-fashioned script. However, since a violent sandstorm blew up just as they were unfolding it, they construed this as an omen and made the twelve rules on it their code of conduct. They read as follows:

The desert postal service

1 Honour the muggroom.

2 Thou shalt not address a white cockerel by name.

3 Thou shalt eat no wood.

4 If thou seest two sticks lying one on top of the other, thou shalt walk backwards over them with thy left foot first, not forwards with thy right. Moreover, thou shalt not devour them.

5 Should a vulture's shadow fall across a fire that has gone out, thou shalt rekindle it three times or a great misfortune will ensue.

6 If thou cross the path of a white cockerel seated on two superimposed sticks, thou shalt not strike it, nor shalt thou address it by name nor partake of the said sticks.

7 Thou shalt bear a name unlike any other in the entire universe. On encountering one of thy brethren thou shalt address him by his full name without a single slip of the tongue. (I shall, in due course, have a tale to tell about this innocuous-sounding rule!)

8 Should a vulture's shadow fall across a white cockerel seated on two charred sticks in the ashes of a dead fire, thou art in a deplorable predicament. Notwithstanding this, thou shalt not (illegible) nor address the cockerel by name, nor devour the sticks, nor strike the vulture, nor greet thy brother in an inadequate fashion.

9 Thou shalt not finkle backwards. (Since none of the Muggs knew what 'finkling' entailed, no one could could do it. Consequently, this rule was one of the easiest to keep.)

284

10 **Thou shalt not finkle forwards.** (See Rule 9.)

11 **Thou shalt not sleep on a dune that drifts in the direction of noon. Should it drift towards evening, thy time has come.**

12 **Thou shalt betake thyself to the city named Anagrom Ataf** and, when thou hast found it, trap it and make it thy home for evermore.

Since there were no white cockerels in the desert and I genuinely had no intention of eating any wood, I had no problem with the rules other than my failure to understand them completely. I found the last rule the most puzzling of all. How could one 'trap' a city? My own view was that none of these rules should be taken too seriously. The truth was, I suspected that they had been written under the influence of sunstroke, but I didn't say as much to the Muggs for fear of hurting their feelings.

And so, on the strength of a crackbrained message-in-a-bottle, the Muggs had devoted themselves to the task of finding, trapping, and occupying a city named Anagrom Ataf. This was not an entirely new idea, it should be added, but the Muggs were the only community to have adopted it as their mission in life.

Anagrom Ataf

The legend of Anagrom Ataf – a city situated somewhere in the Demerara Desert which many claimed to have seen in the distance but none had ever entered – had been current in Zamonia for hundreds of years. It was rumoured to be a pleasanter place to live in than anywhere else on earth. There were no rents to pay, no crime, no air pollution, plenty of parking places for camedaries, and so on – everything, in fact, that anyone could want of a dream city in the desert. Such, at least, were the idyllic conditions reputed to prevail there.

Many people could describe the place, at least from the outside: a city of low white buildings with red and gold roofs interspersed with numerous shady palm trees and an occasional slender minaret. Nothing spectacular, in other words, just a typical oasis city of medium size. But anyone who tried to enter it found that it shrank away like a timid deer and vanished into the desert. It was precisely because no one had ever seen Anagrom Ataf from the inside that it had acquired such a legendary reputation.

Adventurers surmised the existence of fabulous treasures, the old and frail of medicinal springs or fountains of eternal youth, gluttons of a land of milk and honey. Many people even believed that Anagrom Ataf was the gateway to the Garden of Eden and had set out to find it, but none had ever quite got there. The desert was littered with the bleached and sand-blasted bones of those who had pursued this phantom of a city ever further into the waterless waste. Moreover, no one had ever evolved a reasonably convincing scientific theory about this phenomenon. No one, that is to say, except Professor Nightingale.

From the
'**Encyclopedia of Marvels, Life Forms
and Other Phenomena of Zamonia and its Environs**'
by Professor Abdullah Nightingale

Anagrom Ataf. This is a semi-stable Fata Morgana or semi-solid mirage in the shape of an oasis city situated in the so-called →*Demerara Desert*, an arid tract of land on the continent of Zamonia. In temperatures exceeding 320° Fahrenheit, the sugar of which the Demerara Desert consists begins to melt [→*Sugar Flux*], releasing a cloud of fine sugar vapour. If the temperature drops sharply at that moment [e.g. because of sudden katabatic winds], the sugar hardens in mid-air; and if, in addition, the image of a real oasis city is projected on the crystallizing sugar molecules, its layout can become permanently imprinted on them. This produces the semi-solid mirror image of a city that can be blown hither and thither by the wind, creating the impression that it is moving of its own volition.

I, on the other hand, took the view that Anagrom Ataf had resulted from centuries of muggroom-eating and from the monotony of the desert – that it was the idealized image of a city dreamed up by people half dead from thirst. But still, I had no intention of depriving the Muggs of their dreams. Anagrom Ataf was the only thing that kept them going.

The Muggs roamed by day and slept by night. I myself considered this nonsensical, because it would have been much easier for them to make progress during the relatively cool nights than in the

287

scorching heat of the day. They would have consumed less water and found their bearings more easily. There were hardly ever any clouds over the Demerara Desert, so the night sky was always clear and well lit, particularly when the moon was full, thanks to the highly reflective crystalline surface.

But the Muggs feared the night in a way that reminded me of the Minipirates. When dusk approached they looked for a camp site near some source of water. It was always a great pleasure to watch the Muggs searching for an underground reservoir. They began by consuming vast quantities of muggrooms to sensitize themselves to the proximity of a spring. Then they tottered across the twilit desert with their arms outstretched like inebriated albatrosses. If a Mugg began to rotate on the spot and hum like a top, it meant that he had found a watercourse. The others had then to hurry to his assistance, because he couldn't stop spinning by himself. Many Muggs, having mistakenly strayed too far from the group in search of water, continued to rotate for hours before they were found. This left them feeling dizzy for days, and care had to be taken to prevent them from falling off their camedaries again and again.

Alarming stories Once a source of water had been found and a temporary borehole sunk, huge camp fires of camedary dung were kindled and everyone sat down to talk and make music. The Muggs' conversations abounded in old wives' tales about the threats night presented. The most innocuous stories concerned Sugar Gnomes (more of them later), but others were considerably more frightening and bloodthirsty. There was, for instance, the legend of the Darkmen, who were made of night and had stars for eyes. Unwitting Muggs who travelled by night were borne up into the sky by these creatures and then hurled to earth, burning up like meteorites on the way. The Muggs spoke in whispers of huge snakes that looked in the dark like dunes and could swallow whole caravans at a single gulp. They also told the story of the Drowsy Dunes that slept all day, to awaken at dusk and transform themselves into treacherous quicksands. They knew stories about wind-, sand- and cactus-sprites that did their dirty work in the dark, about invisible crevasses, deadly scorpions, desert demons, and sand pirates. These tales were reason enough to avoid travelling at night, light a ring of camp fires around the caravan each evening, and spend the night in the shelter of the flames and the tribe.

I cannot pretend that these stories made going to sleep any easier. *A sleepless night* One night I lay awake longer than usual. As if I didn't find it difficult enough to sleep on the hard desert floor, I heard the weirdest noises in the darkness.

Sand coyotes were howling and prowling around the camp with glowing red eyes, rattlesnakes rattling the tips of their tails, monstrous cicadas chirping in their thousands. Rustling, crackling sounds were audible in every direction, for at night the desert awoke to a life that lay in wait by day. A seven-tailed hydrascorpion was dancing in a circle, seemingly in time to the music that had ceased long before.

Dust-moths fluttered around the camp fires, and every conceivable kind of insect came crawling out of the darkness, eagerly seeking the proximity of the flames. Stilt-legged spiders stumbled over stones, earwigs and venomous lizards vied for places in the foremost rows around the embers.

None of this worried the Muggs. They had mummified themselves tightly in their lengths of cloth and were blissfully snoring, whereas I kept an anxious eye on the small creatures that teemed on the desert floor. A multicoloured rainbow adder wormed its way up to me; I lashed out at it with a stick and drove it towards the camp fire. Dazzled by the firelight, a fat tarantula staggered around me in circles; that, too, I drove off with my stick. Four big dust-moths danced above my head, a cicada the size of a loaf jumped over me and sang its maddening song a mere two feet from my ear.

I began to realize that I wasn't made for life in the desert. I could only hope we very soon reached a spot that would enable me to get my bearings sufficiently to go my own way. Meanwhile, I kept a wary eye on my surroundings. I could always sleep on my camedary the next day. If another unpleasant creature crept up on me, I would use my stick to fend it off.

Only a few yards away and to my front, the sand began to stir. Some insect must have overslept and was now struggling to the surface with the aim of helping its colleagues to terrorize me. I watched the process intently. There was a minute eruption, and the desert floor broke open. What came to light was no insect, however; it was a bony finger.

From the
'Encyclopedia of Marvels, Life Forms and Other Phenomena of Zamonia and its Environs'
by Professor Abdullah Nightingale

Subterranean Sandmen, The. Of all the →*Demerara Desert's* unpleasant life forms, so-called Subterranean Sandmen are probably the most unpleasant. Before they can awaken and emerge, four conditions must be met:

1 Cogitating Quicksand. The first prerequisite is →*Cogitating Quicksand*. Zamonia's largest deposits of Cogitating Quicksand are to be found in the numerous quicksand swamps of →*Nairland* and in certain parts of the →*Demerara Desert*.

2 Disreputable Cadavers. The second prerequisite is that one or more persons of evil repute should have sunk into this quicksand and given up the ghost.

3 Dehydration. The third prerequisite is that the quicksand has, in the course of the centuries, been baked by extreme heat into firm, sandy ground, and that it has absorbed its capacity for cogitation from the skeletons buried in its depths.

4 Victims. The fourth prerequisite is that one or more persons should bivouac for the night above the skeletons lurking in the sand. If all these conditions are met, there occurs the phenomenon referred to by Grailsundian demonologists as a 'Malign Awakening'. Like ticks, the skeletons spend a long time in a trancelike or hibernant state before coming to life, burrowing their way to the surface, and killing any unwitting creature that happens to be asleep there.

A second finger broke through the desert floor, then a third, a fourth, and finally a whole hand.

A 'Malign Awakening'

The ground beside it broke open for a considerable distance, and a skull emerged. The same thing happened at several places inside the ring of camp fires. All the insects vanished into the night. Skeletons were now protruding from the ground waist deep, some of them wearing remnants of their former clothing, rusty helmets and coats of chain mail. Many were even brandishing notched sabres, which indicated that the quicksand's victims had once been desert pirates.

The Subterranean Sandmen had come to life.

'Help!' I shouted. 'Wake up, all of you!'

The first skeleton had now dug its way out completely. Its bones were encrusted with pale brown sugar, which lent it a singularly unreal, ghostly appearance. It threw back its death's-head and clattered its teeth together – an act which doubtless corresponds, in skeletal circles, to a triumphant laugh.

The Muggs had meantime scrambled to their feet and were blearily staggering around. More skeletons were breaking through the surface all over the place.

Subterranean Sandmen, The [cont.]. As already mentioned, one of the preconditions for the Sandmen's emergence is their disreputable character. In most cases they are former criminals, desert pirates or murderers who have fled from the law and escaped into the wilderness. When coupled with the quicksand's negative attributes, this produces a life form that leaves little to be desired in the way of savagery.

The Muggs shrieked and clung to each other but made no move to defend themselves. Their peaceable nature forbade them even to take up arms against bloodthirsty skeletons. They clustered together, wailing, while more and more Sandmen arose on every side.

I hurried over to a camp fire and pulled out a big, blazing piece of wood. Fire – everyone was scared of that! Then, running up to one of the skeletons, I hit out with my torch. The hissing flames parted the darkness, my weapon struck the skeleton's shoulder, and for a moment we were both enveloped in a shower of whirling sparks. The skeleton threw back its head and clattered its teeth to gruesome effect. Then, quick as a flash, it wrested the torch from my hand, rammed it down its throat, and bit off the glowing tip, which slithered through its ribs to the ground. Having retained some of the embers in its mouth, it spewed them out into the darkness in a stream of sparks. Last of all, it casually tossed the remains of my now useless torch over its shoulder and into the desert.

The skeleton fixed me with its empty eye sockets, the Muggs clung to each other more tightly than ever.

Next, the skeleton raised its right arm and described a small circle in the air with its bony forefinger. This was the signal for the other Sandmen to take up their positions. They formed a big ring round us. By this time I, too, had joined the Muggs, feverishly trying to think of some way of fighting off the Undead. Fire was no use, that much was clear.

Subterranean Sandmen, The [cont.]. There is no point in defending oneself against Sandmen. Even discounting the fact that the layers of sugar-sand encrusting their bones render them invulnerable [e.g. to fire or cuts and thrusts with a sword], they no longer have any vital organs to pierce. Moreover, even if it were possible to kill a Sandman, it would make no difference to him because he is already dead. The best advice that can be offered to those who experience a 'Malign Awakening' is to resign themselves uncomplainingly to their fate.

The ring of skeletons drew closer. When a camedary strayed inside the cordon, a dozen skeletons pounced on the poor beast and hauled it off into the darkness. Its desperate bleating rang briefly in our ears, then ceased abruptly.

The Sandmen were now within a yard of us. Their teeth grated together as they conversed in their skeleton tongue, probably discussing how to share out their prey. I shrank back into the throng of trembling Muggs and almost fell over: I had trodden in the half-drilled borehole leading to an underground stream. My hind leg remained stuck in the mud. Two Muggs hurried up and helped me to extract my paw from the ooze. There was a sucking sound, and I was free. A thin jet of water emerged from the hole and shot into the air.

The Sandmen stopped short. One of them indicated the spurting water with his jawbone and ground his teeth hideously. I seized the drilling pole that lay beside the hole and rammed it in with all my might. There were many puzzled exclamations, both from the Sandmen and from the Muggs. Then the muddy hole emitted a subterranean belch, and a jet of water as thick as a tree trunk broke surface and shot into the night sky.

For the first time in ages, it was raining in the desert.

The Muggs still failed to see what underlay my course of action, but the Sandmen had already grasped what lay in store for them. Fat, heavy drops of water came pattering down on the skeletons. Dumbfounded, they put their skeletal arms over their skulls and tried to shield them from the downpour. But the water permeated their bony frames unhindered, soaking the mixture of bonemeal, sugar – sand, and malevolence. One skeleton lost an arm, which simply fell to the ground and broke into three pieces. Another's leg dissolved – it flailed its limbs for a moment, then measured its length on the ground. The skull of another skeleton toppled off, while that of yet another dissolved into gruel and trickled into its thoracic cavity. Jawbones fell off into the mud.

The Sandmen were liquefying.

At last the Muggs grasped what had to be done. Seizing the pole, they rammed it repeatedly into the borehole to enlarge the aperture and reinforce the jet. The downpour grew steadily heavier.

The Sandmen staggered helplessly around, trying to escape their fate. Skeletons completely dissolved and oozed to the ground like porridge.

The Muggs went prancing through the rain. I myself took care to see that none of the skeletons got away.

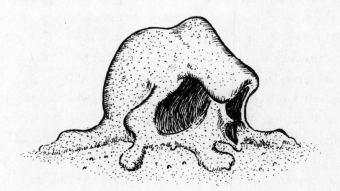

Meantime, nearly all of them had liquefied and seeped back into the ground from which they had come. The few skulls that still lay here and there, grinding their teeth, were carefully trampled underfoot by the Muggs. Before long, not a single trace of the Sandmen remained. The Muggs slapped me on the back and congratulated me on my vigilance.

We decided to move on by night, for once, and pitch camp in another spot.

I decide to quit

The Sandmen incident clinched my decision to try to leave the Demerara Desert and strike off on my own. These were definitely not the surroundings in which I wanted to spend my remaining lives. It was becoming ever clearer to me that the Muggs' way of life was not, in the long term, compatible with my own. Living with them was not quite as easy as it had at first appeared. As time went by I noticed a number of whims and peculiarities which would have driven even the most easygoing bluebear to distraction.

The curse of long names

For a start, the message-in-a-bottle's Rule No. 7 had prompted them to adopt terribly elaborate but hopelessly unimaginative names such as *Tabitha Tetrachotomous Sunsister*, or *Polycarp Polyethylene Glycol*, or *Cosmo Uncuncle Universuncle*. For fear of failing to observe the rule and choosing a name that occurred twice in the universe, they burdened themselves with appellations whose main characteristic was their great length and monstrous number of syllables. What made matters more difficult was that, in conformity with the second part of the rule, they insisted on being addressed by their full name. Nicknames and other forms of abbreviation were not only taboo but reputed to bring bad luck.

Pelpemperem Papriami Parmisani was relatively easy to memorize because it possessed a certain melodious quality, but tongue-twisters like *Clapcan Caplacan Planplacpaclan* presented greater difficulty. If you got so much as a single syllable wrong, the Mugg in question would be deeply offended and trail around after you for days, complaining bitterly. You then had no choice but to perform a ritual act which the Muggs called 'muggrifying'. This entailed sprinkling your head with sugar-sand and shouting out the relevant name, word perfect, until the injured party graciously forgave you. Depending on the complexity of the name and the extent of the injured party's disgruntlement, this could take days. The result was that I did my best to steer clear of any Muggs whose names were exceptionally complicated. One, for instance, was called *Charch Chachcherachchech Chechchachcherachchach* and another *Fneckfepffepperepell M. Shrabshubshabremshubram* (I didn't dare ask what the 'M' stood for). To this day I have a suspicion that many Muggs deliberately chose names that would trip you up, so as to be able to wallow in righteous indignation. Why? Because there was so little else to do in the desert. I was particularly wary of one Mugg, whose name – I shall never forget it – was *Constantine Constantinople Canstontinaple Tennineeightsevensixfivefourthreeone*. The catch was that his surname was easy to remember because it consisted of the numerals one to ten, less two, recited backwards. You concentrated so hard on missing out the two that – no idea why – you always ended up saying it. The said Mugg persisted in dogging my footsteps, and he managed to engage me in conversation every time. The outcome was more or less as follows:

He (I shall use 'he' rather than have to keep writing 'Constantine Constantinople Canstontinaple Tennineeightsevensixfivefour-threeone') *(casually)*: 'Hello, Bluebear.'

I *(sighing)*: 'Hello, er…Constantine Constantinople Canstontinaple Tennineeightsevensixfivefourthree…one.' *(Phew!)*

He: 'Muggly weather today, eh, Bluebear?'

I: 'Yes, really muggly…*(groan)* Constantine Constantinople Canstontinaple Tennineeightsevensixfivefourthree…one *(Phew!)*

He: 'The weather wasn't as muggly yesterday, though, was it, Bluebear?'

I: 'No, the weather yesterday wasn't as fine as it is today, *(very quickly)* Constantine Constantinople Canstontinaple Tennineeightsevensixfivefourthreeone, not by a long chalk.'

He *(impressed)*: 'Well…I must be going, Bluebear.'

I *(so relieved that I lose concentration)*: 'See you around, then, Constantine Constantinople Canstontinaple TennineeightsevensixfivefourthreeTWOone – Aaargh!'

He *(throwing up his hands in feigned indignation)*: 'Oh, how could you be so hurtful! No one has ever subjected me to such…*(and so on and so forth)*

I spent the next three days showering myself with sugar-sand and faultlessly shouting out a name I really don't care to write down again. In the end, heaven be praised, I thought of a way out of this intolerable dilemma. I appeared before the assembled Muggs and solemnly announced that I myself had assumed a new name. I had a perfect right to do this, being a Mugg probationer, but had never taken advantage of the fact. From now on I was to be addressed as

Tihiviranipiri Kengklepperkengkereng Tadjifioparifztugghhtrtrhhgsrtgh Keek Kaak Kokkeek Barp Bluebear the Threehundredandfiftyeight- thousandsixhundredandeighth. This was the longest name any Mugg had ever given himself. After that, peace descended on the dunes. No one dared to engage me in stupid chitchat any longer – in fact I even started to feel a bit lonely.

After three months spent trekking through scorching heat in a series of nonsensical zigzags, spirals, and wavy lines, the Muggs were beginning to get me down. What contributed to my irritation were their everlasting cries of 'Muggly!' and their constant indecision, their monotonous musical soirées and unvarying diet (i.e. muggrooms).

I consider myself a peace-loving creature, but I'm bound to confess that life with the Muggs was so irksomely peaceful that I some- times itched to start a little quarrel. Their monotonous talk of Anagrom Ataf (other subjects of conversation included sand quality, wind strength, and muggroom recipes), the sticky, sugary atmosphere, the discordant bleating of the camedaries, the annoying sugar-flies that tried to sup the little fluid I had inside me from the corners of my eyes – taken in combination, all these things were enough to make one run off into the desert, screaming, and devour a cactus. But I pulled myself together and faithfully followed the bleating caravan on its journey to nowhere.

One day – we had been on the march since dawn, and even the toughest Muggs were showing signs of fatigue – I noticed that the ground was stickier than usual. It was becoming harder to detach our feet from the desert sand with every step we took. We might have been walking across a sheet of glass with suction cups attached to our soles.

The Sugar Flux

The Muggs had also noticed this.

Confused cries of 'Sugar Flux! Sugar Flux!' arose.

From the
'Encyclopedia of Marvels, Life Forms
and Other Phenomena of Zamonia and its Environs'
by Professor Abdullah Nightingale

Sugar Flux. Cane sugar melts at a temperature of 320° Fahrenheit and congeals into an amorphous mass as it cools, becoming hygroscopic and, when it has settled, crystalline. Continuous heating at 320° Fahrenheit turns cane sugar into fructose or glucose, but at 374° into bitter brown caramel. During the summer months, temperatures in the central areas of the →*Demerara Desert* can exceed 200°, particularly when boosted by lack of wind. In basin-shaped tracts of land [flat valleys, dried-up lakes] this may result in the process known as Sugar Flux, during which the desert becomes caramelized for miles around, later to solidify when the temperature drops.

These periods of Sugar Flux present a threat, not only to the sand eels and rattlescorpions whose favourite habitat such areas happen to be, but also to the unsuspecting traveller who finds himself in the midst of a sea of deliquescent sugar. First trapped without warning by the feet, the helpless victim sinks ever deeper into the molten carbohydrate until it envelops him completely like a prehistoric insect in amber. Either that, or - an even worse fate, perhaps - the caramel cools before it wholly engulfs him, imprisoning him waist-deep in congealed sugar and condemning him to a miserable death by thirst.

We were indeed in an area of basinlike conformation, and – what was more – right in the middle of it. Our only hope was to make as quickly as possible for a small range of sugarhills some two miles away. I mounted my camedary and, in company with the rest of the caravan, galloped towards the hills as fast as the steadily softening desert floor allowed.

But the Sugar Flux was quite far advanced. Bubbles of hot caramel were already bursting everywhere, and little pools of liquid sugar had formed. The camedaries repeatedly got stuck, extricated themselves with a supreme effort, or fell headlong. When that happened, the rider had to abandon his beast and baggage and make good his escape on foot.

Half a mile from the hills my camedary stuck fast in a pool of sugar. I had to jump off and leave the poor beast behind. I waded on through the molten sugar, which was liquefying more and more. It was like a nightmare. I found it harder to extricate my paws with every step I took, as if hot, sticky hands were trying to capture me and drag me down to my death.

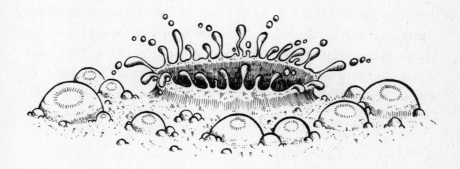

I mustered all the reserves of strength in my legs, just as I had when racing the Spiderwitch, but the molten sugar was growing steadily hotter. The Muggs vociferously urged each other on, the camedaries bleated in mortal fear, the sounds of our panic-stricken flight were multiplied a hundredfold by the sides of the basin, which we reached at last.

We climbed over the edge of the basin, summoning up the last of our energy, and shoved and hauled each other and the camedaries to safety just before the molten sugar began to boil. Our losses that day were fourteen camedaries and a ton of muggrooms.

It dawned on me that, quite contrary to their intentions, the Muggs led an exceptionally hard life – the hardest, perhaps, in all Zamonia. Their daily wanderings, their everlasting worries about water, the heat, the insects and poisonous snakes, Sandmen, Sugar Flux – I could scarcely conceive of an existence fraught with greater deprivation and danger. In conditions such as those one took pleasure in the smallest things: a cool breeze blowing through a desert valley, a cluster of muggrooms under a stone.

Desert art

One of the desert's few pleasant distractions was the variety of sculptures created there by the sugar-laden wind. Many had grown to the size of a mountain massif and others were only two or three feet high, but it was always interesting to study their shapes and look for familiar images in them. There was the Valley of the White Trees, in which stood a whole forest of sugar sculptures resembling snow-covered fir trees three hundred or more feet high. There was also a lake with big billows of sugar from which jutted the backs of crystalline whales that blew fountains of sugar high into the air.

Another sculpture looked like the huge, sugar-encrusted head of a Bollogg (some Muggs even claimed it really was one), and the desert was dotted with little, beckoning Sugar Gnomes (the Muggs said they came to life at night in order to rob them of muggrooms and blow in the ears of sleeping camedaries).

Even whole caravans seemed to have congealed into sugar. On one occasion we sighted at least a hundred sugar camedaries and as many Wolperting Whelps, all amazingly lifelike in appearance. One Mugg said it was a genuine caravan that had been overtaken by a sugarstorm. These storms, which were very infrequent, occurred when a night frost, unfavourable katabatic winds and drifting sugar dunes combined to produce this rare natural phenomenon.

Appalled by this idea, we didn't dare to verify his assertion by examining one of the sugar sculptures. We hurriedly rode on, trying to banish the eerie spectacle from our minds.

I made a habit of memorizing the sculptures and their location, gauging the time it took to travel from one to another, and using these data to draw a map of the Demerara Desert in my head. Although this pastime was intellectually stimulating, it made no sense because the Demerara Desert was forever changing shape.

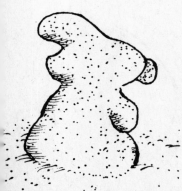

Another diversion was the large number of messages-in-a-bottle we came across. For instance, we kept finding the same message embodying the twelve aforesaid rules inscribed in the same handwriting and the same order. This reinforced the Muggs' determination to observe them. We also found bottles containing heart-rending missives, final farewells from adventurers dying of thirst who did not share the Muggs' instinctive ability to find underground watercourses. Other bottles held absurd maps drawn by people with a warped sense of humour and purporting to show the location of buried treasure – the height of irresponsibility, in my opinion, because they might have sent gullible persons astray. Most of the letters were banal, however – just tedious descriptions of the desert landscape, accounts of their solitary authors' circumstances, and loving messages to their families. Many, too, were quite insane and smacked of sunstroke. One of them we found to contain a tornado timetable.

Anyone who came across a message-in-a-bottle was duty-bound to read it out to the whole caravan. One afternoon, when yet another had turned up, we halted and gathered around the dune from which the finder read it aloud:

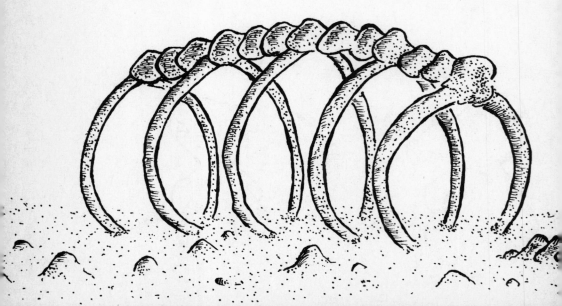

'Impic Alps, so far away,' the Mugg began,
'hearken to my sad refrain…'

I hurried over to him and snatched the message out of his hand.

> *Impic Alps, so far away,*
>
> *hearken to my sad refrain!*
>
> *Will there ever come a day*
>
> *when I see you all again?*

It was one of Fredda's efforts – her favourite poem, in fact. So she, too, had crossed the Demerara Desert! The piece of paper on which she'd written the poem was comparatively new and unfaded, which convinced me that I couldn't have missed our own era by much when I fell through the dimensional hiatus, perhaps by no more than a few weeks or days.

Fredda's message-in-a-bottle made me even more dubious about what I was doing. I resolved to part company with the Muggs as soon as we chanced to reach the edge of the desert once more. Until then I would have to possess my soul in patience.

Where, I wondered, was Fredda now?

So much for pleasant distractions. Apart from roaming the desert and looking for water, the Muggs devoted most of their time to closely observing the state of the weather so as to guard against surprises.

In addition to Sugar Flux and a wide variety of sugarstorms, catastrophic sugarwater floods occurred on the rare occasions when it rained, and vast expanses of quicksand masqueraded as dry land. The Muggs even reported that the Demerara Desert was sometimes infested with swarms of carnivorous locusts. They had

adapted themselves to these conditions by keeping a close watch on their surroundings and learning to assess them. The slightest change could herald some impending danger and give them time to take precautions.

They knew two thousand different names for sand. Coarse-grained sand had a different name from fine-grained, pale sand a different name from dark, and there was an incredible multiplicity of names for intermediate textures – for sand that was sticky or dry, rough or smooth, glassy or opaque. Although I myself would never have noticed these shades of difference, a Mugg could determine from two hundred yards whether a sand dune consisted of *glomm*, *slythe*, or *blunk*. By studying the layers of different kinds of sand the Muggs could tell with a fair degree of accuracy whether or not a sugarstorm was in the offing and which of roughly five hundred different types of sugarstorm to prepare for.

One day around noon, as if in response to an inaudible word of command, the caravan came to an abrupt and unexpected halt. Nearly all the Muggs had raised their heads and were sniffing the air.

'Sharach-il-Allah!' said someone at the very rear of the caravan.

'Sharach-il-Allah!' another Mugg chimed in, and before long a babble of cries arose from every throat.

'Sharach-il-Allah! Sharach-il-Allah!'

From the
'Encyclopedia of Marvels, Life Forms
and Other Phenomena of Zamonia and its Environs'
by Professor Abdullah Nightingale

Sharach-il-Allah. Some five hundred kinds of sugarstorm occur in the Demerara Desert, ranging from dinky little dust devils to hurricanes and tornadoes [→*Eternal Tornado, The*]. The most dangerous form of sugarstorm, which travels horizontally, is commonly known by the Arabic name 'Sharach-il-Allah,' or, loosely translated, 'God's Sanding Block'. This compresses sugar-sand to such an extent that it bakes itself into a solid, concretelike mass shaped like a brick and several miles long. Travelling at speeds of up to 250 m.p.h., it buffs away all that stands in its path, whether animal or human being, building or mountain. If a Sharach-il-Allah is approaching, the only thing to do is to bury yourself as deeply as possible and hope that the storm fails to find you.

The Muggs had gone to ground quicker than a bunch of chipmunks in a thunderstorm. Where a whole, panic-stricken caravan had been milling around a moment ago, nothing could now be seen but a level expanse of desert. All that betrayed where holes had been dug were a few little mounds of pebbles. Not even the baggage had been left behind. Most astonishing of all, even the camedaries had vanished. Their muffled, flabbergasted bleating could just be heard through the layer of sugar-sand that now covered them.

I alone continued to stand rooted to the spot, staring spellbound in a westerly direction. A grey, absolutely rectangular shape was blotting out the sun and sky and approaching at breakneck speed. A hot gust of wind, an innocuous harbinger of the storm, blew a handful of dust in my face and roused me from my trance. I tried to dig myself a hole, but unfortunately I lacked the Muggs' long experience of excavating sugarstorm shelters.

Digging a hole... It's easier said than done. You might think you could dig a hole in a sandy desert with your bare hands, but anyone who actually tries to do so will receive a valuable lesson on its powers of resistance. Effortlessly shovel aside a few cubic inches of loose sand, and you will come to a surprisingly compact layer of dried mud five million years old with little, sharp-edged stones and splintered seashells baked into it, not to mention a network of fossilized, prehistoric tree roots. Strongrooms could be built of such material. By the time I'd scraped away a layer some two paw's-breadths deep I'd snapped off four of my claws, which are quite strong. Beneath the layer was a massive block of granite probably one mile across. Had I actually managed to dispose of this, I would doubtless have come upon some prehistoric reinforced concrete or a thick layer of diamonds. So I resigned myself to my fate, gazed at the wall thundering down on me like a rabbit mesmerized by a snake, and waited to be sanded to death.

The Sharach-il-Allah raced towards me like a gigantic brick. It was about a mile wide and would reach me in twenty seconds at latest. This meant, since I was right in the middle of its leading edge, that I would have to run 1000 yards in no more than 9.0 seconds to escape it – a speed roughly ten times the current world record. This

God's sanding block

309

wholly superfluous calculation, which occurred to me only seconds before my death by abrasion, convinced me yet again that mathematics is of only limited practical use in real life. I ran to and fro, tore out my fur, and adopted what was, after all, the only sensible course of action in such a predicament: I went out of my mind.

Yes, I went insane. Sheer terror had caused my brain to suspend normal service – at least, I could find no other explanation for what happened before my very eyes. Not more than five hundred yards away, a ghostly apparition interposed itself between me and the oncoming, brick-shaped storm. It took the form of numerous little buildings and minarets, and it was white as snow.

I'd gone crazy, of course – an entirely pardonable reaction under existing circumstances. Even the most hard-boiled veteran of the desert would have lost his reason at the sight of a Sharach-il-Allah, so I found it quite understandable that my brain should pretend that an idyllically beautiful architectural complex had kindly come to my rescue and interposed itself between me and the hurricane. With a mighty grating, grinding screech, the sandstorm slowed like a gigantic train whose emergency brakes have been applied. It came to a stop just beyond the white apparition, paused for a moment, then changed direction and went thundering off to the left. Another few moments, and it disappeared over the skyline.

From the
'Encyclopedia of Marvels, Life Forms and Other Phenomena of Zamonia and its Environs' by Professor Abdullah Nightingale

Conventions Observed by Exceptional Natural Phenomena, The. In view of the fact that natural phenomena such as catastrophic tempests, the Northern Lights, volcanic eruptions, meteor storms, et cetera, never occur simultaneously, it may be assumed that they observe something akin to a set of rules - a sort of highway code respected and complied with by all large-scale natural phenomena. No hurricane would intrude on a devastating earthquake, just as no tornado would spoil the effect of a mirage. Little research has been devoted to the origins and practical operation of this code. Gullible souls credit storms with minds and volcanoes with the power of thought, but the truth, as ever, is probably far more banal and down-to-earth. The subject need only be computed, catalogued, tabulated, made the subject of numerous doctoral dissertations, and formally included in the university syllabus.

But the apparition remained. It continued to hover, shimmering, above the desert when the Muggs dug themselves out of their holes and patted the sugar-sand from their robes. If it really was a hallucination, it was a collective and very celebrated one. I was convinced of this by a Mugg who, pointing to the white city with outstretched arm, reverently murmured, 'Anagrom Ataf!'

'Anagrom Ataf!' chorused the whole caravan. 'Anagrom Ataf!'

A few of the more impatient Muggs tried to storm the city at once, needless to say, but it was just as the old wives' tales had foretold: if approached by a living creature, be it only a camedary, Anagrom Ataf retreated precisely as far as the intruder had advanced.

After several fruitless attempts, therefore, we pitched camp nearby and confined ourselves for the next few days to observing the city at a distance.

Having simultaneously defied the Sharach-il-Allah *and* sighted
Anagrom Ataf before anyone else, I had overnight become a
person worthy of respect. When I strutted across the sand in camp
the Muggs deferentially stepped aside to let me pass. No one tried
to engage me in complicated conversations, and at meals I was
given the biggest portions of muggroom. I often saw little knots of
Muggs with their heads together, quite obviously whispering
about me.

On the the morning after the first sighting of Anagrom Ataf, a
delegation of Muggs came to my tent and asked me to trap the city.

'*Trap* it?'

'It's in the rules. Paragraph twelve.'

'Why me, of all people?'

'You're the one who tamed the Sharach-il-Allah. You're the one
with the book in his head. You're the *Chosen One*.'

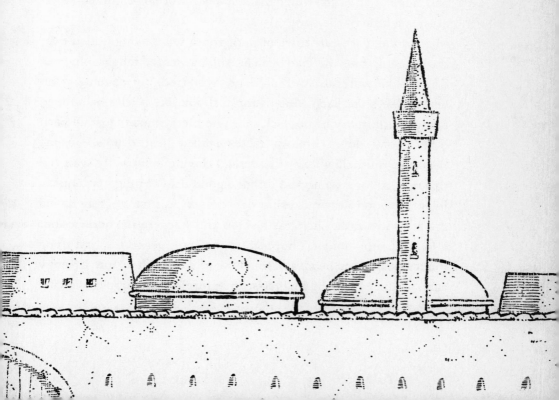

'The Chosen One! The Chosen One!' chorused the entire tribe, which had by now assembled outside my tent. It seemed that they had all conspired to ensnare me. I was touched, to tell the truth, and found it hard to suppress a certain sense of pride.

'No, really, fellows!' I said, all modest and defensive.

As one man, the delegates went down on their knees and presented me with some great big pieces of the smoked muggroom that was normally reserved for high days and holidays. Meantime, the Muggs outside the tent continued to chant 'The Chosen One! The Chosen One!'

When the Muggs proclaim a person The Chosen One, he has to be prepared for a post-election party of the first order. The Muggs were past masters at holding post-election parties. First, the delegates picked me up by all four paws and bore me out of the tent. Then they swung me to and fro a few times and tossed me high into the air, to be caught by a multitude of hands. After that the crowd carried me around in a circle for an hour or so, shouting and singing, and each Mugg made it a point of honour to carry me at least a little of the way.

Drunk on muggroom juice

Meanwhile, vast quantities of muggroom were being grilled over the big camp fires that had been lit, and fermented muggroom juice flowed like water. Last of all, dancing started, but dancing to no discernible step. Each Mugg simply shook like a jelly or hopped along as if bitten on the backside. The merrymakers jostled each other, blew down hollow cactus stalks, beat drums, or just bellowed unintelligibly at the desert. Having bemusedly watched this revelry for a while and drunk a good deal of muggroom juice, I ventured on to the makeshift dance floor. At first I merely flailed my arms in a rather helpless fashion and staggered to and fro, but I soon became bolder. I hopped on the spot, yelled the first thing that came into my head, and finally worked myself up into a frenzy such as the Muggs had never seen before. They stopped dancing and formed a circle round me. I didn't notice this at first, but when I did it fired me up still more. I have very little recollection of what happened after that.

The next morning I awoke with a head so fat it filled the whole tent and the feeling that I had made a complete fool of myself.
But the Muggs gave no sign of this. They brought me a fortifying breakfast of muggrooms, then carried me to a wooden platform which they had erected to give me a better view of the city. I mounted it and studied Anagrom Ataf through a telescope. The city was hovering quietly a hand's-breadth above the desert floor. It was a Fata Morgana, of that there was no doubt, but what exactly *was* a Fata Morgana?

From the
'Encyclopedia of Marvels, Life Forms
and Other Phenomena of Zamonia and its Environs'
by Professor Abdullah Nightingale

Fata Morgana. Originally the name of the legendary King Arthur's sorcerous stepsister and Sir Lancelot's spurned mistress, a fairy who was particularly fond of demonstrating her power by means of mirages. The more precise world of science defines a Fata Morgana as an atmospheric mirage that occurs when layers of air of different temperatures - and, thus, different density and re-fractivity - are juxtaposed or superimposed in such a way that the rays of light passing through them are refracted, change direction, and follow a zigzag course. It is also rumoured in confidence that Fata Morganas are cities inhabited by those who have died of thirst in the desert. There is a certain logic in this theory, given that a desert lacks any buildings which the dead could inhabit and haunt. It is only natural, therefore, that they should make their home in wandering mirages.

But this could not deter me from trapping the city. I had a Chosen One's reputation to live up to, after all. The entire caravan, bleating camedaries included, was staring up at me expectantly from below the platform.

Fata Morgana [cont.]. It is quite impossible to trap a Fata Morgana because it always retreats at exactly the same speed as the person or persons approaching it advance. To cite the so-called Nightingalian Unapproachability Equation governing mobile mirages: A [distance] = X [person approaching] ÷ S [speed] x T^2 [time squared]. In other words, the distance between oneself and a Fata Morgana remains constant however quickly or slowly one approaches it.

Professor Nightingale had a brutal way of confronting one with the facts, but it was also he who had taught me the virtues of lateral thinking – not that this was getting me anywhere at the moment. Besides, I would have to leave the platform in a hurry if I didn't want to get sunstroke. It was hotter than it had been for ages.

Just then a Mugg shook the platform.

'Chosen One, Chosen One!' he cried. 'We must strike camp and move to higher ground. It's so hot, we may be in for a Sugar Flux. If we stay down here, it won't be long before we're stuck!'

That was it! The ideal solution! A Sugar Flux was just what we needed! If we couldn't approach the city because it always retreated, we would have to prevent it from doing so. While climbing down from my vantage point I worked out the basic physics of the plan in my head, then sat down on the desert floor and drew my calculations on the sand with a stick.

Nightingale's Fata Morgana research had disclosed that mirages always hover precisely 9.2 inches above the ground. This altitude is constant, unlike their horizontal position, which is unstable. If the said 9.2 inches could be filled with adhesive or something similar, the Fata Morgana would be stuck to the desert floor and immobilized. That, at least, was what my plan envisaged. As I saw it, the sole requirement was accurate scientific computation.

From the direction of the wind, the position of the sun, the temperature, the humidity, the Muggs' information about sugar-sand texture, and my own knowledge of gravitation, geophysics, meteorology, and gastronomy (the category to which the caramelization of sugar really belongs), I could precisely foresee when and where a Sugar Flux would occur in this valley during the next few days. Morover, since Sugar Fluxes always occurred at the lowest point in a dip, it would be child's play to locate it.

What was more complicated was to manoeuvre Anagrom Ataf over that spot without falling prey to the Sugar Flux oneself.

My plan required the city to be surrounded on all sides. The next afternoon, when the temperature was at its highest for several weeks and the air had been completely still for hours, I decided to act. If a Sugar Flux occurred, it would do so within the next hour. I had instructed the Muggs to take their musical instruments and dig in around the city in a big circle. There, doubtless chewing muggroom balls, they patiently awaited my orders.

I myself sat on my platform armed with a primitive cross between a megaphone and a trumpet, which I had fashioned out of a dried cactus stalk.

I had agreed five prearranged signals with the Muggs.

TOOOOOT!

The Muggs on the south side left their holes and marched towards Anagrom Ataf in open order. Predictably enough, the city retreated at the same speed as the Muggs advanced.

TOOOOT-TOOOOT!

The Muggs on the north side dug themselves out, formed up, and slowly advanced on the city. Insofar as a city may be credited with an emotion, Anagrom Ataf seemed disconcerted. It wavered between east and west as the two groups marched towards it at a steady pace, clearly uncertain which escape route to take. Then it decided to glissade westwards.

TOOOOOT-TOOOOOT-TOOOOOOT!

The western contingent struggled clear of the sand, formed line abreast, and set off. The Fata Morgana promptly stopped short and turned east.

TOOOOT-TOOOOT-TOOOOOT-TOOOOOOT!

The Muggs in the eastern contingent burrowed their way out and swiftly took up their prearranged formation. Anagrom Ataf was trapped. The whole mirage quivered like a huge blancmange, incapable of going in any particular direction. The sun had just passed the zenith, the time of day when the ground temperature reached its peak. A Mugg reported the latest reading: 214°. 214°! We needed 215°!

We were one degree short of a Sugar Flux, and the temperature would drop again in the next few minutes. I climbed down from the platform, picked up a big, flat stone, drew back my arm as far as I could, and hurled it under the hovering city like someone playing ducks and drakes. The stone caromed between the Fata Morgana and the desert floor, striking a spark or two. At that moment the first sugar bubble exploded. The friction caused by the skittering stone had boosted the temperature by the requisite one degree: the caramelization of the desert floor had begun at just the right moment.

TOOOT-TOOOOT-TOOOOOT-TOOOOOOT-TOOOOOOOT!

On the last signal, the Muggs hurriedly withdrew so as not to become caught up in the steadily expanding process of caramelization.

This was probably the first time in the history of mirages that a semi-stable Fata Morgana had been fused to the desert floor, so no one could ever before have heard the noise that resulted. Not a very dignified noise (rather vulgar, in fact), it was reminiscent of a Bollogg's fart. Imagine the effect of a wet coffee pot being deposited on a hotplate, only much louder. Bubbling, hissing, whistling, squeaking, rattling sounds ensued. Anagrom Ataf creaked and groaned as if it were being torn apart brick by brick. From time to time one of the big sugar bubbles exploded like a burst balloon.

The city fought hard. It kept rising a few inches, only to be sucked back into the molten sugar. In the end, all the noises died away. Whistling faintly, Anagrom Ataf subsided and, with a dull thud that shook the whole valley, embedded itself in the caramel for good. The city was firmly welded to the desert floor.

Anagrom Ataf was ready for occupation.

We looked anything but a band of intrepid conquistadors when we entered Anagrom Ataf. Eyes darting nervously in all directions, we stole silently along the broad main thoroughfare and into the heart of the city.

No one had ever before captured a mirage, still less entered one. Was it inhabited? If so, by whom? Were they human beings? Monsters? Spirits? Zombies? Were they peaceable or ill-disposed? The suburbs consisted of small, whitewashed, single-storeyed houses, all very spick and span. Washing was hanging out to dry at many windows, but there wasn't a soul to be seen, not even the cats or mongrels so often found in desert cities.

We came at last to the market place, which looked as if all the traders and their customers had been spirited away on a busy market day. There were big stalls laden with fresh fruit and vegetables, sausages and eggs, spices and bread. There were baskets filled with red apples and fat green water melons, cheeses, hams, dried beans, corn cobs, sacks of grain and flour, rice and noodles.

I make a pig of myself

After months of deprivation in the desert and an endless diet of muggrooms, I can surely be forgiven for having fallen on the fresh food like a shipwrecked sailor. I stuffed a banana into my mouth, then a hunk of sheep's cheese, and tossed a handful of strawberries after them. Strangely enough, they didn't satisfy my hunger in the least. I ate a few grapes, half a loaf of bread, two apples, and a small maize cake *au gratin*. Still hungry, I tore off a big piece of ham, devoured two more bananas, a squashy pear and a garlic sausage, then a bowl of figs, half a melon, and a whole pancake. I slurped down four raw eggs, dipped a piece of currant cake in honey, helped myself to some more ham, consumed a wholemeal bun, an entire salami, and two croissantlike pastries with vegetable filling, a bowl of millet gruel with sultanas, and a sticky doughnut that tasted of sugar and cinnamon. I was as hungry as ever. Then someone handed me a piece of muggroom. One bite, and I instantly felt replete.

We combed the whole city systematically, street by street, building by building, room by room. We found signs of human occupation everywhere – half empty plates on the tables, hot stoves, soups simmering to themselves – but never a real sign of life. In other respects everything was perfect: the streets clean, the houses newly decorated and pleasantly cool, the beds made, and a great abundance of things such as anyone would find immensely luxurious after sleeping on the hard desert floor for a long time.

When hours went by and still no inhabitants or householders showed up, I formally proclaimed Anagrom Ataf a Mugg possession. We at once proceeded to share out the houses among ourselves. By sunset Anagrom Ataf was completely occupied and humming with new life. That night we held a little celebration at which the Muggs, too, sampled the food that was lying around. Curiously enough, though, we all felt equally unsatisfied and had to fall back on roast muggrooms and fermented muggroom juice.

The next morning I strolled through the city and inspected a few empty houses. One of them smelt of freshly baked cakes, and the table was laid. When I went into the bedroom I heard a whispering sound behind me. I spun round quickly, but there was no one there, so I left the house feeling a trifle creepy. Eventually I came to the market place, where we'd held our inaugural party the night before. The Muggs were all still in bed (most of them for the first time ever). Hanging over the city was a thin pall of morning mist which would soon, without doubt, be burnt off by the fierce desert sun. I felt sure we'd finished off nearly all the food, but no: the baskets had all been replenished and the hams were as fresh and untouched as if the Sugar Gnomes had been there during the night.

Although the Muggs were slow to take to urban life, they did their level best. Most of them sleepwalked at nights and roamed the streets by day because they missed their perambulations. Indeed, many of them made a thoroughly dejected impression. Until now they had never devoted much thought to how to spend their time; they had simply roamed because roaming was their way of life. Now that they had reached their destination, they didn't know what to do with themselves.

Learning how to settle down
As The Chosen One and trapper of Anagrom Ataf I felt it my duty to help the Muggs settle down. I organized a course in which the art of 'dwelling' was taught. People don't find 'dwelling' too easy, especially when all they've done hitherto is roam restlessly from place to place. I began by showing the Muggs how to sit on chairs, having set up a few in the market place for them to practise on. They went about it very clumsily, either missing them altogether, or knocking them over and falling over themselves, or climbing on them and not daring to get down. They ended by being even more frightened of chairs than before. It was the same with lying in bed. The Muggs couldn't get on with beds, which they found far too soft. Many filled their mattresses with pebbles or lay beside or under them.

Even basic activities like entering a house by the front door did not come naturally to the Muggs. They climbed in through the windows, not knowing how to operate a door handle, or locked themselves in or out or lost the keys. For this reason, many preferred to sleep in the streets. Domesticity was entirely alien to them, and it remained so.

Being The Chosen One, I was in the thick of every problem and had to answer innumerable questions. How do you make a bed? How do you stoke a stove? What do you do with a cupboard? How do you use a broom, a table, a knife and fork? What are stairs for? The Muggs were completely thrown by simple things that domesticated people took for granted. How did you 'dwell', and why? Questions without number.

The greatest problem, however, was the city's instability. Anagrom Ataf was only a semi-stable Fata Morgana, which meant that certain parts of it continually vanished and reappeared after a certain interval. Items of furniture dissolved into thin air, whole houses suddenly weren't there any more. The next day these things would be back in place, and a wall would be standing in yesterday's blank space. Sometimes whole districts vanished one day and reappeared the next. Life in Anagrom Ataf was completely unpredictable. A chair could vanish from under your backside just as you were sitting down. This was harmless enough, but several Muggs had nasty falls when the first floors of the houses they were sleeping in evaporated. One Mugg ran full tilt into a wall that had suddenly materialized in his path. Accidents of this kind occurred almost daily. Before long, everyone was sleeping downstairs and moving very slowly.

Unstable conditions

I found a steaming dish of mashed potatoes on the kitchen table the first time I entered my house. That was why I'd chosen the place, on the principle that there couldn't be much wrong with a house whose kitchen table bore a steaming dish of mashed potatoes.

I emptied the dish every night – though it never took the edge off my appetite – and always found it refilled when I woke up the next morning. Several other Muggs had similar experiences. Empty fruit bowls replenished themselves, dirty clothes were washed and ironed, pieces of furniture had been shifted, doors closed and windows opened – and always surreptitiously or during the night, when everyone was asleep.

A sinister rumour

Before long, a rumour circulated that we weren't alone in Anagrom Ataf. Some of the Muggs thought the Sugar Gnomes were responsible for these strange happenings, other more timid souls attributed them to the spirits of the city's former inhabitants. There were several identical reports of ghostly apparitions, transparent figures that scurried away when challenged. Nocturnal rumblings and bangings could be heard in nearly every house, and many Muggs told of spine-chilling groans and wails that rang out as soon as the sun had set.

Something surprising was happening to the Muggs – something of which I would never have thought them capable: they started quarrelling. At the civic assemblies we held from time to time, there were always one or two who came to blows over some trivial point like refuse collection or the establishment of a communal kitchen. This was very odd, given their traditionally peaceable behaviour.

They began to form little cliques and got in the hair of other little cliques, they took offence at the drop of a hat, they became embroiled in disputes and expected me to settle them. I was the unelected mayor of a city full of discontented, quarrelsome Muggs.

Then there was the lack of sleep. The Muggs, who were used to exerting themselves to the point of collapse, had been so tired after a day's march that they literally 'fell' asleep. Now they spent the whole day loafing around with nothing to do but gather a few muggrooms and look for water. Many Muggs found it impossible to sleep for want of exhaustion, while others were kept awake by the nocturnal noises. Some even claimed that their beds started shaking as soon as they shut their eyes. When they sat up with a start, they saw transparent figures disappear, howling, into the darkness.

So universal irritability was aggravated by constant overtiredness. I myself did not suffer from this – give me a nice soft bed, and I always enjoy a healthful night's sleep – but I resolved to get to the bottom of the problem, so one night I lay in wait. I was determined to solve the mystery of the inexhaustible supply of mashed potatoes in my house.

Accordingly, I sat down at the kitchen table, ate the potatoes (no effect), and waited. The dish had to replenish itself somehow or other, and I intended to witness the process even if I never shut my eyes all night.

Half an hour later I was asleep.

I dreamed of Troglotrolls making poisoned mashed potatoes in the cellars of Anagrom Ataf, though Anagrom Ataf had no cellars. They were stirring their saucepans with big iron forks, making a terrible clatter. That was the sound that woke me.

Standing at the small, coal-fired kitchen stove was the transparent figure of a man who was noisily stirring a saucepan with an iron fork.

The Fatom

I rubbed my eyes to reassure myself that I wasn't still dreaming. The transparent man continued to stir his mashed potatoes. He really was as transparent as a glass of wine. Having scooped the mashed potatoes out of the saucepan with a spoon, he filled the dish and joined me at the table.

'*Bon appétit,*' I said, to be polite.

'*!esiwekiL,*' he replied.

I was conversant with all the Zamonian languages, tribal dialects included, but this meant nothing to me.

**From the
'Encyclopedia of Marvels, Life Forms
and Other Phenomena of Zamonia and its Environs'
by Professor Abdullah Nightingale**

Fatamorganic. The only mirror-image language in Zamonia, Fatamorganic is High Zamonian spoken without an accent but backwards, and is unique to the interior of mirages. It is relatively easy to translate. If in written form, it should be held in front of a mirror; if spoken, it must simply be listened to with one's brain in reverse.

'motaF a ma I,' said the transparent man. 'diarfa eb ot deen on s'erehT. naem I ,elpoep gniracs dna gnitnuah – snoitnetni yltsohg on evah ew tub ,wonk I ,emoseurg ytterp kool eW.'

His voice was thin and reedy.

Not to make matters more difficult than necessary, I shall here translate into Fatamorganic as I go. Once I knew the secret, it was really quite simple. The man had said:

'I am a Fatom. There's no need to be afraid. We look pretty gruesome, I know, but we have no ghostly intentions – haunting and scaring people, I mean.'

A Fatom? I'd come across phantoms in Nightingale's lectures on Grailsundian demonology, but I knew nothing of Fatoms.

From the
'Encyclopedia of Marvels, Life Forms
and Other Phenomena of Zamonia and its Environs'
by Professor Abdullah Nightingale

Fatoms. Translucent life forms belonging to the Restless Spirits Without Cause of Death family. Found only in semi-stable Fata Morganas, they consist for the most part of reflected light, frozen sugar vapour, and diluted spiritual essence in gaseous form.

As already mentioned in the article on semi-stable →*Fata Morganas*, the sugar-sand of the Demerara Desert melts at temperatures in excess of 320° Fahrenheit [→*Sugar Flux*], begins to boil, and gives off a fine sugar vapour. If the air temperature drops sharply at that moment [e.g. because of sudden katabatic winds], the sugar hardens in mid-air; and if, in addition, the image of an actual oasis city is projected on the crystallizing sugar molecules, that image can become firmly imprinted on them. The same thing can happen to the living creatures in such a city. This is how so-called Fatoms originate. Unlike traditional ghosts, they are not spirits of the dead, but forms of existence that may well be still alive.

The thought that I wasn't confronted by the spirit of a dead person promptly made my transparent guest seem more congenial.

Fatoms [cont.] Fatoms must be numbered among the most pitiful spirit forms in Zamonia. They pursue no definite end such as the intimidation of living creatures, nor do they derive any pleasure from their existence in the same way as poltergeists or →*Hobgoblins*. They are merely condemned to repeat, for evermore, the activity in which they were engaged when the semi-stable →*Fata Morgana* came into being.

Certain things were now clear to me. The Fatoms still inhabited Anagrom Ataf but had been in hiding ever since our tactless intrusion. My house spirit had been making mashed potatoes when Anagrom Ataf came into being and was obliged to go on doing so for evermore. Similar things must be happening in the other houses. It was true: we didn't have the city to ourselves.

The Fatom tried to explain the situation. 'Nothing has been the same since you got here. We're scared, and that's not right. *You're* the ones who should be scared – of *us*.'

He sighed and spooned some mashed potato into his mouth. I could see it narrow in his throat and slither down his gullet in a thin stream, like water down a transparent straw. The remainder of the digestive process was mercifully hidden from view by the kitchen table. I really wasn't keen to see how a Fatom's stomach dealt with mashed potato.

The Fatom told me all about life in Anagrom Ataf. He also explained that nothing in the city actually existed, but nothing actually disappeared. Every apple you ate would sooner or later turn up again. That was also why the food never satisfied people: they ate it, true, but it returned to the place they'd taken it from before they could digest it.

The Fatoms had led a life of constant repetition before we threw them out of their stride. A postman kept delivering the same letter, a greengrocer kept replenishing his market stall, and someone, somewhere, was always pouring the same glass of milk. People greeted each other in the street for the millionth time, a flower pot kept falling off a windowsill over and over again, a woman swept her doorstep to all eternity, a man had been hammering the same nail into the wall for a century – such was life in Anagrom Ataf.

What sounded awful to a non-Fatom was the Fatoms' normal way of life. They were content with their ever-recurring repetitions and had become accustomed to them. What frightened them was change, and, in particular, the changes introduced by the Muggs and myself.

The Fatom made the saddest impression any creature (if Fatoms may be classified as such, being only half-creatures) had ever made on me. We had deprived him and the rest of Anagrom Ataf's legitimate inhabitants of the only thing they had left: their repetitious activities. It was quite impossible to go on opening the same door if Muggs were passing through it. How could a street be crossed at the same point, again and again, if the roadway was occupied by a bunch of Muggs arguing about municipal refuse disposal? How could a Fatom go on taking the same nap when camedaries were bleating all over the place?

Life in Anagrom Ataf had become a nightmare. The Fatoms had gone to ground wherever they could. In constant fear of discovery, they hid by day (not well enough to prevent the occasional sighting) and waited for nightfall, when they could at least resume their beloved activities under cover of darkness.

The Fatom emitted a groan in reverse, which sounded as if he'd inadvertently swallowed a moth. I promised him that I would convene a citizens' assembly – all that occurred to me on the spur of the moment. The Muggs must meet these half-spirits for a frank exchange of views, and I would act as interpreter.

The citizens' assembly at Anagrom Ataf was probably one of the most extraordinary political meetings in the history of Zamonia. All the Fatoms and Muggs had gathered in the market place and were eyeing each other suspiciously. I delivered a short speech in both languages, Zamonian and Fatamorganic, in which I appealed to their forbearance, public spirit, and good-neighbourliness. There was no applause.

'What's the use of good-neighbourliness if we don't have anything to eat?' called one Mugg.

There had recently been rumours that stocks of muggrooms were running low. To pick them it was necessary to roam far afield. These cactoid mushrooms grew in a rather solitary fashion. Incapable of being bred, cultivated, or planted in large numbers, they had to be picked wherever they were found.

'And what's the use of good-neighbourliness,' cried another voice, 'if our houses simply vanish?'

The problem of Anagrom Ataf's semi-stability was indeed proving hard to tackle. I had issued a strict ban on using beds that were more than three feet from the ground, but this was more a cosmetic measure than a genuine solution.

Then came the Fatoms' turn to speak. One of them, the real mayor of Anagrom Ataf, delivered a long, plaintive speech which I translated for the Muggs' benefit. He declared that we had no manners and no right to live in Anagrom Ataf. We were causing chaos – indeed, we hadn't the least idea what 'dwelling' in a place really meant.

The Muggs retorted that they had every right to be there. In support of this they displayed their golden rules and drew special attention to commandment number twelve.

It was a diametrical difference of opinion. The citizens' assembly ended in disaster. The mayor kept repeating his speech over and over, the Fatoms and Muggs gabbled at each other without understanding a word. The city could never have witnessed such a commotion in its history. Realizing that agreement would be hard to reach, I decided to try another tack.

I called for silence.

'I've got it!' I announced. 'We'll move out.'

The Fatoms applauded enthusiastically, the Muggs booed.

'Where would we go?' called a Mugg. 'Anagrom Ataf was our destination. How could we roam the desert without a destination?'

That was a relevant, justified, and – off the cuff, at least – unanswerable question. I requested an adjournment. I needed to think.

I roamed the desert for days on end, cudgelling my brains. I could ask the Muggs to accompany me to Atlantis, but that was my goal, not theirs. Experience of Anagrom Ataf had shown that the Muggs were out of place in a city.

Until I found a solution, life in Anagrom Ataf had to go on. The Fatoms resumed their repetitious activities, but they seemed to derive no real pleasure from them under the Muggs' suspicious gaze. The Muggs stuck doggedly to the houses they'd occupied, but the Fatoms, who were now bolder in their movements, made life there somewhat less agreeable. It can detract from your home comforts if you're constantly being subjected to black looks by transparent apparitions seated on the living-room sofa. Discontentment in the mirage city was steadily growing.

On my desert walks I often encountered Muggs attempting to tire themselves out by marching round the city. They watched me avidly as if intent on witnessing the moment when I had my flash of inspiration. It's almost impossible to think under such circumstances. The pressure on me intensified day by day.

I receive a sign One afternoon I could endure the Muggs' presence no longer. I diverged from my usual route and fled several miles into the desert. There, savouring the peace and quiet, I sat down on a boulder and surveyed my surroundings.

Political responsibility wasn't for me, that much was clear. You have to feel some degree of local patriotism if you want to make a credible mayor of a municipality. Personally, however, I found it quite impossible to develop any sense of affection for a semi-stable mirage. Not even the Muggs could do that. Although they stubbornly clung to the idea that they had reached their destination, in their heart of hearts they longed to be back in the desert.

About a hundred yards away was a smallish drifting dune. I caught myself envying its freedom – the freedom to go wherever the wind took it. Some shiny object in the sand was reflecting the sunlight. Things that reflected light were rare in the desert, so my curiosity was aroused. I went over and saw a bottle protruding from a small hummock in the sand. The writing on the message inside was completely faded and illegible, but it gave me an idea.

What we needed was a sign.

Three days later a Mugg came running into the city, hugely excited. He had found a message-in-a-bottle and brought it to me to read. The Muggs still cherished a certain respect for me. I feigned surprise.

'A message-in-a-bottle?' I exclaimed. 'It must be a sign!'

'A sign! A sign!' cried the Muggs who had gathered around me. Some more Muggs hurried up, together with one or two Fatoms. I solemnly read the message aloud. It consisted of four rules:

1 Ye shall not dwell in Anagrom Ataf.

2 If ye dwell in Anagrom Ataf notwithstanding, ye shall depart the city swiftly and without demur.

3 Ye shall go to a city that bears the name ESIDARAP S'LOOF.

4 And, of course, ye shall honour the muggroom.

It was such a brazen device, I felt a twinge of remorse for having employed so obvious a subterfuge. I waited for the boos and rotten muggrooms to start flying.

'Ye shall not dwell in Anagrom Ataf!' cried one of the Muggs.

'If ye dwell in Anagrom Ataf notwithstanding, ye shall depart the city swiftly and without demur!' yelled another.

'Ye shall go to a city that bears the name ESIDARAP S'LOOF!' several other Muggs chanted in unison.

'And, of course, ye shall honour the mugg-room!' the whole caravan shouted as one man.

It was remarkably easy to persuade the Muggs to move out of Anagrom Ataf once they had a new destination. Although none of them knew where esidaraP s'looF was, the location of Anagrom Ataf had been just as much of a mystery. They packed up their belongings at once and saddled their camedaries. Crying 'esidaraP s'looF! esidaraP s'looF!' again and again, they disappeared into the desert without even bidding me farewell. I found this rather disappointing after all the fuss they'd made about The Chosen One, but they probably took it for granted that I was coming along too. If I knew them, they mightn't begin to look for me for several days. The Fatoms were delighted with this development. The fact that I had welded their city to the desert floor was regrettable but irreversible. Besides, it helped to make the place exceedingly prosperous: in the next few years Anagrom Ataf became one of Zamonia's principal tourist attractions. The Fatoms made a fortune out of the fruit and vegetables that dissolved in the tourists' stomachs and returned to them intact for resale. Wherever they pursued their everlasting activities they set out little bowls with the following notices (in Zamonian) attached to them: 'Gratuities of any amount, large or small, will not be considered demeaning.' This earned them even more than the illusory wares of which the tourists could never eat their fill. As for the Fatoms, they acquired a self-confidence they had previously lacked.

The writing on the message addressed to the Muggs was also destined to keep vanishing and reappearing at intervals, because I had written it with a pencil from Anagrom Ataf. However, this only added to its mystique and led the Muggs to venerate their new set of rules still more.

I had taken advantage of the occasion to part company with the Muggs. Instead of roaming the desert with them at an everlasting trot, I proposed to try, at my own risk, to reach Atlantis.

I provided myself with an ample supply of water and set off in a northeasterly direction, that being where the metropolis must lie.

I journeyed far more purposefully than the Muggs, taking my bearings by the sun and conserving energy and water by trying as far as possible to travel by night. Before a week was up, however, my water was was running low and the end of the desert was nowhere in sight – at least, the nature of the terrain and vegetation presented little immediate prospect of my reaching a more temperate climatic zone.

I had been on the move all morning and was taking a short rest, scanning the horizon for a glimmer of hope, when I sighted something very seldom found in a desert.

It was a species of bus stop.

Since the sun had been beating down on my unprotected head with exceptional ferocity for a considerable time, I thought at first that it was a mirage, but curiosity prompted me to examine it more closely.

It was not only real but firmly embedded in the desert floor. It was also, if I had correctly deciphered the symbol on it, a 'tornado stop'. Around it lay a huge heap of the most heterogeneous objects: food, vases, vessels filled with water, gold and jewellery, bales of cloth and sacks of spices.

335

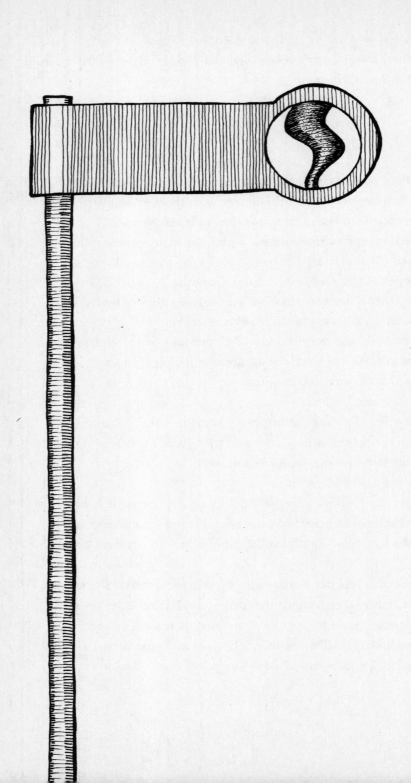

From the
'Encyclopedia of Marvels, Life Forms
and Other Phenomena of Zamonia and its Environs'
by Professor Abdullah Nightingale

Tornado Stops. A curious feature of the Demerara Desert, these are erected on the route of a tornado which is thought to be everlasting, always travels in the same direction, and is popularly known as the Eternal Tornado [→*Eternal Tornado, The*]. Many travellers use this whirlwind as a means of transportation and hitch a ride in it for part of the way.

Today, if someone recommended me to hitch a ride in a tornado to save time or take a short cut, I would direct him to the nearest mental institution. At that time, however, I was at an age when such daring feats represented a challenge. A tornado can travel at immense speeds, so anyone whirling along inside it could cover vast distances in a very short time.

From the
'Encyclopedia of Marvels, Life Forms
and Other Phenomena of Zamonia and its Environs'
by Professor Abdullah Nightingale

Eternal Tornado, The. The Eternal Tornado is the last surviving representative of a generation of whirlwinds that keep to a fixed route. At its southernmost point this route traverses the interior of the Demerara Desert; at its northernmost point it skirts the Humongous Mountains, beyond which lies →*Atlantis*.

So this tornado would not only whisk me out of the desert but set me down in the vicinity of Atlantis. What more could I want?

Eternal Tornado, The [cont.]. The objects whirled along and deposited at tornado stops render it probable that the Eternal Tornado is filled with treasures of all kinds. It is presumed to contain tons of gold, silver, platinum, diamonds, jewellery, pearls, and other articles of value, as well as masses of Zamonian currency from various periods.

The encyclopedia referred to a means of transporation that would get me to Atlantis in double-quick time and was also as jam-packed with valuables as a bank vault. Perhaps I would be able to filch a few of these and arrive in Atlantis a wealthy man. The only problem was, how did you board a whirlwind and how did you get off one? Well, I could at least examine the possibility of doing so. If it seemed too dangerous, I could always give it a miss.

Accordingly, I resolved to wait for the tornado.

Waiting for the tornado Meantime, I took a look at the objects lying around the tornado stop. Vases filled with pearls. A keg of gold dust. A solid silver suit of armour. Goblets, some of gold, others of mother-of-pearl. Twelve place settings encrusted with diamonds. Who would discard such valuables in the middle of a desert? They must have belonged to oasis dwellers in the area. Why had they abandoned these treasures to a meteorological phenomenon?

I waited an hour.

No tornado.

Be patient, I told myself, you can't expect a whirlwind to come along hourly. I sat down and waited another three hours.

Still no tornado.

Evening came, then night, and still not a grain of sand appeared in the sky. I waited the next day and the day after that. Growing bored, I festooned myself with jewellery and strutted around the tornado stop. The local insects and snakes may well have been watching me, whispering together, and fearing for my sanity. I took off the jewellery and sat down on the sand.

There wasn't even a gentle little dust devil in sight.

On the fifth day it all got too much for me. I'd obviously fallen for a practical joke. A tornado stop? Bah! My water reserves were down to half and I hadn't gone a step further. After five days under the sweltering sun, my brain had probably shrunk to the size of a raisin. I decided to move on before I lost the rest of my wits. I shouldered my bundle and set off.

A faint headwind ruffled my fur, a little flurry of dust appeared on the horizon.

It was the tornado.

A whirlwind looks quite innocuous from far away, like a lady's stocking dancing across the countryside in a frenzy. As it slowly draws nearer, however, it imparts a growing sense of help-lessness, indeed, of absolute impotence. It very soon dawns on you that you're confronted by a natural phenomenon which, along with volcanic eruptions, tidal waves and earthquakes, registers ten on the Richter scale. This was no dust devil or feeble little whirlwind that sends a few cactuses sailing through the air; this was a genuine monster of a tornado, a Grade One storm in the heavyweight division – the kind that can wipe out whole cities in seconds or scoop up a body of water the size of the Zamonian Gulf.

The closer it came, the louder the incredible roar it emitted, which might have issued from the throats of thousands of maddened buffalo, lions, elephants, and baboons. Underlying it was a bass note that made the whole desert resonate so violently that cactuses toppled over while the tornado was still dozens of miles away. By the time it was within a mile of me, I could make out the objects that circled it like satellites before being engulfed: boulders the size of houses, cactuses – even a camedary or two.

From the
'Encyclopedia of Marvels, Life Forms
and Other Phenomena of Zamonia and its Environs'
by Professor Abdullah Nightingale

Tornado Stops [cont.] It is a traditional Zamonian custom to erect stop signs on the route of the Eternal Tornado [→*Eternal Tornado, The*]. These serve to guide those who leave sacrificial offerings for the whirlwind, which many of Zamonia's inhabitants worship as a deity. They believe it to be an animate, supernatural being that can be appeased, or induced to grant wishes, by gifts. As mentioned above, the stop signs are occasionally misinterpreted as an invitation to ride aboard this meteorological phenomenon or construed as a challenge by death-defying adventurers. It is said that some naive souls are actually prepared to run the risk of travelling aboard a meteorological phenomenon that eats its way through the countryside while rotating at 5000 r.p.m. Sensible wayfarers, on the other hand, construe the stop signs as a warning - a kind of recommendation to quit the area as fast as possible.

There's still time, I thought. I can still stir my stumps and run for it before the torna –

Before I could finish the word in my head the tornado picked me up by the scruff of the neck like a struggling rabbit. A gigantic hand made of dust, mud and desert sand hoisted me high into the air and whirled me in a circle around the midpoint of the tornado. It could not have been more than a few seconds before I was high enough to overlook the whole of the desert. Anagrom Ataf lay far behind. That was the last thing I saw before being sucked into the tornado's interior. I was hauled backwards through a loose mass of sand, pebbles and desert scrub that engulfed me completely but was so well ventilated by the constant motion that I could still breathe. The most unpleasant thing was the peculiar sensation that overcame me as I sank ever deeper into this mixture of desert sand and pebbles. It was a very frightening sensation, a feeling of utter helplessness accompanied by a presentiment of death. At the same time, all the strength was sucked out of me. My body became heavy and ached all over, as if I were suffering from a bad bout of influenza. And then, quite suddenly, the tornado released me. I fell head over heels and came to rest on a firm surface. It was, as I discovered to my bemusement, a flight of stone steps.

From the
'Encyclopedia of Marvels, Life Forms
and Other Phenomena of Zamonia and its Environs'
by Professor Abdullah Nightingale

Eternal Tornado, The [cont.] Eternal Tornado is the popular term for the last megatornado in the perpetuum mobile category still active in the →*Demerara Desert*. Unlike normal tornadoes, this whirlwind, which is approximately five miles high and half a mile in diameter, possesses certain characteristics no longer found in present-day whirlwinds. Among other things, it apparently goes on for ever.

Another characteristic is the so-called mobile stability that exists in the heart of the tornado, hence the theory that relates it to another violent meteorological phenomenon, namely, the hurricane. One well-known feature of the hurricane is its calm centre, the so-called eye of the storm. Some authorities surmise that the Eternal Tornado originated in prehistoric times, when a hurricane and a tornado collided and became fused together. Although this would conflict with another meteorological theory [→Conventions Observed by Exceptional Natural Phenomena, The], it may be one of those popular exceptions that always prove the rule when scientists are at their wits' end.

This mobile stability, or zone of complete calm inside a raging whirlwind, is so pronounced in the case of the Eternal Tornado that many tornado experts espouse the possibility that a house of cards could be built inside it without collapsing. Although this may be something of an exaggeration, the physical conditions prevailing inside the tornado must be so stable that it would - in theory, at least - be possible to survive there [in very primitive conditions, of course]. Purely in theory, be it noted, because no one would be insane enough to enter a whirlwind of his own free will.

What temporarily alarmed me far more than the discovery of a flight of stone steps inside the tornado was the fact that I couldn't see very well. My vision was blurred, and everything looked less well defined than usual. I should point out that my eyesight is normally as keen as that of an eagle looking through an electron microscope; I can tell the sex of an ant at fifty yards without any technical aids, even in twilight. Now, however, I saw just about as well as an owl in daylight. Everything seemed to be shrouded in a

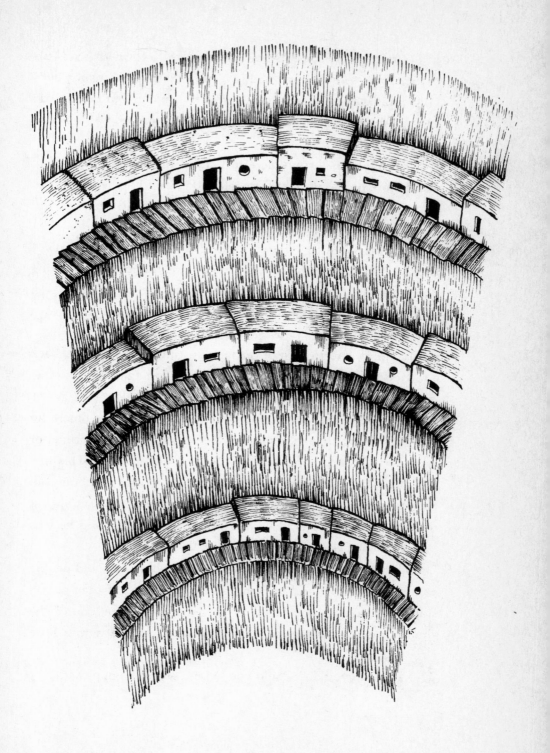

pall of mist, and I had to screw up my eyes to focus them a little better. Some tornado dust had lodged in them, presumably, but I hoped this was only temporary. I tried to stand up but failed to do so with anything like my normal agility. My limbs felt as heavy as lead.

It was only with a supreme effort that I managed, groaning, to stand more or less upright. The fall had evidently taken more out of me than I thought. I felt as if I were suffering from lumbago, and every muscle in my body ached.

Beneath me were the stairs on which I'd landed so painfully. I walked – or rather, hobbled – to the edge and found myself peering down a shaft several miles deep. The stairs went spiralling down it, lower and lower, and the walls of the shaft were lined with small, single-storeyed houses, evidently built of mud.

Overcome by a terrible fit of vertigo, I instinctively staggered back a few paces. When I turned round, I was standing only a few feet from one of the primitive little houses.

The centenarians Out of the crudely constructed doorway stepped an old man. By 'old man' I don't mean a sprightly senior citizen in his prime, or aged between sixty and seventy, but a *really* old man. This one must have been at least a hundred years old, possibly a thousand. He had shoulder-length grey hair and a white beard that almost reached his knees. His face was a mass of wrinkles, and he was leaning on a stick.

He subjected me to a stare of the kind that only very old people can give – so long and piercing that you wonder if they're still staring at you or have died in the interim. I soon found the situation embarrassing, so I tried to break the ice with a little conversation.

'Er...How do you do? Could you tell me where I am, please?'

346

My voice made a noise like the door of a prison cell opening after decades of oil deprivation. I gave a start, it sounded so croaky and unfamiliar. Feeling awkward, I cleared my throat, which probably still had bits of tornado lodged in it.

The old man looked at me pensively but without surprise. Then he gave a gentle smile and said, 'You're in Paradise.'

Of course! That was the answer: I was dead. The whirlwind had broken my neck. I must have suffocated in the mass of pebbles or died of shock. No idea what had finished me off, but I had certainly kicked the bucket. I was dead, I was in heaven, and this old man was none other than...God! Looking the way he did, who else *could* he be?

He had now shuffled to the edge of the stairs. Cupping his hands around his mouth, he called out, so loudly that his voice went echoing down the shaft, 'A new arrival! A new arrival!'

Some more men came out on the stairway. They all had long white hair and yard-long beards and were at least as old as the one I took to be God. Not a word was spoken as they came toiling up the stairs, a laborious and painful process. I myself refrained from speaking because my own voice frightened me. The old men clustered round me and fondled my head with their bony hands in what appeared to be a well-meant form of ritual greeting. Two of them solemnly approached me bearing a large mirror.

'Look in the mirror!' one of them commanded. His tone, though friendly, brooked no refusal. Looking at the greybeards' faces, I detected the sort of tense expectancy displayed by parents watching their children open Christmas presents.

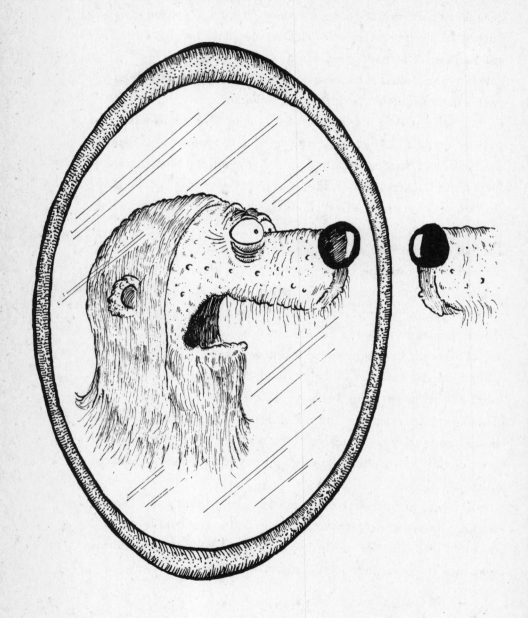

Hesitantly, I looked in the mirror. I had to screw up my eyes before I could make out my reflection, and then…My fur had turned snow-white and was so long on my head that it straggled down my neck to my shoulders. I had a yard-long beard, and there were big, dark blue bags under my eyes. At a rough estimate, I had aged at least a century. I opened my mouth to give a horrified cry, but before I could do so my knees turned to jelly and I lapsed into merciful unconsciousness.

10.

My Life
in
Tornado City

When I came to, I was lying on a comfortable mattress with five of the old men standing round me. One of them handed me a cup of tea. They had evidently carried me into one of the houses. Near the bed on which I was lying stood a table and two chairs. There were also a small stove and a cupboard containing some crockery.

'Feeling better?' asked the greybeard who'd brought the tea. 'It's normal – happens to everyone. It's the shock.' The others eyed me sympathetically.

'The shock, tee-hee!' tittered the smallest of them. 'It knocks everyone sideways.'

'I had a terrible nightmare,' I said, still rather bemused. 'I dreamed I was terribly old – as old as you are – and...' I stopped short, aware that I was being tactless, but the old men continued to smile understandingly. The bearer of the teacup acted as their spokesman. His name, I soon discovered, was Baldwyn Baobab.

'I've got some news for you,' he said. 'Bad news and good news. You grow older very, very quickly when you enter the tornado. You age decades in a few seconds – seventy or eighty years on average. I'm sure you experienced that sensation – it's thoroughly disagreeable. That's the bad news. The good news is, once you're inside here you hardly age at all – only around a minute a year. You can work out for yourself how long a year of life takes: for ever! No matter how old you are, you generally live for another umpteen thousand years – unless, of course, a piano falls on your head. It isn't immortality, exactly, but you won't come closer to it anywhere else. Once you get used to it, you feel you're in Paradise. But don't ask me how it works, old boy. To discover that, you'd need more than one brain.'

From the
'Encyclopedia of Marvels, Life Forms
and Other Phenomena of Zamonia and its Environs'
by Professor Abdullah Nightingale

Eternal Tornado, The [cont.]. The perpetual motion tornado is a meteorological phenomenon that can recur again and again because of exceptionally stable temperatures and atmospheric conditions, which cause it to follow a course known as the Abdullian Double Tornado Pretzel [so called after Professor Abdullah Nightingale, the celebrated amateur tornadologist]. In this mode, the tornado always follows the same course, a series of loops in the shape of a double pretzel some two thousand miles across.

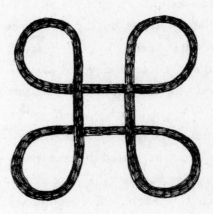

Interesting, but what bearing did it have on the fact that I'd become a doddering old man within the space of a few seconds?

A stable time vacuum prevails inside the Eternal Tornado. In other words, time is propelled outwards and away from the centre of the whirlwind - like moisture in a salad drainer - by the immense centrifugal force it exerts. In the eye of the storm, on the other hand, time is subjected to extreme condensation, with the result that it passes at breakneck speed. Anyone insane enough to penetrate a tornado's outer wall of sand would age decades within the space of a few seconds.

One of the advantages of old age is that you don't get worked up over things so easily, not even over the belated arrival of information from an encyclopedia implanted in your brain. At least I now knew how matters stood. What I still failed to understand was why anyone inside a tornado should age by even a minute a year.

While the tornado is changing its centrifugal direction, an annual process that takes about sixty seconds to complete, the time vacuum fills up with time. This means that, should any living creature happen to be inside the tornado at that moment [an improbable state of affairs, since, as we have already mentioned more than once, no one would be idiotic enough to enter a tornado in the first place], it, too, would be bound to age by one minute.

I informed the old men of Nightingale's scientific explanation, which they greeted with nods and murmurs of approval.
They gave me some readily digestible porridge to eat (one of the tornado inhabitants' favourite dishes), and we drank a few cups of tea together. Once I had regained some of my strength, I actually succeeded in getting back on my wobbly legs.
'This will be your home from now on,' one of the old men said with a sweeping gesture. 'You can choose another house if you don't care for this one. There are still a few vacant in the lower section.'
'Come,' said Baldwyn, 'we'll give you an exclusive guided tour of Tornado City.'

Conditions inside the whirlwind were remarkably stable, as I have said, and approximated to those prevailing in a modern jumbo jet subjected to periodic spells of turbulence. The floor and walls vibrated incessantly but quite gently. A few teacups and old men fell over when the city gave an occasional jolt, but that was all. The deafening external roar produced by the tornado was muffled by its thick integument of sand. All I could detect was a subdued hum, though this might have been because my hearing had deteriorated with age.

From time to time, probably when it rounded a bend, the tornado emitted some mighty creaks and groans. When this happened a few of the loosely laid stairs became telescoped and one or two of the houses teetered a little, but no one took any notice.

The old men had built the stairway and the houses themselves, using all kinds of materials found inside the tornado – a considerable achievement, given their advanced years. On the other hand, they'd had an immense amount of time to play with. They had dispensed with architectural folderols of any kind and subordinated form to function, so all the houses looked more or less the same. In old age, I discovered, one no longer sets much store by outward appearances.

'It really is pure heaven, this place,' I was told by Abraham Kra, the man who ran the city's main storage depot. Like many of Tornado City's inhabitants, he had been travelling with a caravan when the whirlwind overtook him. (I had at first assumed that most of the inmates were victims of tornado stops, but it transpired that I was the only one.)

The storage depot consisted of a longish row of houses situated in

356

the central section of the staircase. It was chock-full of everything imaginable – foodstuffs, tools, shoes, clothes, bath mats, brooms, household goods – and functioned as a kind of department store whose wares were arranged in accordance with some system known only to Abraham.

'All right, so we're a bit unsteadier on our pins than we used to be and our eyesight isn't what it was, but there isn't much to see here anyway.' To Abraham, every cloud had a silver lining.

'So there are compensations,' he went on. 'The best of it is, we don't have to worry about a thing. We don't have to work either, if we don't want to. It's the perfect form of retirement. The tornado supplies us with all we need – more than we need, in fact. People leave the craziest things at tornado stops. Look: white whale caviar, nightingales' tongues in aspic, unicorn goulash – things you only find in gourmet restaurants as a rule. We've got whole farms in here, complete with ducks and chickens, pigs and milch cows.

'Not even the freshest food goes bad because nothing in here grows older. Of course, that only applies to the things that fly in through the hole in the top of the tornado and don't pass through the wall. Here, this cask of milk sailed in two years ago – still tastes as fresh as if it had come straight from the udder.

'People outside believe the tornado is a god, or something of the kind. They often bring their offerings from far away, and have done for hundreds of years. Even kings must have been among them, to judge by the gold and jewellery that comes sailing in here from time to time.

'When the tornado sucks something up, we simply retire into our houses and wait for the shower of goodies to abate. You have to be really careful, though. Last year two of us were nearly killed by a camedary. I myself got a trombone on the head – could only see in black and white for a month afterwards.

'Most of the stuff falls down the shaft, but a few things land on the

357

stairs. We collect what we need. A lot of it is useless, of course. Last year it rained kayak paddles three times in quick succession. I suppose *you* couldn't find a use for a couple of hundred kayak paddles?'

It might be supposed that a person doesn't find it too easy to get used to being eighty years older from one day to the next, but this isn't so. You get used to it very quickly – within three or four days – for the simple reason, no doubt, that there's nothing to be done about it. Being old isn't so bad. It's just that everything becomes a little slower and you act with greater deliberation.

The inhabitants of Tornado City didn't go out much. It was always a bit of a risk, using the stairs, because something could come whirling in at any moment. So we kept our walks to a minimum. The old men spent most of the time in their little houses, pursuing their various hobbies.

I had made friends with Baldwyn Baobab, the first old man to find me on the stairs. I visited his home for a chat at least once a day, and we recounted our life stories.

Baldwyn's story   One day Baldwyn told me how he had ended up in the tornado. 'It was youthful folly, of course. I'd always liked taking risks, but my Reptilian Rescuer idea was by far the biggest risk I ever took.'

I pricked up my ears at the words 'Reptilian Rescuer'.

'I'd heard that, however great a danger you were in, one of those dinosaurs would always rescue you in the nick of time. I'd shot the Wotansgard Falls in a canoe, waded blindly through the Graveyard Marshes of Dull, plunged into the raging waters of the Loch River – and every time I'd been saved at the very last minute by one of those ancient birds.'

358

I thought back on my time with Mac. In those days I'd often wondered how people could get themselves into such dangerous situations.

'I trusted the dinosaurs so implicitly that I became more and more reckless,' Baldwyn went on. 'Things got to the stage where I jumped off Demon Rocks without a parachute.'

The mention of 'Demon Rocks' made me prick up my ears a second time.

'I simply hurled myself into space without a second thought. Only when I'd fallen two thousand feet did it occur to me that visibility was extremely poor that day, and that a heavy drizzle and dense mist were very unfavourable conditions in which to be sighted by a Reptilian Rescuer. After five thousand feet I had my first misgivings. What would happen if none turned up at all?

'At the foot of Demon Rocks lies a glass forest whose crystal treetops are as sharp and pointed as the peaks of the Gloomberg Mountains. But I wouldn't have survived even if there had been a whole warehouseful of mattresses down there, not after falling from such a height.

'I suppressed this disagreeable thought for a while, but after falling another ten thousand feet I was unpleasantly struck once more by the suspicious absence of any pterodactyls. Another thousand feet or so, and I would crash to the ground. I would have welcomed it had the outlines of a flying lizard shown up, if only in the distance, but nothing of the kind occurred.

'While falling the last five hundred feet I realized that it had probably been unprofessional of me to jump in such poor visibility. There wasn't even a bird to be seen, a potential sign that my decision to jump without a parachute had not been based on mature consideration. On the other hand, a parachute wouldn't have done me much good. The treetops would have skewered me more slowly, that's all.

'Fifty feet from impact I came to the conclusion that it had *definitely* been a mistake to risk the jump. I fiercely reprimanded myself, condemned my carelessness, and bitterly deplored my blind faith in the Reptilian Rescuers.

'I had indeed been mistaken, that much was clear. Three feet from being spitted on a glass tree trunk the height of a flagpole I had one of my life's most profound revelations: I was an unmitigated idiot. One foot from impact I mentally underlined this realization twice in red pencil.

'Six inches from impact a flying lizard shot out of the dense mist, grabbed me by the scruff of the neck, and carried me back up Demon Rocks, where he gave me a regular tongue-lashing. I'd had plenty of lectures from Reptilian Rescuers in my time, but I'd never felt so ashamed.

'That pterodactyl really knew how to bawl someone out, believe me! The strangest thing of all was, there was a little bear sitting on its back. Not a white one like you, though. Its fur was blue.'

An old friend That clinched it: Baldwyn had been referring to one of my countless missions with Deus X. Machina. I recalled the dense mist, the poor visibility, and Mac's stubborn insistence on waiting till the very last moment. It had been a genuine feat of navigation, flying almost blind in a heavy drizzle. I also recalled the shamefaced young man we'd deposited on the summit of Demon Rocks.

I had helped to save Baldwyn's life.

A tearful, affectionate scene ensued when I told Baldwyn that the little blue bear had been me. Baldwyn wept because he had encountered one of his rescuers. As for me, I wept at this reminder of my happy cubhood, which was now a thing of the past. Finally we wept because we couldn't help it. We pulled ourselves together after a while, and he continued, sniffing:

'Stupidly enough, that incident reinforced my faith in the reliability of Reptilian Rescuers to such an extent that I started taking even bigger gambles. I floated down the Wotansgard Rapids in a barrel and jumped into an erupting volcano from a dirigible balloon. No risk was too great. And all went well every time – one of those pterodactyls always turned up at the last moment.

'Until the day I decided to defy the tornado. So here I am. Not even a bird showed up – not even at the very last moment.'

Well, Mac and I couldn't be everywhere at once.

Depending on their particular interests, the old men had taken up various hobbies of which most were connected with the things the tornado sucked in. One day it swallowed an entire library, and since then a man named Gnothi C. Auton had been busy retrieving books from the sand, arranging them, cataloguing them, and lending them out. Others specialized in collecting velvet cushions, door handles, or sun umbrellas. They were always engaged in swapping things, cadging them off each other, or bartering them. Thus the biggest social event in Tornado City was the day of the regular flea market, when each inhabitant could barter the junk displayed outside his front door.

'Junk' is putting it a bit strong, perhaps, because some of the things on offer were extraordinarily valuable. There were cut diamonds the size of billiard balls, gold jewellery, whole treasure chests filled with silver coins and strings of pearls, ivory mantilla combs, platinum shoehorns, cutlery and flatware of unbreakable glass from the Impic Alps, ashtrays of volcanic crystal, coffers full of tiny gold bars and barrels of paper money, skilfully fashioned rings and bracelets in a wide variety of precious metals, crowns and sceptres,

Tornado treasures

diamond-studded coffee spoons, caskets of rubies and emeralds, and elaborately decorated kitchen utensils made of highly compressed meteorite dust.

All these had been engulfed by the tornado over the years. Once inside it, however, the most valuable articles were worth least, whereas a few intact fresh eggs or a roll of really soft toilet paper were regarded as absolute luxuries. Cash, gold, and diamonds meant nothing in Tornado City.

I started to collect these treasures notwithstanding. From the flea market I amassed vast quantities of antique gold coins, diamond tiaras, noblemen's coronets, magnificent goblets, silver cutlery. I filled my house with stacks of gold bars and stored sacks of pearls beneath my bed. After a few weeks my home resembled a treasure chamber from the Thousand and One Nights. I swathed myself in splendid robes of silk and ermine, wore a caliph's crown for breakfast, and strutted up and down in front of my house draped in sparkling necklaces of precious stones. At every flea market I bargained for treasures of all kinds: bales of Chinese silk, jade vases, platinum goblets, sackfuls of gold, silver buckets filled with uncut diamonds. I couldn't get enough of them.

By now, I could scarcely move in my house. While sleeping I was pricked by the jagged extremities of the royal crowns I'd stacked on my bed for lack of space. I had to pick my way with difficulty through the luxury goods that lay around all over the place, waded through the diamonds and pearls that covered the floor to a depth of several paw's-breadths, and had to clamber over brimming treasure chests just to get from my bed to the table.

In contrast to this superabundance, I was always short of coffee, sugar, porridge oats, and honey-water – all of them simple, everyday things to which I was accustomed, but which I'd largely bartered away for my treasures. I lived on a strict diet consisting mainly of water and the scraps of food I sometimes found on the rubbish dump.

One morning Baldwyn came to breakfast. He was looking worried. Having grown used to his notoriously bad moods, I thought no more of it. I gave him a cup of potato tea (an infusion of roasted potato skins – a brew I'd invented for want of coffee) and a plate of potato skins, likewise roasted. Donning my ermine cape with ruby buttons and my favourite crown, I waded through my treasures to the kitchen table to keep Baldwyn company. 'You're the talk of Tornado City,' he said, having taken a sip of potato tea and, with a look of disgust, replaced the emerald-encrusted gold cup on its saucer.

'Really?' I said. 'What are people saying about me?' My curiosity was aroused – they probably envied me my treasures. Lying on the table were some sacks of gold. They were obscuring my view of Baldwyn, so I pushed them aside.

'I'm surprised you haven't heard them, the din they're making all day long. They're laughing at you, that's what.'

I shook a little gold dust out of my ears – maybe I hadn't heard aright. I'd become the wealthiest inhabitant of Tornado City in no time at all. I owned the Norselander crown jewels, I controlled the whole of Tornado City's gold and platinum reserves. What was so funny about that?

'Take a look at yourself,' Baldwyn said with a hint of compassion in his voice. 'You look like a circus clown with megalomania. Look around you! What do you want with all this loot? You've got sackfuls of diamonds but you can't offer me a decent cup of coffee. You're swimming in gold but living on scraps. You still haven't caught on, have you? You're going to be here in Tornado City till the end of your days. There's no going back! You can't take it anywhere, all this rubbish you've collected, and it's utterly worthless in here. You still haven't come to terms with the fact that you're the tornado's prisoner like the rest of us.'

Baldwyn rose and struggled across the room to the door, ripping his cloak on a gold sabre in the process. That really infuriated him. In the doorway he paused and turned.

'You're a hundred years old, so grow up at last! The sooner you resign yourself to your fate the better. And get rid of all this loot!' So saying, he made his way down the stone stairs to the public tearoom, where everyone was tearing me to shreds.

I see sense at last

I remained seated at the table for a while, blushing under my magnificent crown. Baldwyn was right, but not quite in the way he thought. I was well aware that my treasures were worthless in here. I had accumulated them because I still secretly hoped to extricate myself – and them – from the tornado. This had completely blinded me to my real objective, which was to escape. Well, things were going to change.

I spent the next few weeks getting rid of all my treasures – no easy task, because nobody really wanted to take them on, still less give me anything genuinely useful in exchange. Usually so decrepit, the old men hobbled past my flea-market stall with surprising agility, so I resorted to a trick: I visited each of the inhabitants in turn and took the opportunity to shower them with sumptuous gifts. In Tornado City, as in every sensible society, to refuse a gift was considered an insult.

I would drop in for coffee and leave a sack of diamonds behind, or pay someone a brief visit and happen to have a casket of gold bangles with me, or come for a game of chess and drape my host in dozens of pearl necklaces. This not only divested me of all my useless ballast but enabled me once more to enjoy what the tornado had to offer in the way of really important things like coffee, bread, and tobacco, for it was customary for a host to repay one gift with another.

Having jettisoned all my ballast, I concentrated on escaping.

I searched the tornado daily for potential escape routes. I combed it for cracks and fissures big enough to squeeze through – I even sniffed the air in quest of a dimensional hiatus.

No matter how much longer I lived inside the tornado, I simply wasn't born to remain in the same place for evermore (even if that place itself covered vast distances!). I wanted another sight of the sea and sky, yearned to breathe fresh air again and gaze across miles of open countryside. If there was a way into the tornado there must also be a way out. That was a lesson I'd learned in the maze of tunnels in the Gloomberg Mountains.

I crawled into every corner of Tornado City in search of loopholes, emergency exits, secret trapdoors. I sounded every wall with my knuckles, burrowed into the rubbish dump like a mole, and mentally reviewed the most adventurous methods of escape – for instance in a home-made balloon, with the aid of a parachute made from underpants sewn together, or in a do-it-yourself helicopter with kayak paddles for rotor blades.

But the tornado seemed as escape-proof as a maximum security prison. Nobody knew what would happen if you burrowed through the tornado's walls. You probably aged still more, so the risk was simply too great. As for escaping by air, this was rendered far too dangerous by the heavy objects that were forever sailing in through the top of the funnel.

I proceeded to pump the old men. It transpired as time went by that nearly all of them had flirted with an escape plan of some kind. They told me of tunnels that had filled up with detritus in a flash, of flying machines that had crashed, of daring dreams and shattered hopes. In the end, I was forced to acknowledge that all my escape plans had already been tried and found wanting. There was only one way out of the tornado: straight through the wall, and that route no one had ever ventured to take.

'No, wait,' said Baldwyn. 'One person did.'

'You mean he made a genuine attempt to escape?' I said eagerly. 'Who was it?'

'Phonzotar Huxo, who owns the post office.'

I knew the dilapidated building at the foot of the staircase. The sign outside said 'POST OFFICE', but I'd always assumed it to be a joke the tornado-dwellers played on themselves. What good was a post office in the middle of a tornado?

'Does someone really live there?'

'He seldom ventures outside his door. Pay him a visit. Phonzotar always welcomes a bit of company.' Baldwyn turned his head aside, so I couldn't tell whether the noise he made was a cough or a smothered laugh.

I paid a visit to the post office the very next day. The interior of the building was dark and untidy. The walls were lined with tall shelves full of dusty, empty bottles, and there were big stacks of faded message forms in the corners. Phonzotar Huxo was seated at a desk piled high with papers, scribbling away in the gloom.

Phonzotar Huxo

'Excuse me,' I said cautiously. 'Is this the main post office?'

'No, it's the bakery!' the old man snapped without looking up. He continued to scribble away, then picked up the message form and inserted it in a bottle.

'I'm sorry...I simply wanted to know how the postal system works here. It must be a complicated business...'

I had evidently struck the right note, because his manner became somewhat less brusque.

'It's quite simple,' he croaked. 'You insert your messages-in-a-bottle in the wall of the tornado and they're forwarded. Incoming mail falls into the top of the tornado. You only have to gather it up.'

'You mean you *do* receive incoming mail?'

'Not so far, but it should be here any minute.'

'Er...How long have you been waiting for it?'

Phonzotar scratched his head. He might have been gazing out across a wide expanse, trying to discern something on the horizon.

'Er...Two hundred years? Three hundred? What's the date today?'

I tried another tack. 'I've been told you tried to leave the tornado once upon a time.'

'It wasn't me, it's so long ago. It was someone else.'

'But you did try?'

'Yes.'

'How?'

Phonzotar looked at me for the first time. He didn't make a demented impression. On the contrary, he looked like a wise old man who knows all the secrets of the universe.

'You want to know, eh? You're new here, I suppose. Can't come to terms with the idea of dying in here, no matter how far in the future? That's it, isn't it?'

I nodded.

'Then I'll tell you something, youngster. Listen carefully, because I'll only tell you once. There's only one way out of the tornado, and that's straight through the wall, as I'm sure you've discovered for yourself.'

I nodded again, too excited to interrupt him.

'I come from a long line of adventurers. According to our family annals, my forefathers first arrived in Zamonia paddling tree trunks. Curiosity alone impelled them to cross the ocean. They did so without any navigational aids, with nothing between them and Davy Jones's locker but a few logs. That's what I call courage, my lad.'

I mumbled some appreciative noises.

'Some of it rubbed off on me. I've never shirked risks, no matter how great they were and how slender my chances of survival. Have you ever sat on a palm leaf and tobogganed down a frozen waterfall a mile high?'

I was forced to admit that I'd not yet had that pleasure.

'That's the sort of thing I mean. When I think of the dangers I've defied! I could tell you a tale or two, youngster...'

I hoped he wouldn't go off at a tangent.

'That's the reason I'm in the tornado now,' he went on. 'And that's why I risked trying to burrow my way out through the wall.'

Yes, yes!

'But I only managed to stick my head in the wall. It felt as if a shaft of lightning had gone in through one ear and out the other.' A look of horror came over Phonzotar's face.

Horrific visions

'Armies of dead men went marching through my head. I heard a noise like a cosmic scream. My brain turned to ice. Then the ice cracked in all directions and disintegrated into tiny particles like snowflakes, and each snowflake was afflicted by a pain of its very own. In the end, everything went black. I found myself looking out into the universe. Seated on a diminutive planet made of glass was a red dwarf who had twelve important messages for me.'

Phonzotar's face brightened.

'I extracted my head from the sand. The next day I opened this post office.'

He proceeded to scribble on another message form. The old man's attempt to escape from the tornado had obviously driven him insane. I thought it appropriate to withdraw.

Just as I was leaving the gloomy room, Phonzotar called me back.

'Hey, take these and stick them in the tornado wall. Express post, very urgent. Well, go on!'

An important message

The old man handed me three bottles. I took them for courtesy's sake and went outside, then drew several deep breaths. The possibility of leaving the tornado by way of the wall could be struck off my list.

I couldn't restrain my eagerness to read what Phonzotar had written. I uncorked one of the bottles and removed the message. It read:

369

1 Honour the muggroom.

2 Thou shalt not address a white cockerel by name.

3 Thou shalt eat no wood.

3 If thou seest two sticks lying one on top of the other, thou shalt walk backwards over them with thy left foot first, not forwards with thy right. Moreover, thou shalt not devour them.

5 Should a vulture's shadow fall across a fire that has gone out, thou shalt rekindle it three times or a great misfortune will ensue.

6 If thou cross the path of a white cockerel seated on two superimposed sticks, thou shalt not strike it, nor shalt thou address it by name nor partake of the said sticks.

7 Thou shalt bear a name unlike any other in the entire universe. On encountering one of thy brethren thou shalt address him by his full name without a single slip of the tongue.

8 Should a vulture's shadow fall across a white cockerel seated on two charred sticks in the ashes of a dead fire, thou art in a deplorable predicament. Notwithstanding this, thou shalt neither lose courage nor address the cockerel by name, nor devour the sticks, nor strike the vulture, nor greet thy brother in an inadequate fashion.

9 Thou shalt not finkle backwards.

10 Thou shalt not finkle forwards.

11 Thou shalt not sleep on a dune that drifts in the direction of noon. Should it drift towards evening, thy time has come.

12 Thou shalt betake thyself to the city named Anagrom Ataf and, when thou hast found it, trap it and make it thy home for evermore.

I went all weak at the knees. I had to sit down on one of the stairs before I took in what I was holding in my hands. I opened the second bottle and read what was on the slip of paper.

1 Honour the muggroom.

2 Thou shalt not address a white cockerel by name.

3 Thou shalt eat no wood.

3 If thou seest two sticks lying one on top of the other, thou shalt walk backwards over them with thy left foot first . . .

The third bottle contained the same message. I felt sick. Two old men walked past and saw me sitting there with the bottles beside me. 'Well, anything important?' one of them inquired jocularly.

The other tapped his head. 'He's been sending these important messages for . . . let me think . . . two hundred years? Three hundred? What's the date today?'

And they walked on, laughing to themselves.

'Thou shalt not finkle backwards!' chortled one.

'Thou shalt not finkle forwards!' said the other. They had to prop each other up to prevent themselves from tumbling down the stairs.

So the Muggs had been traipsing through the desert for centuries because of that demented old man. It was on his account that I'd trapped a Fata Morgana, on his account that we'd put the fear of God into the Fatoms. Strictly speaking, it was his fault that I was imprisoned in this tornado, for if the Muggs hadn't obeyed his message-in-a-bottle we should never have found Anagrom Ataf and I should never have ended up in Tornado City.

I was absolutely shattered. Old Phonzotar had not only got me into the tornado; he had robbed me of any hopes of being able to leave it again. I hurled the bottles down the shaft to join the rest of the rubbish at its foot.

I resolved to turn over a new leaf entirely. It was futile to dream of escaping from the tornado; no route to freedom existed. I would have to resign myself to my fate like all the rest.

I knew that most of them consoled themselves against their imprisonment by engaging in some form of activity, either a definite occupation like tidying the central storage depot or a hobby – collecting things, mainly. One had a large collection of roof tiles and others hoarded chair legs or coffee beans, each according to his particular interest. I spent a long time debating what to collect. Chastened by my humiliating experience with the treasures I'd amassed, I opted for something that possessed intrinsic rather than financial value and was of general interest.

The chronicler of Tornado City
I collected stories. It was my intention to become the chronicler of Tornado City and record the biographies of all its inhabitants. I went to the storage depot, where I procured a thick block of paper, several pencils, and an eraser.

Then I proceeded to question the old men about their life stories.

I was greeted with suspicion at first. None of them was willing to speak freely because it seemed they all had something to hide. In the end, however, they started to enjoy themselves. They felt flattered to be taken seriously, eagerly dredged their memories for forgotten incidents, and became thoroughly communicative.

Where most of the old men were concerned, a blot on their past emerged: all of them had lied about the true reason for their presence in Tornado City. The vast majority began by repeating the story of the caravan overtaken by the whirlwind, but eventually, in response to my probing, most of them came clean. The real reason why they had ended up in the tornado was identical in almost every case: prompted by youthful exuberance or a spirit of adventure, they had obediently waited at a tornado stop until they were whirled away. And one of the reasons for this natural stupidity was that all the inhabitants of Tornado City (except me) were human beings.

From the
'Encyclopedia of Marvels, Life Forms
and Other Phenomena of Zamonia and its Environs'
by Professor Abdullah Nightingale

Human Being, The. A life form belonging to the mammalian family and endowed with speech, this is an erect, ten-fingered creature of moderate intelligence (only one brain). The human being has two arms, two legs, and one head. It does not, however, possess any magical, Nocturnomathic or telepathic faculties, which in Zamonia puts it beyond the pale.

In consequence of the Zamonian war of succession, all human beings were banished from →*Atlantis*. Elsewhere in Zamonia they are found only in small groups and village communities or as lone individuals. The rest have retreated to other continents such as Africa, Australia, or Yhōll.

The few human beings who still lived in Zamonia were hard-bitten adventurers, because it required nerves of steel to live on a continent inhabited for the most part by hobgoblins, trolls, yetis, Wolperting Whelps, and evil spirits of various kinds.

And it was this willingness to take a risk that had brought most of them to Tornado City.

Their true stories were considerably more interesting and bristled with adventures. These decrepit old men had once been the biggest daredevils in Zamonia. The tales they told were filled with hair-raising deeds of daring. I would gladly pass them on for the reader's benefit, but they would make a book on their own. I shall therefore confine myself, so as to convey at least some idea of them, to the three that impressed me most.

1 Yson Bor, the man Death rejected.

One day, Yson Bor decided that he wanted to die. He wasn't suicidal, ill, or in any kind of trouble – on the contrary, he was thoroughly optimistic by nature, young, fit, and full of plans for the future. It was simply that he considered dying the most unpleasant aspect of human existence and wanted to put it behind him as soon as possible, so that he could get on with his life without always being confronted by the prospect of death. He was convinced that, once having died, he would somehow contrive to find his way back to the land of the living.

Yson lived in one of the villages in the Muchwater Marshes, so it seemed logical to pick a quarrel with the Peat Witches that inhabited them, whose songs caused people to lose their way and die a painful death by drowning in the waters of the morass. Yson allowed himself to be bewitched by their singing, marched into the swamp, and duly sank below the surface.

But he didn't drown.

Hard as he tried and eagerly as he drew the brackish water into his lungs, he simply couldn't drown. His lungs breathed the water like fresh sea air. The Peat Witches, who were beside themselves with rage, pelted him with clods of earth and chased him back to his village.

Next, Yson tried to burn himself to death. He had heard of the Hellfires of Midgard, great pools of liquid fire that bubbled up from the bowels of the earth, hot enough to melt rocks and ingots of iron. Unhesitatingly, he hurled himself into the biggest of those pools of fire.

But he didn't burn to death.

On the contrary, he found the fire freezing cold and shivered like someone in an icy bath. Instead of sustaining fatal burns he caught a bad cold.

Having recovered from his cold, Yson went to Baysville, where the biggest millstones in Zamonia ground the wheat from Harvest Home Plain into flour. Each of these stones was as big as a medium-sized village, and each time it turned it pulverized the grain from five whole fields. Yson lay down beneath one, hoping to be crushed to death.

But the millstone didn't crush him.

Instead, it broke into a thousand pieces and buried him. But not even that could kill Yson. He crawled out of the debris a few minutes later, whereupon the angry local farmers drove him out of town.

His other attempts to kill himself, though quite comparable with Baldwyn's suicidal exploits, were equally unsuccessful.

No Reptilian Rescuers came to Yson's assistance – in his case they were superfluous. He merely discovered, on numerous occasions and in a wide variety of ways, that he was invulnerable. But he didn't give up hope. He persisted in trying to kill himself by the most multifarious means.

But he didn't die.

One day there came a knock at Yson's door. He opened it to find Death standing outside. 'Listen to me, Yson,' said Death. 'You can tie yourself in knots for all I care, but *I* still decide when someone dies. I've nothing against you personally, and it's all the same to me if you'd sooner die today than in fifty years' time. But if I turn a blind eye once, *everyone* will want the same privilege, and I might as well hang up my scythe. Just remember this: I'll always be where you're least expecting me, never where you're looking for me – so give up!'

But Yson didn't give up, not even on Death's personal recommendation. He passed through sandstorms and showers of meteorites unscathed, scaled the highest peaks, defied the thunderbolts of a Gloomberg Tempest, and jumped off Demon Rocks no less than three times.

But still he didn't die.

One day there came another knock at his door. A masked man was standing outside. 'Do you want to die?' he asked.

'Oh, yes!' said Yson. 'Can you help me?'

Then the man told him about the Eternal Tornado. No one who tangled with it had ever been seen again.

Yson trudged across the Demerara Desert without any water but didn't die of thirst, was flattened by the Sharach-il-Allah but escaped without a scratch. At long last he was confronted by the Eternal Tornado. Unhesitatingly, he threw himself into the whirlwind, but even that failed to kill him.

'Know what I think?' Yson asked me at this point in his story.

'What?'

'The masked man – that was Death. He sent me into the tornado because he knew it was the place where I would remain alive longer than anywhere else.'

And that was how Yson ended up in Tornado City.

2 Slagoud Morvan Jr., the Bollogg-hunter.

Slagoud Morvan was the least respectful person I have ever met. Compared to him, Knio the Barbaric Hog was a creature of the utmost sensitivity and refinement. Even before he could walk, his father, Slagoud Morvan Sr., made him wrestle with some Ornian Strangleworms – not an educational method I myself would recommend for universal adoption, but one that led him to despise any living creature except himself, be it never so big, strong, dangerous, cunning, poisonous, or good at wrestling.

When the time came, his father asked him what profession he would like to pursue. Slagoud thought it over. He thought it over for a day, two days, a whole week. Slagoud's forte was wrestling, not thinking. He pondered the matter for a month, trying to decide which was the biggest, most fearsome and invincible creature in Zamonia. After a month and two days it came to him: 'I'd like to become a Bollogg-hunter,' he announced.

For the first time, his father began to have doubts, not only about Slagoud's sanity but about the wisdom of using Strangleworms as a teaching aid. But Slagoud was now almost twice as big as his father and a far better wrestler, so he simply said 'An excellent idea, my son' and let him go.

Slagoud travelled throughout Zamonia, defeating the numerous Yetis, Mountain Demons and Strangleworms that barred his path, but not a single Bollogg because he never encountered one. So he settled down at the foot of the Humongous Mountains, which were reputed to be a favourite Bollogg stamping ground. Wait long enough, it was said, and one was sure to come along.

Slagoud waited a year, two years, three years. After ten years had passed he began to wonder whether he ought to change professions. Bollogg-hunting hadn't earned him a penny so far, and he was just debating how to provide for his old age when he suddenly heard a distant commotion:

CRASH!

It was a Bollogg – a belated Bollogg, but still.

CRRASH!

Slagoud went hot and cold by turns. It suddenly occurred to him that he hadn't the faintest notion of how to slay a Bollogg.

CRRRASH!

The Bollogg had almost reached Slagoud's hut. Slagoud was running to and fro, racking his brains as to how he could kill the gigantic creature, when he heard a distant sound.

VROOM!

Another Bollogg⸮

VROOOM!

No. Bolloggs go **CRASH!**

VROOOOM!

It was the Eternal Tornado.
More than that, it was racing towards Slagoud's hut from the opposite direction.

So the tornado and the Bollogg were about to collide exactly over Slagoud's hut. This would have made anyone else run off, screaming, but it gave Slagoud an idea: he would defeat the Bollogg by allowing the tornado to pick him up and whisk him high into the air. Then he could jump off the whirlwind and throttle the giant into submission.

Slagoud sprang boldly into the tornado and was swiftly hoisted into the air. Once up there, however, he discovered that the Bollogg had no head at all and, consequently, no throat he could squeeze. Having come to that final realization, he was sucked into the whirlwind.

And that was how Slagoud came to be inside the tornado.

3 Olsen Olsen of Oslo, the gentleman adventurer.

Olsen of Oslo was the most striking individual in Tornado City. He was the only one without a beard and white hair, and could not have been more than thirty-five. As unlike Slagoud as could be, Olsen of Oslo had the most perfect manners in the tornado. A blue-blooded adventurer whose ancestors came from Northern Europe, he was susceptible to bets of all kinds. He simply couldn't resist a wager, no matter how high the stake or how slender his chances of winning. If someone said, 'I bet a million Atlantean pyras you wouldn't walk through a forest full of sharp-eared werewolves with a bell round your neck,' you could be sure that Olsen would hotfoot it to the nearest bell foundry.

Olsen won every bet he accepted, almost as if Lady Luck had personally selected him to demonstrate her existence. His only problem was, he had so many daredevil wagers running simultaneously, he hardly had time to draw breath.

One night he really did walk through a smallish wood in South Zamonia notorious not only for its omnivorous werewolves but also for their extreme sensitivity to sounds. They had devoured many an innocent wayfarer from the feet upwards, just for disturbing the hush that prevailed in their little wood by inadvertently treading on a rotten branch. Olsen, I need hardly add, had a massive, three-clappered dinner bell suspended from his neck.

When the first four werewolves pounced on him, Olsen tried to take advantage of the occasion to win another wager. He had bet someone (with whom he already had two more wagers outstanding) that he could simultaneously, and in the course of a single night, lift the curse on three werewolves by faultlessly reciting the Dullsgardian Spells backwards.

The moon was full, there were enough werewolves available, and Olsen had wisely taken the precaution of learning the Dullsgardian Spells by heart – backwards, of course. So he recited them aloud in the darkness.

To his amazement, three of the werewolves turned back into what they had been before, namely, a peat-cutter, a troll-hunter, and a journeyman baker. The fourth werewolf had a hearing problem, however, so it didn't resume its original form. It continued to do what werewolves do best: it bared its teeth and flew at Olsen's throat. Just then, Olsen was whisked into the air by a Reptilian Rescuer that had heard his bell clanging on an inspection flight over South Zamonia and waited until the last, dramatic moment.

The Reptilian Rescuer gave Olsen a thorough talking-to and offered to fly him home before he could indulge in any more stupidities. Olsen gratefully accepted. They were overflying the Demerara Desert when he suddenly spotted the Eternal Tornado from above. 'What's that?' he asked the Reptilian Rescuer.

'That's the Eternal Tornado,' he was told, 'the only natural phenomenon whose victims not even we can rescue. It's too dangerous. *I bet you wouldn't dare jump into it yourself.*'

Naturally, Olsen jumped.

And that was how Olsen entered the tornado, the only person to have done so from above and not through the wall – hence his uniquely youthful appearance.

Well, such was the cloth from which Zamonia's last human beings were cut. They weren't all great luminaries, but you certainly couldn't accuse them of lacking guts.

One day the tornado changed its rotational direction.

There was a sudden hush. The roaring and creaking died away. The others merely looked up for a moment and then went on with their daily routine, but I, who was experiencing this phenomenon for the first time, took careful note of what happened. Nothing happened, strictly speaking, until the roaring and creaking began again. Roughly a minute's absolute silence had elapsed in the interim.

Eternal Tornado, The [cont.]. It is assumed that the tornado comes to a complete standstill for the few moments it takes to change its rotational direction [during which the temporal vacuum briefly fills up with time]. This would be the only juncture at which anyone situated inside the tornado [and that, as already mentioned in passing, would mean that he possessed the IQ of a lugworm] could leave it in relative safety. He would have precisely one minute in which to burrow through the tornado wall and make good his escape. During that minute the focal mass of the time inside the tornado's wall changes, flowing backwards at twice the normal speed for sixty seconds. This signifies that, if the wall were penetrated during that period, the ageing process to which those entering the tornado are subjected would be reversed. This is only a hypothesis, however, and has yet to be confirmed by practical experimentation.

This encyclopedia article had scarcely faded from my mind's eye when the tornado got under way again. Another of Nightingale's priceless gems of information! Had he told me a few minutes earlier I could have escaped from the tornado! There would be another chance in a year's time, but how would I know when the year was up? The very thought of Nightingale made me seethe with fury.

From the
'Encyclopedia of Marvels, Life Forms
and Other Phenomena of Zamonia and its Environs'
by Professor Abdullah Nightingale

Zamonian Year, The. The standard Zamonian year is precisely one day shorter than the years on other continents. Time in Zamonia flows somewhat faster because of the greater incidence of dimensional hiatuses, gaining almost exactly twenty-four hours in a full year. This means that a Zamonian year lasts 364 days, or 8736 hours, or 524,160 minutes, or - to be absolutely precise - 31,449,600 seconds.

Aha, so a Zamonian year lasted exactly 31,449,600 seconds – that was intensely interesting! These eternally nonsensical or belated encyclopedia articles were beginning to get on my nerves. I would have given anything to banish them from my head. I now knew how many seconds there were in a year on the Zamonian mainland – seconds which, thanks not least to the encyclopedia, I would never see again.

One moment...

There were precisely 31,449,600 seconds in a Zamonian year.

31,449,600 seconds until the next tornado standstill.

Approximately three minutes had elapsed since the last standstill, or 180 seconds. That made, er...

$$31{,}449{,}600 \text{ seconds}$$
$$- \, 180 \text{ seconds}$$
$$= 31{,}449{,}420 \text{ seconds}$$

From now on I need only count off the seconds backwards to determine the exact time of the next tornado standstill!

31,449,419 . . . 31,449,418 . . . 31,449,417 . . .

The trouble was, I would have to go on counting, not only for a whole year but backwards. That would require immense concentration. I would have to count and think simultaneously.

31,449,395 . . . 31,449,394 . . . 31,449,393 . . .

Was it feasible? After all, I would have to sleep occasionally. No one can sleep and count backwards at the same time, it was an impossibility. Wait, though – I could take it in turns with someone. Baldwyn could take over the counting shift while I slept. He was very dependable as a rule.

31,449,355 . . . 31,449, 354 . . . 31,449,353 . . .

Counting and thinking simultaneously worked, but what about counting and speaking? I tried a little experiment with Fredda's favourite poem:

'Impic Alps, **(31,449,328)** so far away, **(31,449,327)**
'listen to **(31,449,326)** my sad refrain! **(31,449,325)**
'Will there ever **(31,449,324)** come a day **(31,449,323)**
'when I see you **(31,449,322)** all again? **(31,449,321)**.'

There, it went perfectly. I hobbled downstairs to the tearoom and quickly told Baldwyn the sensational news:

'Hello, Bald**(31,449,111)**wyn, I've **(31,449,110)** found a **(31,449,109)** possib**(31,449,108)**ility of **(31,449,107)** escap-**(31,449,106)**ing from **(31,449,105)** the torn**(31,449,104)**ado!'
And so on. I told him about my plan to count backwards. He wasn't too enthusiastic. The thought of counting backwards for half of all the seconds in a year didn't appeal to him.

'It's our **(31,449,056)** one and **(31,449,055)** only chance! **(31,449,054)** Otherwise we'll **(31,449,053)** never know **(31,449,052)** exactly when **(31,449,051)** the right **(31,449,050)** moment **(31,449,049)** comes!'
It was like having numerical hiccups.

Baldwyn reluctantly fell in with my plan.

31,449,023 … 31,449,022 … 31,449,021 …

Drumming up support

Next, I tried to persuade the rest of Tornado City's inhabitants to escape with us. I had no trouble at all with Olsen of Oslo, Slagoud Morvan Jr., Yson Bor and one or two other bold spirits, but the majority presented more of a problem. I found it too tedious to win them over individually (especially as I had to count backwards at the same time), so I convened a general meeting at the assembly hall. There I explained my plan in every detail with the aid of a large blackboard and some coloured chalks borrowed from the central storage depot.

It met with little enthusiasm. The inhabitants of Tornado City had become unaccustomed to changes in their daily routine, adventurous schemes, and, above all, physical exertion. It wasn't easy to do the necessary spadework. My presentation evoked agitated murmurs, and there were even a few cries of 'Balderdash!', 'Youthful impetuosity!', and the like.

'Why should we escape at all? Why escape from Paradise?' was one of the counterarguments. 'We've got all we need. Enough to eat and drink, good books to read, eternal life – or as good as!'

Many of the inhabitants had developed the mentality of long-term prison inmates. They were afraid of freedom, of the world outside, of an unregulated mode of existence.

'Who's to guarantee we'll regain our youth if we go through the tornado wall?' cried someone else. 'We could age still more! We might even die in the attempt!'

A hard argument to refute.

'In here I may have another twenty thousand years ahead of me, probably far more. Outside, fifty at most – *if* your rejuvenation idea works at all. And you call that a good plan?'

I fudged a bit, blathering about free will and a readiness to take risks, fresh air and good eyesight – and tried to remember to count at the same time. All in all, it wasn't a very convincing performance.

'Do you want to end up like Phonzotar Huxo?' called an old man. 'Why, what's wrong with me?' demanded Phonzotar, who had been venturing out into society for some time and was actually present at the meeting. He didn't understand the question.

Many of my audience simply rose and walked out. They were the ones who would never be convinced, not even after a year. The rest, or some three-quarters of the tornado's population, remained seated and were at least prepared to discuss the matter. They included those who hadn't been in the tornado very long, so could hope that their friends and relations were still alive, and those who, even at a ripe old age, had preserved their exceptional spirit of adventure.

15,678,978 . . . 15,678,977 . . . 15,678,976 . . .

Six months went by. In the meantime, a split had developed

between the thirty per cent who were still prepared to escape and the remaining seventy per cent, who had dissociated themselves from us, possibly for fear of becoming infected with our foolhardy stupidity.

We escapers had held regular meetings at the tearoom and made strategic preparations for our exit from the tornado. First came the theoretical part. We ran daily checks on the number of seconds left, drew sketch maps of the tornado, and calculated the strength and height of its walls. We also explored its nether regions for the most favourable jumping-off point. We settled on a spot where the wall seemed comparatively thin and would be about six feet from the ground when the tornado came to a standstill.

13,478,333 . . . 13,478,332 . . . 13,478,331 . . .

Daily workouts We also prepared ourselves physically for our escape attempt throughout the year. All of us were in very poor shape, this being a product not only of old age but of our comfortable way of life inside the tornado, with its ample diet and limited opportunities for exercise. After all, why keep fit when you more or less live for ever? Escaping entailed physical exertion, however, because we would have to burrow through the wall at top speed, jump clear, fall a few feet, land successfully, and sprint off at once before the tornado really got going again. Our bones, muscles and sinews would become rejuvenated during the escape – so we hoped! – but our reflexes had to work as well. Accordingly, we introduced a daily workout ridiculed by the tornado-dwellers who had decided to stay.

We began every day with a session on the stairs, one step down, one step up. Then ten minutes' rest.

9,345,436 . . . 9,345,435 . . . 9,345,434 . . .

Next came fifty press-ups in succession. This, of course, entailed a certain amount of prior training.

8,905,778 ... 8,905,777 ... 8,905,776 ...

Knee-bends for the calf and thigh muscles. A hundred a day.

7,670,886 ... 7,670,885 ... 7,670,884 ...

More step-ups on the stairs followed by half an hour's yoga for purposes of relaxation. Then a round of staircase golf to pass the time.

6,567,113 ... 6,567,112 ... 6,567,111 ...

Chin-ups.

5,654,336 ... 5,654,335 ... 5,654,334 ...

Sit-ups.

4,111,699 ... 4,111,698 ... 4,111,697 ...

Shadow-boxing.

3,458,224 ... 3,458,223 ... 3,458,222 ...

Skipping.

2,444,679 ... 2,444,678 ... 2,444,677 ...

Bending from the waist.

1,343,667 . . . 1,343,666 . . . 1,343,665 . . .

One last session of step-ups on the stairs, then off to bed. And so it went on, day after day, for almost a whole year. We were the fittest centenarians that ever inhabited a perpetual motion tornado.

The great day was drawing near. We spent the last month sharing out our belongings among the rest of the tornado's inmates. I offered my handwritten account of their life stories to Phonzotar.

'No thanks,' he said. 'I'd sooner come with you.'

'Really? After all that happened to you the last time you tried to get through the wall?'

'I've thought it over,' he replied. 'I've lost my wits. Maybe I'll get them back. What have I got to lose?'

86,400 . . . 86,399 . . . 86,398 . . .

The last day came. None of us had slept for two nights. Another two tornado inmates had changed their minds like Phonzotar, and had to be toughened up with the aid of a crash course. The ones who were staying behind threw a touching farewell party complete with home-made cakes and hand-painted banners ('Lots of Luck!', 'Happy Landings!', 'You Suckers!', etc.). Many tearful farewells were exchanged by 'old' friends (the word really meant something in there). Solemn speeches were delivered and old times invoked – in fact I hoped it would all soon be over before a few more of us decided to stay in the tornado for sentimentality's sake. Then we made our way down into the bowels of the tornado.

65,524 . . . 65,523 . . . 65,522 . . .

It was undoubtedly the longest day of my lives to date, even though I was spending it in a place where time didn't exist. As each separate second went by, another drop of sweat trickled down my fur.

12,345 . . . 12,344 . . . 12,343 . . .

Final limbering-up exercises.

1,432 . . . 1,431 . . . 1,430 . . .

All of a sudden, terrible misgivings overcame me. There wasn't a scrap of proof that my plan would really work. I was taking us all to perdition.

233 . . . 232 . . . 231 . . .

Only another four minutes. I could still call the whole thing off.

120 . . . 119 . . . 118 . . .

Two minutes. What if we all ended up like Phonzotar Huxo? A tornado full of demented old men? I decided to abort the operation. Or better not?

60 . . . 59 . . . 58 . . .

Into the last minute. I decided to escape after all.

20 . . . 19 . . . 18 . . .

Call it off.

14 ... 13 ... 12 ...

Escape.

10 ... 9 ...

Call it off.

7 ... 6 ...

Escape.

5 ... 4 ...

Call it off.

3, 2, 1 ... zero!

Okay, let's do it!

The moment of truth The tornado ground to a halt. We had precisely one minute in which to get out of our perambulating prison. Twenty men burrowed into the wall at a time, each group starting at ten-second intervals. Baldwyn and I were in the last batch. Everything went according to plan: after fifty seconds nearly all of us were outside.

Another ten seconds. Baldwyn and I and the others plunged head first into the debris. No unpleasant sensations, no hallucinations. An agreeable, euphoric feeling overcame me as I burrowed through the wall. I could feel my muscles grow taut and the leaden sensation in my legs disappear. I crawled along, thrusting the sand and pebbles vigorously aside and taking care not to get any of the muck in my mouth. My paw broke through, then my head, and I caught my first glimpse of the sky. The desert floor was some nine feet below me. I simply let myself fall, landing rather clumsily on my backside, but got up at once and started to run for it. The rest had already taken to their heels. They sprinted off in all directions, making for the shelter of some rocks.

With a creaking, grinding sound, the tornado got under way again. I couldn't resist the temptation to look back. After all, how often do you get a chance to see a tornado at a standstill? It looked like a rent in the sky, like a mountain rammed summit first into the ground. The creaking sound became a rumble, and a man-sized boulder buried itself in the sand beside me. I turned and sprinted towards a small dune. How supple my limbs were, how strong! I performed a flying somersault over the dune and cowered down behind it.

With a roar, the tornado resumed its progress. More boulders came hurtling over our heads, desert dust whirled around, bewildered scorpions and sand snakes flew through the air.

The tornado stormed off, bellowing like a wild beast, and receded into the distance.

We stood around for a long time, marvelling at our youthful faces, congratulating each other on our appearance, exchanging pats on the back. One of us had brought a little mirror along, and we all competed for a sight of it.

Then we went our separate ways. Yson Bor went in search of death – he'd heard tell of a lake of acid on Paw Island that could even dissolve hardened steel. Slagoud's destination was Harvest Home Plain, because I had told him about my encounter with the Bollogg.

He proposed to wait there until a specimen with a head passed by. Phonzotar Huxo seemed quite lucid. He was not only rejuvenated but right in the head again. What puzzled me most, however, was the baby in his arms.

'This is Olsen of Oslo,' he said, rocking the infant as he spoke. 'We forgot he was the only one to preserve his youth after entering the tornado. Passing through the wall has made him even younger.'

Having spent a while debating who should look after the baby, we eventually entrusted it to Phonzotar, who was mad about the idea. So Olsen's life began again from scratch.

Baldwyn was very keen to visit Baysville, the home of a girl he'd always wanted to kiss.

As for me, I was the only one who wanted to go to Atlantis because human beings weren't welcome there. Baldwyn drew me a little map showing the quickest way to get there. Atlantis was normally accessible only by sea or air because the city stood on a peninsula cut off by the impassable Humongous Mountains, but Baldwyn knew of a short cut. It was probably the most unusual short cut in Zamonia – or rather, if there had been a hit parade for unusual short cuts, Baldwyn's would definitely have topped the charts.

After a three-day trek on foot across the Demerara Desert I reached its outlying dunes. I turned for a last look at the sea of brown sugar and thought back on the life I'd spent there. Having silently wished the Muggs, the Fatoms, the tornado-dwellers and the ex-tornado-dwellers all the luck in the world, I climbed the final slope.

On reaching the crest I was confronted by what was probably the most astounding view in Zamonia. Two or three miles away loomed a mountain range composed of blue-black pyrite crystal. It was totally unsuitable for climbing. The mountainsides were so smooth that one would have needed suction cups to scale them, and the edges were sharp enough to bisect an elephant. But the most astonishing feature was something else: running through the centre of the range was an immense cleft, and in that cleft reposed a head.

A head some twenty miles in diameter.

11.

My Life
in the
Bollogg's Head

Baldwyn Baobab had explained it all.

'It's a Bollogg's head,' he told me. 'Bolloggs are –'

'I know what a Bollogg is.'

'Then perhaps you also know they sometimes discard their heads. Legend has it that this one removed his head thousands of years ago. Then he went off hunting.'

'Hunting? For what?'

'For his head, of course. Bolloggs aren't particularly bright, you know.'

'I'm aware of that.'

'Anyway, this one's head is still lying there, blocking the route to Atlantis.'

'I could climb over it.'

'Thousands of Bollogg fleas live in the parting. Do you know what Bollogg fleas are?'

From the
'Encyclopedia of Marvels, Life Forms
and Other Phenomena of Zamonia and its Environs'
by Professor Abdullah Nightingale

Bollogg Fleas. Of all the large bloodsucking insects in Zamonia, Bollogg Fleas must undoubtedly be the biggest. They can attain a height of eighteen feet and weigh three-quarters of a ton. Bollogg Fleas have a wingless, lopsided body and powerful legs that are admirably suited for jumping. Sprouting from the head are two long antennae for examining prey by touch, and beneath them are a pair of sawlike mandibles and the proboscis with which Bollogg Fleas immobilize their victims and suck them dry. Their favourite habitat is the dense hair on discarded Bollogg heads. They feed mainly on smaller mountain creatures and unsuspecting mountaineers.

'I know what Bollogg fleas are.'

'Good,' said Baldwyn, 'but there's another route.'

'Which is?'

'Very few people have ever dared to try it, and nobody knows if even one of them got through.'

'What route is that?'

'It's the route *through the head*. You go in one ear and out the other – but only, of course, if you manage to reach the first ear without the fleas devouring you. However, it's said that very few of them live in the tips of the hair. The majority lurk in the parting, feeding on golden eagles and pyrite vultures. At least, that used to be the story. It's all so long ago.'

'You mean there's a way through the Bollogg's brain?'

'So it's said. I had a cousin whose godfather had a grandfather who was reputed to know someone whose sister on his mother's side had a boyfriend who tried it.'

'Well? What happened to him?'

'No one knows. Perhaps he went to ground in Atlantis.'

I didn't deliberate for long. 'I'm an expert on labyrinths,' I said. 'I'll try it.'

Baldwyn gave me a lingering stare. 'There's only one problem...'

'Which is?'

He lowered his voice and whispered in my ear:

'They say the head's completely insane...'

From the
'Encyclopedia of Marvels, Life Forms and Other Phenomena of Zamonia and its Environs' by Professor Abdullah Nightingale

Bollogg's Head, The. Several Zamonian legends all state that, in early times, the continent was inhabited by Bolloggs far bigger than the ones surviving today. The most tangible clue to the existence of these prehistoric Megabolloggs is the so-called Bollogg's Head in the Humongous Mountains in eastern Zamonia. It is surmised that one of these huge, primeval Bolloggs deposited his head in the mountain range's deepest gorge and then set off to look for it. The Bollogg's Head is approximately fifteen miles high and about the same distance across. It consists for the most part of dense, matted hair which continues to grow some sixty feet a year. The hair is inhabited by numerous small insects, chamois and nesting birds, as well as by the dreaded →*Bollogg Fleas.*

The interior of the skull is estimated to contain a brain with a volume of roughly fifteen cubic miles, but size and weight are no indication of a creature's intelligence. An elephant's brain weighs on average twelve pounds, whereas that of a Nocturnomath tips the scales at half a pound. It might even be contended that a creature's intelligence decreases in inverse relation to the size of its thinking apparatus. The bigger the brain, the more widely separated its various lobes and the poorer their lines of communication. Better than a large brain, therefore, are several well-connected smaller ones. It is further surmised that the Bollogg's Head is not dead but asleep, because it allegedly emits periodic snores and mutters unintelligibly from time to time.

My ascent to the ear was disagreeable rather than genuinely difficult. If every mountain were hairy, mountaineering would be child's play. There were handholds everywhere. The hairs were not only as strong as ship's ropes but matted, tangled and knotted in a way that presented plenty of aids to climbing. What I found most unpleasant of all was the smell of the matted tufts, which had been proliferating unwashed for thousands of years, the feel of the gooey sebacious matter, and the very peculiar sensation aroused by scaling a gigantic head.

A living mountain

The one thing I had to beware of was dandruff. Flakes of Bollogg scurf are as big as soup plates, weigh a couple of pounds apiece, and can, if dislodged, sweep you away like an avalanche.

They covered the head in layers like roof tiles, and one tug at the wrong hair could set hundreds of them in motion. Two such avalanches of dandruff descended on me. I escaped the first by taking refuge beneath a greasy, matted strand of hair, the second missed me by only a few feet. But I made good progress. The weather was superb: not a breath of wind and no rain in prospect. Within an hour I had covered two-thirds of the distance and was taking a breather on a tuft of hopelessly knotted Bollogg hair.

After a brief rest I resumed the ascent with renewed vigour. The Bollogg's earlobe, an immense, fleshy overhang, was dangling less than a hundred feet above me. I skirted around it on the right so as to be able to climb straight into the auricle. Sprouting from the ear within arm's reach of me was a long hair – a distasteful sight, admittedly, but a perfect means of swinging myself straight into the cavity.

Except that the hair began to move.

Instead of swinging straight into the ear, I was swung to and fro on the end of the hair. What with a sheer drop of several miles beneath me and no kind of handhold but a slippery growth, I could not have held out for long. But then – as if the hair had changed its mind – it hoisted me over the rampart of flesh and into the shell of the ear.

The thing I'd been holding wasn't a hair: it was the antenna of an outsize Bollogg Flea. I let go at once and landed with a thud, not that this did much to improve my situation. The huge creature was standing between me and the entrance to the ear, rubbing its forefeet together like a someone sharpening a carving knife.

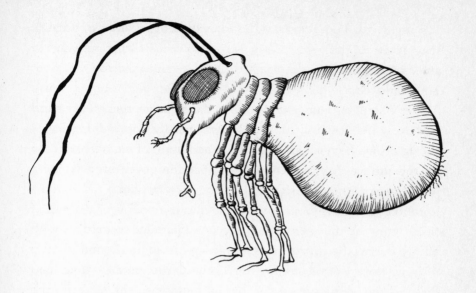

I had absolutely no time to panic; I had to act at once. I took a step to the left. The flea followed the movement with its massive body, but I promptly swung right and slipped between its legs. The flea was too bulky to react in time, which enabled me to sprint into the interior of the ear.

Ponderously, the huge insect turned and took up the pursuit with long, powerful strides. A few yards ahead of me was a large pool full of what I took to be rainwater. It was dark brown and looked extremely uninviting, but I had no reason to be fastidious. I boldly dived head first into the murky brew, hoping that Bollogg Fleas couldn't swim.

The earwax pool

Whether or not this was a mistake was hard to judge. It seemed to be a wise move where the Bollogg Flea was concerned, because it remained rooted to the spot on the edge of the pool and did not attempt to dive in after me. On the contrary, it made a peculiar movement resembling a sympathetic shake of the head, then turned and walked outside again.

It wasn't such a wise decision from my own point of view, because the putative rainwater turned out to be Bollogg earwax, a substance quite as potentially lethal as a morass or a bed of quicksand.

The evil-smelling sludge encompassed me like a huge, greasy hand and drew me down. I thrashed around wildly with my forelegs – not a very well-considered course of action, but at least it kept me on the surface. My desperate doggy-paddling even brought me a little closer to the opposite bank of the earwax pool.

Sprouting from the bank and trailing into the pool was a clump of black hairs the thickness of a finger. As I paddled towards it with all my might, the earwax closed over my head and found its way into my nose, eyes and ears, rendering me temporarily blind and deaf. I even swallowed a substantial helping of the sludge – the most disgusting sensation I ever experienced.

In my horror and disgust I forgot to paddle and sank still deeper into the soft, warm ooze. All that now protruded from the pool was one of my paws, which groped for the clump of hairs. My final movement was less of a grab than a farewell wave. I was utterly exhausted.

Someone or something – it was hard to tell which in such a pre-dicament – grasped my paw. At least it didn't feel like a flea's antenna or anything else of an insectlike nature, so I clung to it and allowed myself to be hauled to the surface. I hung on tight and lashed out with my hind legs until they encountered terra firma. Then I crawled out of the pool on all fours and wiped the earwax from my eyes to see who had saved my life. A transparent, pulsating blob of light, it made – even at first sight – a strangely despondent impression.

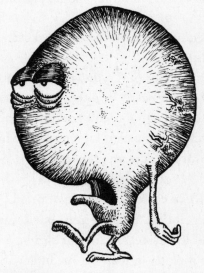

'My name is 1600H,' it said. 'I'm an idea.'

'Delighted to meet you,' I replied. 'My name is Bluebear, and I'm a bluebear.'

We stood there rather awkwardly for a while, at a loss to know what to say next. For want of a better idea, I started to wring the earwax out of my fur.

'You were lucky I happened to be nearby,' the idea said. 'Many people have drowned in that pool. Bollogg earwax is treacherous stuff.'

'You can say that again. Many thanks, you saved my life. I owe you one.'

'Don't mention it. I'm glad to have been of service for once. I'm not much use as a rule.'

'How do you mean?'

'Well, I'm an idea, but a bad one. Everyone began by making a tremendous fuss of me, but they eventually discovered that I wasn't a good idea. When that happens, people simply drop you. There are masses of us roaming the passages in this brain. We're the dregs of the cerebral community. Could *you* find a use for a bad idea?'

'I'm not sure. All I'd like to know is the quickest way through the head and out the other side.'

'You don't need an idea for that, you've already got one: *"Through the head and out the other side."* Whether or not it's a good idea I couldn't say. It's diabolically difficult and dangerous, getting from one side of the brain to the other. Do you know how many miles of cerebral convolutions there are in here?'

'No.'

'Neither do I, but there must be millions of them.'

That was an exaggeration, I suspected, but I was beginning to realize that the whole business wasn't as simple as I'd thought.

'What you need is a plan – a plan of this brain, so you don't lose your way. A plan made by a planmaker, I mean. Do you follow me?'

'No.'

'The plans in this brain are made by planmakers. They're good craftsman but very fussy. If you need a shoe you go to a shoemaker. If you need a plan you go to a planmaker. I know one who lives quite near here. Like me to take you to him?'

Ideas, so 1600H told me, took their names from the hour, minute and second at which they occurred to someone. Most such names were much longer, for instance 2346H/46M/12S or 1321H/32M/55S, and so on, but 1600H really had originated on the stroke of 4 p.m.

'The trouble is, lots of us have the same name. After all, new ideas crop up almost every second of every day. I know fifty other ideas named 1600H, and guess what? They're all equally bad. Four p.m. doesn't seem a particularly favourable time for good ideas...'

Entering a head by way of an ear gives one a vaguely burglarious sensation. I have to admit that I felt rather guilty and uneasy, somehow, like an uninvited guest sneaking in by the back door.

In the auditory canal

Little daylight penetrated the passage at our backs. 1600H shuffled on ahead of me, wearily pointing out items of interest from time to time like a tourist guide who has seen them all far too often before. ('Look up, and you will now see the massive temporal bone.')

I had to be careful not to lose my footing on the precipitous slope, which was slippery with earwax. Before long our path was barred by a wall resembling an expanse of parchment.

'That's the eardrum,' 1600H explained. 'I know a hole we can get through.'

The tympanic membrane of the Bollogg's ear was, in fact, as riddled with holes as a Swiss cheese, but most of the apertures were no bigger than a fist. 1600H led me over to one the size of a football.

'The eardrum is very elastic,' he told me. 'We must simply squeeze through.'

Ideas were very elastic too, it seemed, because 1600H slipped through the aperture just like that, whereas I managed to negotiate it only with his active assistance and by pulling in my stomach hard. We now found ourselves in a large cavern. Something appeared to be moving on the roof, high overhead, but the ambient lighting was now so poor that I couldn't make out what it was.

'Those are the hammer, anvil, and stirrup of the ear,' said 1600H. 'Don't ask me why they're called that, but they're said to play an important part in hearing.'

On reaching the other side of the cavern we had to squeeze through another perforated membrane ('We're now climbing through the cochlear or "snail" window, as it's called') and then climb a kind of staircase ('We're now ascending the majestic cochlear spiral').

There was no light at all now, discounting the meagre phosphorescence given off by 1600H's body (doubtless the faint afterglow of an abandoned idea). In labyrinthine surroundings once more, I wondered how I could have been stupid enough to land myself back in a situation so alarmingly reminiscent of my experience with the Troglotroll.

The passage ahead of us seemed to spiral inwards like a snail shell, becoming steadily narrower. We were now crawling along on our hands and knees.

'Not much further,' said 1600H, doing little to reassure me.

He crawled into an even narrower tunnel that branched off the main passage. Its walls were lined with slimy cables of many different colours.

'Those are nerve fibres. This is the auditory nerve canal. We've now reached the innermost part of the ear.' The Troglotroll had uttered optimistic remarks of a similar nature.

The passage terminated in a small aperture rendered visible by the faint light beyond. 1600H slipped through it with practised ease.

'Come on!' he called from the other side. I squeezed through the hole with a considerable effort.

We were now in yet another passage, a big tunnel along whose walls minute specks of light were racing like demented sparklers. The sparks seemed to have voices, faint but clearly audible little voices that whispered or muttered, murmured or giggled as they sped past us. They varied in size and colour, some being white and others red or green. They came from all directions, from behind and ahead, above and below, making me feel as if I were in the middle of a miniature firework display. Sometimes two sparks collided, combined to produce a dazzling flash, and raced on into the darkness, chattering together. I paused to stare in amazement, turning my head this way and that like a spectator at a tennis match.

1600H answered my unspoken question. 'They're thoughts,' he said. 'We're now inside the Bollogg's brain.'

From the
'Encyclopedia of Marvels, Life Forms
and Other Phenomena of Zamonia and its Environs'
by Professor Abdullah Nightingale

Bollogg Thoughts. Strictly speaking, these are any ideas promoted by means of cerebral activity from a →*Bollogg*'s realm of perception and sensation to that of the conceptual, judgemental, and inferential. In a wider sense, however, they are ideas relating to matters not directly perceived by a Bollogg or possibly inaccessible to its senses; in other words, ideas conjured up not only by the power of memory but also by the Bollogg's imaginative faculty.

As usual, the encyclopedia's explanation had turned up too late, at the wrong moment, and couched in insufficiently comprehensible language.

To put it rather more simply: a thought is intermediate between a feeling and a spoken sentence. This is much the same in Bolloggs as in other creatures capable of thought.

I felt I ought to comment on this, but nothing occurred to me.

Precisely. That is another very good definition of thought.

I sometimes had the peculiar feeling that Professor Nightingale was calling me on the telephone, as it were, and that it wasn't the encyclopedia inside me speaking at all.

Bollogg Brain, The. The Bollogg's immense cerebrum consists of two parts or so-called hemispheres traversed by deep furrows [sulci] and subdivided by a principal fissure [sulcus maximus]. The cerebrum is assumed to be the seat of consciousness, memory, and volition. Also based there are fear, humour, hunger, and – depending on the character of the subject – modesty or megalomania. The cerebellum of a discarded Bollogg head is uninteresting because it controls the tactile sense and muscular coordination, both of which help to facilitate physical movement, and these, since the discarded head no longer possesses a body, are completely redundant.

1600H pointed to the specks of light flitting along the wall of the tunnel.

'There are a lot of different ideas in here, you can tell them apart by their colours. The red ones are commonplace, everyday ideas – those are in the majority. The yellow ones are worries, of which there are also plenty. The blue are questions the brain keeps asking, and the green are answers. If a blue question collides with a wrong green answer, absolutely nothing happens.'

410

Just then a green flash collided with a blue one, setting off a few sparks. They circled each other in a puzzled kind of way before whizzing off again.

'You see? If the blue question bumped into the correct green answer, they'd merge and become a solution. See that big orange flash there? That's a solution.'

In fact, several of these orange flashes were racing along the wall of the tunnel. 1600H drove his fist into his palm.

'If two solutions collide they produce an idea – a good one or a bad one, whichever. I'm a bad one.' He sighed. 'Here comes a good one.'

A glowing blob of light rounded the bend a few feet behind us. At *A good idea* least twice the size of 1600H, it was lit up from within like a Christmas tree and hummed like an electricity pylon as it strode majestically past us.

'Hello, 1600H,' it said in a condescending tone.

'Hello, 2100H/36M/14S,' 1600H replied humbly.

'How does a Bollogg manage to have a good idea?' I asked. 'I thought Bolloggs were mentally rather ill-equipped.'

We were walking side by side along the tunnel, which seemed to meander on for ever. At brief intervals, numerous neuron paths branched off it to left and right. Meanwhile, we were surrounded by a continuous, multicoloured stream of racing thoughts, questions, answers, and solutions.

'They don't become stupid until they remove their heads. The heads themselves are far from daft. Only the bodies are stupid.'

'Then why did this one remove his head, if he was so intelligent?'

1600H glowed red for a moment. He hummed and hawed, then:

'Well . . . That was one of his bad ideas . . .'

'Why are you blushing?' I asked.

1600H groaned. 'To be quite honest, the bad idea was me.'

We rounded a bend beyond which I expected to find yet another passage. Instead, the tunnel suddenly opened out to reveal an impressive view of a cerebral valley, one of the enormous cavities that sometimes occur in a Bollogg's brain. Thoughts were flashing across the roof of this cavern like colourful comets speeding across a dark firmament. Below us lay a tangled maze of cerebral convolutions, narrow little lanes in which thousands of ideas scurried around like the inhabitants of an oriental medina.

'That's the Valley of Discarded Ideas,' 1600H said sadly. 'My home.' We descended into the valley by way of a switchback neuron path.

1600H explained the hopeless predicament of the bad flashes of inspiration that lived in the valley. To justify their existence they

spent their days roaming the lanes and trying to marry themselves off in the vain hope that two bad ideas might produce a good one.

It was like a fish market. Blobs of light stood on every street corner, loudly extolling their own alleged virtues. Others kept clutching me by the arm and claiming to be the idea of the century. Many stood around in groups, arguing over which of them was the best. None of them took offence at my unusual appearance, they were all too busy pursuing their futile activities.

1600H was detained and engaged in conversation. Meanwhile, the crowd swept me on. When I reached a fork and turned to look, I found that I'd lost 1600H in the seething mass. I decided simply to stay where I was and wait until he was borne past on the tide.

Something caught hold of my arm and accosted me. 'Hey, want an idea? You look like you could use a good one.'

The bearded idea

The first thing that struck me about this idea was his mouth odour. He pressed against me, wafting his foul breath into my face. The second thing was his beard. None of the other blobs of light were bearded, but this one had a beard that covered his body almost completely from the nose down. I concluded that I was dealing with a particularly stale specimen.

'What are you offering?' I asked, to be polite.

The idea gave me a lopsided grin. 'Er . . . This is my idea: *How about short-circuiting a few nerve fibres?* Well, how about it? Are you game?'

'You think I should short-circuit a few nerve fibres?'

'Yes. A good idea, don't you think?'

I couldn't help laughing – a tactless thing to do, as I realized too late.

'Yes, well, I know I'm not the Fount of Wisdom . . .' The bad idea sounded positively hostile all of a sudden. 'What did you expect – the secret of perpetual motion? Picky, aren't you!'

I looked around for 1600H. The situation was getting unpleasant. The walking beard eyed me suspiciously. 'What sort of creature are you, anyway? You don't look much like an idea to me. You wouldn't by any chance be from the other side of the brain, would you?'

The idea clutched my arm and raised his voice. 'Hey, everyone! Look what we've got here!'

The noise and bustle around me died away, all eyes turned in my direction. The pressure on my arm increased.

'This young gentleman thinks he's too good for us!'

Curiosity turned to anger, the busy hum of voices gave way to malevolent mutters.

'What's he doing here?' called someone. 'He's probably one of the riff-raff from the right hemisphere!'

414

The other ideas formed a close-packed ring round me. This incident seemed to be presenting them with a welcome diversion from their futile activities. 'He looks quite different from us!' cried a high-pitched voice from the crowd.

'I'm just passing through!' I said defensively, but my words were drowned by the general tumult.

'He's a spy!' crowed the bearded idea. 'He's planning to steal our good ideas!'

That really got my goat. I wrenched my arm away and gave the idea a shove. 'Don't talk rubbish!' I yelled. 'What is there to steal here? Not a thing! You're just a bunch of totally useless, crack-brained notions!'

The mob fell silent. There are times when the truth is the worst possible thing you can come out with. The ideas looked more hostile still, the ring drew still closer. It was the bearded idea that uttered the clincher.

'We ought to throw him into the Lake of Oblivion!'

I was seized by numerous hands and hoisted into the air.

'Yes! Throw him into the Lake of Oblivion! He's a spy! Into the Lake of Oblivion with him!'

I was borne off by the mob like a cork on the high seas.

'Into the Lake of Oblivion with him!' croaked the bearded ringleader. 'And then we'll start a revolution. This time they've gone too far. We'll reduce the whole brain to chaos. They've trampled us underfoot for too long. Into the lake with him!'

Bollogg Brain, The [cont.]. Situated in every Bollogg's brain is a so-called *Lake of Oblivion*, a pool of liquid forgetfulness not unlike a lake of boiling pitch. Anyone or anything that falls into it dies of oblivion, a peculiarly drastic form of demise because nothing remains of the deceased, not even a vague recollection.

415

To die of oblivion – to vanish for ever without leaving behind the smallest memory, to simply dissolve without having etched myself into the minds of my contemporaries – was the most unpleasant end I could conceive of. I had been born to become famous – even, perhaps, immortal. What now confronted me was the diametrical opposite.

The Lake of Oblivion seethed beneath me like boiling lava, sending up sulphurous fumes that almost took my breath away. I was poised on a cliff above it with four ideas holding me tightly by the forepaws while the bearded one stood beside us and harangued the others, who had gathered around the lake, in a demented voice.

'This is the beginning of a new age!' he cried. 'We shall seize control of the brain. Away with the old order! Long live anarchy! We shall fill every corner of the brain with chaos. And this creature – this henchman of the old cerebral establishment – will be our first victim. On the count of three, throw him into the Lake of Oblivion!'

I racked my brains for a means of escape, but it would have been pointless to start a fight with so many opponents.

'One!' cried the bearded idea.

What did liquid forgetfulness feel like? Was there a chance of escaping from it by swimming?

Bollogg Brain, The [cont.]. Liquid forgetfulness, which consists of equal parts of hydrochloric acid and Bollogg bile, is inhabited by millions of voracious mortality bacteria. Anyone taking a dip in the Lake of Oblivion is as unlikely to survive as if he had jumped naked into the crater of an active volcano.

'Two!' The ideas thrust me to the edge of the cliff.

'And...' The bearded one raised his arm in readiness to give the crucial signal.

'STOP!' bellowed an imperious voice.

It was 1600H. My diminutive friend had managed to elbow his way through the throng. He strode resolutely up to the ringleader, who recoiled, looking rather taken aback.

Then he did something I really hadn't been expecting: he seized the bad idea's beard and wrenched it off. It was false! What came to light beneath it was the most repulsive sight I'd ever seen. Not even the offspring of a Hobgoblin and a Troglotroll could have looked more loathsome.

'You fools!' cried 1600H. 'Don't you know who this is? It's *Insanity*!'

The crowd let out a yell and drew back. The idea that had turned out to be Insanity spread his sharp claws and hissed: 'Don't touch me! I'll bite anyone who dares to lay a hand on me, and you know how infectious I am! *Sssssss!*'

The crowd parted like a piece of cloth ripped down the middle. Nobody wanted to come into contact with Insanity, who forged a path through the others, hissing and lashing out with his claws.

'Out of my way! *Sssssss!* I'm Insanity, so take care! *Sssssss!*'

Insanity vaulted some cerebral furrows and gained the mouth of a tunnel. There he turned and shouted, 'One day you'll all be mine! As for you...' He levelled a finger at me. 'I'll settle accounts with you personally! *Sssssss!*'

Then he disappeared into the tunnel, followed by the echoes of a peal of laughter that made all my fur stand on end.

1600H addressed the crowd. 'Have you nothing better to do than fall for Insanity's stupid tricks?' he demanded.

Sheepish murmurs and shuffling feet. Odd words of apology could be heard: 'Sorry... we only thought... pretty good disguise...'

'This is Bluebear, who's passing through,' 1600H continued. 'He's my personal guest, and I want you all to treat him accordingly, is that clear?'

The mob dispersed in silence. Then they started scurrying around and hawking their wares as if nothing had happened.

'He keeps trying it on,' 1600H told me when we had left the Valley of Discarded Ideas and were walking along a quiet tunnel. 'Insanity is the most evil creature imaginable. He creeps along the cerebral passages and tries to inflict as much damage as possible. He saws through nerve fibres and causes short circuits in the synapses. He's a master of disguise and intrigue. His object is to drive the whole brain insane.'

'But that's stupid,' I said. 'He'd destroy himself.'

'You're right. There's only one explanation for his behaviour.' 1600H tapped his forehead and lowered his voice. 'He's not quite right in the ...'

The Planmaker was occasionally a cube that hovered about three feet above the ground. He lived in a spacious cavity beside an exceptionally quiet cerebral convolution. The cavity was completely empty apart from him. I said he was *occasionally* a cube, because he was forever changing shape and texture. At the moment he was a cube illuminated from within, and abstract symbols were flickering on each of his rectangular sides.

One side seemed to be displaying a paper pattern for a man's shirt, another a weather map, another the ground plan of a cathedral. Then the surfaces changed once more. They now displayed a chart, a timetable, and a view of some solar system or other.

The Planmaker changed shape completely from one moment to the next, becoming a pyramid, a tetrahedron, or an entirely smooth sphere inscribed with all the orbits followed by our planet. He also rotated continuously on his own axis, which made it quite a strain to watch him.

His voice seemed to issue from deep within him. It was a high-pitched, almost sing-song voice, and it gave an electric crackle whenever it uttered a sibilant, but it wasn't disagreeable.

'All right, ƒynchroniƒe your watcheƒ!' the Planmaker said in an authoritative tone.

1600H glanced at his wrist – he wasn't wearing one at all – and mechanically replied, 'Sixteen hundred hours.'

'Er, nineteen hours forty-seven minutes,' I called out at random.

The Planmaker looked triumphant. 'ƒixteen hourƒ ƒeven minuteƒ! Exƒellent!'

This, I assumed, was a form of ritual greeting.

'Permit me to introduce Bluebear,' said 1600H. 'He's passing through and he needs a plan of the brain so as to get to the other side. Can you help?'

'Tƒƒ...' hissed the Planmaker, and transformed himself into a rotating disk bearing a medical diagram of a brain.

'A brain map, eh?,' he mused. 'It'ƒ bound to take a while. Don't you realiƒe how complicated a Bollogg'ƒ brain iƒ? How many mileƒ of passages there are inside it? If all the passages in this brain were put together, they'd stretch from the earth to the moon. You don't by any chance need a map of all the moon's craters, do you? I could sell you one for a song...'

A very handsome map of the moon, with the craters neatly drawn in, appeared on the back of the rotating disk.

'Come now,' 1600H cut in. 'How long will it take?'

'Two months,' lisped the Planmaker. 'At least.'

'How much?'

'Seventeen thousand scintillas.'

'Seventeen thousand scintillas? Come off it!' said 1600H. 'Ten thousand, not a scintilla more.'

The Planmaker turned into a truncated cone resembling the fez of a Moroccan carpet dealer. His upper surface was now displaying something that looked like the street map of a casbah.

'Sixteen thousand.'

'Twelve thousand five hundred.'

'You're simply ruining me, but it's a deal! Twelve thousand five hundred scintillas two months from now, same place, same time. Synchronise your watches!'

The Planmaker turned back into a cube, which was evidently his favourite shape.

'Sixteen hundred hours,' said 1600H.

'Fourteen twenty-nine,' I lied.

'Sixteen fifty-six,' cried the Planmaker, and showed us out of his cavern. 'It's high time I started work.'

Not content with having saved my life on two occasions and helped to procure me a map of the brain so that I could cross it, 1600H now proposed to shame me by generously offering to put me up.

Scintillas

I had to stay somewhere for the next two months, after all, so 1600H invited me to overnight in his small sleeping cave. It was a modest cerebral furrow near the Lake of Oblivion, whose sulphurous vapours came drifting over at times, but it was relatively peaceful. This was to be my base for the next two months, and it was from there that I had to get hold of twelve thousand five hundred scintillas. I had heard of these at the Nocturnal Academy, where I smoked my first Gloomberg algae cigarette in a scintilla shower.

From the
'Encyclopedia of Marvels, Life Forms
and Other Phenomena of Zamonia and its Environs'
by Professor Abdullah Nightingale

Scintillas. These are the bedrock of any brain, being the basic material from which thoughts can develop: thoughts that have yet to be thought, so to speak. Just as a butterfly can evolve from a caterpillar, so a scintilla can become a thought. Invisible at first, scintillas abound throughout the Zamonian atmosphere. Once they have penetrated the brain (I can recommend my scintilla shower as a means of accelerating that process), they assume the form of plump little worms that vegetate in the cerebral cortex. They occur in various colours. Many are red, many others ochre, golden yellow, copper-coloured, silver, green, grey, violet, pale brown, or dark blue, but all have a metallic sheen. Scintillas are, so to speak, the currency of every cerebral community, the basis of every idea, and the stuff of dreams.

How to come by some scintillas, that was my problem. They were like money: they didn't lie around in the street, nor did people simply chuck them at you; you had to earn them somehow. If I wanted to make some scintillas I needed a job. Once again, it was 1600H who came to my assistance.

'Are you imaginative?' he asked me.

I admitted to possessing limited but adequate powers of imagination. 'That's a rare talent. Imagination can earn you a mint of scintillas in here. You could become a dream composer. Dream composers are always in demand.'

A Bollogg's head sleeps all the time, so it must also dream continuously. Situated just behind the Bollogg's eyes, 1600H informed me, was the dream organ, the instrument on which dreams were generated. The dream organ had to be manned day and night without a break, otherwise the Bollogg's head would wake up – a disastrous development, because it would throw the whole brain into confusion. The head would try to walk or eat or perform some other action for which it needed the body, and this would create short circuits in the nerve fibres, or, at worst, enable Insanity to seize power. Thus the brain had to be lulled with a never-ending supply of dreams, a task that had, over the millennia, subjected dream composers to a certain amount of wear and tear. Anyone who felt he had a vocation could become a composer of dreams, and this means of earning scintillas was practised by good and bad ideas alike. Work had to go on round the clock without a break, so the composers relieved each other in shifts and job vacancies always existed. Scintillas were paid into a cerebral exchequer by all the brain's inhabitants, a form of taxation that funded the dream composers' salaries. They got ten scintillas an hour, not a princely sum, but it was at least a start.

The dream organ wasn't a musical instrument, of course. It was just a name for a big, multicoloured nexus of thousands of nerve endings in a cavity behind the Bollogg's eyes. Different dream

The dream organ

images were generated in the Bollogg's brain according to which nerve ending you plucked or how hard you squeezed it. It took me a while to discover which endings produced which images, but I eventually, with constant practice, mastered the technique. The images were projected on the back of the Bollogg's eyes, which formed one of the walls of the organ loft. Most of my colleagues simply squeezed and tugged the nerve endings at random until their shift was over. This produced the sort of confused dreams nearly everyone has: disjointed, fragmentary recollections, bizarre nightmares, indiscriminately jumbled scenes from the past. I was attracted by the possibility of welding seemingly unrelated images into meaningful compositions; of constructing stories that made more sense than dreams of having forgotten to put one's trousers on. If the image of a lion were wedded to that of an antelope – to take a simple example – the result would be a life-or-death chase lasting minutes on end. That was more exciting than simply projecting a haphazard series of images the way other composers did. Stored in the Bollogg's brain were some incredible memories of antediluvian times: motion pictures of gigantic lizards doing battle, of Cyclopses playing football with mountains, of volcanic eruptions, earthquakes, floods, meteor showers, primeval storms, tidal waves, extinct monsters, and wars with other families of giants. The Bollogg must have been so tall that his head projected almost into space. He could make out every last crater on the moon, see Mars and Saturn – indeed, survey the whole of our solar system.

There were images from the childhood and adolescence of the Cyclops, when he was still small and rode mammoths and wrestled with giant gorillas. He pelted other young Cyclopses, who merely laughed at him, with rocks the size of houses. He had traversed the whole of Zamonia several times and preserved some superb landscape shots of it in his memory. He had witnessed almost all of Zamonia's early history and seen all its creatures, extinct ones included. Dinosaurs scuttled around at his feet like rats, volcanoes looked from his standpoint like dainty little soup bowls. He could wash his hair in a storm cloud and, if thirsty, drain a sizeable mountain lake. No one who aspired to compose magnificent dreams could have wished for more grandiose material.

Many nerve endings produced no images but aroused or intensified emotions like joy, sorrow, suspense, or fear. I soon knew all the stops by heart. Without even looking, I knew exactly how much pressure would generate which image or which emotion.

I discovered that certain nerve endings produced music, acoustic recollections of the Bollogg music the giant must have heard in his youth. It wasn't very sophisticated music, as the reader may imagine, but it had a charm of its own and went excellently with the monumental images available. I could now superimpose dreams on suitable melodies and rhythms.

My dreams developed according to how I combined these images, sensations and melodies. I could produce happy dreams, exciting dreams, even nightmares.

1600H usually watched me while I worked.

I began by putting together small but carefully devised pictorial compositions and action sequences, which I underpinned with the right kind of music and brought to a climax.

I generated the image of a predatory dinosaur, for example, combined it with that of a zebragazelle, and a thrilling chase began. An erupting volcano in the background? A throbbing tympanic accompaniment provided by Cyclopses rhythmically beating whole oak trees together? Why not! And if an upbeat finale was required, I allowed the zebragazelle to escape by squeezing the appropriate nerve ending harder to make it run faster.

As time went by my dream compositions became longer and more complex, almost symphonic.

I once staged an eventful dream thriller based on the Bollogg's experiences during the ten-thousand-year Cyclopean Wars, battles waged in primeval landscapes with clubs whose impact shook the whole of Zamonia. I skilfully spliced together scenes that were widely separated in time: the fight between two primeval Cyclopses that started the war, the resulting mass hostilities, and the decisive battle in the Impic Alps, in which thousands of Cyclopses took part. I spanned centuries with lightning cuts and condensed millennia into a few minutes. Only the boldest dream composers could do that.

I also concocted a few nightmares out of the giant's phobias, which were mainly to do with small, scuttling creatures – from a Bollogg's viewpoint, all life forms apart from himself. I soon abandoned such dreams, however, because they made the head very restless. It started to pant and snore so loudly, I was afraid sheer terror would wake it up.

Little by little, word got around in the brain that my dream compositions possessed special merit and were well worth seeing. The spectators who began to throng the organ loft during my shifts proved an added incentive to produce dreams of the

426

highest quality. Whenever I wasn't manning the organ myself, I watched my colleagues at work and strove to learn from their mistakes.

After a few weeks 1600H asked me how many scintillas I'd amassed. I counted them. There were less than three hundred. I needed most of what I earned for my own consumption. I had to eat, after all, and the only food available in the Bollogg's head was scintillas. They didn't taste too bad, either. *Art and commerce*

1600H was critical of my unbusinesslike approach. 'You won't get out of here in under ten years,' he told me.

He was right. The few scintillas I earned from composing would never enable me to accumulate the twelve thousand five hundred I needed for the Planmaker.

'You could charge for admission,' 1600H suggested.

'Admission? To what?'

'To your dreams. The other ideas are crazy about them.'

No such thought would ever have entered my head. For me, dream composition had become an art, an activity transcending the sordid acquisition of scintillas. You didn't demand payment for art! I indignantly rejected the suggestion.

'You accept ten scintillas an hour.'

True. There was a contradiction there.

'Charge them all one scintilla a head, and you'll have the twelve thousand five hundred in no time.'

My performances were always sold out. Spurred on by scruples about selling my art, I strove to repay the ideas for their admission fees by offering them dream delicacies of an increasingly subtle and sophisticated nature. The cerebral convolutions were thronged with long queues of ideas eager to attend my shows. My dreams were the talk of the Bollogg's head.

1600H took the entrance money.

Box-office successes

Major disasters were my most popular productions, and the Bollogg's memory had a lot to offer in that field. The giant had witnessed every conceivable kind of natural disaster in the course of his long life, from asteroid strikes to the Great Flood, and had seen them from a unique perspective. How many people had observed a mile-high tidal wave or a Gloomberg Tempest *from above*? How many had looked down into an active volcano? Who could walk through a shower of meteorites as if it were a warm summer drizzle? Those were images which only a Megabollogg's memory could conjure up.

Also popular were peaceful nature films of steppe unicorns grazing, sea serpents mating in Shivering Sound (a truly edifying sight!), or Cyclopses hunting the Tyrannomobyus Rex bare-handed.

The Bollogg, who had evidently gone diving in the primeval Zamonian Sea, had preserved some unique images of contemporary submarine life: monstrous octopuses fighting huge, glowing jellyfish with countless transparent tentacles, whole schools of primeval sharks with luminous teeth, submerged continents on the ocean bed, ghost cities with shellfish-encrusted skyscrapers populated by colossal crabs and twin-headed moray eels. The Bollogg had seen ghost ships' graveyards, seething submarine volcanoes, bird-headed fish that seemed to be on fire within, enormous manta rays with pectoral fins as colourful as butterflies' wings, spiral fish composed of light.

He had dived ever deeper, down into dark, unfathomable abysses inhabited by creatures of lava that performed amazing underwater ballets. He had swum through the coral forests of the Zamonian Riviera, among red, turquoise and cobalt blue trees of shell limestone, and across meadows of yellow fireweed on which grazed whole herds of seahorses as big as unicorns.

My audiences were enthralled. Seated at the dream organ like some ecstatic pianist, I used to pull out all the stops. Sometimes I simply improvised, but instead of projecting a haphazard series of images on the Bollogg's retina I followed a dramatic pattern based on colour. Having summoned up shades of yellow only – streams of lava, flaming sunrises, deep-sea buttercups opening, undulating fireweed – I would then go over to shades of red – exploding meteors, poppy fields, galloping primeval horses with fiery manes – and underscore it all with grandiose music.

These voluptuously self-indulgent compositions of mine verged on kitsch, I must confess, but the material was just too tempting.

And the public loved it. Before two months were up, I had my twelve thousand five hundred scintillas.

'All right, ʃynchroniʃe your watcheʃ!' commanded the Planmaker, turning into a cube, a sphere and a trapezohedron in quick succession. *The brain map*

'Sixteen hundred hours,' said 1600H.

'Nineteen hours thirty-seven minutes,' I sang out.

'ʃixteen hourʃ ʃeven minuteʃ!' crepitated the Planmaker, a cube once more.

The map he'd made was truly worth every scintilla. It not only showed every cerebral convolution in detail, together with the principal short cuts and dead ends, but was beautifully drawn. Inscribed on finest cerebral cortex in dark red ink (Bollogg blood?), it resembled a treasure map and was a masterly aid to orientation. I would be able to find my way out of the other ear unerringly and in double-quick time. The map also made it plain that I might have taken years to do so without it.

Route

Destination

Brain

Left Hemisphere

Map

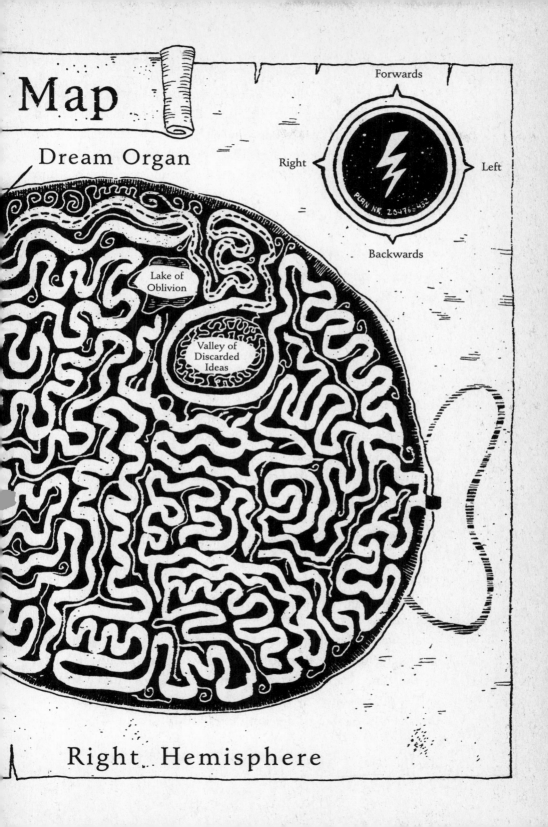

Dream Organ

Forwards

Right

Left

PLAN NR. 20476-433

Backwards

Lake of Oblivion

Valley of Discarded Ideas

Right Hemisphere

'It'ſ quite ſimple, juſt follow the dotted line,' the Planmaker explained. 'Don't let any bad ideaſ lead you aſtray. Don't let them perſuade you to take a ſhort cut or take one yourſelf. Life iſ a winding path. One ſometimeſ haſ to make detourſ. That'ſ my humble opinion, anyway.' I deposited my sack of scintillas on the ground and thanked him politely.

'Check your watcheſ!' cried the Planmaker, turning himself into a ball.

'Sixteen hundred hours,' murmured 1600H.

'Seventeen thirty-eight,' I called.

'End of office hourſ,' said the Planmaker. 'It'ſ high time I ſent you on your way.' Still in the shape of a ball, he bounced a couple of times and hustled us out of his office.

Before I set off for the other ear I decided to give a farewell performance, admission free.

I wanted to compose the best dream I could assemble at the organ, the crowning glory of my œuvre. I called it simply:

The Bollogg's Dream

Underwater shot of the primeval sea. Classical Cyclopean music. Fire-squid float upwards like flaming captive balloons. A Tyranno-mobyus Rex comes into shot, we follow it. Tyrannomobyus swallows a school of sharks. Torpid after its meal, it swims on. This is the moment when the Bollogg, which has been watching it all the time, leaps on to the monster's back. A titanic struggle ensues. Imprisoned in the giant's iron grip, the colossal whale thrashes the water wildly until exhaustion sets in. The Bollogg rides landwards on its back, but instead of dragging it ashore and devouring it, he releases it. Tyrannomobyus swims off into the sunset. The music swells.

Dissolve to:

Primeval Zamonia. The sky is a glowing expanse of every conceivable colour. Comets shoot across the sky. Listen! Distant thunder. No, not thunder!

Cut to:

A battle in progress. A hundred Bolloggs are belabouring each other with huge cudgels on a lowland plain. We plunge into the thick of the fray. Twenty minutes of mayhem conveyed by a swift succession of cuts.

Dissolve to:

A Bollogg wearily trudging home to his sweetheart. Romantic music. The Bollogg maiden is sitting in a valley, uprooting huge oak trees and weaving them into a garland. The Bollogg craves a kiss for his success in battle. The music abruptly turns dramatic. The Bollogg maiden rejects his advances. He hasn't brought her a gift, she intimates. He might at least have captured an enemy's cudgel.

Cut to:

The Bollogg trudging through a shower of meteorites. Melancholy music. What can he bring his beloved? If only he'd strangled that stupid whale! There, listen! Distant thunder! Has another fight broken out? No. It's a volcanic eruption.

The music sounds suddenly upbeat. The Bollogg approaches the volcano. He gazes down affectionately at the dear little mountain, then proceeds to pluck it. Very carefully, he digs it out of the ground. He has to dig really deep to extract the lava stem intact, right down to its fiery root. That done, he bears away the active volcano like a tulip on its long stem of pumice stone – gingerly, so the lava doesn't dribble down over his fingers.

Cut to:
The Bollogg maiden sulking in the valley. The Bollogg hands her the erupting volcano. She smiles. The ice is broken. She rewards him with a kiss. Romantic music. Cut to the primeval sky. Blazing meteors explode like gigantic fireworks.
The End.

I found it hard, saying goodbye to 1600H. He'd done so much for me, and I couldn't do anything in return.
'It was fun to do something useful for once,' he said. 'Besides, your dreams were really great. The standard of dream composition is bound to go downhill again. Let's not prolong the agony.'
And he shuffled sadly off, back into the Valley of Discarded Ideas.

I proceeded in the opposite direction, following the map eastwards. The recommended route skirted the Lake of Oblivion and followed a switchback cerebral convolution leading to the other hemisphere.

The route to freedom

When I came to the lake I was assailed by evil memories as well as sulphurous fumes. I walked swiftly past it and set off up the switchback. If I hurried, the trip would take me only a few days.
'You don't propose to run off just like that, do you? We've a score to settle. *Sssssss!*' said a snarling voice I hadn't heard for quite a while. It was Insanity, who had been lurking behind a cerebral ridge.
'I've been waiting for ages to get you on your own,' he went on. 'Very popular you were, you and your dreams, but now you're all by yourself.'

'Leave me alone,' I said. 'I haven't done anything to you.'

'I'm Insanity. *Sssssss!* I don't have to have a reason for doing something evil.'

'You're insane!' I said. Nothing more original occurred to me on the spur of the moment.

'*SSSSSSS!*' snarled Insanity, very loudly now. 'Don't say things like that, not to me!'

'What else, then? That you're *bats in the belfry?*'

Insanity rolled his eyes and seemed to double up in agony. He couldn't bear to hear the truth, I suppose.

'Never say that again!'

'What would you prefer? That you're *a screw loose?* That you're *off your rocker?*'

I'd found a way of tormenting him.

'*SSSSSSSSSS!* Take that back!'

'Sorry, no can do. You're *bananas*! Is it my fault you're *cracked?* All right, so you've *lost your marbles* and *come unglued*, but can I help it if you're *loony, screwy, gaga, cuckoo, not all there, nutty as a fruitcake, a couple of prawns short of a sea-food salad* . . .'

Sadly, I'd run out of synonyms.

It was all too much for him. He sprang at me with a snarl and wrested my map of the brain away.

'Now let's see you fish it out of the Lake of Oblivion!'

And he ran off in the direction of the lake.

Here's a piece of good advice: Never tell Insanity to his face that he's not quite right in the head. It makes him really *mad*.

Insanity raced to the clifftop from which he'd intended to hurl me into oblivion. I sprinted after him, even faster than I had from the

Spiderwitch. On the edge of the cliff he halted and, with the map between his fingertips, held it poised over the seething brew. Green bubbles of corrosive acid burst with an ugly sound.

'I hereby solemnly commit you to oblivion,' he said in an unctuous voice. Then he let go.

I boldly leapt forwards and just managed to grab the map, only to lose my balance and tumble over the edge. As I fell I succeeded in clinging to a small cerebral fissure with my free paw.

There I dangled like an overripe fruit, one forepaw lodged in the crack, the other holding the map. Beneath me lay the Lake of Oblivion, above me loomed Insanity.

He leant over with an evil grin.

'So I'm not all there, eh?'

It was time to be diplomatic.

'I didn't mean it that way! It was just a joke in poor taste!'

'Oh well, if I've lost my marbles it doesn't matter if I let you fall into the Lake of Oblivion. It won't be *my* fault. After all, I'm not responsible for my actions.'

Insanity prised one claw out of the crack. I was now suspended by only four claws.

'Don't!' I cried.

He prised out another claw. That left three.

'Did I hear something? No, must have been the voices in my head. I'm off my rocker, don't forget.'

Another two claws. Only one left.

'Goodbye, then. Another few seconds and you'll cease to exist, even as a memory.' He set to work on the last claw.

Quite suddenly, Insanity went flying over me and plunged head first into the Lake of Oblivion.

'AAAAAARGH!' he gurgled as the mortality bacteria closed over him. The lake hissed and bubbled, giving off noxious putrescent gases.

There was a hideous crackling sound, and Insanity sank from view. 1600H bent down and grasped my paw.

'Honestly, you can't be left alone for a minute.'

He hauled me up.

'I've always wanted to do that,' he said, watching the last of the ugly bubbles Insanity had left behind.

'That was a really good idea!' I told him.

1600H blushed and bridled. 'I came back because I remembered the pool of earwax. There must be one inside the other ear as well. How do you propose to cross it unaided?'

I was genuinely relieved to have 1600H's company while crossing the brain. In other respects it was a very tedious trek along endless, monotonous cerebral convolutions and across knotted ganglions and excrescences of cogitative tissue. Ideas were rarer in the left-hand half of the brain. Most of the ones we did encounter had lost their way, so we were able to redirect them with the help of our map.

I seized every opportunity to tell them how 1600H had disposed of Insanity. He always writhed with embarrassment like an earthworm, but I thought it might earn him somewhat more respect in the cerebral community. It was my only way of repaying him a little.

Things were more boring in the left-hand half of the brain, which was largely populated by reflexes and thought patterns. These took the form of little spheres and cubes in various shades of grey that floated along the passages, humming monotonously to themselves. No creative processes occurred in this part of the brain. No ideas were originated or debated here. This was where orders were

executed and stocks of ideas filed. It was the brain's administrative centre.

We felt like ants that had strayed into the wrong nest. Although the ideas we met politely stepped aside to let us pass, they did so with a resentful hiss. Foreign bodies and anomalies were clearly not appreciated in this half of the brain.

All the walls were dotted with recesses of various sizes, many rectangular, others hemispherical. The whizzing spheres and cubes would look for a suitable niche and park in it, still humming to themselves. Then they flew on once more.

CRRRASH!

A very faint noise, accompanied by a very faint but perceptible vibration.

'Hey, what was that?' said 1600H.

'No idea.'

CRRRASH!

There it was again. The tunnel walls shook slightly.

'What can it be?' asked 1600H.

'Concussion?' I said flippantly.

'I've never known anything of the kind in here. We'd better hurry.'

The further we went, the stronger the tremors became. Scarcely perceptible at first, they steadily increased in violence. The rhythmical, repetitive sounds reminded me of something, but what?

The floor of the tunnel gave a sudden lurch. 1600H and I staggered to and fro.

'What's going on?' I exclaimed. I, too, was becoming nervous.

'Search me.'

Another, more violent lurch.

By now the reflexes and thought patterns were racing along the passages in an even more hectic and erratic manner, humming and muttering in extreme agitation. 1600H detained a dark grey cube as it flitted past. Their conversation was incomprehensible to me, unfortunately, being telepathic. They hummed at each other for a while, then 1600H let the cube whizz off again.

'Well?' I asked. 'What's wrong?'

'The brain is waking up,' said 1600H.

CRRRASH!

Time presses
It seemed egotistical of me to quit the Bollogg's brain at such an historic moment, but we had now reached the lake of earwax on the far side.

'You must go,' said 1600H. 'Don't worry about us. We'll manage, even if the brain really has woken up. The old place could do with a bit of a shake-up.'

440

We plucked out a few thick hairs and tied them together (it's far from easy to tie knots in hair, but I hadn't lost the skills I'd acquired during my time with the Minipirates). Then, having made a noose in one end, I lassoed a fat wart on the other side of the pool. 1600H pulled the hair rope taut and held it tight while I went across it, paw over paw, and gained the far bank without difficulty. I doubt if I'd have made it without his help.

We exchanged a farewell wave. Then 1600H went back into the ear with the brain map under his arm.

He was the best bad idea I ever had.

CRRRASH!

I made my way out of the ear. It was around noon, and the sun was shining down on Zamonia. Not a Bollogg Flea in sight. In the distance I could see Atlantis, an endless expanse of buildings bathed in sunlight. At last! All I had to do was climb down the Bollogg's head.

CRRRASH!!

Why did I find the sound so familiar?

CRRRASH!!!

I caught a familiar scent. It was the smell of danger.

CRRRASH!!!!

Every crash made the Bollogg's head vibrate. The last one sent me reeling. I fell over and landed on my backside.

CRRRASH!!!!!

I now knew the answer: only a Bollogg's footsteps sounded like that. The primeval giant had come back to retrieve his head.

The worst thing that could happen now was that the Bollogg should replace his head before I managed to get off it.

To judge by the vibrations, he was already very near. I scrambled quickly out of the ear and set off for the valley below.

Feverishly, I slid down a strand of hair. The vibrations had ceased – an ominous sign, because it denoted that the Bollogg had reached his destination.

Then the sky went dark and I saw a primeval Megabollogg for the first time. He must have been a hundred miles in height. The upper half of his body was obscured by cloud, but his shoulders were probably in space. The colossus crouched down. The largest life form on earth was bending over the head he'd removed so many aeons ago: he was about to replace it on his neck.

I clambered down as fast as I could. Sometimes I simply let go and clutched at tufts of hair as I fell. I could do that because the slope wasn't vertical, more like a steep slide, but it was dangerous even so. If I once missed a handhold I would hurtle down out of control, and I still had several miles to go.

442

Then the heavens parted and two hands appeared among the clouds. As big as medium-sized islands, they were black and covered with primeval calluses. The giant gave off a revolting smell. Many square miles of Bollogg hide, unwashed for thousands of years – the reader can have no idea of the stench, nor do I propose to describe it in detail here. Suffice it to say that I almost passed out – only for a moment, but long enough to make me miss the next tuft of hair. At breakneck speed, I tobogganned into the valley on the seat of my pants.

The Bollogg had now grasped his head. The desert sand was still about a mile away. Although the slope was becoming less steep and correspondingly less dangerous, it slowed my rate of descent. The Bollogg picked up his head. The hairy track beneath me gave a lurch. I pitched forwards, turned several somersaults, and continued to slide down it on my belly. The track drew taut. Only a few yards to the ground.

The descent

On this occasion, too, it was the giant's sluggish movements that largely contributed to my escape. A Bollogg was slow, but a Megabollogg was monstrously slow. I was able to stand up and run the remaining few yards. At long last, I sank to the hard ground.

I crawled a bit further on all fours, then scrambled to my feet. A very rare spectacle was unfolding high above me: the replacement of a Megabollogg's head.

443

The gigantic Cyclops twisted his skull to and fro with an unpleasant, crunching sound. Then came a click that rang out far across Zamonia: the head had snapped into place. For the first time for many thousands of years, the Bollogg was surveying his surroundings through his single, cyclopean eye. I prayed he wouldn't decide to make for Atlantis. Eventually he turned and headed south towards the Zamonian Gulf. Perhaps he felt like taking a dip in the sea.

So did I, as a matter of fact.

12.

My Life
in
Atlantis

I could hear it from far away, that sound which only very big cities can produce: a sound consisting of all sounds rolled into one: the hum of voices and the cries of animals, bells ringing and the chink of coins, children's laughter and hammers beating metal, knives and forks clattering and a thousand doors slamming – the grandiose sound of life, of birth and death, itself.

I made for the city like a dog hauled along on a leash, slowly and rather fearfully at first, then faster and faster until I broke into a loping run. Atlantis seemed to exert a magnetic attraction. The louder the hum of the city became, the more I itched to find out who or what was making all those sounds.

At last I stood panting outside the gate (only one of many, but that I didn't discover until later). Looming over me were two black marble columns at least sixty feet high. They bore a plaque engraved with the following words:

ATLANTIS
CITY WITH A
FUTURE

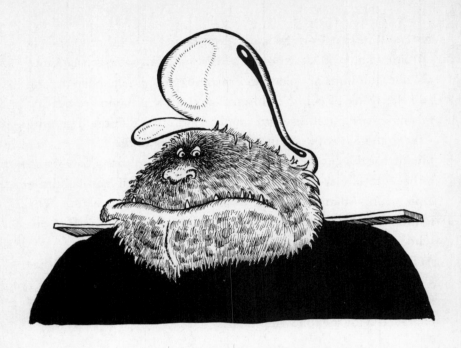

Between the columns stood an impressive individual three times my size and three times as hairy, with glassy red eyes and twice as many teeth in his mouth. In his hand was an implement that would have lent itself to innumerable uses, on his head a military-style peaked cap of blown glass. Although I didn't know it at the time, he was a trooper in the municipal guard, a unit traditionally recruited from Yetis alone. The Yeti looked down at me sternly and tapped his cap with the implement. The glass gave out a high-pitched 'Ping!'.

'Hello there! Are you a human being, or directly related to, or on close terms with, or related by marriage to, or financially dependent upon, or romantically involved with, any member of the human race?'

'No,' I replied. 'I'm a bluebear.'

'Of course you are, I'm not a halfwit. I have to ask, it's my job. Welcome to Atlantis, the city with a future! You see that Gryphon up there?'

He levelled his tool at the summit of a minaret jutting into the sky behind him. Seated on the topmost parapet was a huge Gryphon. 'Yes,' I replied.

'It's a genuine Gryphon. Do you know what that means?'

'No,' I said.

'It means it's a genuine Gryphon.'

He gave me a long, enigmatic look, then waved me on. Just as I was slinking past him with my head down, the ground suddenly shook. It was only a slight tremor. The Yeti and I swayed a little, then it stopped.

'What was that?' I asked.

'An earthquake. It's harmless, we get lots of them. Welcome to Atlantis.'

From the
'Encyclopedia of Marvels, Life Forms and Other Phenomena of Zamonia and its Environs' by Professor Abdullah Nightingale

Atlantis. Capital and seat of government of the continent of Zamonia. Classified as a megalopolis, Atlantis is divided into five administrative districts, each of which really constitutes a kingdom in its own right: Naltatis, Sitnalta, Titalans, Tatilans, and ...

Thanks, but we already know that. At the time of my arrival, Atlantis was by way of being the world centre for non- or half-human life forms. Human beings were simply not admitted in consequence of the Zamonian war of succession. It happened like this:

Human beings used to make up one-third of the population of Atlantis until they and the Norselanders became embroiled in a dispute over who should be mayor of the city, which in practice meant governor of all Zamonia. City Hall had been controlled by the Norselanders for several generations, and the mayoral office continued to be handed down from father to son until, one day, the inhabitants condemned this as nepotism and demanded free elections. Some heated arguments ensued, at first of a verbal nature only, but the opposing camps ended by resorting to violence.

The Zamonian war of succession
In the course of the wholesale free-for-all that broke out during a debate in the municipal senate between human and Norselander politicians, a Norselander was pushed out of the window in the general confusion and broke his ear (the structure of a Norselander's ear is very complex, with a fragile osseous system.) With considerable diplomatic skill, the Norselanders took advantage of this incident to form an alliance with almost all the city's other non- or semi-human life forms, thereby imposing what amounted to a strict local ban on humans. The latter resentfully emigrated to other continents, where – in a spirit of defiance, so to speak – they founded metropolises such as Rome, Constantinople, and London, from which semi- or non-human life forms, and Norselanders in particular, were debarred in their turn.

The ban on human beings
What resulted was the breach between humans, semi-humans and non-humans that persists to this day. That is why dwarfs, demons, Troglotrolls, witches, and other non-human manifestations hide themselves away from human eyes. A similar fate attended the few humans remaining in Zamonia, who either steered clear of Atlantis or went off into the desert like the ones I got to know in Tornado City.

The Antlerites
So Atlantis was ruled by Norselanders. These rather disagreeable creatures allegedly hailed from Norway, or possibly from Iceland. They were reputed to have reached Atlantis by clinging to Viking ships – a myth, perhaps, but one that does at least say much for their stamina.

Norselanders were elks with human bodies (they walked erect) and extremely long, sensitive, protruding ears. It's hard to say what made them, in particular, such good politicians; perhaps it was their ultrasensitive hearing. According to one Atlantean proverb, a Norselander could hear the wind change before the wind itself became aware of it.

Other denizens of Atlantis included Florinthian Klodds, a very sociable species of large dogbat with wings and dark fur; Melanosprites; Grailsundian Hazelwitches; North Zamonian Zombies; Harvest Home Hamsters; Glacier Gophers, whose ancestors came from Greenland; Shivering Sound Shrews; and scampering hordes of Muchwater Mannikins.

Klodds, Hazelwitches, Glacier gophers, and other Atlanteans

Most of the inhabitants of Zamonia originated on other continents. Among them were the Italian Doombirds. These strange hybrids, a cross between a human and a chicken, resembled normal farmyard fowl in outward appearance but spoke in deep bass voices, generally of impending disaster.

Beneath Atlantis's numerous bridges resided the Bobkins, a timid race of likeable, helpful little gnomes who voluntarily collected the city's refuse at night. Also living on the waterfront in corrugated iron shacks were the Wildlings, a fascinating bunch of hybrids, at times half human, half fish, at other times half goat, half insect. Much to everyone's relief, they kept themselves to themselves.

Bufadistas and Bluddums

At the street corners sat Bufadistas, toadlike creatures from Portugal who sang melancholy ditties about unrequited love and other injustices. Passers-by were rudely pestered for coins by fearsome-looking Bluddums (from the waist up, shaggy black bears with huge projecting teeth; below that, bony humans with blood-red skin and preternaturally large feet). Bluddums were always to be found where uncouth behaviour was called for.

Zamonian Wolpertingers

Zamonian Wolpertingers were universally respected but ever so slightly feared because of the mock battles they staged with much clashing of antlers. Their ancestors came from Lapland. Antlers apart, they looked almost like normal canines, except that they were ten feet tall and walked on their hind legs. Most Wolpertingers hired themselves out as bodyguards or bouncers.

Kukbuks

Kukbuks baked little yeast cakes on open grass fires and sold them so cheaply that they had, to all intents and purposes, become a staple food. Very small, spherical in shape, and entirely covered with fur, Kukbuks were of pure Zamonian stock. Legend had it that they grew in the Graveyard Marshes of Dull.

Rickshaw Demons

Responsible for transportation were Chinese Rickshaw Demons, unutterably hideous creatures with huge calf muscles. They simply perched you on their humpbacks, however much you weighed, and raced off like the wind.

The African Tangawangas were Sedge Gnomes not much bigger *Sedge Gnomes*
than children of three but immensely quick, strong, and pugnacious. The Irish Druids, by contrast, were peaceable but not
wholly innocuous. They were said to be able to turn you into a
harp or a lump of peat if you insulted their native island.

The Central Indian Trifakirs, though something of a pest, were *Trifakirs*
quite harmless. They always appeared in threes, of course, and
made a practice of handing out muddle-headed philosophical tracts.

The Noontide Ghouls, who hailed from Asia and preferred to get *Noontide Ghouls*
up to their tricks in the middle of the day, looked like paper cut-
outs. Nobody knew what to make of them. Ghosts that appear
during the day are not very impressive, after all, because they

forfeit their spooky appearance. Having a disembodied spirit in your home in broad daylight is merely a nuisance, nothing more. The Noontide Ghouls were undeterred, however, and would continue their monkey business even when you ignored them and got on with your lunch.

Draks

The Draks, amusing little minidragons belonging to the goblin family, were good-natured, well-meaning house spirits. They had nothing in common with big, fire-breathing dragons apart from their physical resemblance. Just as a dolphin isn't a fish but a mammal, so Draks weren't dragons but – well, something else. They even brought you good luck if you treated them with respect, and by respect the Draks meant mainly first-class board and lodging. But keeping them was rather like going in for the lottery. You could pamper them for years and get nothing in return, whereas someone else could invite a Drak to a meal just once, and the next day he would find a bucketful of gold on his doorstep. Draks also had a curious knack of transforming themselves into wet dogs for brief periods, something they particularly liked to do on high days and holidays.

Toothworms

Toothworms occupied the lowest rung on the social ladder. Originally natives of the Swiss Alps, they were somehow out of place in a big city. Persons of stable temperament were repelled by their subservient, grovelling manner, but Bluddums liked to keep them as salaried domestic pets and used them to fetch their newspapers for them.

Gryphons

Gryphons, which were breathtakingly beautiful lion-eagle cross-breeds, had huge black wings like angels of death. They were Atlantis's unofficial police force and primarily responsible for the fact that conditions in such a vast, chaotic city were so relatively peaceful. Everyone respected the Gryphons, not only because of their physical superiority but, above all, for their Solomonic integrity and sportsmanlike fairness. Like symbols of justice carved in granite, they perched almost motionless on the tops of the city's skyscrapers, minarets, and pyramids, their keen eyes scanning the busy streets below. You had to have witnessed the arrival of a Gryphon to know how authority should be personified. Its wings created more noise and turbulence than a tornado, and when it dug its talons into the ground and opened its mighty beak to emit a roar worthy of a whole pride of lions, you stopped whatever you happened to be doing.

The Gryphons were assisted by Gargylls, a winged species of gnome whose appearance varied greatly. This was because the Gargylls of Atlantis came from a wide variety of continents and had interbred over the millennia.

Gargylls

Some specimens had the bodies of humpbacked dwarfs and semi-human faces, others reptilian tails and dragons' heads, and others webbed feet and gnomelike features, but all had small, leathery wings. They took care of any minor misdemeanours – traffic offences, cases of shoplifting, nocturnal breaches of the peace, et cetera – that would not have warranted the intervention of a

Gryphon. It was the Gargylls' rather sinister appearance and somewhat brusque manner that accounted for the remarkably low crime rate in Atlantis. The stone figures of these creatures still to be seen on churches or old buildings in many modern cities were carved by sculptors who at one time lived in Atlantis.

Hoopoes The Hoopoes also had wings but enjoyed considerably less respect. Indeed, nearly everyone pursued them because of the rumour that their feathers brought good luck in matters of the heart. This meant that only the proximity of a Gryphon could make a Hoopoe feel reasonably secure. Not only were seated Gryphons encircled by the usual fluttering Gargylls; a big flock of Hoopoes would also be jostling for position on some nearby gutter.

Big-Footed Bertts Big-Footed Bertts were half duck, half Bush Witch; more precisely, women with ducks' bills up top and ducks with very big women's feet below. They were entirely harmless, even though they cursed everything and anyone that crossed their path. Quacking and vituperating, they restlessly roamed the streets of Atlantis on their own, and it must be accounted a blessing that no one understood their language except the Bertts themselves. Their profanities became truly dramatic when two of them happened to bump into each other. If this occurred at night, sleep was out of the question within a radius of three miles.

Dragons Atlantis had its dragons too, of course – over five hundred of them, so it was said, though they were never seen. Sewer Dragons lived in the subterranean part of the city (of which more later) because they really belonged to the Scaleworm family, whose members favoured cool, damp, unstressful conditions on account of their high blood pressure. For the present, all I shall say of them is this: *Yes*, they really can breathe fire; *no*, they don't abduct damsels in distress; *yes*, they have human voices (at least, the one I encountered did); and *yes*, they can become very, very vicious if you cross their path at the wrong moment.

Duodwarfs walked around all over the place, quarrelling with themselves. Pathetic creatures belonging to the genus *Contradicens*, they comprised a speaking head and a speaking stomach that were always at odds over everything, no matter what.

Duodwarfs

Chimeras were extremely annoying and unpopular creatures. Members of the overweight Pressuresprite family, they were enabled by their batlike wings to gain access to any bedroom by night, there to perch on the chests of slumbering citizens and give them nightmares. This did no one any good, not even the Chimeras themselves, so the Norselanders (with the Gryphons' tacit consent) declared them fair game. The only result, however, was that the Chimeras transferred their roosts and hatcheries to even more secluded places, of which Atlantis had plenty. It was even rumoured that the Chimeras had discovered the secret tunnels leading to the Atlantean pyramids and installed themselves there.

Chimeras

The Popples, who were wood goblins and skilled craftsmen, did a roaring trade in pixie stars, which they produced with the aid of fretsaws. Pixie stars were thought to be the only effective antidote to Chimeras – if sawn aright, and only Popples were reputed to be able to saw them correctly. At least one pixie star hung in almost every Atlantean house, yet the nightmares occasioned by Chimeras persisted. This gave rise to a rumour, not only that Popples turned out shoddy work occasionally, but that they were really in cahoots with the Chimeras.

Vampires are a subject in themselves. Atlantis teemed with them, and one really shouldn't lump them all together. For a start, it entirely depended what they lived on, and very few of them lived on blood. Those that did were unpleasant creatures of whom most lived in the ruins of the Italian cathedral, which no one in his right mind entered after sunset. Contrary to all modern descriptions, bloodsucking vampires looked like big, dark-furred cats with baboonlike faces and the short, leathery wings of a bat. Also contrary to all the legends about them, they were not necessarily dependent on blood and quite capable of living on a normal diet – even on garbage, if they pulled themselves together.

There were also blood-*drinking* vampires that acquired their blood by legal means. They purchased it from one of the numerous Atlantean bloodbroking establishments. These vampires included Dwerrogs (ferretlike creatures with projecting teeth and good manners), Yhôllian Bloodslurpers (obese mountain demons with two faces), and Transylvanian Werewolves, which traditionally ran the said bloodbroking businesses.

The remaining, considerably more innocuous vampires were dependent on smell, touch, and hearing. One example of the first category was the Olfactil, an extremely thin vampire some four feet long and equipped with as many as fifteen noses. Olfactils

fed exclusively on body odours of all kinds. Although superficially unattractive, this habit had a very practical side. If you
smelt strongly of sweat after taking physical exercise, an Olfactil
had only to nestle against you for a few seconds and inhale
through its numerous noses for the unpleasant smell to disappear
completely.

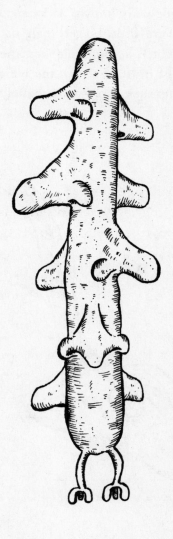

There was also a rather less popular and considerably smaller Olfactil variety with only four noses but eight legs. It specialized in halitosis, and would clamber on to the faces of sleeping people at night to inhale their mouth odour. To wake up in the small hours and find a little, snuffling Olfactil on your cheek could be a traumatic experience.

Earspoonlets

Even more innocuous and equally beneficial to society were the acoustic vampires popularly known as Earspoonlets, which lived on speech. They were little bigger than dachshunds but had hearing organs of which a young elephant need not have been ashamed. They spent most of their time lying around in public places and pricking up their ears – an extremely amusing sight.

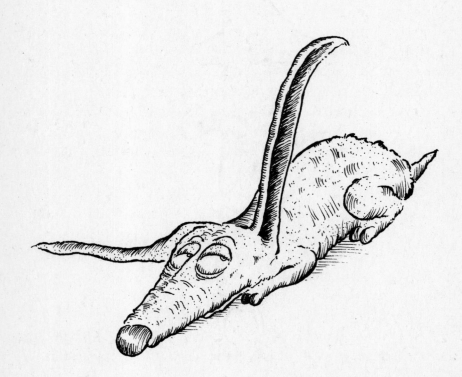

Earspoonlets were capable of storing up all they heard for months and regurgitating it before it was fully digested. Thus, they were much in demand as itinerant purveyors of information or witnesses of arguments. You could easily annoy them by noiselessly opening and shutting your mouth as if talking. This made them bounce around like mad things, vainly trying to catch the words they thought they were missing.

The pixies or elves were not quite as likeable, and certainly not as *Pixies* cute and innocent, as their modern reputation would have us believe. More like unpleasant insects – like highly intelligent wasps, so to speak – they were absolutely mad about anything sweet, which was why no one anywhere in Atlantis could eat a slice of cake without sharing it with at least one elf. The killing of pixies was prohibited because it not only brought bad luck but was even alleged to spell the downfall of Atlantis. This rumour had gained such general currency that no one could recall where it had originated, but I secretly suspected that it came from the pixies themselves. They probably kept whispering it in the inhabitants' ears at night, the cunning little creatures.

As for the Fangfangs, they were *genuinely* disagreeable individuals! *Fangfangs* They were really forest demons from the thickets on the outskirts of the city and had no business in a civilized metropolis, but once in a while a drunken gang of them would stray into Atlantis. Not even the Yetis at the gates could turn them away because Fangfangs were not subject to any definite exclusion order.

The Norselanders had been drafting one for years, but not, it was whispered, with any great enthusiasm because they themselves were indirectly related to the intruders. Discounting their size and close-set human ears, Fangfangs bore a close superficial re-semblance to Norselanders.

The uncouth creatures were very tall, even by Atlantean standards, and could attain a height of thirty feet. They always operated in groups of 150 to 200, and the destructive power of such a contingent was equal to that of a medium-sized Bollogg. If a gang of them entered Atlantis, a fight was bound to break out sooner or later. It was usually the Bluddums they came to blows with, or, oddly enough, the diminutive Tangawangas, who would stand no nonsense from anyone. Whenever this happened, it took a dozen Gryphons to restore order and escort the troublemakers out of the city.

Hackonians

The Hackonians were quite another kettle of fish: universally popular, soft-hearted, incorrigibly romantic, and never at a loss for a word of praise.

They were also known as Blarneykites because they spent the whole time paying people unsolicited compliments, flattering them, admiring their work or their appearance, and – without payment-rhapsodizing about everything and everyone in general. If you were feeling a bit depressed, your best plan was to visit a Hackonian tavern, where your spirits were bound to be restored.

The Hackonians came from Hackonshire in south-west Zamonia, a region separated from the rest of the continent by a long trench. Legend had it that Wotan, a god with little appreciation of good nature, was so infuriated by the Hackonians' amiability that he severed their homeland from Zamonia with his huge axe. However, the resulting cleft was more likely to have been an ancient canal excavated by Zamonia's earliest Venetian Midgets.

The Mandragors resident in Atlantis were rather affectionate semi-human plants of the deadly nightshade family. Originally from Greece, they had rootlike arms and legs that enabled them to cling to people. This they constantly did, because it was all they'd learnt to do. They were eternally mystified by their failure to be richly rewarded for this trick, as they had been in their native habitat, where it was customary to pay Mandragors for their embraces because they were reputed to bring you good luck when ploughing. *Mandragors*

Also from Greece but quite different in temperament were the Raving Maenads, devotees of the god Dionysus who liked to dress up in animal skins and dance through the streets until they passed out. They had women's bodies and wildcats' faces, and were always accompanied by a band of Satyrs, gifted flautists and winebibbers with human features and muscular, goatlike legs. The Venetian Midgets were mineworker trolls from Tuscany, extremely industrious and fond of singing but proud, vindictive, and inveterate strikers on principle. *Raving Maenads*

Anyone looking for an intellectual challenge sought out the Witthogs. These were very slim, philosophically gifted semi-pigs with a markedly ascetic streak. They lived exclusively on tea, milky porridge, and conversation. There were two or three of them to be found in every tearoom in Atlantis, and it was only too easy to be drawn into a philosophical debate. If you weren't careful, a Witthog would argue the chair away from under you and sit down on it himself. You had only to make some untenable *Witthogs* assertion, and a Witthog would flatly contradict it. You did well not to overstep the mark, however, because a Witthog was always prepared to fight a duel on behalf of his own opinion. And Witthogs were amazingly nimble swordsmen.

Midgard Serpents and Twerpps

From time to time a colourful Midgard Serpent would slither through the streets, as long and massive as an anaconda but harmless as an earthworm. Scurrying along behind it came the swarms of Twerpps who collected the serpent's slimy trail in buckets to make a soup alleged to render one immortal. (This was never proved because the Twerpps, who lived to at least a thousand in any case, consumed it all themselves.)

Baalbek Wormlets

Baalbek Wormlets were nothing of the kind – that's to say, they weren't wormlets or even worms, but big, spotty giants with bulls' heads and three sinewy arms. No one knew how they got their name, because they bore not the slightest resemblance to worms and came from Easter Island, not Baalbek. They had good manners but peculiar habits, one of which was to bury themselves waist-deep in loose sand and mutter unintelligible prayers.

It would be an impossible task to enumerate all the life forms that inhabited Atlantis. Here are a few of the continent's many other ethnic groups and tribes: Danish Dunefolk, Halfway Humans from the Humongous Mountains, Antarctic Fridgitrolls, Japanese Bonsai Mites, Monastocalves, Melusines, Ghorks, Obliviogs, Nineslayers, Gibbetkins, Elverines, Norns, Lemurs, Poophs, Ronkers, Rumple-stilts, Burrps, Thimbleskins, Dogheads, Auntifers, Anklemen, Paradise Worms, Bozzums, Waterkins, Gogmagogs, Semi-mummies, Pratts, Voltigorks, Cinnamen, Swamazons, Ventisnipes, Bovisimians, Cucumbrians, Zebraskans, Aquadjinns, Shadow Pygmies, Hellrazors, Swamp Orks, Snowscoops, Silvanosprites, Peat Witches, and a whole host of almost unclassifiable mini-groups and lone individuals of every kind. Even Bolloggs were admitted to Atlantis, though only if less than fifty feet in height and equipped with a head.

A bluebear attracted no attention in such surroundings.

Oh yes, to complete the picture I should add that there were also the so-called Invisibles, social misfits and radical dropouts who had retreated to the ancient, disused sewers of Atlantis. They never showed themselves in the streets by day. Only at night (and very seldom even then) did they crawl out of their tunnels and into the open to perform the few really essential tasks that compelled them to remain in contact with the world above.

There was even a rumour that the ones who did come to the surface were not true Invisibles but their aides and intermediaries. *Genuine* Invisibles were said to be really invisible and not of this world. This, at any rate, was what parents told disobedient children, not forgetting to add a dire warning that Invisibles had a

The Invisibles

fondness for kidnapping fractious youngsters and hauling them off to their catacombs.

The creatures that lived beneath the streets were rather like the sacred cows of Atlantis. Although they made no contribution to the common good, the city's inhabitants cherished a natural respect for them, partly out of fear and partly from superstition. At all events, it was the Atlanteans' inviolable custom to throw surplus foodstuffs, obsolete household equipment and other donations into the ancient sewers as sacrificial offerings to those who dwelt in darkness. All they would hear was an eager, rustling sound in the depths, and the gifts disappeared.

This was why Atlantis had no beggars, no pavement dwellers, and no genuine poor – or none that were visible, at least. Anyone who couldn't cope with the world of daylight vanished into the sewers and was never seen again.

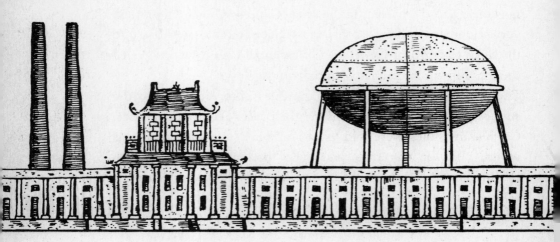

The city displayed every conceivable form of architecture plus a few more besides. Representatives of every nation that ever sailed the seas in ships had visited Atlantis at some stage and left their architectural traces behind.

The descendants of some Egyptian pirates had erected – as Egyptians tend to do – several huge sandstone pyramids whose entrances were still being sought when I arrived in Atlantis. The dead were reputed not only to live inside them but to go about their daily business there in the normal way. These gruesome rumours did not deter Atlanteans from using the terraces, which were almost completely overgrown with grass and creeper, as picnic sites on fine summer days. At night, however, when the pyramids creaked and groaned and weird bell music issued from deep inside, they gave them a wide berth.

Arabs had constructed minarets and labyrinthine kasbahs made up of low, whitewashed buildings. They were also responsible for those urban districts that consisted almost entirely of tents. The Italians, who had built vast cathedrals with lavishly decorated

interiors and erected huge, ostentatious statues, preferred to live in narrow alleyways flanked by houses with peeling stucco walls and washing lines suspended between them. The Italians were also fond of ruins, so they partially demolished their showplaces and abandoned them to the weeds and wild vine. What made these ruins so interesting, once they had been gnawed by the teeth of time, was that they were ruins *of* ruins – and more ruined than that you can't get.

The Menhir Gnomes from Normandy had erected monoliths in every sizeable square and opened little cafés around the sides. There they served coffee so strong that it made your head wobble for hours afterwards if you weren't used to it. At night the Granite Dwarfs from the South of England, who were at loggerheads with the Menhir Dwarfs, knocked the monoliths over or constructed bizarre sculptures with them. It was one of Atlantis's abiding mysteries where the little creatures found the strength to do this. The most superficially primitive but – because of their monstrous size – visually impressive buildings in Atlantis had been erected by

the Australian Ant People. These were anthills of immense proportions, many of their towers being several miles high. The Ant People, human below the waist and formicine above, were respected for their diligence. The streets were spotless, thanks to the indefatigable way in which they collected refuse free of charge and incorporated it in their towers. Thus the latter were really nothing more than ever-growing rubbish dumps with firmly cemented exteriors.

The Ant People's physical strength was impressive. They could carry objects a hundred times their own weight, but they were less well endowed with intelligence. It was impossible to converse with them about anything apart from refuse collection and anthill construction, and even that had to be done in a sign language for which you really needed two antennae growing out of your head. (You could also put your fists to your ears and waggle your forefingers, but, as I have already implied, it wasn't worth the effort.) Most of the city's temples were Indian, but so were the numerous rice kitchens on the outskirts, which were run by Semielephants.

These creatures were largely human but endowed with a pale blue elephantine head and six arms, which rendered them even more suited to running a fast-food restaurant than the four-armed Poophs (though the latter were better cooks). Since they could also use their trunks for prehensile purposes, they were capable of simultaneously stirring saucepans, shaking frying pans, filling plates, slicing onions, rinsing rice, washing up, and taking the customers' money. Though delicious, all their curry dishes tasted the same.

The Japanese Bonsai Mites inhabited a bonsai plantation of around twenty square yards, the smallest urban district in Atlantis but immense by their standards. The Bonsai quarter, whose inmates were little more than one inch high, was regarded as one of the city's favourite tourist attractions and enjoyed special protection. Enclosed by a strong wire-mesh fence, it could only be viewed from outside and was additionally guarded by an impressive contingent of Yetis. A glass roof shielded it from the elements, because a single raindrop would have been sufficient to kill a Bonsai Mite stone dead.

Big as skyscrapers, Atlantis's warlike-looking sandstone castles with hundreds of arrow slits had been built by Saracen pirates but were now used mainly for storing junk. Proliferating inside them, so it was said, were innumerable Kackertratts, extremely unpopular creatures of which more in due course.

There were whole city districts whose builders had vanished without trace, strange towers and halls constructed of materials to be found nowhere else in Zamonia, plastics and metals of sensational durability. Most of these buildings consisted of a material resembling burnished copper but much harder and more imperishable. Although they had allegedly stood for thousands of years, no downpours or meteor storms had dulled or scratched their gleaming surfaces. Their windows were huge, circular, multicoloured crystals that concentrated the light in a very economical way and distributed it over the interior spaces. The floors and ceilings were made of a glasslike substance that glowed green in the dark and seemed to breathe. Erected in the squares in these city districts were monstrous statues five times as big as

those of the Italians. Portrayals of creatures unlike anything that existed in Zamonia or elsewhere in the world, these statues were – surprisingly enough – of polished wood, though the wood came from trees as hard and durable as high-grade steel.

Many of these buildings were governed by the strangest natural laws. Water flowed uphill in them, and they were allegedly haunted on a vast scale. The furniture – insofar as the outlandish objects jutting from their walls, floors and ceilings could be described as such – was said to hold nocturnal conversations. Not even the most hard-boiled citizens of Atlantis ventured to occupy these buildings, even though all their doors stood open. It was whispered that the Invisibles had lived there before they retreated to the sewers.

Pagodas a hundred storeys high were a Chinese legacy. The Chinese had also, for some unknown reason, tried to bisect the city with a great wall but had lost interest at some stage, so all that remained of it was a low mound eighteen inches high, twenty miles long, and breached in numerous places. The Vikings had left behind hundreds of elongated timber buildings now used by Smorgard Dwarfs, who tended the cauldrons of water that steamed on eternal fires inside them. Atlanteans liked to meet there on cold days to sweat and pay the dwarfs to thrash them with bundles of reeds – in their opinion, an aid to good health. In accordance with the proverb that a greenhouse arises wherever two Dutchmen meet, the Dutch had glassed-over whole city districts. These were now used for growing their giant tomatoes by Corn Demons of Celtic stock.

Modes of transport

The Venetian Midgets had nostalgically criss-crossed the entire city with canals on which they liked to spend their leisure hours rowing colourful gondolas and belting out sentimental arias. You could get almost anywhere by way of these canals provided you had a boat and knew your way around. Other forms of transportation included the underground tramway system, the aforesaid Rickshaw Demons, some domesticated Midgard Serpents, Giant Snail coaches (romantic but slow), a large number of captive balloons, and a Zamonian version of the streetcar powered by Nightingalian ant-motors.

The underground tramway was a complex network of tracks operated by dwarf miners and propelled by gravity. You entered an underground station somewhere in the city and were loaded aboard one of the tramcars, which were usually coupled together in tens. Then, having blown his horn, a dwarf miner in the leading car would release the brakes and off you went, hell for leather, through tunnels illuminated by blazing torches. *The tramway*

Travelling by tramway was not for the faint-hearted. You went downhill all the way from A to B, the sole motive power deriving from the gradient and the weight of the cars and their occupants. At many points the cars reached a speed of 100 m.p.h. or more. On bends the showers of sparks were very impressive, and there were derailments from time to time.

At Point B you alighted with trembling knees and regained the daylight by way of a long spiral staircase. The tramcars were hoisted by means of ropes and tackle on to different tracks that led in many other directions. If your nerves were strong enough, you could reach almost every part of Atlantis by changing several times.

Suspended above the city from pylons were cables along which captive balloons travelled. This guaranteed that the balloons, most of them equipped with spacious gondolas, were not too dependent on the winds. If the air currents were unfavourable, passengers could lend a hand and drive the airship along with the aid of a large propeller. Provided for this purpose was a long crankshaft running the length of the gondola within easy reach of every seat. The streetcar network was a municipal, tax-funded system on which *Tethered balloons*

473

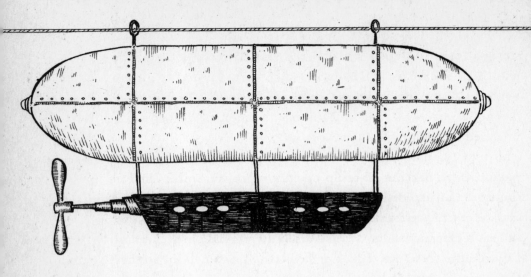

citizens could travel free of charge. It was manned by a permanent staff of Ant People, who were, logically enough, experts at maintaining ant-motors.

Ilstatna Boulevard

Cutting right across Atlantis was a broad boulevard known as the Ilstatna, an exclusively commercial thoroughfare offering every known commodity and service in the contemporary world, including restaurants to suit every nationality and outlandish dietary requirement.

Zamonian Wolpertingers, who were good chess players, had taken advantage of this to establish a chain of Wolpertinger Chess Cafés. Here, while eating snacks and drinking strong beer, customers could lose to a Zamonian Wolpertinger at chess. (Nobody had ever defeated a Zamonian Wolpertinger, perhaps because nobody dared to.)

The furdressing salons were mainly patronized, of course, by furry creatures. They were run by Melusines, a hairless type of dwarf with a penchant for gossip and a positively artistic way of wielding brush, comb, and scissors. I went there at least once a week, passing garlic bakeries, Twerpp tailoring establishments, Chinese laundries, tooth-pulling clinics (run by Bluddums), fortune-tellers' tents in which Italian Doombirds made dire predictions, betting shops, footcare studios, herbal tearooms, malediction bureaux (where you could pay shamans to curse your enemies), dance halls, cryptic bookstores (containing books found exclusively in Atlantis and written in still undeciphered languages), spitting taverns, (where, for a small charge, you could spit to your heart's content on sawdust-covered floors), briquette boutiques, fried ham stalls, cafés, boxing booths, beer gardens, and other products of Atlantean business acumen.

The inhabitants of Atlantis had requirements that far transcended those of human beings. Gnomes, for example, no matter where they hailed from, found it hard to resist footwear made of reeds, with the result that there were countless shoe shops selling grotesque shoes woven from that material. Although non-gnomes would pass such establishments shaking their heads, they would be thronged with gnomes avidly trying on one reed shoe after another. Irish Druids, for their part, had a love of austerity that manifested itself in their businesses as well. Druid shops were the bleakest places imaginable. All that most of them contained were some rickety shelves on which lay a few mossy stones, misshapen twigs, and pieces of damp driftwood, yet in business hours the Druids fought to get at these wares as if they were the Ornian crown jewels. Atlantis also had its so-called rumour cookshops. Run by Ornian Dune Toads, these were small establishments in

Other life forms, other customs

475

which you could partake of rumours. The 'cooking' was done at large, circular wooden tables round which the toads sat busily smoking cigarettes and whispering together. Little by little, their whispers, slanders and unverifiable allegations combined to produce an interesting rumour that could be picked up, taken home, and passed on – for instance, that the mayor of Atlantis secretly dined on the contents of trash cans at night.

Hide thrasheries were gloomy little establishments, most of them situated in basements, where Yhôllian Dervishes thrashed uncured hides with heavy iron carpet beaters, singing melancholy songs in Yhôllian the while. Only those who brought their hides to be beaten knew the purpose of this procedure (but they preserved a stubborn silence on the subject).

And that was probably the whole secret of Atlantean society. Few minded what their fellow citizens got up to as long as they themselves were left in peace.

Atlantean politics Politics had really been a dead letter since the Zamonian war of succession. In very early times the various urban districts had been ruled by kings. Then, by employing a series of diplomatic stratagems, the Norselanders had taken over the reins of government while the kings confined themselves to ceremonial duties. The latter did little more than attend the opening of new supermarkets, run marathons for charity, deliver graveside addresses at the funerals of prominent citizens, or turn up on major sporting occasions. (One exception was King Snalitat XXIII of Tatilans, who had lost his reason at some stage during the Zamonian war of succession and ran naked through the streets making unintelligible government announcements. His last edict was that all Norselanders over the age of thirteen be painted yellow and lined up in a row to have their feet tickled.) The people of Atlantis really governed themselves, a system that worked well at times, less well at others, and sometimes not at all. Total chaos broke out about once a month. Either one of the dwarf communities would draw attention to some form of discrimination by clogging the sewers with toilet paper, or the Rickshaw Demons and the Venetian Midgets would call a solidarity strike, thereby paralysing the entire transport system and cutting off supplies of fuel. Absolute chaos in such a confined space very soon became intolerable, however, so everything calmed down after two days at most and before any sensible strike demands could be put, let alone met. Then everything returned to normal.

Atlantis really functioned like an anthill. Although at first glance it looked completely chaotic and conformed to no discernible system, it held together and served a single common purpose: the survival and functional efficiency of a gigantic and alarming, wonderful and incomprehensible city.

To someone who had spent most of his previous life at sea, in the desert, on small islands, or in enclosed labyrinths, such a massive concentration of different life forms and cultures was like a blow with an invisible club. I must have resembled someone who had just been hit on the head as I tottered through the streets of Atlantis open-mouthed, continually turning on the spot to marvel at some unfamiliar sight. Several hours went by before I paused at an intersection, each corner of which was guarded by a black marble lion at least three hundred feet high.

A culture shock

477

It was late afternoon by now. Atlanteans were strolling, jostling and shoving each other around me, my feet were beginning to ache, and I hadn't the slightest idea exactly where I was, where I wanted to go, or what there was for supper.

I had hitherto been used to being given my food or finding it in my natural surroundings. Nightingale's lessons had taught me that different laws prevailed in big cities, which meant, among other things, that you paid for your meals – with money, to be precise.

I had already noticed that Atlantean money consisted mainly of gold, silver and copper pyramids of various sizes. In a Pooph-run pizzeria, for example, you could buy a delicious maize pancake smothered in just about everything a person could eat.

During the last hour a Pooph pizza had become, for me, the most desirable object in the universe. Pizzas were obtainable on almost every street corner, and wherever you walked or stood you could see chins draped in skeins of cheese from one of those pancakes with the alluring aroma.

'Pretty impressive, gah?' said a voice beside me.

A Tobacco Dwarf named Chemluth Havanna

It was a Tobacco Elf, a Southern Jungle Dwarf of the Rain Forest family, creatures who normally liked to pursue their nefarious activities on tobacco plantations and had more or less normal dwarfish habits – that much I knew from Nightingale's classes. They were recognizable by their tastelessly garish home-knitted caps, olive complexions, absurdly curly moustaches, and the gargling sound they made whenever they said an R. They also tacked a 'gah' on to every remark they made. Depending on the context, this could mean all manner of things.

(Incidental note: Zamonian was spoken in Atlantis by common consent, fortunately, but every little ethnic group had smuggled its own dialect into the language. Many interspersed all they said with saliva-rich sibilants, others with hoarse bellows, and others prefaced every word with an 'Eh⸮'. The easiest to understand were educated Druids, who spoke academically precise High Zamonian. Least comprehensible were the Horned Imbicels, who communicated in a croaking sing-song – they sounded like an opera singer with a moth in his throat. But nobody conversed with the Horned Imbicels in any case, so that problem – like so many others in Atlantis – resolved itself.)

'Yes indeed,' I said absently, being engrossed in the sight of a Bluddum who was disposing of a Pooph pizza in three quick gulps. 'The lions, I mean.'

I awakened from my Pooph pizza trance. 'Oh, the lions ... Yes, they're very fine. Beautifully carved. Lovely and smooth.'

'Gah, they weren't carved,' the dwarf replied almost lovingly. 'They were hand-polished – with paper handkerchiefs! Can you imagine how long it takes, gah, to polish a sculpture like that out of marble – with tissues⸮'

I tried to express my admiration.

'An amazing feat,' I said, and meant it.

'They're inhabited, gah. Four thousand apartments in each lion. Running hot and cold water, gah. No balconies, of course, but a mechanical elevator with music!'

He began to hum a Zamonian pop song.

'I don't see any windows.'

'You can only see through the windows from inside. Clever, gah⸮'

'Brilliant!'

'They belong to me.'

'What⸮'

'Gah. The lions. I own them.'

'That's, er, very impressive. Many congratulations.'

'Like to buy one?'

'What?'

'Like to buy a lion? Gah? They're going very cheap.'

'The trouble is, I don't –'

'Now listen to me!' The dwarf lowered his voice and glanced anxiously in all directions. 'I've taken to you, gah. That's why I'm going to quote you a crazy price, gah: ten pyras.'

He proceeded to slap his own face to punish himself for making such an altruistic proposition.

'Gah, gah!' he cried at every slap. 'What an idiot I am! I'll never make a good businessman.'

I gave him a lingering stare. In Atlantis, ten pyras would just about buy you a pizza.

I felt offended. I must have looked an utter nincompoop for him to have tried to bamboozle me with the oldest tourist trick in the world.

'Okay, gah!' he said, and improved his offer. 'Call it five pyras.'

And that was how I got to know Chemluth Havanna, who became my best friend in Atlantis.

Once I had made it clear to Chemluth, *first* that I hadn't escaped from a funny farm and *secondly* that I didn't have a pyra to my name, he promptly changed his tactics. He was determined to make money out of me somehow – quite how, he didn't yet know, but he stuck to me like glue.

'You're something special, gah? You're blue! You're a bear! You're a rarity! Gah?'

So he trotted along behind me, doing his best to talk me into all kinds of deals.

'Just stand on a street corner. You sing, I'll go round with the hat.'

'I can't sing.'

'We'll sell you to the zoo. At night I'll come with the pass key and let you out.'

'I've no wish to go into a zoo.'

Chemluth Havanna knew of a safe place to sleep, at least. We walked for all of two hours, and the further we went the stranger the neighbourhood became.

We began by trudging for miles along narrow, roughly cobbled alleys spanned by washing lines. Then the houses became sparser and gave way to ruined palaces, colonnaded temples thickly overgrown with brushwood and creeper, and stone monuments of which many were threaded with cracks and had largely collapsed. It was evident that no one lived here apart from some feral cats that insisted on rubbing against our legs.

A blue flash darted from the cobblestones, described a big electric arc, and disappeared down a crack. The alleyway was momentarily bathed in pale blue light.

I gave a start and jumped back at least my own length. Chemluth made a dismissive gesture.

'Greased lightning,' he said. 'It's harmless.'

From the
'Encyclopedia of Marvels, Life Forms
and Other Phenomena of Zamonia and its Environs'
by Professor Abdullah Nightingale

Greased Lightning. Natural phenomenon observed exclusively in the city of Atlantis for the past several hundred years. Generally bow-shaped and blue in colour, electrical discharges come shooting out of the ground, usually at night. Although no adequate scientific explanation of them has yet been found, it has at least been ascertained that these shafts of lightning pose no health hazard other than the possibility of death by mental trauma.

We crossed a broad, open square in the midst of which a black obelisk fully sixty feet high projected skywards from a dried-up fountain. Several dozen cats lay in the basin, purring and licking their paws. Beyond the obelisk stood the biggest cathedral I'd so far seen in Atlantis. It was built of white marble and surmounted by a green cupola, a good third of which had fallen in.

'Our sleeping quarters,' Chemluth said with a grin.

A flight of steps as wide as one of the city's thoroughfares led up to the entrance, which was guarded by two stone Cyclopses the height of a house. The door – or rather, gates – stood open. As big as the stern of a three-master, one of the gates had come off its hinges and crashed to the floor of the nave a long time ago, to judge by the tufts of grass, thistles, nettles and small trees sprouting from its joints. A swarm of pigeons fluttered into the air as we stepped over it into the ruined cathedral. Some lean brown shapes scurried off into the shadows at our approach.

In the cathedral

We climbed another big flight of steps to a gallery. The interior of the cathedral looked absurdly ill-constructed, probably because of its dilapidation. Steps led nowhere, half-demolished arches jutted pointlessly into space, fallen columns and shattered fragments of the cupola barred our path, overgrown with weeds.

The sun's dying rays slanted down through the dilapidated roof, dramatically illuminating the headless, armless statues in the cathedral's niches. At one point a huge half-relief carved into a red marble wall portrayed a robed Grim Reaper wielding his scythe.

I didn't care for the place, but it would soon be nightfall and I couldn't afford to be choosy.

'At least there aren't any Kackertratts here, gah?' Chemluth remarked while we were collecting some big wads of moss to sleep on.

'Kackertratts? What are they?'

'What are Kackertratts? Hard to say, gah. Who knows?'

From the
'Encyclopedia of Marvels, Life Forms and Other Phenomena of Zamonia and its Environs' by Professor Abdullah Nightingale

Kackertratts. Unpopular animal mutation combining the genes of pigeons, rats and cockroaches. Four to five feet long, Kackertratts are large canal rats with pigeons' wings, birdlike beaks and legs, and the antennae and digestive organs of cockroaches. Their sole legacy from the rat is a long, rubbery tail. Even the most painstaking autopsies have failed to discover the Kackertratt's brain. The body's control mechanism is therefore assumed to be located somewhere in the gastro-intestinal tract, which forms the bulk of the creature's innards. Also lacking is a heart, but this deficiency is offset by an outsized liver capable of digesting the most poisonous foodstuffs and facilitating the circulation of the blood, which resembles putrid egg yolk in smell and consistency. Kackertratts prefer to hunt for their food under cover of darkness. Their diet consists mainly of household trash and carrion, but they will also attack sizeable living creatures in times of famine. Kackertratts are the only known scavengers that devour the bones, toenails and eyelashes of their prey.

'Ugh! Are you sure there aren't any Kackertratts here?'
'You can never be absolutely sure of anything, gah?'
I was beginning to have my doubts about Chemluth's qualifications as a tourist guide.
'How often have you spent the night here?'
'Oh, often!'
'How often?'
'Lots of times.'
'Come on, how many times?'

'Er . . . Once.'

'Once? Honestly? When was that?'

'All right, tonight's the first time, gah? There always has to be a first time. Happy now? Can we get some sleep at last? Gah?'

It took Chemluth Havanna only a few minutes to make the transition from rhythmical breathing to a dreamer's happy little whimpers, whereas I lay awake for ages. The events of the day, the many impressive sights I'd seen, my pangs of hunger, and, first and foremost, our eerie sleeping quarters – all these conspired to give me no peace.

Even if half ruined, why should such a magnificent building be deserted? I had seen people living in tents and corrugated iron huts, so why not in this part of the city, where hundreds of grand buildings stood empty, mouldering away to no purpose? I remembered how the local inhabitants had stared after us, shaking their heads, as we made for the cathedral. I thought of my uncertain future in this bewildering city. And then I fell asleep after all, overcome by sheer exhaustion.

I dreamed that Chemluth and I were moving into an apartment in *A dream* one of the marble lions. It was really a vast kitchen-living room equipped with several luxurious stoves on which mighty beefsteaks were sizzling. I dreamed of big ovens in which sybaritically-topped Pooph pizzas were blowing cheesy bubbles, of huge saucepans in which rich soups simmered over open fires.

It was my job to sample these soups with a ladle several feet long. Whenever I managed to spoon some up, however, the apartment grew bigger and bigger and my ladle longer and longer, with the result that I couldn't put it to my lips. I lost my temper and hurled the ladle through a window, whereupon dozens of Kackertratts came fluttering in through the hole and proceeded to gobble everything up. One of them alighted on my chest and began to nibble my eyelashes. Its weight was unendurable. I felt I was suffocating, because the creature was also devouring my breath. Then I woke up – and the reality was almost worse than my nightmare. An eight-legged Lesser Olfactil sat perched on my cheek, inhaling my mouth odour with avid squeaks. Meanwhile, a fat Chimera had hunkered down on my chest and was regarding me with an impudent grin.

No dream!

I let out a yell and brushed the Olfactil off my cheek. It landed on the flagstones, scuttled off zigzag fashion, and disappeared down a crack. I lashed out at the Chimera with my fist, but it skilfully dodged the blow, fluttered into the air, and vanished into the shadows with a bleating laugh.

I leapt to my feet, screaming, and bombarded Chemluth with reproaches. Still half asleep, he hadn't a clue what was wrong.

'You had a bad dream, gah,' he said indifferently. 'Go back to sleep.'

'It wasn't a dream! There was a thing on my chest, and another on my face!' (At that stage I didn't know what Olfactils and Chimeras were, but it wouldn't have made much difference to my state of mind if I *had* known.)

I was far too agitated even to sit down. I stood there, breathing heavily, and scanned the bewildering maze of shadows in the cathedral's interior. Darkness flickered over the walls like black flames. Something uttered a snarl.

'There are animals of some kind in here,' I whispered.

'Poof! A few rats, perhaps,' said Chemluth, trying to reassure me. 'Lie down again, gah?'

The timbers overhead creaked, and I was briefly showered with flakes of plaster. Tiny particles of some ancient mural painting rained down on me. Peering at them in the moonlight, I made out beautifully painted foliage, fragments of hands, apples, angels' wings, eyes. Then a little bell tolled – a single, muffled note as if a large bird had flown into it.

The sound lay heavy on my heart.

Silence returned.

Chemluth slowly sat up, staring past me wide-eyed. He pointed to something behind my back.

'Gah!' he said.

I heard the flutter of heavy wings; then something raked my head with its hard, sharp talons and disappeared, snarling, into the darkness. Warm moisture was trickling down my neck. Afraid that some disgusting creature, probably a Kackertratt, had excreted its unspeakable bodily fluid on to me, I explored the warm, sticky substance with my paw. Although it looked jet black in the moonlight, I knew it was blood. It took very sharp talons to pierce a bluebear's fur.

'Blood?' I queried.

'Vampiros!' Chemluth replied.

Then came the first attack.

Snarling, a streak of black lightning sped towards me from the darkest corner of the cathedral. A muscular cat the size of a full-grown mastiff, it had the face of a maddened baboon and accelerated its progress through the air by flapping the short wings that sprouted from its shoulders.

And then, just before it reached me, something strange happened: the whole sequence of events seemed suddenly to go into slow motion, and I was pervaded by a profound feeling of calm.

The cat (monkey? bat?) took an infinite length of time to cover the last yard between us, time enough for me to study its musculature, draw my own conclusions therefrom, calculate its angle of attack, take one step forward, and simultaneously lean over backwards, with the result that my attacker missed me altogether.

I had a clear view of the monkey-cat's grimace of dismay as it soared over my head. I even had time to draw back my forepaw, slowly and powerfully, and deliver a well-aimed blow to the creature's solar plexus that catapulted it out of its trajectory and sent it sailing through the air for yards. With a crash, it landed on its back on the hard marble floor, then bounced around the nave like a broken clockwork toy, yelping with pain.

'Gah!' Chemluth said respectfully. 'That was quick!'

The process that had seemed so infinitely slow had actually lasted only a split second. Although it didn't dawn on me until later, this marked the awakening of my innate predatory instincts. I was a bear, after all. Those instincts had been dormant, thanks to my previous upbringing, but something had now been unwise enough to attack me and activate my atavistic, ursine defence mechanisms. I threw back my head and let out a spine-chilling roar whose reverberations took a long time to die away.

Then two of the vampire cats sprang at me simultaneously. I ducked, and one went crashing into the remains of a column behind me. The other I plucked out of the air by the hind leg. Whirling it around my head three times like a hammer thrower, I hurled it back in the direction it had come from. It must have hit some of its own kind, because a chorus of angry, agonized snarls went up when it landed.

Then peace returned.

'Haha!' chortled Chemluth. 'That's that, gah, they won't be back. Vampires are cowardly creatures!'

He spat contemptuously on the ground and tried to give me an admiring slap on the back, but only succeeded in patting my elbow because of our difference in height.

At that moment, some fifteen vampire cats converged on us from all directions while five more attacked us from the air.

Like all Tobacco Elves, Chemluth was ignorant of fear. It wasn't that he was courageous, because you can't be courageous unless you know what fear is and overcome it. It was simply that Tobacco Elves were completely devoid of that emotion because they had green blood in their veins and no adrenalin. Tobacco Elves *noticed* when they were in danger but simply didn't care. If attacked by a nine-foot jungle gorilla, they wouldn't stop to think that they might come off worse but plunge into the fray without more ado. Infinitely superior opponents were often so disconcerted that they turned tail. This made Tobacco Elves extremely efficient and redoubtable fighters despite their small stature. Being a jungle dweller himself, Chemluth knew where best to hit predatory apes and jungle cats: on their moist, sensitive noses. Hit the mark, and one well-aimed thrust with a finger was enough to put a vampire cat out of action for minutes on end.

Chemluth excelled at a South Brazilian sport known as *flamencação* (he even possessed a colourful embroidered belt that marked him out as an adept of the ninth grade). When performing this elegant cross between flamenco dancing, karate, and bullfighting, he simply stood there, scarcely moving from the spot, with one hand on his hip and the other poised above his head like a cobra about to strike at any moment. Simultaneously, he turned on his own axis with little, mincing steps and stamped his foot from time to time (lending the contest an almost balletic rhythm), then swiftly stepped aside so that a vampire cat sailed past him into space or went crashing into a wall.

Flamencação

Every now and then, clamping two fingers together and striking downwards with lightning speed, he would drive them into an adversary's nose or a sensitive spot below the ribs, humming a bossa nova as he did so.

Less deliberate and well-rehearsed, my own technique was spontaneous and instinctive. I was amazed at the strength that had been slumbering unutilized within me. The bear is regarded as one of the most dangerous wild animals on this planet, but that I had yet to grasp because I'd been too busy roaming subterranean labyrinths, sitting on a school bench, and engaging in other non-ursine activities. One blow from my paw sufficed to send a vampire cat somersaulting through the air; one bite, and another of the creatures retreated into the shadows, whimpering with pain. I dished out punishment with speed and vigour, never missing the mark, never making an unnecessary move or neglecting to keep my guard up, like a professional boxer equipped with claws.

If the vampires had really been as cowardly as their reputation suggested, they would long ago have quit the field of battle. But they persevered no matter how much we hurt them or how hard they landed on the ground. They merely withdrew into the dark corners of the cathedral and then resumed the attack.

They had a simple but effective tactic: they operated in shifts. When half of them became tired they withdrew to lick their wounds and the other half took over. Chemluth and I were exhausting ourselves, whereas they could recoup their energy again and again. They were bound to defeat us in the end.

One big vampire cat had crept up behind me and buried its fangs in my fur, another was crouching in front of me, clawing painfully at my legs, and a third was fluttering overhead, snapping at my muzzle. My strength had run out at last, I realized. Scarcely able to lift a paw, I was debating whether to drop my guard and abandon myself to my fate when the vampires backed off and withdrew as if in response to a secret word of command.

Badly dishevelled and gasping for breath, we were suddenly all alone. The air was throbbing to an unfamiliar, ominous sound, an electric pulsation rather like the chirping of enormous crickets.

'*Cacatratas!*' said Chemluth.

'What?'

'Kackertratts, gah! Lots of them.'

Twenty or thirty feet away the floor of the cathedral seemed to have come alive. A jostling mass of creatures was advancing on us. Here and there I could see long antennae quiver in the night air. From time to time, when a Kackertratt fluttered wildly into the air, one could briefly discern its hideous silhouette in the moonlight before it sank back into the milling throng.

'I thought there weren't any Kackertratts in here!' I hoped the subdued reproach in my voice was clearly perceptible.

'Oh, Kackertratts – they've no style!' Chemluth snorted contemptuously. 'Always turning up where they're not wanted.'

That wasn't altogether true. The Kackertratts had temporarily saved our lives, at least. Only so as to kill us themselves, perhaps, but still: the vampire cats had beat a retreat. They were obviously creatures endowed with common sense.

'I know,' Chemluth suggested. 'We'll simply make a dash for the door.'

Of course. Why not?

Kackertratts [cont.]. Persons who encounter one or more Kackertratts would be well advised not to move too quickly, but to favour a fluid, balletic mode of progression. Kackertratts react to abrupt, hurried movements only. Not possessing a brain, they assume that anything in fluid motion is water.

That was a tip from the same stable as the one that adjured you to remain absolutely still when a Tyrannomobyus Rex swam towards you or an angry Phorinth charged you with its horn lowered. I found it very difficult to muster sufficient faith in this piece of advice. My instinct would have been to run down the steps screaming and waving my paws, but I did my utmost to move like a ballerina in slow motion.

'Walk very slowly!' I hissed between my teeth. 'Then they'll mistake us for water.'

Chemluth stared at me mistrustfully. 'Gah? They'll think we're water? What gives you that idea?'

'I've got an encyclopedia in my head. It sometimes tells me things like that,' I whispered as I descended the steps with my forelegs out sideways like a tightrope walker on a slanting rope.

'Gah, so you've got an encyclopedia in your head. I understand...'

'Well, not an encyclopedia exactly. It's really a Nocturnomath with seven brains. He can see in the dark and open a can of sardines by will-power. I can hear him inside my head.'

Chemluth gave me the sort of look you give a delirious fever patient.

'Listen,' he said, 'you've temporarily lost your wits, but that's all right, gah? It's no disgrace, considering the danger we're in. I'm taking over command, gah? We'll simply run down the steps with our arms out, yelling blue murder.'

I looked down the steps.

'No,' I said, 'that's just what we won't do.'

'Why not?'

'Because.' I jerked my snout at the bottom step.

Another contingent of the Kackertratt army was climbing the steps. Thousands more were following in line abreast from the cathedral door. The huge insects were pouring into the cathedral

through broken windows and cracks in the walls. We were completely surrounded.

'We're going to die,' I said.

'Gah, we're going to die.' Chemluth didn't contradict me for once, but I could tell that he was looking for some way of putting a good face on the situation.

Nothing occurred to him.

The Kackertratts came swarming up the steps in a broad black wave. The electrical crackle of their Kackertrattian language was amplified many times over by the cathedral's echoes.

Something was moving beneath my foot: in the gloom, I had trodden full on a Kackertratt! I leapt aside in disgust and picked up a piece of stone, intending to smash the insect's skull. I was raising it above my head in both paws when I saw I hadn't trodden on a Kackertratt at all. The step was sinking. So was the one below it and the one below that.

In the midst of the flight of steps was a hole big enough to admit a horse.

Chemluth jumped into it without a moment's hesitation.

'Gah!' he called from below. 'Come on, jump! It isn't deep!'

I hurled the stone at the mass of Kackertratts, shattering one of the insects' chitinous shell with an ugly splintering sound. It was the worst thing I could have done at that particular juncture.

The Kackertratt emitted the kind of sound a saw would make if it could scream. Hundreds of its fellow insects took up this cry, shot into the air, and flew straight at me.

I jumped into the hole.

I landed on my hind paws less than six feet down, suffering only a slight pain in the ankle joints. Above me, stone grated on stone as the steps slid shut. A Kackertratt just managed to wedge itself between them, only to regret it a moment later when they neatly cut it in half. The darkness below was as profound as in Nightingale's darkroom.

'You're safe here,' said a voice. I couldn't even tell whether it was *A talking trumpet* male, female, or demonic. It sounded like a trumpet endowed with the power of speech.

'Follow my voice, I'll guide you to the surface. This way ... this way ...' Those were the only words the voice uttered, again and again, as we stumbled after it through the gloom: 'This way ... this way ...'

I don't know how many times I fell over. It was pitch black, and there were plenty of obstacles. Now and then, one of the shafts of greased lightning that had startled me so much would go snaking along the wall of the tunnel, but so swiftly that it failed to show up our guide. I couldn't make out *where* he (or she, or it) was, even in its blue glow.

At last we entered a tunnel that was at least dimly illuminated. Thin fingers of light stabbed the darkness through some little holes in the roof.

'That's a manhole cover,' said the voice. 'You can get out here.'

Although the visibility was a little better, I still couldn't make out the owner of the voice. He (or she, or it) must have been standing right beside me, but there was nothing to be seen. We climbed an iron ladder, pushed up the manhole cover, and emerged into the open air. We were in a dark side street leading to a main thoroughfare humming with big-city life. There was no sign of the voice.

'That was one of the Invisibles,' Chemluth explained.

'Invisible people, you mean?'

'Gah. They're invisible.'

Side by side, Chemluth and I made our way in silence to the Ilstatna, the big shopping street where we hoped to drum up some breakfast. Chemluth had become rather subdued, perhaps because he felt embarrassed to have landed me in such a predicament.

He made strenuous efforts to cadge a few pyras and placate me with a modest breakfast at a Wolpertinger chess café, where Wolpertingers sat over their chess boards from early morning onwards, growling angrily whenever their opponent made a move.

After the events of the night I realized that anyone who hoped to survive in this city needed a roof over his head. For that you needed money, and to get money you needed a job. I was firmly resolved to look for work. Chemluth found this a highly unappealing idea.

'Work?' he said with distaste. 'No, let's go busking. I'll sing, you dance.'

'I'm not a dancing bear.'

'Gah,' he sighed. 'I realize that.'

Various jobs Finding work in Atlantis was no problem. For the first few weeks Chemluth and I worked in a furdressing salon. There was always a demand for hairpickers, whose job it was to remove tufts of hair from combs and brushes, sort them into their various types, and deliver them to the wigmakers. We spent our days and nights teasing troll hair out of brushes, sorting it carefully, and putting it in paper bags. It wasn't exactly pleasant, coaxing former cave-dwellers' often rank and greasy hair out of a comb, especially when you got your fingers bitten by the lice that infested it.

We soon moved on to one of the spitting taverns that employed sweepers to clear away the nauseating mishmash of sawdust and spittle and scatter fresh sawdust in its place, twenty-four hours a day. It was easy work, but not particularly hygienic. You had to be constantly on your guard to dodge jets of saliva, because sweepers were the customers' favourite target.

Our next employer was a bloodbroker. You could work in such establishments as a labeller responsible for ensuring that the many different kinds of blood did not get mixed up. This was a definite step up the professional ladder. I felt like a salesman in a wine merchant's. You had to have a precise knowledge of each type of blood in stock, determine its origin, blood group and vintage, and tell whether it came from a troll, a dwarf, an elf, or some other creature.

Working for the bloodbroker

There was green blood from Irish goblins, white blood from Flemish aquasprites, blue blood from aristocratic Norselanders, yellow blood from Rickshaw Demons, and, of course, red blood of every shade ranging from dark red Minotaur blood to the translucent red of the Hackonians (a rosé, so to speak).

It was not overly pleasant to watch our Werewolf bosses at work. Anyone who sold his blood was not only looked down on but treated accordingly. On one occasion, in the days before I started work at the bloodbroker's, I myself had donated some blood. I was made to sit on a crude wooden chair while one of the Werewolves prepared to insert the needle. Then he bent over me and asked, 'With or without anaesthetic?'

'With, please,' I replied.

The last thing I saw was his fist as it slammed into my jaw.

After that we worked as 'screamers' for a waxworks. Bearing in mind that Yetis and Rickshaw Demons were an everyday sight in Atlantis, the reader may perhaps form some idea of the horrific

The House of Horrors

exhibits a waxworks had to display in order to terrify the city's inhabitants. It was our job to hide behind the wax figures and, if customers were not sufficiently intimidated, freeze the blood in their veins with spine-chilling screams.

Although this was quite fun for a few days, we grew hoarser and hoarser. Besides, the job was not without its dangers, and we abandoned it after our third set-to with a family of Yetis.

It would undoubtedly be easier to list the jobs we *didn't* sample than the ones we actually took. To name only some, we worked as street sweepers and lamp trimmers, leaflet distributors and cemetery gardeners, chess café waiters and trouser pressers, errand boys and night watchmen, barkers and billboard scrapers, newspaper boys and fish sorters – none of them forms of activity requiring much in the way of qualifications. I should have liked to do a job that made the most of my comprehensive Nocturnal Academy education, but this was harder than I had thought.

To obtain a teaching post you had to have spent years working your way up through Atlantis's intricate educational system, and nearly every learned profession required hard-to-get permits from mysterious government departments. You could get nowhere without a Norselander rubber stamp, and that was available only to those who queued up for months on end, paid bribes to the competent authority, or had a Norselander in the family. All the professions were controlled by obscure committees. In short, organized chaos prevailed here as elsewhere. So I resigned myself to these temporary jobs until a profession worthy of my qualifications came my way. The high point of my career to date was topping-spreader in a Pooph pizzeria. And Chemluth was my assistant.

Chemluth Havanna, I regret to say, was an inveterate womanizer. He went in search of suitable partners whenever time permitted. Even during the period we spent trying a wide variety of temporary jobs, I counted seventy-seven occasions on which he made assignations with Atlanteans of the feminine gender. I've never quite grasped how he managed it. Let's not beat about the bush: Chemluth was a dwarf, and dwarfs are small by definition. He wasn't particularly handsome either, what with his potato nose and clawed feet, but he evidently had what it took. He had only to accost some completely unknown female in the street, and within half an hour he would be holding hands with her in a café and crooning romantic rain-forest ditties in her ear.

Chemluth the womanizer

Whether it was his fiery gaze or the numerous Rs he rolled in his throat, no Atlantean female of any species was proof against his charms. He dated dwarfs, gnomes, Norselanders, elves, druidesses, and once, even, a Yeti's fiancée. This earned him a thorough thrashing from her Yeti brothers.

But none of these relationships lasted longer than a day, and the reason for their swift dissolution was always the same.

'Gah, not enough hair,' Chemluth would sigh whenever he returned from one of his assignations.

He hankered after a girl that had more hair than all the rest – no ordinary pipe dream, but such was Chemluth's ideal – and even in a city like Atlantis, which harboured many creatures even more hirsute than a bear, he failed to find the female of his dreams.

The corkscrew tower

We were now able to afford a small apartment in East Lisnatat: two rooms, kitchen, and a lavatory on the landing (which we unfortunately had to share with several Bluddums). It was situated in one of Atlantis's five Babylonian corkscrew towers. These were gigantic skyscrapers in the shape of truncated cones with huge stairways spiralling up the outside, hence their name. All the towers had been left half-finished, the Babylonians' typical mode of construction and one that doubtless accounted for the fact that they never really managed to gain a foothold in the real estate business. No one had ever completed these ruins because of their total failure to comply with building regulations, so City Hall leased them at extremely low rents rather than leave them unoccupied and abandon yet another building to the Kackertratts.

Another reason for the affordable rent was the exterior stairway. This being the only means of reaching your apartment, the higher up you lived the more strenuous the climb – and the lower the rent. We lived on the 200th floor, right at the top. The view of Atlantis was enough to knock you sideways. So was the wind that blew in through the unglazed windows.

But on balmy summer nights we enjoyed sitting outside on the stone steps, watching the blue streaks of greased lightning that flickered all over the enormous city. Whole streets would become rivers of blue light for seconds at a time, while we sat up there like gods, as if we had created it all.

Life in a Babylonian corkscrew tower may safely be described as adventurous. Only the more reckless and less vertigo-prone denizens of Atlantis dared to occcupy these half-ruined buildings, a fact that made them risky to live in. Our own tower was populated mainly by Troglotrolls, Mountain Dwarfs, Bluddums, and Yetis, an uncouth bunch with little consideration for their neighbours. The South Zamonian Mountain Dwarfs celebrated at least one wedding a week because they were always swapping spouses, and every wedding was the occasion of a riotous party at which all their relations were present by invitation and a brass band played Mountain Dwarf music. Mountain Dwarf Music was played on phnagguffs, instruments resembling alphorns with cymbals mounted on them. The phnagguffists bashed the latter with an iron drumstick while blowing into the mouthpiece. Phnagguffs were so long that they projected out of the windows, which made the noise pollution even worse, but this counted for little because there wasn't a door or window pane in the entire building. The rest of the wedding guests did their utmost to drown the phnagguff music with curses, that being the traditional way in which South Zamonian Mountain Dwarfs congratulate a bride and groom.

There was no point in complaining, not unless you thought it desirable to be beaten up by a gang of Mountain Dwarfs and dangled upside down from the 200th floor until you apologized, a procedure to which Chemluth was subjected at six o'clock one morning, when he begged a Mountain Dwarf brass band at least to muffle their iron drumsticks with hand towels.

The Bluddums in the next-door apartment were clearly in some shady line of business. They slept by day, snoring loudly for the most part, and were visited at night by other Bluddums with whom they performed strange rituals that entailed coughing in unison into tin buckets. When a Bluddum goes to the lavatory you mustn't expect him to emerge for three hours. You will also have to wait another hour before you can enter it without losing consciousness, and the noises he produces inside are even more horrific than those he makes when coughing into a tin bucket.

The Yetis, though good-natured types at heart, had a regrettable tendency to sleepwalk when the moon was full. They would breeze into other people's apartments and throw out any pieces of furniture small enough to go through the windows. No one had the temerity to wake a somnambulant Yeti because it was rumoured that someone had risked it and gone the way of his furniture.

Getting home could be a perilous adventure in itself, particularly in winter, when the outside stairway was slippery with ice and a blizzard was blowing, or during violent summer thunderstorms, when the shafts of lightning made you feel like a target in a shooting gallery.

All our homes were open to the elements, as I have said, so a little cloud could sail in one window, deposit its load of rain on the living-room carpet, and disappear out the other. During thunderstorms, dense black masses of cloud would come rolling in and blind us until some ball lightning exploded inside them. The reader can have no idea how loud a thunderclap sounds at source. One went off right beside my head while I was asleep, and I've had this high-pitched whistle in my left ear ever since.

On hot summer days our elevated position was a great advantage because we were always fanned by a cool breeze, but in winter the apartment was constantly blanketed in snow. We built ourselves a little igloo to sleep in until the spring sunshine melted it.

But the apartment was our home, my first real home, paid for out of money I had earned myself (120 copper pyras a month) and relatively safe from vampires and Kackertratts, none of which would venture into a building occupied mainly by uncouth louts with hands the size of coal shovels.

Only when the earth shook (as it did at least once a week) did we wish we lived in a smaller, stouter structure. It was said that no building in Atlantis had ever been demolished by an earthquake, but in my opinion it was only a matter of time before this happened, at least in the case of a corkscrew tower. The walls and floors groaned like spirits in torment, plaster rattled down cavities, and furniture promenaded across the apartment as if it had come to life. Earthquakes could be life-threatening if you were on the outside stairway, and I was nearly shaken off into space on two occasions.

The Pooph pizzeria

Working at the Pooph pizzeria was the first job I had in Atlantis that taught me a lifelong skill, namely, cooking. The restaurant's head chef and proprietor, a potbellied Pooph named Nabab Yeo, was a master of his craft, and had been awarded four golden spoons by the Association of Norselander Gourmets.

Pizzas, being designed for fast-food customers and counter sales, were not the only items on the menu.

The back kitchen was where Nabab cooked in earnest for a regular clientele of well-heeled epicures. Whenever I got the chance I used to peer over his shoulder and watch him prepare his specialities.

That was how I learnt to braise pork chops in beer, simmer boiled beef to a turn, rinse scalded artichokes, and gratinate oysters (with a mixture of chopped spinach, Gruyère cheese, and breadcrumbs).

Nabab Yeo

Nabab showed me the only authentic way of preparing spaghetti (boil for twelve minutes, don't rinse, simply remove from the hot water, allow it to drain, pour melted butter over it, fold in two raw egg yolks, squeeze a clove of garlic over it, mix well, and serve); how to simmer an oxtail over a low flame until you can flake the meat with a spoon (cooking time: five hours minimum); how to poach eggs in red wine till they're soft as wax; how to beat a veal

504

cutlet (with the flat of a large knife, never with a meat mallet!);
what cheese goes best with rocket (South Zamonian pecorino);
and how to eat a poussin (in your fingers only). Nabab not only
divulged a never-ending series of recipes but knew the correct
answers to the most abstruse nutritional problems. Being a
historian of dietetics in his spare time, he was a walking gourmet's
encyclopedia. He could tell you the calorific value of every
foodstuff, both existing and extinct. He knew every edible plant
and spice that had ever grown in Zamonia. There used, for
instance, to be a spice named pelverin that could turn any food into
a delicacy. It was extracted from the pelv, a plant the Bluddums had
eradicated because they thought it harboured the Devil. Nabab
told me of plants that yielded yogurt, of the legendary
megastrawberries of Dullsgard, which could reputedly grow to the
size of a house, and of pimmagons, peat eggs that tasted like baked
bananas.

But he waxed truly rhapsodic when he spoke of his special field,
the blending of flavours. Nabab Yeo believed that a menu should
embody as many different ingredients and courses, spices and
calories, as possible. It was breathtaking, the audacious
combinations of tastes he produced. I once saw him braise a fish in
honey and deep-fry a salted peach. He stuffed chickens with liquid
chocolate and tossed noodles in cinnamon, but none of his
customers ever complained; on the contrary, the restaurant rang
with their cries of delight. The greater the number of foods a
creature consumed in its life, the more meaningful its existence:
such was Nabab Yeo's philosophy.

I was not privileged to assist him, because Chemluth and I worked
shifts in the pizza section, where I had risen to the rank of senior
topping-spreader thanks to a bright idea that occurred to me one

day: I took one pizza, complete with topping, and superimposed it on another. This double pizza not only led to my promotion but became one of the restaurant's best-sellers. Chemluth, my assistant, deftly tossed me the olives, onion rings, slices of salami, sardines, mushrooms, and gobbets of tuna and ham with which I decorated my works of art. There were always a few Atlanteans watching us at work with their noses flattened against our window. This presented Chemluth with a welcome opportunity to show off in front of members of the fair sex and make dates with them, especially when the females in question had exceptionally luxuriant heads of hair.

At home, whenever we weren't trying to grab some sleep between Mountain Dwarf weddings, I used to pass on some of the knowledge I'd acquired at the Nocturnal Academy. In return, Chemluth taught me a few *flamencação* movements.

At night, smitten with homesickness, he would speak of his native tobacco plantations. Hearing him sob as he raved about their creeper-entwined beauty, I couldn't help recalling Qwerty Uiop's equally emotional accounts of the 2364th Dimension.

Wednesdays in Atlantis Wednesdays were the best thing about Atlantis. The middle of the week was a traditional holiday there. Everyone stopped work and celebrated the fact that half the week was over.

On Wednesdays the whole of the city's working population slept late, picnicked in the parks, or attended one of the cultural functions of which Atlantis had more to offer than any city in the known world.

Pizza Sandwich à la Bluebear

Ingredients for the dough:
10 grams yeast, 200 grams flour, pinch of sugar, 1/4 teaspoonful salt

Topping:
150 grams mozzarella, four puréed tomatoes, six sardines,
four slices of salami, five halved olives,
100 grams raw ham, one can of tuna, some fresh basil,
onion rings, capers, grated parmesan.

Method of preparation:
Mix the dough ingredients with two tablespoonfuls of water,
knead well, leave for 30 minutes, then roll out.
Apply topping in the following order:
tomato purée, mozzarella, remaining ingredients.
Repeat the entire process,
cook both pizzas in the oven for 15 minutes,
place one pizza on top of the other,
and serve piping hot.

A glance at one page in the *Atlantean Advertiser* revealed a whole host of current attractions. The following are only a selection:

Zemm Zeggliu and the Norselanders, a combo from West Zamonia, were playing at a rave in the **Banned Bunker**, a kind of subterranean dance hall beneath one of the city's lakes. There were no genuine Norselanders in the band, of course (they would have been far too snobbish), merely Bluddums disguised as Norselanders. This was pretty daring in itself, because the Norselanders were very quick to take offence and didn't hesitate to sue other creatures for defamation.

The **Colodrome**, a huge theatre with 34 stages, was presenting a marathon performance of *The Voltigork's Vibrobass*, an experimental drama by Wilfred the Wordsmith. It lasted 240 hours and employed a cast of 3000 actors. The spectators relieved each other in shifts, but this did not render the production any less intelligible because Wilfred's play was intended as an attack on pure meaning and repeated the dialogue, with only minor variations, every twelve hours. Chemluth, who had seen parts of the play, was very disappointed by it. He'd been bewildered by the fact that the actors delivered their lines backwards and were permitted to eat their meals on stage.

Psittachus Rumplestilt, the author of *How Dank Was My Valley*, was signing copies of *How Dank Was My Valley II*, the sequel to his best-seller, in the **Topers' Tavern**, a literary café on the outskirts of the Italian quarter.

The **Zamonian Wolpertingers** had issued a general invitation to a **chess marathon** at their favourite establishment, **The Desperate Endgame**. Their advertisement promised the victor free beer and immunity from physical violence.

The **Big-Footed Bertts** were organizing a protest march down **Ilstatna Boulevard**. Participants, who were invited to suggest what the protest should be about, would be provided with plenty of blank placards and banners to write on.

Culrossian Porg, a former troll-hunter turned trollophile, was chairing a public meeting at the **North Lisnatat Youth Hostel**. Those attending this event, which was bound to expose him to criticism of his former activities, would doubtless be limited to infuriated trolls and, possibly, to avowed trollophiles.

Professor Yobbo G. Yobb, the founder of Yobbism, was scheduled to lecture and insult his audience at the **Muchwater Museum**.

The **Rickshaw Demons** were organizing piggyback races in **Atlantis Park**, free of charge, to improve their image with the younger generation. (They had been trying to do this for years, but they were so hideous that no child ever turned up, and the Rickshaw Demons would probably find themselves deserted yet again, paper hats and free bottles of Demon Lemonade notwithstanding.)

The **Consortio Flagellantium**, a group of fat, toad-headed Italian tenors, were scheduled to perform some ancient choral works on an open-air stage in Silnatat, simultaneously thrashing each other with fresh stinging nettles to attain still greater expression in the upper register.

The **Museum of Ineffabilities**, which displayed objects people didn't care to talk about, was presenting a special exhibition entitled 'Zamonian Dental Instruments through the Ages'. Anyone who saw what Bluddums employed to perform extractions without anaesthetic was guaranteed to clean his teeth five times a day thereafter.

'Flash' Fangfang, the lightning tamer, was giving a show in the **Square of Lost Souls**, a kind of open-air theatre in central Lisnatat. 'Flash' had discovered that the shafts of greased lightning which flickered through Atlantis at night were attracted to water. Accordingly, he arranged buckets of water in ever-changing geometrical patterns at places in the city where this phenomenon occurred with particular frequency. The lightning shafts cavorted from bucket to bucket in an extremely graceful manner, producing a type of balletic *son et lumière*. Needless to say, 'Flash' cordoned off these sites well in advance and pocketed a fat entrance fee.

Melliflor Gunk, the darling of every female Atlantean less than two hundred years old, was giving a recital that had been sold out for months. Stripped to the waist and accompanying himself on a diamond-encrusted harp, he sang all his songs, which told of eternal love and the purchase of exorbitantly expensive engagement rings, with tears streaming down his cheeks.

The **Half-Baked Meat Helmets**, an avant-garde theatrical company from South Zamonia currently appearing in a nightclub cellar, allowed audiences to pelt them with coins in return for an admission fee.

Heavily attended, no doubt, was the **gebba match** between the urban districts of Tatilans and Titalans for the Rickshaw Cup (another image-boosting venture on the part of the PR-minded Rickshaw Demons). Gebba was the prototype of football, the sport so popular today, except that the teams numbered as many as 5000 players and the game was played, not with a ball, but with 400 wooden discs of various colours. These had to be kicked into an indeterminate number of small round goals, which in turn were closely defended by forty goalkeepers. The venue was the **Gebba Palace**, a building on twenty floors. This made it impossible to maintain an overall view of the game, which lasted all day but could also continue, with numerous periods of extra time, far into the night. Every gebba match was followed by days-long arguments over who had really won, a question that often defied elucidation. Victory and defeat were immaterial, however, because taking part was all that mattered.

Yes indeed, Atlantis had many forms of entertainment to offer, but the main event on Wednesdays, beyond a doubt, took place in the city's **Megathon**. This was the **Duel of the Congladiators**, for which Chemluth obtained two tickets to celebrate my invention of the pizza sandwich.

From the
'Encyclopedia of Marvels, Life Forms and Other Phenomena of Zamonia and its Environs'
by Professor Abdullah Nightingale

Congladiators of Atlantis, The. Popular idols endowed with an ability to con an audience in an entertaining manner. Professional congladiators regularly engage in so-called Duels of Lies at the Megathon in Atlantis, where they compete for the title 'King of Lies' by exchanging fictitious stories. Audiences assess and evaluate the contestants' relative entertainment value with the aid of a rather complicated scoring system. In order to practise this profession, aspirants must undergo intensive training at the Liars' Institute, rising by degrees from assistant liar to certified congladiator. The congladiators of Atlantis belong to the Self-Employed Guild. They combine the talents of a conman, comedian, stage actor, samurai, heavyweight boxer, chess grandmaster, and - of course - Roman gladiator.

Congladiators are more idolized in Atlantis than any other kind of talented entertainer. Popular congladiators have schools and observatories named after them. To keep his name on everyone's lips, the reigning King of Lies has it stamped on every loaf of bread baked in Atlantis. The most popular of all time was →*Nussram Fakhir the Unique*, who held the title for twelve years before relinquishing it of his own free will.

The Megathon

The Megathon was a circular, roofless stadium with tiers of seats for approximately a hundred thousand spectators and a small stage in the middle. We entered it by one of the four main gates and looked for our row – one of the cheaper ones, naturally. The stadium was completely sold out, as it was for every Duel of Lies. The upper tiers at the back, whose occupants got in free because they could see almost nothing, were largely monopolized by roistering Bluddums and Yetis who belched, bellowed the names of their favourite congladiators, and pelted other spectators with gnawed corn cobs (it was a traditional feature of duels of lies that grilled corn cobs and hot beer were sold at the entrance to the stadium).

Seated in the front row were Norselanders, city dignitaries, celebrities, and – of course – Reganaan Salias II, the current mayor of Atlantis. The central tiers were occupied by Atlanteans of every conceivable kind, all mixed up together: Draks, Venetian Mannikins, Poophs, Waterkins, Anklemen, Woodentops – duel-of-lies enthusiasts were drawn from all social classes. The only absentees were the Invisibles, not that one knew this for certain because they couldn't be seen in any case.

High above the spectators, stationed at regular intervals on the circular stadium wall, were the Gryphons and Gargylls whose task it was to keep order. Duels of Lies were emotional occasions, and the hard-bitten fans of certain congladiators had a tendency to brawl. Bluddums, in particular, seized every opportunity to vandalize seats and swear at inoffensive spectators.

Corn cobs and hot beer

Chemluth and I were seated in the twentieth row, each holding a steaming beer and a sizzling corn cob. Chemluth was a prey to mixed emotions. He had just broken it off with a troll girl because she had turned up for their date with her hair bobbed in the latest fashion. That was the real reason for our presence in the Megathon: Chemluth declared that the best aids to banishing one's cares were a hot beer, a corn cob, and a thrilling Duel of Lies.

I began to enjoy the show even before it opened. The excited chatter of a hundred thousand spectators, the solemn phnagguff music played by the Mountain Dwarf band in the orchestra pit, the scent of toasted corn cobs – all these generated an atmosphere that enthralled me from the very first. I shuffled excitedly to and fro on my seat and asked Chemluth at five-minute intervals how soon the show would start. He himself, having already witnessed several such duels, was considerably calmer.

'A while yet, gah. They like to boost the suspense by keeping the audience on tenterhooks.'

The Mountain Dwarf orchestra was now playing a phnagguff arrangement of the Zamonian national anthem. Everyone rose and joined in, the Bluddums loudest of all:

All hail to thee, Zamonia,
beloved native land,
encircled by the ocean blue
and girt with silver sand . . . and so on.

Having got that over, we could resume our seats. Next, some Norselander mimes mounted the stage of the Megathon and launched into an unutterably boring routine that illustrated the history of the mayors of Atlantis. This drew enthusiastic applause from the ringside seats.

Then came the master of ceremonies, who announced the contestants in an awe-inspiring voice: Mutra Singh, an Indian fakir, and Deng Po, a former Rickshaw Demon. He laboriously enumerated the two congladiators' victories and defeats, their relative weights, their hobbies and favourite authors, their star signs and dates of birth. Then, unaccompanied and with no discernible musicality, he sang a song in Old Zamonian, a language unintelligible to ninety-nine per cent of his audience. Although this ritual invariably evoked impatient murmurs and hisses, it was a centuries-old tradition.

At long last the supporting bouts began. Not to be compared with the main event in terms of form and quality, they served as a warm-up and provided ambitious young congladiators with an opportunity to prove themselves in front of a sizeable audience. Two youthful tyros would mount the circular stage, stand there looking diffident, and verbally joust in a rather puerile way.

They tried to sell each other ill-constructed tall stories and, at the same time, accuse each other of lying – a pretty unedifying affair, and one that usually culminated in the following type of dialogue:

'It just isn't true!'
'It is!'
'It *isn't*!'
'It *is*, so!'

I was very disappointed. After all the fuss people made about congladiators, this struck me as quite pathetic. Resentful that so much good money had been wasted on the tickets – enough to buy me a month's ration of honey – I conveyed my displeasure to Chemluth.

'Wait a bit, gah,' he told me. 'It's all part of the show. They're beginners – they need practice.'

The Duel of Lies   The main bout began at last. Two large, thronelike chairs, gilded all over and set with precious crystals, were trundled into the arena. Mounted on the high back of each, like a clock or tachometer, was a huge dial. The chairs were also attached to a complex system of cables. Then another piece of equipment was pushed on to the stage: a big silver box with an outsize, stylized ear projecting from either side.

'That's the applause meter. The louder the applause, the more points.'

I realized that the spectators' reaction played a substantial part in assessing each performance. The applause meter registered the volume and converted it into points for the contestant in question. The duellists eventually mounted the stage. They wore traditional velvet duelling cloaks, blue for the challenger and red for the reigning King of Lies. The spectators rose from their seats, simultaneously humming and strumming their lower lips. This produced the thousandfold 'Brrrr!' with which audiences customarily paid homage to the contestants.

Urged on by their fans, the pair approached their chairs with stately tread and sat down. Then a mighty gong was struck in the orchestra pit and the duel commenced.

As challenger, Deng Po had to start the contest. Singh sat back with a relaxed air. Having held the title for the past six months, he calmly awaited the challenger's opening move. Deng Po began with a story from his native land, a delicately constructed fairy tale in which, if my memory serves me, an important part was played by sundry Chinese wind and water sprites. His delivery was crisp and devoid of stage fright, and he embellished his story with one or two humorous interjections and a dramatic dénouement.

The audience applauded politely, the applause meter registered 2.5, and Sing embarked on his response. He countered with a story from his own native land. This dealt with the discovery of rice, to which Singh laid personal claim, and with an epic novel which he had allegedly written with a fly's eyelash.

Far more suspenseful than his opponent's, Singh's story embodied a wealth of hair-raising scientific details and razor-sharp witticisms. He also possessed greater histrionic ability. He enunciated better, his gestures were more assured, and his talent for mimicry captivated the audience. He scored a straight 6.0 on the applause meter.

Deng shrugged off this initial setback. His second story, a kind of fisherman's tale from the China Sea, described the catching of a huge fish made of solid gold. He had clearly saved it with a view to raising the stakes. His delivery was better, too, and his gestures were more confident. He embroidered the story with fictitious biological facts about goldfish and satirical asides aimed at the Chinese fishing authorities. These evoked uproarious laughter from his audience, especially the Rickshaw Demons. He scored 3.8 on the dial, not bad for a challenger at this early stage in the contest.

But here my powers of recall fail me a little. I can't remember the adversaries' tall stories in every detail, but I do know that their duel developed into an equal and exciting contest lasting over three hours. The stories became more and more ingenious and imaginative, the details more subtle, the jokes more fanciful. The audience bestowed its favour sometimes on Singh, sometimes on Deng, but the needle never came to rest below 4.0, some indication of the high standard of the lies on offer.

In the end, rather predictably, victory went to the more experienced Mutra Singh. Deng Po had not yet learnt to pace himself, it seemed, because he definitely flagged during the final phase. He had used up his best material in the middle of the duel, whereas Singh saved his best stories for the end. Deng eventually threw off his cloak as a mark of submission, for a Duel of Lies continued until one of the contestants resigned.

Singh, who had won deservedly but not spectacularly, was carried around the Megathon for an hour by boisterous Bluddums. Then the Mountain Dwarf orchestra struck up a Zamonian lullaby and the gates were opened to allow the spectators to disperse into the darkness.

Slightly tipsy after our hot beer, we discussed the contest as we walked home. The night was sultry, and Atlantis was bathed in a flickering blue glow by the shafts of greased lightning that rampaged through the streets.

Chemluth, who had placed a small bet on the outsider, was correspondingly disappointed with his performance. I was thoroughly delighted by the whole affair because it was so new to me. Never had I been so carried away by a cultural event. It fascinated me that an activity as disapproved-of as lying could be turned into a thrilling sport. I had chewed several of my claws to the quick, and I couldn't help chuckling retrospectively at some of Singh's brilliant punchlines.

But something else kept nagging me. During the contest I had put myself in the duellists' place and devised my own tactics, my own tall stories – indeed, I had sometimes been faintly disappointed by what they themselves had come out with. This seemed pre-sumptuous of me, so I didn't dare tell Chemluth, but I genuinely felt I could match the performances I had seen that night, if not improve on them.

The congladiatorial contest preoccupied me for days afterwards. I couldn't concentrate on my work – much to the delight of our customers, because I anointed the pizzas far too liberally – and became more and more dissatisfied with my job as a pizza-topper. True, I earned good money, worked in warm surroundings and always had plenty to eat, but surely that couldn't be the acme of my professional career.

The restaurant was particularly full one night, and Chemluth and

I had to work flat out to keep up with demand. The weather was hot and sultry, the stoves had been stoked until they were white-hot, and we were both streaming with sweat.

But my thoughts strayed out into the open air and back in time. They roamed through the streets of Atlantis to the Megathon and the night of the Duel of Lies. I analysed the congladiators' tactics and mistakes, ran through the entire contest in my mind's eye, dreamed up my own tall stories – and topped the pizzas more generously than ever. I was so preoccupied, I failed to notice that Nabab Yeo had planted himself in front of me and was giving me a dressing-down. Waving his four arms wildly in the air, he brandished a ladle under my nose and accused me of trying to ruin him. He had often done this before without getting under my skin, but this time I threw my apron at his feet and strode off. Chemluth, who was glad of an excuse to quit the job, followed suit.

An earthquake I was on my way to the exit when the ground suddenly fell away from under my feet. Airborne, I flailed around with my forelegs and hind legs, then landed on my back. The ground was shaking so violently that all the tables in the restaurant went walkabout and big flakes of plaster showered down from the ceiling. The staff and customers let out a chorus of panic-stricken cries. Chemluth dragged me under a table, to which we clung by the legs. The jolting persisted for a while, and more and more customers came crowding into our refuge. Then the tremors abruptly ceased. One of the pizza ovens had burst, spewing a stream of red-hot coals into the restaurant. The floor was littered with plaster, broken crockery, and splintered glass. It was the most violent earthquake to have occurred since my arrival in Atlantis.

To settle our nerves we strolled up and down Ilstatna Boulevard for a while.

'Never mind, gah,' said Chemluth. 'We can still go busking. I'll sing, you can dance.'

Money was no immediate problem because we had a little put by. The rent was paid, our store cupboard was full, and, as I have already said, jobs were always to be had in Atlantis. What irked me far more was that there were still four days to go to the next Duel of Lies. I could hardly wait.

For the next two months we found temporary work as messenger boys, sandwich-men, gherkin sorters, fish descalers down at the harbour, and vinegar stirrers at the mustard factory, but I never missed a Duel of Lies. Mutra Singh – I was now one of his greatest fans – turned in some of his finest performances.

But then, having held the title for eight months, he lost it.

We were back in the Megathon one Wednesday evening, nibbling our corn cobs and waiting for the main event. Mutra Singh seemed to have become a fixture. Nobody ever went more than eight or ten rounds with him, and it was a pleasure to attend his sportsmanlike and tactically adroit duels. Chemluth was wearing a shirt on which he had painted Mutra's congladiatorial emblem, and we joined the Bluddums in chanting his fan club's refrain: 'Singh, Singh, Mutra Singh! Singh, Singh, Mutra Singh!'

It was catchy, albeit not very original.

Tonight's challenger was an unknown. All we knew was that he styled himself Lord Olgort, presumably a *nom de guerre*. We were so confident of Singh's ability to see him off that we'd staked a few modest pyras on him.

Betting had lately become a small but steady source of income. Our improving knowledge of form had enabled us to forecast the winner of many a main and supporting bout.

I made notes during every Duel of Lies, ran through the bouts at home, devised mendacious strategies, and committed the names of all the previous Kings of Lies to memory.

Ambrosiac Nassatram, Crontep Cran, Nussram Fhakir, Brutan Cholltecker, Chulem Chertz, Salguod Smaddada Jr., Colporto Poltorky, Gnooty Valtrosa the Implacable, Yongyong Tumper, Husker Pothingay, Elija Moju, Barimbel Cornelis, and the rest – I knew the intermediate phases, duration and result of every Duel of Lies that had ever been held in Atlantis.

Chemluth sometimes poked fun at my fanaticism, but he never missed a contest either.

We hurled our gnawed corn cobs at the stage because the congladiators were keeping us waiting yet again. Mutra Singh finally appeared and ascended his throne. We sang a few more songs in his honour, then silence fell. The gong sounded, and his challenger mounted the platform.

It was the Troglotroll.

A surprise

I couldn't have been more surprised if I'd seen myself walk out on to the stage. Of all the creatures I'd encountered in my previous lives, he was definitely the one I least wanted to meet again. How could such a degenerate individual have managed to become a congladiator while I spent my time rinsing out vinegar buckets in a mustard factory?

Highly indignant, I told Chemluth about my acquaintanceship with the Troglotroll.

'Gah!' said Chemluth. 'So he's a scoundrel, but no matter. As long as he's a good liar...'

He was certainly that, as I knew from experience.

520

As challenger, the Troglotroll had to open the contest. He presented a pathetic description of his childhood, the way everyone trampled him underfoot, and so on – all the nauseating nonsense familiar to me from our previous encounter. But a surprising rapport grew up between him and the audience. He interwove his life story with a tissue of lies about the labyrinthine tunnels inside the Gloomberg Mountains and his self-sacrificing efforts to extricate those who had lost their way in them. Although it turned my stomach to hear him, he contrived to lie his way into his listeners' hearts and move them to tears. Their rapturous applause registered a colossal 8.0.

Mutra Singh could only manage 6.5.

I'm bound to admit that the Troglotroll really had what it took to be a congladiator. His stories were original and told in a lively manner. He was also a surprisingly gifted actor. He could mimic voices brilliantly and had a range of expressive gestures that rendered his delivery convincing in the extreme. Above all, he could lie with a lack of scruple exceptional even in a congladiator. He was as flexible as a plasticine figure, had exceedingly elastic face muscles, and displayed a sense of humour, albeit a very peculiar one.

Mutra Singh, the courteous gentleman gladiator, seemed rather stiff by comparison. He had now been in office for quite a while, so the spectators were well acquainted with his technique. The Troglotroll gave promise of something new. When even Chemluth suddenly started applauding the crazy gnome, I realized that Mutra Singh was in trouble.

Much to my indignation, the Troglotroll won the next four rounds. I found Singh's stories far better and clapped and whistled when the meter was registering his score, but the spectators definitely favoured the Troglotroll. They even let him get away with many a feeble pun and ill-constructed tale as long as he pulled enough funny faces. It was part of the beauty, but also the tragedy, of this sport that the spectators were the ultimate judges of who sat on the throne.

Singh won only three out of fifteen rounds. In Round 16, after the Troglotroll had registered 9.5 on the applause meter, he threw off his cloak. He was close to tears.

The Troglotroll, or Lord Olgort, as he now styled himself, was Atlantis's new King of Lies.

My ambition is aroused

Far from dampening my enthusiasm for the sport of lying, the Troglotroll's accession to the royal throne fanned it into a blaze. Mutra Singh had prompted me to enjoy the sport as a spectator; the Troglotroll kindled a desire to participate in person. I secretly dreamed of deposing him with all Atlantis looking on.

We continued to attend every Duel of Lies. Lord Olgort stoutly defended his title against all comers and assembled a steadily growing crowd of supporters. I alone remained sceptical of his methods.

I disliked his whole style, his self-ingratiating tricks, his nauseating tendency to please an audience at all costs. Like a tree swaying at the whim of the wind, he bent in any direction that seemed most likely to garner applause. He took no risks, purely intent on appealing to the lowest common denominator. And appeal he certainly did, with an unerring precision that surprised me. Even Chemluth thought him good.

'Gah. He's funny,' he said whenever I started to find fault with Lord Olgort.

One night, as we were leaving the Megathon, I caught sight of a poster.

Hey, You!

Yes, you! Ever get the feeling
life is passing you by?

Do you resent being a face in the crowd?
Does it bug you to lead a humble, low-paid, anonymous existence?

Would you like to wow huge audiences, earn a fortune in pyras,
become a popular celebrity, and wallow in applause?

WHY NOT BECOME A CONGLADIATOR?

It's child's play! Anyone can learn!

For details inquire at the FILTHY FLEECE,
No. 20,567 Ilstatna Boulevard

I didn't breathe a word about my plan to Chemluth, not at first, or
he would have called me a megalomaniac.

Not until the next day, when I was on my way to the 'Filthy
Fleece', did misgivings first assail me. Was I capable of performing
in front of a sizeable audience? I had displayed some talent as an
entertainer on Hobgoblin Island, but this was quite another kettle
of fish. I was shaking like a leaf with stage fright when I entered
the taproom of the 'Filthy Fleece'.

The tavern was a gloomy dive, and far seedier than I'd expected. Although it was still early in the day, a few boozers, most of them Bluddums, were seated at the tables wreathed in acrid cigar smoke. Could this really be the reception centre for congladiators? Perhaps I'd misread the address or fallen for a stupid practical joke. I was just turning to go when a voice awakened some unpleasant memories.

'By Wotan's tonsils, landlord, where's my beer?'

'Exactly!' bleated someone else. 'By Wotan's tonsils!'

I slowly advanced on the voices through a dense pall of tobacco smoke. I was now near enough to make out the dim figures of three drinkers. 'By the Megabollogg!' one of them bellowed. 'Do I have to get unpleasant?'

I vigorously flapped a paw. The haze parted to reveal an inebriated Bluddum and two old acquaintances.

They were Knio and Weeny, neither of whom had changed much. They had both grown a bit, especially Knio, and short-sighted Weeny was wearing a monocle which I immediately recognized as Professor Nightingale's cyclopean lens from the Unperfected Patents Chamber. I went up to the table.

'Hello, Knio! Hello, Weeny!'

They gave a start and instinctively groped under the table, perhaps for concealed weapons. Weeny leant forwards, adjusted his monocle, and peered at me.

'Bluebear?'

'Bluebear?' Knio echoed.

They sent the Bluddum away and invited me to have a beer with them. Although I declined the beer, pointing out how early it was (whereupon they both laughed heartily and clinked mugs), I sat down and we chatted awhile about the old days and how we came to be in Atlantis.

'Man, was I glad when my time with the old fart was up at last,'
Knio roared at the top of his voice as usual. He was evidently
referring to Professor Nightingale.

'I never understood a word of what he was spouting. A complete
waste of time. The university of life, that's what counts.'

Knio waved his beer mug at the tavern's occupants, and a couple
of Bluddums returned the toast. He and Weeny seemed to be
regulars. Nightingale's transmission of knowledge by means of
intelligence bacteria did not work with everyone, that much was
clear.

'I was a hopeless case, the old man didn't take long to hoist that
in.'

Knio rapped his head with his knuckles, producing a sound like a
hammer hitting an empty safe. The intelligence bacteria had
probably bounced off his skull.

'It worked with me!' Weeny broke in. 'But I've forgotten it all again, tee-hee!' He likewise raised his mug of Yeti Beer and brandished it as if to demonstrate the reason for his loss of memory.

'I'm suffering from a disease. There's a name for it, but I've forgotten that too, tee-hee!'

From the
'Encyclopedia of Marvels, Life Forms
and Other Phenomena of Zamonia and its Environs'
by Professor Abdullah Nightingale

Gnomic Cretinism. This is a very rare syndrome occurring only among Gnomelets. The constant use of a Gnomelet's brain for trifling purposes makes the items of knowledge stored there feel unwell. They commit mass suicide by diving into the so-called Lake of Oblivion, a cerebral area found in Bolloggs' brains as well as in those of Gnomelets. The resulting gaps in a Gnomelet's education steadily increase until its brain becomes a complete intellectual vacuum.

Knio and Weeny were still the same ignorant knuckleheads they'd been during our schooldays together. I chalked up a few more minus points to be set against Nightingale's educational system.

'Then he sent us off into that tunnel, that labyrinth of caves. Man, that was some ordeal, I can tell you! It took us two hours to find the exit, but we made it in the end, by all the Gryphons!'

Two hours! *They* had found the exit after two measly hours, whereas *I* had taken half a lifetime – yet another indication that fortune doesn't always favour the righteous.

Knio gave a hoarse laugh. 'I grabbed one of those creatures that scurry around the passages – a Troglotroll, know what I mean? Like the fellow who's King of Lies these days. He tried to fool us and get us lost, but I grabbed him and hit him on the head until he showed us the way out.'

Weeny took up the story. 'Then we made our way through a forest. A creepy place, that, huge cobwebs everywhere, brrr! We actually found a spider at one point – a colossal specimen, but dead, luckily for us. It had probably starved to death – all shrivelled up, it looked.'

'I'd have dealt with it,' grunted Knio, and took a swig of beer.

So I really had killed the Spiderwitch! I was glad to have met the pair of them, if only because of that information.

'Yes, and then we went to sea,' Weeny went on. 'We built ourselves a raft out of tree trunks and launched it in Bear Bay, beyond the Great Forest. Unfortunately, we forgot the rudder.'

Knio guffawed. 'No idea how long we bobbed around out there without a bite to eat. We were completely at the mercy of the waves – we almost went mad. I even imagined I could hear the waves chattering together. Things got so bad, Knio tried to eat me.'

'That's not true!' Knio growled, blushing.

'It certainly is! You sank your teeth in my leg!'

'Only in fun...'

'Come off it! Anyway, luckily we sighted land at that very moment. It was Atlantis harbour. We bummed around for a while and then took this job. We're congladiator scouts. Tell us, though: What brings *you* here?'

I refrained from giving them a detailed account of my arduous journey to Atlantis and came straight to the point. 'I saw that poster, and I thought...'

'You want to become a congladiator?' Knio and Weeny glanced at each other.

'Well, I'd seen a Duel of Lies, and I thought I could do just as well.'

Knio grinned. 'So do lots of folk. Still, why not? You never know till you've tried. Come on, we'll introduce you to the boss.'

We made our way across the taproom to a wooden door, I in the lead, Knio and Weeny whispering and giggling at my heels like a couple of schoolboys. They obviously felt sure I would make a fool of myself. I cursed myself for having ventured into this shady dive. Knio pushed the door open and thrust me into a back room.

It was even murkier than the taproom. The air was filled, not with white cigar smoke, but with dense black phogar smoke, which made it almost as dark as Nightingale's darkroom.

From the
'Encyclopedia of Marvels, Life Forms and Other Phenomena of Zamonia and its Environs'
by Professor Abdullah Nightingale

Phogar. Strictly speaking, a recreational drug extracted from the Phorinth flower, which is related to the tobacco plant and found only on Thumb Promontory, Paw Island. The cigar-shaped umbels of the Phorinth flower contain equal parts of nicotine, tar, and black pollen. Their nicotine and tar content is approximately a hundred times that of a traditional cigar, and the smoke is as black and acrid as that given off by burning pitch. Only creatures without lungs or hearts [e.g. Shark Grubs, Iron Maggots, Kackertratts] are physically capable of smoking a phogar without expiring on the spot.

Seated at a table strewn with playing cards and pyras of every size was a Shark Grub. I had never seen one before. Very rarely found in Atlantis, Shark Grubs were said to be very secretive. I could see little more at first than a dark, corpulent figure with a mouthful of shark's teeth.

From the
'Encyclopedia of Marvels, Life Forms
and Other Phenomena of Zamonia and its Environs'
by Professor Abdullah Nightingale

Shark Grub, The. A crawling maggot of the gill-breathing, semi-insect family, distantly related to the world of fish. Shark Grubs, which are seldom seen, prefer to live in opaque conditions and shroud themselves in phogar smoke [→*Phogar*]. They are highly intelligent [except when compared to Nocturnomaths] and notorious for their ability to accumulate money in swift and mysterious ways. Often charming and affable in demeanour, the Shark Grub has a special aptitude for imposing its authority on groups of weak-willed individuals.

The Shark Grub scrutinized me for a while, chewing on his phogar. Standing in the corner of the room, arms folded and eyeing me suspiciously – I'd mistaken him at first for a statue – was a full-grown Zamonian Wolpertinger. He wore the traditional uniform of a Wolpertinger bodyguard, a troll-hide waistcoat and trousers and a steel helmet adorned with two short horns. Only Atlantean VIPs could afford to employ a Wolpertinger bodyguard.

'What do you want, youngster?' the Shark Grub inquired in a resonant, surprisingly amiable voice. 'You've got blue fur, a great rarity in Atlantis. My name is Volzotan Smyke, but you may call me Smyke.' I was immediately won over. For a maggot, the Shark Grub had good manners.

'He wants to become a congladiator,' Knio and Weeny blurted out simultaneously.

'Shut up!'

Knio and Weeny fell silent. Smyke seemed to wield a certain amount of authority.

'If he wants to become a congladiator, he can surely speak for himself. What's your name?'

'Bluebear,' I replied, trying to sound calm and self-assured.

'Hm... Bluebear... An excellent name, for once. We can do without a pseudonym. That's good, because effective pseudonyms are hard to devise. Where do you come from?'

'Nowhere. I wasn't even born, I was found in a nutshell.'

'So you weren't even born... That's good, too – very good. One of the most barefaced lies I've ever heard. And who found you?'

'Some Minipirates. Nobody knows they exist because they're so small. I myself was equally small in those days – I could fit into a nutshell, as I said, but I grew so big on plankton they had to put me ashore.'

'Minipirates!' bellowed Smyke. 'I like that! You've got imagination!' I was beginning to like him despite myself.

'Where did they put you ashore?' He leant across the table. For some reason, I seemed to be arousing his interest.

'On Hobgoblin Island. That's where the Hobgoblins live. They feed on negative emotions, so I had to weep for them – in fact I became something of a star on Hobgoblin Island. I've got plenty of experience as an entertainer. On many nights the forest graveyard was sold out when I wept. I –'

Smyke's uproarious laughter stopped me in my tracks. His rolls of fat were wobbling like a blancmange. *'The forest graveyard was sold out when he wept!* That's a good one! Stop it, please... No! Go on!' Tears of laughter were rolling down his cheeks. Was he poking fun at me? Maybe I ought to say something more weighty, I thought – something that would demonstrate my seriousness and intelligence.

'I've got a large vocabulary. I was educated by the Babbling Billows.'

'Babbling Billows? That's too much! Any other references?'

'There's a talking encyclopedia in my head which –'

'A talking encyclopedia in his head? The youngster's a natural! Go on, go on!'

'Well, then I made my way across the desert and found a city – no, I'm wrong, it wasn't a proper city, it was a semi-solid mirage. But it was full of Fatoms that spoke backwards, and the houses kept vanishing, which made living conditions impossible. After that I lived inside a tornado. That's why I'm really nearly a hundred years old, but when the tornado went into reverse I became younger again. Well, inside the tornado was a city inhabited by men of a hundred who... No, wait, I forgot to tell you about falling into a dimensional hiatus! I landed in a dimension where they play music on instruments made of milk, and...'

By now, Smyke was rolling around on the floor with laughter. Laboriously, he struggled up from behind his desk.

Suddenly realizing that this brief summary of my life must have made me sound mentally deranged, I thought it wiser to skip the story of the Bollogg's head, say no more, and disappear, never to return, as soon as I'd put this embarrassing situation behind me.

'Stop, that's enough! Save it for your performances!' cried Volzotan Smyke. 'You're sensational! I'm putting you under contract. I'll be your agent. You'll get ten – no, five per cent of all the takings, is it a deal? I'm going to make you rich and famous. Sign on the dotted line.'

He had removed a form from a drawer and deposited it on the desk. Knio and Weeny thrust me nearer. I bent over the document, but I couldn't read a word of it, the print was so tiny and the lighting so poor.

'Sign!' Weeny whispered in my ear. 'It's the chance of a lifetime. Sign before he changes his mind.'

What did I have to lose? I'd gone there to become a congladiator, so why not take the plunge? I picked up a pencil and wrote 'Bluebear' on the dotted line in big, bold letters.

I go into training Once I had told Chemluth the news, we spent a long time discussing our plans for the future. Chemluth was to be my second and trainer. You didn't become a congladiator just like that. Smyke had impressed on me that it required nonstop, intensive training.

Anyone can stand up and tell a straightforward lie – there's no artistry in that. Getting your listeners to believe that lie, therein lies the secret. Like any great art, that of lying calls for diligence and the application of numerous layers. Just as a painter superimposes layers of pigments and glazes, or a composer constructs scores out of melodies and rhythms, vocal and instrumental parts, or a writer weaves a web of words on many levels, so a liar piles lie on lie to form a masterpiece. A good lie must resemble a stout brick wall, patiently constructed course by well-laid course until it's firm as a rock.

It must also mingle fact with fiction, kindle hopes and dash them, lay false trails, perform narrative twists and turns, and proceed by stealth. Above all, the face must lie too. Any tall story, however elaborately constructed, can be blown apart by the wrong facial expression. An ill-timed twitch of the eyebrow, a hesitant flicker of the eye, and the cleverly woven tissue of lies is reduced to tatters. I have seen great congladiators come unstuck because they blinked at the wrong moment.

Most congladiators trained by constantly lying to their friends and acquaintances so as to remain in form. I myself rejected such training methods, not only because they soon drove all your friends away, but because I found them boring. I went in search of a bigger audience.

I went down to the shore and lied to the sea. I went outside the city gates and bamboozled the mighty Humongous Mountains. I climbed the highest corkscrew towers in Lisnatat and conned the sky itself. Yes, I lied to the elements, and the roar of the breakers and the mountains' reverberations were my applause. This is the only way to gain a feeling for great, dramatic rodomontades. Anyone crossing swords with the elements must accept the possibility of being washed out to sea by a wave or struck down by a thunderbolt or an avalanche. It stimulates the imagination and hones the reflexes, makes you cunning and alert.

On one occasion during training, a thunderbolt really did miss me by a hair's-breadth as I stood at the top of a corkscrew tower with a storm in the offing. I was well into my stride, lying fit to turn the sky black, when I became too big for my boots. Just as I was exuberantly cobbling together a half-baked lie, a huge shaft of lightning bore down on me. I managed to leap aside, but it cut the top of the tower in half. That was an object lesson. A congladiator couldn't afford to be guided by his emotions. Every lie, no matter how dramatic and spontaneous its delivery, had to be based on cool calculation.

Reading matter   Another important training aid was the reading of highbrow, middlebrow and lowbrow literature. Writers being second only to politicians at lying, they also make the best teachers. I adopted the daily pre-workout habit of reading three books after breakfast, none of them less than three hundred pages long. I even sacrificed half my night's sleep in order to read more books. I absorbed the entire œuvre of Wilfred the Wordsmith in two hundred volumes – all the novels, novellas, short stories, stage plays, reviews, letters, speeches and experimental sound-poems he had ever written, as well as his twelve-volume autobiography.

I also read the complete works of Count Zamoniac Clanthu of Midgard, a best-selling author despised by the Zamonian literati, who was really an innkeeper named Per Pemmf and had devoted his life to writing thrillers. All his books told how the hero, Prince Sangfroid, underwent hair-raising adventures in which he vanquished a monster with at least three heads and rescued a red-haired princess from its clutches. They also paved the way for Prince Sangfroid's next adventure, in which the presence of a monster and a princess was guaranteed. Reading matter of this kind did not expand my vocabulary, perhaps, but it did nourish my imagination, and a well-fed imagination was one of the most important weapons in the congladiator's armoury.

My grounding in the classics, on the other hand, I obtained from the stage works of Gongolphian Golph, chronicler of the Zamonian war of succession. The main characters in all his plays were Norselander aristos who delivered unintelligible speeches in rhyming couplets and were pushed out of windows in the third act, if not before. Golph's dramas enhanced my knowledge of Zamonian history and my ability to extemporize in rhyme.

Another piece of required reading was *The Song of the Trout*, an epic poem made up of four thousand sonnets. Allegedly written in the course of several centuries by two hundred Mountain Dwarfs who preferred to remain anonymous, *The Song of the Trout* had nothing at all to do with trout (the only one it featured didn't sing and was promptly eaten). It dealt with certain skirmishes between human beings, dwarfs, giants and gods, all of whom tried to outwit each other. Unlike Count Zamoniac's thrillers, *The Song of the Trout* had more than one hero – some two hundred of them, as I recall, and all of dwarfish stature.

I read *How Dank Was My Valley*, principal work of the regional writer Psittachus Rumplestilt, a poet from the Muchwater Marshes, where a massive shower of meteorites had transformed the countryside into a vast expanse of wetland. *How Dank Was My Valley* was a heart-rending saga of life among the reed-dwellers. Any aspiring liar must be versed in grand emotions, and they occurred on every page Rumplestilt wrote. Sensitive souls, those reed-dwellers: the sight of a snapped bullrush was enough to send them into paroxysms of grief, shame, hatred, rage, or local patriotism, whichever. This I found most instructive.

But the congladiator's most valuable literary aid was *The Shortest Legs in Zamonia*, the autobiography of the master practitioner Nussram Fhakir the Unique. It describes his fairy-tale rise from peat-cutter in the Graveyard Marshes of Dull to celebrated congladiator so compellingly and in such obsessive detail that no budding exponent of the art could afford to shirk memorizing as much of the book as possible. It taught me all about the congladiatorial profession, at least where theory was concerned.

I must make it clear from the outset that the spectator's conception of a congladiator's training was wide of the mark. There was no official syllabus or diploma, no form of initiation or prescribed course of instruction. There was really only one rule, namely, that everything should accord with the wishes of Volzotan Smyke.

The tycoon

Smyke was the uncrowned king of the congladiators. Talented individuals were encouraged, developed or demolished to suit his plans of the moment. I very soon grasped this because he liked having me around, and I was often privileged to be present when he engaged in his multifarious business activities.

Smyke not only ran the congladiatorial contests but controlled the Gebba League and the entire port of Atlantis. He dealt in smuggled phogars, pickled belly of pork, Yhôllian antiques, troll hides, blood plasma, coconuts, fake pixie stars, sugar cane, Yeti Beer, and anything else imported or exported by sea.

He knew every shipyard and every captain and vessel in the harbour, was honorary harbourmaster, chairman of the Gebba Players' Association, honorary congladiator, and treasurer of the Atlantean Choral Society. He owned the Megathon and most of the city's corkscrew towers. He maintained a private army of Yetis, Bluddums and Wolpertingers to guarantee his personal safety, controlled thirty per cent of the city's furdressing salons, and took a sauna with the mayor once a week. No, Smyke wasn't just the uncrowned king of the congladiators, he was the uncrowned king of Atlantis itself.

The night of my first public appearance came sooner than I would have liked. I was to have a little sparring match with another young and inexperienced congladiator as a preliminary to the main bout starring Lord Olgort (who was improving with every duel).

I didn't feel sufficiently well-trained for it, which was why the said evening found me fidgeting in my dressing room beneath the Megathon while Chemluth massaged my neck and tried to calm me down.

My first contest

'Just go out there, gah? He's only a little fish and the rounds won't be scored, so what's the big deal? Relax, gah. Your neck muscles are all –'

The door of the cubicle flew open and Knio and Weeny burst in. Behind them, smoking a fat phogar, Volzotan Smyke squeezed through the narrow doorway. Bringing up the rear was Rumo, his Wolpertinger bodyguard, whom I still found slightly intimidating. I secretly hoped they'd come to cancel my bout.

'Now listen, youngster,' said Smyke. 'We've got a problem... Our man, the one who's scheduled to fight Lord Olgort, has gone sick at the last moment. I want you to take his place.'

Chemluth was as flabbergasted as I. 'He's not ready! He's never had a fight. It's crazy, gah!'

Weeny held up a piece of paper. It was my contract. He adjusted his monocle and proceeded to read aloud:

'Clause 14a: The party of the second part undertakes to engage in any Duel of Lies to which the party of the first part assigns him. Should he refuse, a fine of –'

Smyke cut him short.

'Stop browbeating him with that stupid contract! If he won't do it, he won't.' He took a couple of puffs at his phogar and rested one of his numerous hands on my shoulder.

'There's a far more important consideration, my lad. A chance like this may not come your way again so quickly. Many congladiators wait years for a title fight, and many never get one at all. I'd think it over carefully...'

I thought of the Troglotroll. I thought of the labyrinth.

I thought of the Spiderwitch.

'I'll do it,' I said.

'I won't do it! I won't do it!' I cried as they escorted me to the stage, but nobody heard me. What with the bellows of the Bluddums, the blare of the Mountain Dwarfs' band, the hum of a hundred thousand voices – the despairing wails of a novice congladiator on the verge of swooning with stage fright were completely drowned. I had never felt so terrified.

'Just be yourself, gah?' was Chemluth's advice.

But myself was the last person I wanted to be at this moment. I would gladly have swapped places with any member of the audience, whether snooty Norselander, boisterous Bluddum, or pathetic Duodwarf. Best of all I would have liked to be an Invisible, because then I could have slunk away unnoticed. What an idiot I was! How could I have exchanged a comfortable seat on one of the spectators' benches for the challenger's throne? That was the hottest and most uncongenial hot seat in the whole Megathon. Nobody liked unknown challengers. The audience yearned to see them taken apart by the reigning King of Lies – that's what unknown challengers were for. A few minutes ago I had been scared of a sparring match, and now I was on my way, without any duelling experience, to a main bout with a popular champion.

If I hadn't been so pushy I would now be sitting up there with a hot beer in one paw and a buttered corn cob in the other, looking forward to a thrilling contest. Instead of that I was feeling sick – sicker than I'd ever felt in my life. My stomach was behaving like a caged beast, lashing out in all directions and scratching and biting my innards like a cat in a sack. I was so agitated that I temporarily forgot my own name and what I was doing there. My knees were so weak that Chemluth had to support me, and pints of sweat were running down my back into my challenger's cloak. Challenger! How could I have let it come to this? I wanted to turn and run away, out of the Megathon, out of Atlantis, back into the desert – back into the tornado, for all I cared. Anything would have been better than the prospect of mounting the stage.

But Chemluth was holding me by the right paw and Smyke by the left, and the Wolpertinger was grimly marching along behind me. There was no escape.

Although there were only ten steps leading to the challenger's throne, they seemed endless. I wouldn't be able to climb them without losing my balance or my senses. Smyke and Chemluth let go, leaving me with no support at all. The first step seemed to be made of rice pudding or some equally yielding substance. There was no terra firma under my feet. I must have looked like a drunk trying to stand up straight, but I managed to climb the second step. It was a little more resistant than the first, but still as soft as a swansdown pillow. I debated whether to enlist the use of my forelegs and go down on all fours. The third step merely swayed like a ship in a moderate sea but appeared to be of some solid material. The fourth was quite firm and didn't sway either, nor did the fifth and sixth.

The challenger's throne

539

I made it. It was just nerves, excitement, the first time. My stage fright waxed and waned, a perfectly natural phenomenon familiar to everyone who appears in public. Sooner or later you calm down of your own accord. In an excess of self-confidence I half turned and looked over my shoulder. I found myself confronted by a restless sea composed of thousands of hostile faces. Everything started swaying again. My legs turned to spaghetti. I staggered to the right, I staggered to the left, and then I opted for the only correct course of action: I took the remaining steps in one enormous stride and flopped down on the throne. The audience gasped with relief. My nerves subsided altogether.

Invisible support   It was as if magical forces were flowing into me. I sensed the presence of those who had sat there before me – sensed the presence of my idols: Mutra Singh, Ambrosiac Nassatram, Salguod Smaddada, Gnooty Valtrosa, Husker Pothingay, Elija Moju, Barimbel Cornelis, and – of course – Nussram Fhakir the Unique. I could sense their proximity, even though they were long dead or retired or had disappeared. All had once been challengers, all had once sat here before overthrowing the King of Lies and ascending the victor's throne. I felt as if Nussram Fhakir were standing behind me in the flesh and speaking to me. He whispered that this was *my* night, that the royal throne was being defiled by an unworthy Troglotroll, and that it was my responsibility to efface that blot on its dignity.

Or had sheer stage fright simply scattered my wits?

Lord Olgort   Then Lord Olgort was carried in. He was somewhat surprised at first to see me on the challenger's throne, but after a moment he seemed to relish the sight. He gave me a look of mingled anticipation, curiosity, and compassion, like a cat with a captive bird in its claws.

Strangely enough, this left me completely unimpressed. Being the challenger, I had to tell the first story. I didn't even have to think, nor did I need to recite any of the lies I'd learnt by heart and saved for an emergency.

My first story seemed to come from outside, as if my idol had whispered it in my ear. It percolated my brain and emerged from my lips as a flawless tissue of lies. Such, at least, is my recollection. Of the story itself I remember as little as I do of any of the other tales I told on that magical night, but it must have been pretty good: I scored 9.0, the highest number of points any novice's opening gambit had obtained in the annals of the Duel of Lies.

The Troglotroll was history, even after the first round, but he didn't know it. That's to say, he seemed to have at least an inkling of the fact, because his riposte, despite its customary originality, was delivered in slightly hesitant tone of voice. Minor though they were, no one had ever heard him betray such shortcomings. People were accustomed to his lamentations and feigned subservience, but this was genuine uncertainty, and that an audience never forgave. A King of Lies was always measured against his peak performances. The Troglotroll's feeble opening effort earned him a mere 3.5 points.

I was even better the second time. The past masters in my head advised me to pay more attention to the histrionic frills, employ dramatic gestures, intensify my mimicry. Although my story lasted only three minutes, I managed in that short time to reduce the whole audience to tears twice and unleash four gales of laughter. Frenetic applause ensued.

The meter registered 9.5 points.

Lord Olgort strove to save the situation, but it was past saving. It was as if, in the very first round, I'd given him a punch on the nose from which he simply couldn't recover. In a quavering voice, he told a lousy story that was not improved by the fact that he lost the thread several times. He was close to tears. A smattering of sympathetic applause.

One point only.

My third effort combined everything: dramatic structure, congladiatorial technique, histrionic gestures. I played on my listeners' emotions as I had on the dream organ in the Bollogg's head. Cries of horror, tears of joy, whoops of laughter – my innate talents, for such they undoubtedly were, drew all these forth within the space of thirty seconds, because this time I wanted to make it *really* short. The tension in the Megathon released itself in a universal gasp of astonishment when I delivered my punchline. All that remained was deafening, protracted applause.

Ten points, the maximum possible.

Victory and defeat

It is shocking to see a Troglotroll become smaller than he already is. Lord Olgort ran from the stage, sobbing. In this sport, victory in the third round was unprecedented. I had not only dismissed the Troglotroll but become King of Lies in record time.

And that was only the beginning of a long run of good luck.

Volzotan Smyke was almost weeping when he came to my dressing room. He pressed me to his bloated stomach.

'I could shed tears over all the money I stupidly bet on your opponent, my boy,' he sobbed, 'but these are tears of happiness. To think I've been privileged to see this day! For a long time I thought

Nussram Fhakir the Unique would be the last born congladiator to quit the stage, but you – you're his reincarnation! Let me give you a hug.'

He gave me a hug.

Only a week later I successfully defended my title for the first time against a Waterkin who made it as far as the fifth round, when the audience booed him off the stage.

In the following seven months I had twenty-eight fights and won them all, twenty-seven in seven rounds or less and one in the tenth against a stubborn Irish Druid who refused to be driven from the stage, even when the audience pelted him with corn cobs. Betweentimes I fought sparring matches with the best in the profession and won them all by a mile.

Smyke, who never budged from my side from then on, anticipated my every wish and showered me with gifts and tokens of appreciation. Chemluth and I were assigned our own Rickshaw Demons, who were at our beck and call day and night.

Chemluth took advantage of my popularity to make the acquaintance of sundry hirsute females. He always had a different one next him at the ringside as he grandly shouted instructions I scarcely needed. None of these affairs lasted, unfortunately, and I got the impression that Chemluth scarcely noticed the girls any more, as if he'd abandoned hope of ever finding the right one.

We had long ago moved out of the corkscrew tower, of course, and now lived in the green hills of North Naltatis, a luxurious Atlantean suburb where every house commanded a breathtaking view of the city's sea of lights at night.

I owned a villa with fifty-two rooms, three swimming pools, and a personal duel-of-lies stage on which I could practise when at home. I never trained, however, because I was a spontaneous talent. Practising spoiled my style.

I had to give one performance a week, which meant that I could relax for six days out of seven – not a bad ratio of work to leisure. Smyke made every effort to keep me amused and create an environment devoted exclusively to my well-being. I had two chefs, one for cold buffets and another – my former employer Nabab Yeo, the Poophian master chef – for hot dishes. At my service twenty-four hours a day were a Cucumbrian masseur and a Witthog who, while I was being massaged, soothed my nerves by reading aloud from the works of Wilfred the Wordsmith.

I had become an important figure – if not the most important – in Atlantean public life. My desk was piled high with invitations to parties, soirées, dinners, galas, exhibitions, and charity functions. Smyke determined which ones I should accept. Three hours of every day were set aside for press conferences. It might be thought that no one can be interesting enough to produce printable copy for three solid hours a day, but the Atlanteans were so obsessed with their congladiators, and with the title holder in particular, that the press published every word I uttered, from scraps of Nocturnal Academy knowledge to recipes, weather forecasts, and detailed descriptions of my fur care. Sometimes I merely spouted trivialities, but even they were printed verbatim and lapped up by my fans.

The *Atlantean Advertiser* had a central section twice the size of the rest of the paper and devoted to me alone. I published cookery books (written by Nabab Yeo, but it was enough that I ate what he wrote about) and a book of tips for aspiring congladiators (every young Atlantean aspired to become a congladiator, so it was a sure-fire best-seller). I also published a work on the moral aspects of lying in which I extolled it in sport but condemned it in personal relationships. Stylistically I took my cue from Nussram Fhakir's autobiography – in fact, to be quite honest, I copied many chapters from it word for word. All these publications sold like hot cakes, and many bookstores in Atlantis carried nothing but books by me.

My private circle was always the same. It included Chemluth, of course, but also Smyke and his hand-picked entourage: Rumo the Wolpertinger bodyguard, one or two Yetis, and – in recent weeks – Lord Olgort, who was now just the Troglotroll again. He had ingratiated himself with Smyke and would happily perform the most menial tasks for him. He made coffee and fetched beer, held doors open and umbrellas up, and was forever playing the court jester. In short, he was Smyke's personal doormat. He even tried to make up to me, but he left me completely cold. I had lost my desire for revenge, in fact I sometimes felt a little sorry for him.

Our conversations and activities related solely to the Duel of Lies. We discussed my own bouts and the supporting programmes, we visited training camps and watched sparring matches, and I talked with probationers and gave advice. I discussed new tactics with Chemluth or listened to Smyke, who could describe great duels of the past like no one else.

I no longer found it possible to conceive of anything outside my profession.

I had reached the very top of the tree.

A year went by. I had fought nearly sixty major and over a hundred minor bouts without losing a single one.

The duels developed into such a routine that I no longer felt even slightly nervous before a Wednesday night performance. I had long ago ceased to brief myself on my opponents' technique. I didn't even want to know *who* they were; I simply went on stage and defeated them. It was as easy as washing my paws. Sometimes I deliberately performed below par to spin out the contests and render them more exciting, but as a congladiator I was simply unbeatable.

For several weeks now, the city had been imprisoned in a bell jar of sultry air, the heat and humidity made worse by a hot wind from the Humongous Mountains. The inhabitants of Atlantis, all of whom were suffering from headaches and rheumatism, seized every opportunity to relax or cool off. I had taken to giving my daily interviews while lolling on a cork mat in one of my garden swimming pools. From there I dictated my views on the weather for the reporters to take down in their notebooks:

'In my estimation, it's far too hot for this time of year. A spot of cool weather wouldn't come amiss. The humidity is far too high as well. A little thunderstorm would be just the ticket at present. Our Norselander politicos ought to get that into their thick heads for once.'

I had no idea what politics had to do with the weather, but a few derogatory remarks about Norselanders and their intellectual capacity always went down well with the public. The reporters scribbled away busily.

Volzotan Smyke was transacting business from a deck chair, as he usually did. His assistants, who included Bluddums and other underlings such as the Troglotroll, were constantly scurrying to and fro with letters and newspapers and whispering to him. I didn't object to this. It was a daily occurrence, and I had absolutely no wish to know what Smyke was up to – even thinking about it made me nervous, so I concentrated on my public relations work. The only time I sat up and took notice was when the sinister Wolpertinger came up and muttered something in Smyke's ear.

Rumo's chilly gaze could still unnerve me. Smyke became very agitated and hurriedly took his leave, explaining that he had some urgent business to attend to. That wasn't unusual because Smyke *always* had urgent business to attend to.

As if the Norselander politicians had taken my advice to heart, there really was a thunderstorm early that evening.

No ordinary storm, it seemed to come, not from above, as normal storms do, but from below – from the depths of the earth. Although the city was hemmed in and the sun obscured by dark rain clouds of quite normal appearance, the shafts of lightning came straight from the bowels of Atlantis. They were the familiar blue streaks of greased lightning, but bigger and more numerous than I had ever seen before. *The storm*

We stood on the terrace of my villa and watched the fantastic spectacle. It was Wednesday, and my bout was due to start in two hours' time. A cold wind sprang up, but instead of blowing out of the atmosphere it seemed to issue from the sewers. Manhole covers flew high into the air, followed by shafts of greased lightning as thick as tree trunks, which shot up as far as the clouds.

Whirlwinds were massing, thin, elongated vortexes that roared briefly before vanishing into the sewers. Volzotan Smyke told me that such thunderstorms occurred in Atlantis only once in a hundred years. This was the third he had witnessed, and I could count myself lucky to have seen even one.

'The Invisibles are angry,' declared one of the Bluddums, who was notoriously superstitious.

Smyke just laughed.

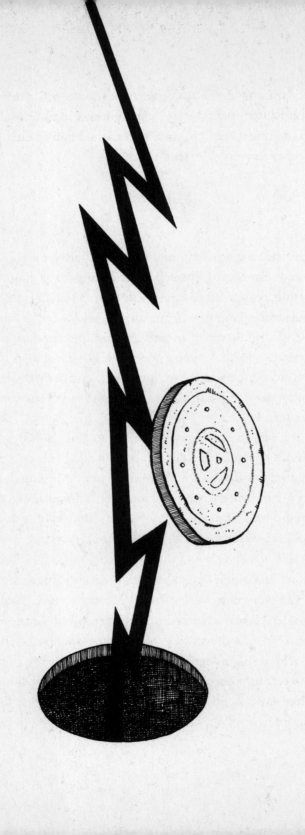

Then the clouds dispersed in places and a cool east wind blew the remains of the sultry heat away. The natural spectacle had refreshed the air. Perfect climatic conditions for a Duel of Lies. We set off for the Megathon.

Shortly before the contest, my fifty-ninth main event, Smyke entered my changing room without an escort and sent Chemluth out because he wanted a word with me in private. The Shark Grub seemed to have something important to say. He never found it hard to speak his mind as a rule, but on this occasion he squirmed like a snake.

An intimate conversation

'Listen, I'd like you to do me a favour tonight. These last few months I've anticipated your every wish and granted it without being asked, as you know. This time, for a change, I'd like you to do something for me.'

'Of course, Smyke.'

'I want you to lose tonight.'

I couldn't have been more surprised if he'd announced that Atlantis was about to sink beneath the waves.

'It's like this: you've become too good. Bets are the crucial part of any Duel of Lies, commercially speaking, but since everyone knows you always win, nobody ever places a bet on your opponents. That's why we can't make a profit any more. Listen, you need only lose once, just tonight. Next week everything will be back to normal. You'll relinquish the title for one week only. I've bet a whole heap of pyras against you, my boy – every bean I possess, to be precise. If you win tonight I'm ruined, and you know how fond of money I am. So don't disappoint me.'

And he waddled out without waiting for an answer.

The phogar smoke followed him like a faithful pet.

I made my way into the Megathon in a daze. I hadn't dared to tell Chemluth, not wanting to involve him. For the first time in my reign, my knees were as weak as they had been when I ascended the challenger's throne on the verge of my very first duel.

To the spectators' annoyance, my opponent kept me waiting. Exasperated Bluddums started hurling corn cobs.

I had no idea of my opponent's identity. I didn't mind that in the ordinary way – I took on all comers. It didn't really matter tonight, either, since I was destined to lose in any case. I had decided to grant Smyke's request. What else could I do?

Then the gong sounded in the orchestra pit and my challenger was ushered in.

It was Nussram Fhakir the Unique.

I now realized why Smyke had chosen this particular night. The master of all congladiators was staging a comeback! Astronomical sums must have been wagered on both contestants. I was the Invincible, but he was the Unique. Even among congladiatorial grandmasters, Nussram was regarded as the undisputed champion, the greatest and most talented liar of all time.

Nussram Fhakir the Unique

We had all read his works and studied his duels. He had devised the Nussram Opening, a standard introduction which all congladiators had subsequently plagiarized in countless different ways, and the Fhakir Variant, a fraudulent ploy that enabled the contestant to go on lying in five hundred different directions. He was the inventor of the so-called White Lie, a subterfuge so delicate, so charming,

550

and constructed with such subtlety, that you simultaneously fell for it and forgave it as if it had never happened. He introduced the Twin Untenability, a con trick roughly comparable to performing a double somersault without a net or looping the loop blindfolded. He also created the Self-Sustaining Fiction, a kind of verbal boomerang which only the finest liars could deliver. He inflicted fourteen successive defeats on Rasputin Zarathustra (a pseudonym), the Norselanders' expert conman. He was the creator of the so-called Nussram Shuffle, a tactic that entailed marking time at a dizzy speed, or so it seemed. This exhausted his opponents and wore them down until the crucial moment, when he floored them with a well-aimed lie.

He also pioneered the Zebrascan Zigzag, an audacious move modelled on the wild hare's escape technique and the ballerina's pirouette. He had personally compiled a liegarithm table embodying thirty-six thousand falsehoods and duelled with twelve of the best congladiators of his generation simultaneously, defeating them all. Nussram Fhakir was a legend, a genius, the Nightingale of the sport of lying. It would not be hard to lose to him – I would do so one way or another. I should perhaps mention that he was a Vulphead, a creature with a human body and the head of a fox. Vulpheads were the offspring of rare matings between Wolperting Whelps and Werefoxes. A peculiar blend of human being, fox and Wolperting Whelp, they were tolerated in Zamonia but not particularly popular. Although they lacked the dangerously aggressive instincts of the Werefox and the physical strength of the Wolperting Whelp, they were sufficiently like both to engender instinctive respect.

The Vulpheads' lack of animal strength was offset by their above-average intelligence. I should also add, perhaps, that they possessed a certain dangerous charm whose effect on the fair sex was particularly marked.

Generally speaking, Vulpheads had a hard time of it in Zamonia. Most of them led a solitary, nomadic existence. They travelled the continent alone, finding employment as skilled carpenters. Nussram Fhakir, as his autobiography recounts, was the only Vulphead ever to have risen from the status of peat-cutter and itinerant carpenter to that of congladiator. For this achievement he was idolized by other members of his race.

'Pardon my belated arrival!' he purred, favouring the audience with a courtly bow. 'I had first to escape from the lead-lined chambers of Baysville, where I was imprisoned unjustly and against my express wish. I succeeded in doing so only by losing a hundred pounds in a single day, thereby enabling myself to slip through the bars of my cell. Unfortunately, it took me some time to put them on again rather than inflict the sight of my emaciated body on you, my esteemed audience. In order to gain the last few pounds I had to consume various cream gâteaux, an elk ham, and several yards of sausage, and that took me a few minutes longer than I'd allowed for.'

Although the applause meter had not yet been switched on, Nussram was already beginning to bombard the audience with charm and throw out ideas as if he had enough and to spare. Not even I dared to dispute his brazen assertions, and I was so entranced by my idol's appearance that I joined in the general acclamation.

I wondered why Smyke had made such a fuss. Against an opponent like Nussram I would lose as a matter of course, however hard I tried. What was more, I would do so with pleasure.

He mounted the challenger's throne with easy grace, fastidiously brushing a few invisible crumbs off his cloak.

'It's ages since I sat here,' he sighed wistfully. 'The challenger's throne, eh? Most uncomfortable. Getting used to it takes time.'

The spectators laughed and clapped at this allusion to his congladiatorial past.

'Except that it's hardly worth getting used to. We shall soon be changing places.' Nussram gave me a piercing stare. I quailed.

The audience laughed still louder.

He levelled a finger at me, so accusingly that I retracted my head like a tortoise.

'Is that my opponent?' he demanded scornfully. 'That blabberer?'

'Bluebear!' I ventured to correct him.

'Or Bluebeard, whatever,' he retorted.

The audience smirked.

'You know what they say about bears,' he whispered to the audience, loudly enough for me to hear him quite well. 'Never leave your larder open when there's one around.'

553

Titters of amusement.

I already knew that Nussram tried to unnerve an opponent in advance by using tricks of this kind. His autobiography devoted a whole chapter to the subject. He regarded it as an art form in its own right to detect an adversary's weak points and use them to demoralize him. Entitled '39 Ways to Humiliate', the relevant chapter described thirty-nine methods of intimidating an opponent before the first round. It was the only chapter I didn't care for, I must confess. Being in favour of a straight fight, I set no store by such tactical ploys. Every congladiator had his own methods, however, and Nussram Fhakir's had enabled him to win many a contest before it actually began.

I kept calm, therefore, and strove to ignore his harmless jibe. Obesity had been a sore point with me since the episode on Gourmet Island, so I was easily riled, but on this occasion professional imperturbability was called for.

'I once knew a bear who was such a glutton that it gobbled up the calories other people lost while slimming.' Nussram had sat back, looking relaxed. He clearly found this new dig amusing.

'The bear was so overfed when it died,' he pursued, 'its stomach lived on for another month!'

I betrayed no emotion of any kind. On the contrary, I treated Nussram to a courteous smile and signified my respect for him by performing a respectful little bow.

Quickly grasping that he wouldn't get anywhere with me like this, he changed tack.

'You weren't born, so I've heard. At least, that's what it said in the newspapers.'

The spectators fell silent. This was no courtly jest; it was hitting below the belt. It was also a subject calculated to rattle me.

Nussram turned to the audience. 'How is that possible? Did he sprout from the soil like a cabbage? If my opponent was never born, how can he be here? Perhaps he isn't here at all – perhaps I've already won the contest. I may as well go.'

A few embarrassed chuckles could be heard. For the first time, I began to doubt my idol's sense of fair play.

'It almost pains me to see him sitting there all on his own, the poor cabbage.'

It seemed that the best way to lose one's respect for an idol was to meet him in the flesh.

'Cabbage is right! I do believe he's turning green!' Nussram couldn't refrain from elaborating on his crude witticism.

Volzotan Smyke surreptitiously shook his head to indicate that I mustn't lose my temper. But it was too late for that. Although I preserved my nonchalant smile, I was beginning to seethe inwardly. Nussram would have done better to stop right there.

'Even an orphan has more relations than this bluebear.' He laughed, but no one joined in. 'Perhaps I should adopt him.'

I had been genuinely prepared to lose this duel with pleasure as a tribute to my idol and a mark of my respect for his achievements, but now I not only wanted to win the contest; I wanted to beat Nussram Fhakir the Unique more soundly than any congladiator had ever been beaten in the history of the sport.

No, I not only wanted to defeat him; I wanted to destroy him, crush him, take him apart. For as long as he lived, I wanted him to break out in a sweat whenever my name or the congladiatorial profession was mentioned. He had wounded my Achilles' heel and twisted the knife once too often. My idol no longer, he was merely another of my numerous opponents.

I couldn't have cared less that he was Nussram Fhakir the Unique.
I was Bluebear the Invincible.

The gong sounded and the duel began.

Rounds 1-10

Seated in the front row as usual were Smyke and his entourage:
Knio, Weeny, Rumo the Wolpertinger, a bunch of Yetis, and
several of Smyke's congladiator protégés. Beside them, all
unwitting, sat Chemluth Havanna. Smyke was smiling graciously
in all directions but nervously shuffling around on his seat. He
gave me another meaningful look to indicate what he expected of
me.

Being the official challenger, Nussram Fhakir had to open the
contest. He began by serving up a story about a Gryphon whom he
claimed to have taught to lay huge boiled eggs. Although it wasn't
very original, he told it with such vocal delicacy and such a wealth
of elegant, expressive gestures that its lack of originality didn't
count against him. Moreover, his disrespectful remarks about
Gryphons drew hearty laughter from the Atlantean audience –
discounting the Gryphons themselves, of course, who were
stoically guarding the stadium. The applause, which was correspondingly generous, earned him a cool eight points.

I knew that he was infinitely superior to me in finesse, experience,
and technique. There was no point in attempting to outdo him
with a tall story on the grand scale. Many another young
congladiator had tried this and come to grief on Nussram's ability
to ride a punch, so I decided to lower my sights. I opened with a
story I'd dreamed up a long time ago and saved for an emergency,
so to speak, in the event that nothing better occurred to me. It was
a good, solid yarn that described how I'd been pursued by pirates

while sailing the high seas with a cargo of hamsters. The point of the story, which depended more on humour than Nussram's, was that I'd ended by harnessing sufficient energy from the hamsters' little treadmills to propel the ship along and enable us to escape. I told it straight, without any frills, and it earned me a well-deserved six points. The first round had gone to Nussram. Smyke relaxed.

My opponent opened the second round with a story about Norselander diplomacy. A dry-as-dust subject, one might have thought, but he turned it into a thrilling story of espionage in which he had penetrated the Norselander diplomats' innermost circle by gluing their ears shut. He seasoned his story with one or two sideswipes at the politicians present and was rewarded with malicious laughter from the audience. In the end he even went so far as to claim responsibility for having started the Zamonian war of succession by inadvertently pushing the aforementioned Norselander out of the window.

Thunderous applause, nine points. I was beginning to grasp that Nussram held a home team's advantage. He was far better acquainted with local developments, the current history of Atlantis, and the needs of its inhabitants.

For the present, to put it in congladiatorial language, I would have to keep my guard up and ride his punches.

Nussram preferred to keep his stories in an Atlantean context, whereas I continued to set mine at sea. I countered with a robust yarn about voyaging with a cowardly crew who were simultaneously frightened by sea sprites and a thunderstorm. To reassure my men, I said, I caught the shafts of lightning in my paws and swallowed them, thereby impressing the sea sprites so much that they fled. My story wasn't of a calibre likely to put an opponent like Nussram Fhakir in his place, but I told it well. Polite applause, five points.

Nussram refused to let these early successes lure him out of his shell. He preserved his composure and displayed none of the lapses of concentration that sometimes afflicted inexperienced congladiators in such situations.

His next effort dealt with greased lightning. He launched into a long and ultimately unresolved account of what the Invisibles might or might not be up to beneath Atlantis. This took the form of a personal report, a confidential piece of gossip that skilfully made the audience his accomplices.

Nussram asserted that the Invisibles had originally come to Atlantis from another planet (as proof of this he cited the buildings in the city in which water flowed uphill), and that they had subsequently been driven into the sewers.

He further stated that they harboured a frightful secret in their subterranean world, and that the greased lightning had some connection with it. Instead of divulging the nature of this frightful secret, however, he left it to his listeners' imagination.

Although utterly devoid of humour and pathos, Nussram's story was so skilfully told that it sent shivers down one's spine. He had also touched on a taboo subject which, although it affected everyone, nobody really cared to broach: What did the Invisibles really do down there? While I was telling silly seaman's yarns, Nussram was dealing with topics of the day.

A moment's breathless silence followed. Then frenzied applause rang out. Ten points – the maximum. Nussram Fhakir had demonstrably lost none of his old expertise.

Having little to set against this, I countered with a rather feeble story about falling into the hands of Yhôllian cannibals who proposed to eat me. I contrived to chill the water in the cauldron by requesting a final peppermint which cooled my breath to such an extent that I froze the water and was eventually able to sell it to the cannibals as peppermint sorbet. This puerile effort earned me a well-merited three points, the lowest score I had ever obtained.

And so it went on for a while, much to Smyke's delight and Chemluth's consternation. Nussram served up one brilliant story after another, scoring top marks, while I produced offerings of average quality and earned no more than respectful applause.

I wasn't gambling on a quick victory, as the reader can see. Congladiatorial duels were not subject to any time limit. They continued until one of the contestants gave up, so I relied on my youthful reserves of energy and hoped that my older opponent would flag. Duels of Lies imposed a great strain on the vocal cords, and that was one of my strengths. I could gabble on and on without tiring, for days if necessary, thanks to my crash course with the Babbling Billows. But there was no reason to under-estimate my opponent. His store of fresh ideas seemed in-exhaustible, and his charm and acting ability were unimpaired after ten rounds.

Round 11

In the eleventh round Nussram essayed a surprise change of tactics: he deserted his secure narrative base, Atlantis, and ventured out into my own world of fantasy – doubtless to prove that he was just as much at home there as I.

Set in the Zamonian Alps, his next tall tale concerned a singing horse with which he had jointly won a yodelling competition. He imitated the horse's voice with great comedic accuracy, and his equine vocal impression went down well with the audience. Result: nine points – a high score, as usual.

The yodelling horse

I decided that the time had come to modify my own strategy. Instead of telling short, pointed stories in humorous vein and garnering a meagre score, I must now retain the public's interest by presenting myself in a glamorous light. So I told the story of Molehill Volcano.

'I . . . can . . . fly.'

Such was my preamble. I projected the words, one by one, at the Megathon's huge, circular auditorium, thereby assuring myself of the spectators' attention. You could have heard a pin drop. Smyke awoke from a blissful daydream (he was probably counting his winnings) and Chemluth nervously kneaded the hat in his hands.

The story of Molehill Volcano

'One day, in the course of my extensive travels, I visited Nairland, the blank space on the map of Zamonia.'

A murmur ran round the arena. No one had ever set foot in Nairland, I knew. Originally pronounced 'Neverland', then 'Ne'erland', the name had eventually come to be spelt as it sounded. It was a district wreathed in legends and rumours more fantastic than all the myths that clung to the Gloomberg Mountains, the Demerara Desert, and the Great Forest put together.

At the mention of 'Nairland', my mind's eye displayed an article from Nightingale's encyclopedia. Instead of being disconcerted by this piece, I spontaneously decided to quote it verbatim:

**From the
'Encyclopedia of Marvels, Life Forms
and Other Phenomena of Zamonia and its Environs'
by Professor Abdullah Nightingale**

Nairland. Somewhat banal compound place name used to designate a region of Zamonia that has hitherto remained completely unexplored. This is not because of its exotic location; on the contrary, it is situated in a central, readily accessible position in the middle of Zamonia, and can easily be reached on foot or by rickshaw taxi. It is simply that no one dares to enter the area. The greatest and most audacious explorers have travelled to its borders, only to give up and turn back. Nairland emits a subconscious signal that advises all comers to give it a wide berth. It is surmised that Nairland consists of telepathic quicksand of a fine-grained, fluid consistency that warns of its dangers by thought transference. The only thing definitely known about the area is that a volcano rises at its centre. Because this can only be seen from hundreds of miles away, and because it looks at long range as innocuous as a molehill, it is known as 'Molehill Volcano'.

The audience rather grumblingly took note of these items of information, which were widely known in Zamonia. Everyone was acquainted with the rumours about Nairland.
'One day, I was on my way through the salt marshes of the Dullsgard Plateau with a letter from the governor of Ornia for the mayor of Grailsund...'
Another murmur of dissatisfaction from the sensation-hungry audience, who resented being burdened with so many boring details.
'...and a gift for my sweetheart, who was also waiting for me.'
This drew a little gasp from the female members of the audience. 'Sweetheart' and 'gift' were words that gave promise of a romantic dénouement.
I presented a detailed description of a gold ring I'd ordered from the finest Twerpp goldsmith in Florinth. I dwelt at great length on the carat value of its layers of gold, the nature of the lucky signs and the wording of the lover's vows I'd got him to engrave inside the ring. The females listened intently, whereas some of the males uttered groans of boredom and a couple of Bluddums blew raspberries.

I then added – in passing, so to speak – that the ring had cost me every pyra I possessed, and that I wasn't absolutely certain it would fit because, when ordering it, I had gauged the size by eye alone.

Next, I described my sweetheart, modelling her appearance on the dream creature that had lured me into contact with the Spiderwitch's hypnotic fluid. My heart almost broke when I described the girl bluebear to the audience, her image had etched itself so deeply on my memory. This agony of mind made my description all the more vivid. My female listeners sighed and unfolded their handkerchiefs in expectation of a tearful, joyful reunion.

'I was rapidly traversing the salt marshes at a spot where the arundineous vegetation of the tundralike terrain gave way to mossy flora of a stunted nature ...'

More muttering from the audience. The Megathon had no time for geographical and botanical minutiae.

'... when I heard the voice of the Nairland *quicksand* in my head.'

The muttering ceased.

Quicksand...

The word alone augured suspense. It denoted an unseen danger lying in wait for innocent victims – a danger, moreover, that led to an agonizing death or a dramatic rescue. Quicksand was simply unbeatable when it came to bringing an audience under your spell, and if the quicksand could talk into the bargain, so much the better.

'**"Stop!"** I heard the quicksand say in my head. **"Not another step, or you'll sink into me!"**

'I came to a halt. In my eagerness to get to Grailsund, I had completely failed to notice the change in the terrain. I had left the salt marshes far behind me and was on the very edge of Nairland. I could see Molehill Volcano smoking away in the distance.'

I knew that my listeners, many of whom had seen Molehill Volcano from far away, would now be seeing it in their mind's eye.

'I thought awhile. Making a detour around Nairland would entail an additional trek on foot of a good two months, if not longer. What was all the fuss about Nairland, anyway? Nobody had ever set foot in the place, so how did people know it was genuinely dangerous? **"I told them,"** whispered the quicksand. **"I'm a *well-meaning* quicksand. That's very rare – a contradiction in terms, in fact. Just go away. Go, before it's too late."'**
To talk in the quicksand's voice was risky from a storyteller's point of view. Many of those present were familiar with that voice, having heard it in their heads during their own excursions to the borders of Nairland. Atlanteans regarded it as a favourite vacation treat to travel there and be sent back home by the quicksand. The voice had to have a rough, sandy quality, but it also had to be elegant, alluring, and dangerous, so I made it sound like a cobra slithering over emery paper, a hoarse rattle of the vocal cords mingled with a menacing hiss.

'Perhaps it's just a trick, I told myself. Perhaps Nairland is full of undiscovered treasures or unexploited mineral wealth. Perhaps that voice was merely a subtle acoustic effect of some kind – perhaps it was just a collection of remote-controlled sound waves. The most incredible things do exist! A graduate of the Nocturnal Academy isn't so easily hoodwinked.

"'There's no treasure here, my dear, only me, the Cogitating Quicksand. Tread on me, and you'll sink as you'd sink into the Graveyard Marshes. I'll clog your throat, your nose, your ears, and then... Oh, how I hate this aspect of a quicksand's existence, the smothered screams and the grisly cadavers rotting away in my depths. That's why I urge you, out of the goodness of my heart, to go away. Push off! Stretch your legs a bit. There's a very scenic route that leads past Devil's Gulch. The mountain demons there are harmless, they only pelt you with edelweiss. Then turn south-east and ford the River Dank near Baysville – you can wade across, it's so shallow. After that –"

'"You're trying to fool me. You're hiding something."

"'No I'm not."

'"Yes you are."

"'No I'm not."

'"Yes you are."

"'All right, if you insist. Come on in. I'm not a quicksand at all, I'm nice, firm desert sand and the crater of Molehill Volcano is full of gold and diamonds. You can forget about that ring for your sweetheart. You could steal her a fortune here, you've no idea!"

'"How did you know about the ring?"

"'I'm a mind-reader, after all. Your lips haven't moved while we've been talking, or hadn't you noticed?"

'I reflected for a moment, weighing the situation up. In one pan of the scales I placed my common sense, my natural caution, and the quicksand's advice; in the other my curiosity, my native stupidity, my suspicion that I was being thoroughly duped, and a few hundredweight of gold and diamonds for my beloved. Guess which side the scales came down on?'

The female spectators drew a deep breath, the males gripped the arms of their seats. The Waterkins, who were neither male nor female, put their hands over their ears. Chemluth bit his cap.

'I took three paces and *sank into the quicksand.*'

I allowed the sentence to resonate awhile. Everyone was expecting a dramatic, drowning man's aria and a last-minute rescue, possibly effected by a Reptilian Rescuer. But nothing of the kind. I simply sank.

Glug-glug.

I inserted a long pause for effect. I shot a sidelong glance at Volzotan Smyke. He was trying hard to preserve a nonchalant air, but I could see his gills quivering with suspense.

'So I'd been wrong and the quicksand was right: I was going to die with my lungs full of sand – deservedly so, what's more! I had not only rejected the quicksand's generous advice but offended it as well. I deserved to die.

'"**Nice of you to look at it that way,**" the quicksand trickled into my ear, "**but belated remorse won't help you now. You're done for, I'm afraid.**"

'"Is there nothing to be done?" I thought back. "Couldn't you possibly solidify a little, so as to give me a foothold and enable me to struggle out?"

'"**Sorry, I'm a quicksand, not a slab of concrete or a lifebelt. Solidifying is completely against my nature. I warned you but you wouldn't believe me, and this is the result. Oh, how I detest being right all the time! Now comes the smothered screams bit ... Soon you'll be just another of the many**

skeletons in my ... Please forgive me, that was tactless! I'm afraid I really can't do anything more for you, except ..."

'Except? That sounded like a glimmer of hope!

'"Except what? Except what?" I demanded eagerly.

'**"Well ... The most I can do is swallow you quicker. It speeds things up a bit. Many people prefer it. The dying part is just as unpleasant, but at least it doesn't take so long."**

'"Many thanks."

'**"Don't mention it."**

'The quicksand was merciful. I sank still deeper into the morass.'

You could have heard a Minipirate's harpoon drop. Thousands of pairs of eyes and one or two cyclopean orbs gazed at me. Smyke leant forward.

And then something utterly unexpected happened – unexpected by me, not the audience: my breath gave out. It wasn't the quicksand that took the wind out of my sails, it was my quicksand story. I had talked my way into this situation in the hope that something would, as usual, occur to me.

But nothing did. This had never happened to me before.

Panic-stricken, I looked across at Nussram Fhakir, who was regarding me derisively. His congladiatorial instinct told him that this was no pause for effect; I had simply lost my thread.

The audience stared at me expectantly.

Outwardly, I remained quite calm; inwardly, I searched my brain for an idea like someone rummaging in a drawer for a missing sock. Still nothing.

Nussram leant forwards slightly, looking like a cobra poised to strike at any moment.

Quicksand Moles, said the encyclopedia in my head. The message was so abrupt and surprising that I promptly recited it aloud:

Quicksand Moles of Nairland, The. Insectivorous mammalian species distantly related to the Zamonian White-Bellied Lemming. Quicksand Moles are thickset burrowing animals with large, paddlelike, fossorial feet and little intellectual capacity. They live exclusively in the extensive quicksands of Nairland, and the ritual self-destructive behaviour they display at regular intervals is associated with Nairland's most prominent geographical feature, the Molehill Volcano. Quicksand Moles attain a length of up to nine feet and can travel through quicksand like fish through water.

'So I sank ever deeper into the quicksand!' I cried, gazing around the auditorium. 'All at once my feet touched something soft and furry! Before I knew it, I was seated on the back of a large animal. **"That's a Quicksand Mole,"** said the quicksand. **"Can you hold out?"**

'"Not for much longer," I telepathized. "I'm out of breath."

"It's your only chance. Hang on tight – the creature's bound to be making for the volcano. It's time again, I can tell from the tremors."

'I had no idea what it was time for, but I didn't care. All I wanted was to extricate myself from the quicksand, because I really was running out of breath.

'Agile as a dolphin, the mole glided through the quicksand so fast that it swirled around my ears. I clung tightly to the creature's fur, determined not to let go until we surfaced. But we didn't surface. We were diving still deeper.'

We didn't surface. We were diving still deeper . . .

Great! I was talking my way still deeper into the mire. The audience gasped for oxygen.

'Down and down we went at a steep angle. My last hour had come! I had only a single atom of breath left inside me, and both lungs were squabbling over it.

'**"You're there!"** the quicksand told me. **"You're off the hook –
more by luck than judgement."**
'And then, quite suddenly, we were out. Air! Oxygen at last!'
Yes, at last. The audience breathed deeply.
'What had happened?' called an excited Norselander.
What indeed? Good question. What *had* happened?
I didn't have a clue.
'What had happened?' I cried dramatically to the audience. 'What
had happened?'
I feverishly racked my brains.
'We had made our way through the quicksand to an underground
cavern, *that's* what had happened! We'd emerged into a huge air
bubble beneath Nairland. More moles were standing around, all
shouting at once:
'"This is the place, this is the time! This is the place, this is the time!"'
Now that I was over the worst, I lied blithely on.
'What place? What time? All I could tell was that we were in a sort
of immense well shaft. The walls around us were of solid quicksand,
and the shaft culminated in a circular hole through which daylight
was coming. It must have been several hundred feet above me.
'"This is the place, this is the time!" cried the moles.
'"Place-ace-ace!" the walls threw back. "Time-ime-ime!"'
I surveyed the amphitheatre once more. It was as silent as the
Great Forest. Nussram was studying his fingernails with an
ostentatious air of boredom, Smyke was conferring with Rumo the
Wolpertinger. Chemluth signalled to me. He drew a finger across
his throat to intimate that I should wind things up. No congladiator
had ever spoken at such length.
But I was just getting into my stride.
'I asked one of the moles to explain. Not to burden you with the
whole of his long, solemn discourse, which was interspersed with
numerous digressions into the history of the Quicksand Moles,

here is a brief summary: Molehill Volcano is an active volcano that erupts regularly every seven years on the seventh of the seventh at seven minutes past seven. There are a few pedants who claim that it actually does so at seven-tenths of the seventh second of the seventh minute past seven on the seventh of the seventh . . .'

The audience groaned in torment.

'. . . and so on,' I said hastily, 'but that's irrelevant here. The fact remains that every self-respecting Quicksand Mole over the age of seven betakes himself to Molehill Volcano on that day.'

Volcano. . . If there was one word that thrill-seeking audience found more entrancing than *quicksand*, it was *volcano* – just so long as you added that it was an active volcano on the point of engaging in its favourite activity: *erupting*. And to disclose the precise time at which an active volcano would erupt was one of the biggest favours you could do a bunch of duel-of-lies addicts. The turmoil in the stadium was steadily increasing. Even Nussram covertly cocked an eyebrow, but no one was paying any attention to him by this time. I lowered my voice and went on:

'The volcano gave a mighty rumble. It sounded like a Bollogg gargling with a thundercloud. An ominous feeling welled up inside me like . . . *like lava in a volcanic crater!* I asked the mole what day of the month it was.

'"The seventh of the seventh," he replied.'

I now did something unprecedented: I took a breather. No, not a pause for effect but a proper breather – a coffee break, so to speak. It had occurred to me that I still had a sandwich in my pocket. Chemluth had packed it so that I could fortify myself before the duel, but I'd forgotten all about it in my agitation. I ceremoniously unwrapped the sandwich and proceeded to eat it.

The audience groaned and muttered. Smyke excitedly conferred with his advisers. Chemluth had pulled his cap down over his face. Although no intermissions were allowed for during a Duel of Lies, they were not expressly prohibited. I had discovered a loophole in the regulations.

I blithely continued to eat, chewing each mouthful seven times and pausing now and then – inserting breaks in the break, as it were. No one in the history of the Zamonian entertainment industry had ever dared to tease an audience in this manner.

When I'd finished I neatly folded the greaseproof paper and put it in my pocket. Then I sat back on my throne, twiddled my thumbs, and hummed contentedly to myself as if I'd altogether forgotten where I was. Another minute, and they would lynch me.

Then, quite suddenly, I shot out a paw at such lightning speed that the spectators almost fell off their seats.

'THE VOLCANO ERUPTED!' I cried. 'And we were at its heart!'

A female Norselander in the front row fainted, but nobody took any notice.

'The plug of congealed lava on which the moles and I were standing was propelled upwards by the volcanic eruption. It was... It was... How can one describe the sensation of being spewed out by a volcano?'

I thought awhile.

'It feels like being fired from a canon mounted on the back of a rocket in flight. The pressure to which we were subjected forced us down on to the lava plug. We were squeezed as flat as pancakes as the circle of daylight raced towards us, faster and faster. With us aboard, the plug shot ever higher into the air – many, many miles into the sky.'

A very brief pause for effect.

'Then, when the plug reached its apogee, a remarkable thing happened: we became detached from it and hovered there as if weightless. We were now so high that we could look straight into outer space, a pleasure usually denied to all but Megabolloggs.'

My listeners could not, of course, know that I had enjoyed a Bollogg's-eye view of the cosmos while seated at the dream organ, so they were highly impressed by my detailed description of our solar system. I was unstinting with my scientific data concerning the various planets, their surface structure and atmospheric pressure – all of it knowledge acquired at the Nocturnal Academy. Having tormented the audience for some half an hour with deadly boring astronomical details, I abruptly went on:

'And then we started to fall.'

Several spectators with weak nerves left the auditorium. Minor commotions broke out here and there, and bottles of smelling salts were handed around.

'The Quicksand Moles uttered cries of delight. No wonder! Being blind, they couldn't see what I could see: the earth rushing up to meet us – or us rushing towards it, whichever.'

The Norselanders waggled their ears, a sign of extreme agitation.

'The moles had spread their legs and were soaring around me, squeaking, like a flock of swallows. They really looked as if they were flying. And now comes the most surprising part: they really *could* fly.'

Every jaw dropped.

'Yes indeed, anyone can. Even you!' I pointed to a female Norselander who was gazing at me open-mouthed.

'The only requirement for someone learning to fly is sufficient altitude. Jumping off a roof or out of a captive balloon isn't good enough. *Only a volcano can propel you to the altitude you need in order to learn how to fly.* The only trouble was, I was scared stiff. I'd wrapped my arms and legs tightly around me and was plummeting earthwards like a bullet. The moles couldn't help me because they couldn't see me. In order to fly, you have to spread your arms.'

'Then spread them, you idiot!' shouted an angry Bluddum in the upper circle.

I had almost overdone the suspense. I would now have to give my listeners what they'd earned.

'I spread my arms – and flew! No longer plunging earthwards, I circled slowly and majestically like an eagle as I made for the ground in a wide spiral. Some of the moles had already landed. Beneath me lay Grailsund, the town for whose mayor I was carrying an important message – the town where my sweetheart lived. I not only landed there as gently as a feather, I landed right on the lap of my beloved, who was sitting waiting for me in the garden. As I came in to land I felt in my pocket for the gold ring. What? I was sure I'd put it there, but no: no ring!'

My female listeners cried out in dismay.

'Had I lost it in the quicksand? Or in the volcano? During the flight? The possibilities were legion. Panic-stricken, I rummaged around in the grains of quicksand in my trouser pocket. Nothing. No ring!'

The first handkerchiefs were being moistened. Sobs could be heard.

'**"Look in the other pocket,"** advised the quicksand.

'I felt in the other pocket, and sure enough, there it was! I removed it just before alighting on my sweetheart's lap, and, while our lips met in a kiss, slipped it on her finger. And lo, it fitted perfectly.'

Silence. Utter silence.

The spectators were beside themselves, even the more refined among them. Seats were wrenched off their bases. The Megathon had never known such an ovation.

It was a pretty good story, admittedly, but I hadn't been counting on such a response. What I didn't know at the time was that I had invented the happy ending, the romantic story with an upbeat dénouement.

All Zamonian stories before my time, especially those told by congladiators, had either had no ending at all, just a punchline, or a tragic ending replete with misery, mourning, and murder. The hero died, the heroine died, the villain died, the king and queen died – together with all their subjects, of course. Every Zamonian story of the period culminated in the death of all concerned.

How Dank Was My Valley, the dramatic regional novel by Psittachus Rumplestilt, ended with all the principal characters drowned by rain. Wilfred the Wordsmith's most widely read novel, *The Roast Guest*, featured twelve thousand deaths alone, and several million more occurred in his whole œuvre, most of them in the last few pages. There were writers' schools which not only taught that the entire cast of characters in every artistic work of fiction had to die but suggested the most subtle ways of accomplishing this: with sword or glass dagger, poison or faked accident, disease or act of God. Every author vied with his confrères to devise the most bloodthirsty, tragic and corpse-strewn finales, and those who succeeded were hailed as geniuses.

Literary prizes were awarded for the novel with the most downbeat ending. In many Zamonian theatres the spectators in the first few rows wore washable clothing because most stage productions showered them with artificial blood. Any authors presumptuous enough to submit novels with non-tragic endings were booted out of their publishers' offices.

I was satisfying a need of which my listeners had been quite unaware. Handkerchiefs were produced throughout the auditorium and tears of joy shed over my story's happy outcome. Many spectators were embracing one another, half laughing, half weeping. Chemluth was dancing a little rain-forest jig.

Only two people showed no emotion. One was Volzotan Smyke, who simply stared at me with his cold, sharklike eyes while his toadies jabbered excitedly. The other was Nussram Fhakir the Unique. If I had impressed him, he certainly didn't show it. He gazed impassively at the spectators and waited for them to subside. I had only won one round, after all, whereas he had ten to his credit. To repeat:

A Duel of Lies continued until one of the contestants resigned. The number of rounds and their duration were not laid down. Many rounds were over in five minutes, others lasted an hour, and there had been duels that went on for forty rounds.

Ours was destined to last ninety-nine.

Rounds 12-22

Every one of the next eleven rounds went to me. The spell had been broken, Nussram's home advantage was forgotten, and the tide of public sentiment turned in my favour. It wasn't that my opponent did badly. His stories were as brilliant as ever, but I always beat him by a point or two.

To be honest, I continued to gamble on the females in my audience. All my ensuing lies had a romantic flavour. They told of grand passions, eternal loyalty, lovers' vows, dramatic partings, broken hearts. All had a happy ending, and all featured a ring. When the females applauded, their escorts applauded even more loudly to please them. After eleven stories, however, I ran out of plots that could be interwoven with the romantic bestowal of gold rings. Besides, the audience's interest in lovesick princesses was noticeably waning.

Rounds 23-33

Sensing that his moment had come, Nussram Fhakir switched to quite another thematic field: Zamonian demonology. This was one of his specialities, as I knew from reading his autobiography. There were more demons in Zamonia than anywhere else in the world, and Atlantis had the highest concentration of them.

There were Mountain Demons, Earth Demons, Air Demons, Water Demons, Animal Demons, Swamp Demons, Sedge Demons, Moss Demons, Dwarf Demons, Megademons, and the aforementioned Rickshaw Demons. Even if he wasn't a demon himself, every inhabitant of Atlantis was acquainted or friendly with, or married or related to, one or more of the creatures.

The public attitude towards demons had changed over the years. All they had done in former times was terrorize and intimidate other life forms, prowl around mainly at night, ambush travellers in forests, howl in chimneys on stormy nights, scare children, and so on. As the demon population steadily increased, however, so their mischief-making became routine. It was quite unexceptional for a Three-Tongued Moss Demon with a bloodstained axe lodged in his skull to peer over the foot of your bed, wailing like a nocturnal phantom, when you retired for the night.

People walking in the woods were no longer startled when a gnome jumped out from behind a tree and pulled awful faces at them. Not even children took fright when Coal Demons rampaged around beneath the cellar stairs. The inhabitants of Zamonia had gradually become inured to demons. No one was afraid of them any more.

The demons' behaviour itself underwent a change. They adapted to social conventions, took ordinary jobs, and fitted into the urban scene. Before long it became commonplace to buy your bread from a demon or have one pull you through the streets in his rickshaw. There were demons in every bowling club and choral society. They swept the streets and sat on the city council. Even some of the most celebrated gebba players and congladiators were demons.

On the other hand, they were still very ugly. Contorted faces, long yellow teeth, exposed gums, rolling eyes, lolling tongues, hirsute ears, multicoloured lips, horned heads, facial warts, bristly hair – all these were typical features for which little could be done. The vainer demons made repeated attempts to remedy them, however. They had their teeth whitened and their lips bleached, tried to keep their tongues under control and refrain from rolling their eyes too wildly, concealed their horns under grotesque hats, wore tailormade clothes, and did their utmost not to be conspicuous.

Nussram exploited this social aspect in his next group of stories. They were simply dolled-up demon jokes (which were very popular in Atlantis), but he lent them an artistic gloss with a variety of demon impressions and daring political allusions, and, above all, an intimate knowledge of demonological conventions that could only have stemmed from personal experience. He imitated the lisping speech of the Rickshaw Demons, the clumsy movements of the Balinese Shadow Ghosts, the squinting eyes of the Japanese Grimacers. He had a perfect command of all their dialects, the swallowed consonants of the Grailsundian Gallows-bird, the stuttering delivery of the Gloomberg Goblin, the keening of the Irish Banshee.

Although every story was a masterpiece of parody, Nussram didn't tread on the demons' corns. He managed to portray their eccentricities and bizarre habits in such a sympathetic way that the numerous demons in the audience applauded him loudest of all.

My own stories were less memorable, but I stood my ground. Although six of the eleven rounds went to Nussram, I scored a respectable number of points. The level of applause for Nussram continued to be high, whereas mine was in the medium range.

Rounds 34-45

Then came a phase when fatigue set in, for the audience as well as for us. We both had to ease off a little, recoup our energy, rest and refresh our imagination. The spectators' attention span and capacity for enthusiasm had definitely diminished. The Megathon became restive. Many of the audience stood up and regaled themselves with corn cobs and hot beer.

So the next twelve rounds were shared and the scores remained comparatively low. Neither of us registered more than five points, our stories were too feeble and the applause was too half-hearted. We both resorted to routine tricks, told new versions of old stories, picked up the thread of each other's jokes, and marked time, narratively speaking. In an attempt to conserve our strength, we fought like weary boxers leaning on each other for a round or two.

Rounds 46-57

I managed to make up some ground in the next dozen rounds. Nussram Fhakir was showing slight but unmistakable signs of fatigue.

Reserves of energy

I now understood why Smyke had been so insistent on my losing: in the long run, the age difference was making itself felt. I was simply in better condition, with more staying power and younger vocal cords. Nussram's lack of stamina (perceptible only to a pro) sent me into a state of restrained euphoria. We had now fought nearly sixty rounds and were roughly level on points. I was back in top form. Stories kept popping into my head as they had during my first congladiatorial contest with the Troglotroll. What was more, I bubbled over with such *masses* of ideas that I lumped several stories together in one round, using enough material for five, and tossed ideas around with wild abandon. The audience came to life again.

Although it was contrary to all the rules and against all common sense to be so extravagant with one's repertoire of lies, I felt I'd tapped an inexhaustible supply. There were plenty more where those came from.

I told of my adventures on the Island of Sirens, of my ability to fashion a work of art out of any piece of wood, of the point I'd snapped off Neptune's crown. I told of an elevator that had taken me to the centre of the earth, of collecting crocodile tears on the Amazon, and of painting the Aurora Borealis on the sky with the tail of a comet I'd ridden. I presented insights into my professional life and described how I'd worked as a star decorator, hiccup curer, equator supervisor, underwater policeman, wave comber, and tide conductor. Speaking in the strictest confidence, I informed the audience that I had been responsible for salting the oceans, icing the Polar Circle, and drying out the Demerara Desert.

I gesticulated, performed convincing impressions, made generous use of my stage voice, and twisted around on my throne to squeeze the last laugh out of my listeners, who were once more, at long last, disposed to be enthusiastic. I was rewarded for my efforts with some more maximum scores, and none of my stories obtained fewer than nine points.

Nussram, meanwhile, was looking overtired. Although he continued, on the acting level, to serve up some brilliant theatrical fictions which any younger congladiator would have envied, an expert could tell from his diminished body language that he was soft-pedalling.

My own strength abated too, not gradually but all at once. With fifty-seven rounds behind me I was ten clear rounds in the lead and should now have put on speed, but every muscle in my face hurt from talking and grimacing, my throat was parched, and my tongue was as swollen and rough as sandpaper. Worst of all, my brain had dried up.

I couldn't think of a single idea.

And that was when Nussram Fhakir really turned up the heat.

Rounds 58-77

I hadn't expected that. Nussram had been fooling me all the time. It was a tactical ploy. He'd leaned on the ropes, so to speak, recouped his strength, and showed me up like a greenhorn. I was completely burnt out – I had senselessly squandered my best ideas, intoxicated with the certainty of victory, whereas he seemed to be in better shape than he had been at the outset.

I had underestimated two things. In the first place, there was the immense amount of experience he'd amassed during a reign twelve times as long as mine. He had not only told thousands of stories but heard and memorized thousands more, a fund of material from which to assemble entirely new ones. Secondly, he'd enjoyed a long rest. It was six years since he'd trodden the boards, whereas I had fought one duel after another for the past year. I was finished; he was on the brink of a new beginning. He now came up with an utterly novel variant of the congladiatorial duel, a revolutionary way of presenting lies which he had devised during his self-imposed absence from the stage and now played like a trump card.

Nussram's musical innovation

He raised his hand, and at his signal the stage was invaded by a band of Voltigorks, each armed with a bizarre instrument. I registered two troll-hide drums, two Florinthian trumboons, a crystal harp, three musical saws, two Hackonian alphorns, two vibrobasses, and a Yhôllian concertina. The musicians formed up behind Nussram's throne and awaited his word of command.

Astonished whispers ran round the auditorium. It was neither expressly permitted nor forbidden to underscore lies with a musical accompaniment. It was simply that no one had thought of the idea. So that was what Nussram had been up to during his mysterious absence: he had devoted himself to music and developed and trained his voice in that artistic discipline; he had devised new lies and arrayed them in musical attire. As a former admirer I couldn't help secretly taking my hat off to him. He had reinvented the art of lying.

His first musical lie took the form of an operatic aria, with a slow, heart-rending trumboon solo overlaid by Nussram's sonorous tenor as he sang the words in Old Zamonian. It didn't matter that very few of the audience understood the libretto. They knew what it was about, like all arias, because the music translated the words into emotions. It dealt with great things like love, betrayal, death, and – of course – infamous lies. Nussram used the short flight of steps in front of his throne for histrionic interludes. He pranced skilfully up and down them, crawled around on them, pounded them with his fists. In conclusion he fell down them with consummate artistry, simulating his own death, and breathed his last in a deep bass voice.

I had to admit that Nussram was not only a talented singer but a gifted composer. The melodies really did have great appeal. Needless to say, he scored ten points. The audience went absolutely wild – more enthusiastic than at any other stage in the duel.

As for me, I failed even to complete my next story. I was booed to a standstill for the first time in my career. All the audience wanted was to see and hear what my opponent had devised for his next offering.

The musicians rearranged themselves. I had expected Nussram to pursue his proven operatic line still further, but his next story was a complete change in every respect: type of music, tempo, volume, even his own appearance. Discarding his congladiatorial cloak, he treated the audience to the sight of his bare chest, which was remarkably muscular for his age. This earned him a few gasps from the fair sex. Then – there's no other way of putting it – he swept the board.

The troll-hide drummers struck up a steady rhythm, actively supported by the Voltigorks in the vibrobass section. The brutal but infectious beat made the Megathon shake. Then the musical saws came in with an electrifying melody that caused the first few spectators to stand on their seats and set even my knees twitching. Nussram, who had switched to a smoky bass register, was shaking his hips – rather inanely, in my opinion, but the audience liked it. Even the concertina's shrillest chords enlivened the atmosphere. It was all I could do to refrain from clapping the rhythm myself and preserve a stoical demeanour. Meantime, the spectators were shaking their hips like Nussram.

This was not only an entirely different way of telling lies but a wholly new conception of music. All that had previously been known in Atlantis were tragic operas, a wide variety of folk music, and the trashy, sentimental ballads of the crooner Melliflor Gunk. This was a novelty. Nussram really did have guts: he was staking everything on a single card.

The story itself was almost unintelligible because of the din (it dealt with the acquisition of eternal youth by means of hip-shaking), and I doubted whether it could be called a lie at all, but Nussram's success spoke for itself.

Another ten points, another deafening ovation. Me, I had only to open my mouth to be booed.

Nussram's next mendacious tale was clearly audible because he employed a harp accompaniment only. Having donned his cloak again, he presented a musical account of the origin of the Impic Alps in a high-pitched, eunuch's soprano. His song took the form of a fictitious saga which only just fell within the rules but was benevolently accepted by the audience. The melody was genuinely moving, albeit in a different way from the operatic aria. This time, Nussram was appealing to Zamonian love of country.

Then he proceeded to yodel. Accompanied by the Hackonian alphorns, he warbled a curiously rhythmical melody that evoked wild applause, especially from the Mountain Dwarfs present. He also underlined the beat by leaping around in a circle and slapping his thighs with the flat of his hands, a procedure spontaneously copied by the audience.

Finally, he reverted to a dramatic song that spoke of the mountains' rosy glow and his inextinguishable love of his native land.

The Bluddums sobbed at this. It was rather too sentimental for my taste, but there was no stopping Nussram. He scored ten points.

All that remained for me was to tell my next story despite the booing.

Nussram cleared his throat and ruffled his hair so that it hung over his face in wild disarray. He took over the Yhôllian concertina and delivered the most delicate tissue of lies in a voice of which any Irish Druid would have been proud. With glassy, tearful gaze, he sang in a sobbing tremolo of his sweetheart, who had been devoured by a vicious Tyrannomobyus Rex. She was still alive in the whale's belly, however, and regularly sent him messages in a bottle.

The Voltigorks formed a hoarse-voiced choir and joined in the refrain, which described the drinking habits of the sea gods. The audience joined in too, swaying rhythmically. The words of the song culminated in a dramatic rescue operation in the course of which Nussram not only extricated his sweetheart but strangled the whale with his bare hands. I couldn't repress a silent, scornful laugh at this. Not so the audience. Ten points for Nussram, corn cobs and boos for me.

By now, Volzotan Smyke had relaxed completely. The stadium had never before witnessed such enthusiasm for one contestant and such scathing rejection of the other. Nussram Fhakir was staging a sensational comeback.

And so it went on for fifteen rounds, in each of which he changed his style of music, his voice, his appearance, and his narrative technique. He sang a mournful blues to the wailing saws, belted out an ecstatic war song in time to the troll-hide drums, presented operatic interludes, sang *a cappella* in a voice as clear as glass, played the vibrobass like a virtuoso, conducted his orchestra with lordly gestures, belaboured the crystal harp with his feet, tap-danced up and down the steps, and performed a few acrobatics of which I genuinely wouldn't have believed him capable at his age. And he scored ten points every time. Meantime, the Bluddums had set some greasy corn cobs alight and were waving them in time to the music.

I now had to display a congladiatorial quality that had never been tested in me before: the nerve to withstand boos and catcalls. Only the toughest possessed this, and many a congladiator had failed to pass the ordeal. But no duel was over until you resigned. The true congladiator showed genuine greatness when he held his ground at this, his darkest hour, and resisted the urge to run, sobbing, from the arena.

I stood there, straight as a ramrod, as the gnawed corn cobs whistled past my ears. It was the nadir of my artistic career. Everything within me itched to flee the stage and crawl into the sewers, but I stood fast and endured all that came my way: boos, catcalls, hisses, corn cobs, beer mugs – even dismantled seats and an entire Bluddum hurled bodily on to the stage by his cronies. I didn't sit down although these humiliations were even harder to endure while standing because they turned my hind legs to jelly. I even forced myself to stand on one paw to show how little they affected me.

The audience knew that boos alone could not drive a congladiator from the stage. Negative reactions were also recorded on the meter; the louder the boos, the higher the score, so they eventually calmed down. Once you've passed that point, you're over the worst. The manifestations of displeasure gradually ebbed and were replaced, first by peevish mutters and then by subdued applause. Audiences resemble wild beasts; they must first be tamed by iron will-power. Only the finest congladiators were capable of this.

Nussram knew this too, which was why my endurance earned me more respect from him than all my stories put together. He was now learning, at long last, that he'd met his match.

The applause did not begin to wane until his last five musical numbers. His two concluding vocal offerings earned him only nine and eight points respectively. After the seventy-second round his repertoire was exhausted, and he only gave encores. The spectators, tired of clapping and stamping their feet, had resumed their seats.

The Voltigork orchestra waddled off the stage, peace returned, and I bravely told my next fictitious story. The audience was ready for a quieter style of presentation. Resistance to me had largely subsided.

Rounds 78-90

Our scores in the next thirteen rounds were the lowest of the duel to date. The spectators had been physically drained by Nussram's musical interlude, and he himself was close to collapse. He had undoubtedly assumed that I would throw in the towel at some stage in his recital, but it hadn't happened: I was still on my feet and his repertoire was exhausted. He fell back on routine stories, repeated some well-tried material, and scored minimum points. As for me, who was having to fight my way back from the brink of the abyss, I could likewise count myself lucky if I scored more than two or three points.

Rock bottom

In the end, three low-scoring rounds went to him and ten to me. The audience was running out of enthusiasm.

'That's enough, that's enough!' chanted a handful of Yetis.

We had fought ninety rounds and won forty-five apiece. We were absolutely dead beat, both of us. Our histrionics were limited to an occasional, feeble wink or a twitch of the eyebrow.

The audience applauded out of politeness only, and none of our stories scored more than a single point. Shame forbids me to disclose their contents, but they really hit rock bottom. Our brains had been wrung dry of every last drop of imagination. Neither of us was willing to give up, of course, not after such a protracted battle. We seemed to be heading for a draw. I scanned the audience in search of inspiration. I needed something on which to base my next story.

My eye fell on Smyke, who was still regarding me coldly. He had started it all, and I couldn't help remembering how he had laughed when I described some episodes from my past. His belief that they were elaborate lies had been the making of my congladiatorial career.

Episodes from my past . . .

Just a minute!

If Smyke had enjoyed them, why not the audience? He had an unerring nose for what was in demand. It wasn't quite fair, because they weren't fictitious at all, but who could prove that? Besides, Nussram's musical interlude hadn't been entirely in accordance with the rules.

Round 91

I began with the Minipirates. I described their nightly firework displays and their unsuccessful attempts to capture other vessels, my rapid growth on a diet of plankton and my ability to tie a knot in a fish. The spectators, who had almost forgotten what a good lie was, pricked up their ears. They were still in a state of lethargy, so the applause was nothing to write home about (three points), but I'd caught their attention again.

That was a beginning. The beginning of the end.

Nussram threw off his torpor with an effort. He was surprised, not having expected me to recover, but he pulled himself together and quickly stitched together a threadbare lie. It earned him two points.

Round 92

My next story dealt with Hobgoblin Island. I carefully built up the suspense in the dark, shadowy forest, then gave a vivid description of the spirits' first appearance, imitating their frightful songs and movements. There followed a detailed account of my performances as a tear-jerking tenor and the Hobgoblins' grisly eating habits.

A preliminary smattering of laughter and a cry of 'Bravo!', followed by some solid applause. Four points.

Nussram was too much of a pro to be overly impressed. Delving deep into his box of tricks, he concocted quite an ingenious double lie out of two classic fictions on which congladiators had been ringing the changes for centuries. The knowledgeable audience saw through this stratagem, however, and punished him with one measly point.

Round 93

Then came my escape by sea. My description of the Babbling Billows aroused general amusement. I imitated their voices in the thick of an argument, slopping around on my throne as I did so. I told of my vocal training and presented a few samples of my vast vocabulary. The appearance of the Tyrannomobyus Rex provided the requisite suspense, followed by a happy ending, and my account of Gourmet Island whetted the spectators' appetite for a sequel. Back in the swing once more, they laughed uproariously and ordered hot beers. Five points.

Nussram preserved his icy calm. As nonchalant and relaxed as he had been in the first round, he spun an elegant yarn about a balloon flight to the moon. I was nonetheless struck by his incipient signs of uncertainty. Although an outsider would never have noticed such an infinitesimal hint of nerves, I detected a very slight but recurrent tremor – the top joint twitched no more than a millimetre, perhaps – in the third finger of his left hand.

Despite its neat construction, Nussram's story was a hackneyed piece of work cobbled together out of some well-known Zamonian fairy tales. The audience graciously awarded him three points.

Round 94

My appetizing accounts of Gourmet Island led to increased corn-cob consumption, my description of the Gourmetica insularis to cries of horror, my last-minute rescue by Mac to sighs of relief. Six points.

Nussram countered, but he countered badly. I knew the story – a brilliant one, admittedly – from his autobiography. It described how he had driven Cagliostro the master charlatan off the stage and into the sewers. He had changed a few names and put the end at the beginning. That didn't fool me, but it did fool one or two inexperienced spectators, because he notched up five points. His finger stopped twitching.

Round 95

My time with Mac the Reptilian Rescuer was made of the cloth from which all good congladiatorial stories were cut: last-minute rescues – any number of them! I told of Baldwyn's leap from the Demon Rocks, of the Wolperting Whelps, of the headless Bollogg's crushing of the dog farm. Frenzied applause. 7.5 points.

This visibly disconcerted Nussram Fhakir, though his discomfiture was apparent only to me and a few genuine experts in the audience, one of them being Volzotan Smyke, who shuffled around on his seat in agitation.

Nussram maintained his wooden mask of self-confidence for the audience's benefit, but I could quite clearly see how, for a tenth of a second, the pupil of his right eye contracted by a fraction of a millimetre. The story he told was not only stolen, but stolen from *me*. However, he had refurbished it so skilfully that I was the only one to notice. Such was the increasing climate of enthusiasm that he scored an unmerited six points.

Round 96

My time at the Nocturnal Academy provided me with scope for extravagant boasts about my state of knowledge. I quoted at great length from the encyclopedia in my head and described the physical attributes of Professor Nightingale, Qwerty, and Fredda. Knio and Weeny slapped their thighs at this but said nothing. I edited them out of my reminiscences and proceeded straight to the maze of tunnels in the Gloomberg Mountains. I also forbore to mention the Troglotroll, preferring instead to give a detailed account of my dramatic, metamorphotic plunge into Great Forest Lake.

Eight points.

Nussram now did something that cost him a lot of good will: he rehashed my own story, substituting the Wotansgard Falls for the Gloomberg Falls and himself for me. Even my punchline was only scantily disguised.

Two points. It served him right, in my opinion.

Round 97

The Great Forest, my illusory love affair, the spider's web, my marathon escape from the Spiderwitch... This was unbeatable stuff, and Nussram knew it.

During my performance there appeared on his brow, barely discernible with the naked eye, a tiny bead of sweat. If there were weight categories for beads of sweat, this one would undoubtedly have been classed as a flyweight. It was smaller than a bisected speck of dust, smaller perhaps than a single molecule of water. It may even have been the smallest bead of sweat in the entire history of perspiration, but *I* could see it, and I was sure it felt to Nussram as if it were as big and heavy as a full-grown Chimera.

As a result, his next story was not only weak in content but presented, for the very first time, with a slight tremor of uncertainty in his voice. This made itself felt on the applause meter: nine points for me, four for my opponent.

Round 98

My account of falling through the dimensions evoked gasps of astonishment at the brazen presumption of my mendacity, yet it was all true. By normal congladiatorial standards, this story was almost experimental and abstract, revolutionary and avant-garde. I mimed the state of Carefree Catalepsy and gave an impressive description of the vastness of the universe, the beauty of the Horsehead Nebula, the bizarre carpetways of the 2364th Dimension, and my return to earth by way of the dimensional hiatus from which I had left it – an impossibility in the truest sense of the word. The sheer audacity of this last assertion was an unprecedented gamble from the strategic point of view, but my quick-witted audience rewarded it with 9.5 points.

The small army of beads of sweat that now adorned Nussram's brow were now visible to the spectators in the ringside seats. He launched into his next story, but at the very first sentence one of them trickled down his forehead and clung to his left eyebrow like a tiny, stranded mountaineer. When he tried to continue, he dislodged a whole avalanche of salty droplets. They stung his eyes, but he dared not brush them away for fear of exposing his weakness.

He faltered for the first time in his long professional career, started again from the beginning, lost his thread once more, and finally dried up in mid story. His cloak was sodden with the sweat streaming down him.

The spectators were absolutely dumbfounded. No congladiator, not even the most inexperienced apprentice, had ever failed like this before. For the first time in the annals of the Duel of Lies, there was no reaction at all, just a deathly hush. No score.

Round 99

My laborious trek through the Demerara Desert brought the audience out in a lather of sweat as well as Nussram. My vivid account of the paroxysms of mirth induced by muggrooms infected the spectators, who roared with laughter. They were equally carried away by my description of the Sharach-il-Allah, the taming of Anagrom Ataf, and life in a semi-stable mirage. I concluded with Tornado City, its population of old men, and the successful outcome of our escape attempt.

Thunderous applause. Ten points, my highest score for some time. That was it: I'd exhausted my repertoire at last. I couldn't recount my interlude inside the Bollogg's head. People could have seen the Bollogg retrieve his head from Atlantis, after all, so I'd have given myself away. I have never come closer to draining the dregs of my imagination.

If Nussram had even the ghost of an idea, he would triumph. The feeblest, most desiccated idea, the lowest possible score, would be enough to defeat me.

He rose and made a dramatic, sweeping gesture of a kind he'd often made in the course of the duel when soaring to new heights after a lapse of form.

'I've a very unusual announcement to make,' he said solemnly. 'Something quite unprecedented – something no audience has ever heard from me before.'

The old fox. The Unique. He'd dropped me in it again. I had no idea what he was going to produce from the depths of his box of tricks. Whatever it was, I would submit with good grace. He'd done it: he really was the champion.

He removed his congladiatorial cloak and, with another sweeping gesture, dropped it at my feet.

'I resign. Well done, my boy.'

Then, head erect, he proudly strode from the stage.

The duel was over.

Pandemonium An incredible commotion broke out. Many of the audience jumped up at once and hurried to the betting counters to collect their winnings, the rest swarmed on to the stage to carry me around the Megathon. I just caught a glimpse of Volzotan Smyke yelling at his entourage and pointing in my direction. Chemluth waved his cap excitedly. Then I was seized by the crowd.

I bobbed like a cork on a sea of hands, was tossed to and fro. This being an old congladiatorial tradition, it had to be endured. I'd experienced it often enough, but not in such a violent form. They tugged at my paws, shook me like a rag doll. The spectators were beside themselves – I was genuinely afraid of being torn limb from limb.

Four Bluddums were wrenching at my forelegs and four at my hind legs. I was on the point of being quartered when the earth began to shake.

No one took any notice at first. Tremors were an everyday occurrence in Atlantis, and this one wasn't unduly powerful, just a rumble overlaid by the general din. Then the rumble became a low, menacing roar. The Bluddums let go of me, and I fell to the ground.

I had never known the ground to vibrate so violently. Everyone was shouting at once, and the Megathon had started to disintegrate. We could count ourselves lucky that the building had no roof, or there would probably have been some fatalities. As it was, a few columns fell over and smashed a corn-cob vendor's stall. A few Yetis were splattered with hot fat, but Yetis were durable creatures.

The Norselanders and the Big-Footed Bertts were shouting loudest. A huge crack transected the steps and the base of the arena, engulfing dozens of seat cushions and part of the stage, complete with applause meter. A big shaft of greased lightning darted out of the fissure and disappeared into the night sky.

Then the earthquake abruptly ceased.

Someone gripped me by the shoulder.

'Come on, we'd better get out of here, gah!'

It was Chemluth. He told me, while we were hurrying to my cubicle to collect our belongings, that Volzotan Smyke was more than a little incensed by my behaviour.

'We must get out of Atlantis, gah. It seems you've lost him a whole heap of pyras.'

'I know.'

'You know?'

'Yes. I'll explain later. We'll collect our stuff and push off, but I must change first, at least. I can't go wandering around in my duelling outfit.'

We dashed through the gloomy catacombs under the Megathon. All the torches had gone out, probably extinguished by falling plaster or the blasts of air that issued from the ground during Atlantean earthquakes.

I pushed the door open. Chemluth lit a match and dimly illuminated the cubicle. Hastily divesting myself of my con-gladiator's cloak, I pulled my clothes on.

'What now, gah?' asked Chemluth.

'Search me.'

'We don't have any money, gah, and Smyke's spies are every-where. We won't get far.'

'Let's take to the sewers.'

'Join the Invisibles, you mean?'

'Or whoever lives down there. It's our only chance.'

Someone knocked three times. We both jumped.

Volzotan Smyke put his head round the door. 'May we come in?'

The cubicle filled up with Yetis and Bluddums. Rumo the Wolpertinger stationed himself in the doorway and lit the room with a blazing torch.

'Glad we caught you, my boy. We must celebrate your victory.' Smyke's tone was as suave as ever. 'However, you'll have to foot the bill for your victory party. I'm flat broke.'

I tried to explain things. 'Listen, Smyke, it's like this. Nussram provoked me and –'

'I'm not only broke, oh no!' sighed Smyke. 'I didn't just stake all my money on Nussram. No, no, I staked everything I owned.

Buildings, businesses, stocks and shares – I've lost *everything*. And all because you refused to do me a measly little favour.'

'Listen, Smyke, I'll earn it all back. I'll work for nothing...'

'You still haven't caught on, have you? As a congladiator, you're all washed up. No one will challenge you after that duel tonight. You've defeated Nussram Fhakir. Who would take you on now? Who would bet on your opponent? Your duels have become totally uninteresting.'

I hadn't looked at it that way.

'Don't worry, I'm not going to kill you. I've got something far more subtle in mind. You're going to experience hell on earth. I'm sending you to the Infurno.'

The Infurno?

From the
'Encyclopedia of Marvels, Life Forms
and Other Phenomena of Zamonia and its Environs'
by Professor Abdullah Nightingale

Infurno, The. Popular term for the mechanical innards of the *SS Moloch*, the gigantic ship that cruises the Zamonian Sea. It is surmised that the engine room of this legendary ocean giant is equipped with thousands of furnaces that have to be stoked incessantly to keep the vessel under way. Saunalike temperatures are reputed to prevail in the Infurno. The working environment, too, is extremely unfavourable. There is no trade union participation, for instance, and the pay is extremely employee-unfriendly. Zamonians use the term Infurno as a synonym for Hell or unpleasant living conditions ['It was sheer Infurno!'], and unqualified persons responsible for bringing up children often threaten them with the

Infurno as a way of calling them to order ('Be good, or you'll end up in the Infurno').

There is no scientific proof of the Infurno's existence because no reputable scientist has ever dared to examine the *SS Moloch* at close quarters.

Smyke made a dismissive gesture. 'Put him aboard the *Moloch* – him and that dwarf sidekick of his!'

One of the Yetis spoke up. 'We're worried about our families, Smyke. The earthquake...We'd like to find out if our homes are still standing. Can't we finish them off here and now?'

Rumo the Wolpertinger stepped forward. 'I'll take them to the *Moloch*.'

'Good,' said Smyke, 'you do that. But make sure they really go aboard. I know you can't stand Bluebear, so no little "accident" on the way, is that clear?'

'Understood.'

Rumo seized Chemluth and me by the scruff of the neck and hustled us along the underground passages ahead of him. He was about five feet taller than me, and his fist alone was twice the size of my head. Wolpertingers are said to be more than a match even for Werewolves, so I tried to be polite.

'Where are you taking us?'

'To the harbour.'

'Are you really putting us aboard the *Moloch*?'

'Shut up!'

He shoved us down a gloomy side passage – the start of the sewers. Taking an algae torch from the wall, he thrust us along in front of him.

After we had stumbled along the tunnel for a mile or two, he came to a halt.

'There,' he said, 'that's far enough.'

Far enough? Far enough for what? He's going to kill us, I thought. He simply can't be bothered to escort us all the way to the harbour. Chemluth adopted a *flamencação* stance.

For the first time ever, Rumo removed his helmet in my presence. There was a big red fleck on his forehead.

'Know who I am?' he asked.

'Harvest Home Plain,' I thought. *'The dog farm, the Wolperting Whelps . . .'* I remembered the tiny puppy with the red fleck, the one we'd rescued from the Bollogg.

'Wolpertingers never forget,' he said. 'You saved my life once. Now I'm saving yours.'

He extended a mighty paw. I shook his index finger.

'Why didn't you reveal your identity before?'

'I knew you'd get into trouble sooner or later, I knew it the first time I saw you. It happens to everyone who gets mixed up with Smyke. Besides, you wouldn't have believed me. It was wiser to wait.'

He peered in all directions.

'Listen: things are happening in Atlantis – really big things. They've been going on for thousands of years... It won't be long before they come to a head. Er...'

He groped for words.

'It's the Invisibles, they... er... how can I put it?'

He scratched his massive canine skull. Wolpertingers were handy with their fists and good at chess, but eloquence wasn't their forte.

'Well, I can't really explain it, but, er... Fredda...'

'Fredda?' How did the Wolpertinger know Fredda?

'Well, er... It's all to do with the greased lightning and the earthquakes... Another planet... We're flying and Zamonia is sinking – no, it's the other way round. Heavens, how can I put it?'

I didn't know either.

'Listen, someone else will explain it to you – someone you know. You're expected down below, in the bowels of Atlantis. I can't take you there, I must go back and get ready for the great moment. My family... I've sent for someone who'll show you the way. He should be here any minute.'

Rumo was speaking in riddles. Either he was slightly cracked, or he was deliberately trying to confuse me.

'Gah!' Chemluth exclaimed. 'Someone's coming.'

Footsteps were approaching.

'Ah, there he is,' said Rumo. 'You can trust him.'

A figure emerged from the gloom. It was the Troglotroll.

'Don't let my resemblance to a Troglotroll mislead you into doing something rash,' said the Troglotroll. 'These days I'm only a Troglotroll on the outside, so to speak. Inside, I've been completely decontaminated, ak-ak-ak! From now on I'm your saviour.'

I tried to convey my dislike of Troglotrolls to Rumo.

'I understand your misgivings,' he said, 'but I've personally taken steps to guarantee this troll's change of heart.'

He bent down, seized the Troglotroll by the throat, and whispered to him, baring his teeth in an ominous way. 'Remember what'll happen to you if a hair of Bluebear's head is harmed?'

'I remember,' the Troglotroll said humbly. The recollection clearly didn't appeal to him.

Rumo wished us luck. Then he handed the torch to the Troglotroll and disappeared into the darkness.

Anyone who has been led astray by a Troglotroll remains a lifelong sceptic where that labyrinth-dweller's qualifications as a guide are concerned. The further we followed him into the bowels of Atlantis, therefore, the greater my misgivings became. We began by wading through sewers knee-deep in brackish water while green-eyed rats scurried between our legs and squeaked at us malevolently. Then we descended a long, steep, slippery flight of steps, largely overgrown with moss, that took us at least a mile into the depths. Where did it lead?

Doubts about the Troglotroll

'It's a short cut,' said the Troglotroll, as if he had read my thoughts. 'These are the Invisibles' ruins. No one ventures down here except rats and Sewer Dragons. This part of Atlantis must have originated many thousands of years ago. Nothing here is like it is on the surface, ak-ak!'

Pullulating on every side were shadowy creatures: rats, woodlice, millipedes, spiders, caterpillars, and multicoloured glow-worms that twinkled in the darkness. Bats kept fluttering around our heads. The walls streamed with moisture that seemed, in some curious way, to be flowing up them.

The tunnels became steadily bigger, and overhead, flashing at brief intervals, were blue and green lights resembling jellyfish attached to the roof by suction. We waded on through an evil-smelling soup. Something slimy wound itself around my leg.

'Just a Snake Leech,' the Troglotroll explained. 'They don't bite, they only suck a little.'

After walking for half an hour we came out in a spacious tunnel illuminated by even more roof lights. Lying at the far end was something big – something alive. It looked like a breathing mound of scales. 'Oh!' said the Troglotroll. 'How unpleasant! A Sewer Dragon!'

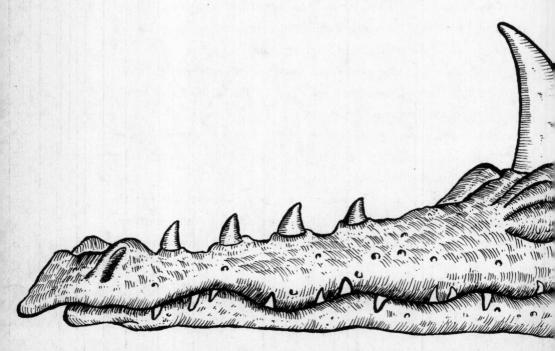

From the
'Encyclopedia of Marvels, Life Forms
and Other Phenomena of Zamonia and its Environs'
by Professor Abdullah Nightingale

Sewer Dragon, The. Socially debased member of the Great Lizard family [Saurii] formerly resident on the surface. A cold-blooded, forked-tongued creature of elongated stature [up to 75 feet long], it is generously equipped with teeth [as many as 900 incisors and molars] and covered with a scaly hide consisting of multicoloured plates of horny skin abounding in warty humps, crests, and folds. Sewer Dragons thrived in the marshy terrain Atlantis used to be before it dried out and became a built-up area. Unable to cope with life in the metropolis, they retreated to its extensive sewers. Sewer Dragons feed on anything assimilable by a Sewer Dragon's efficient digestive system, which means almost anything including wood, basalt, animals, human beings, Halfway Humans, and - not to put too fine a point on it - other Sewer Dragons.

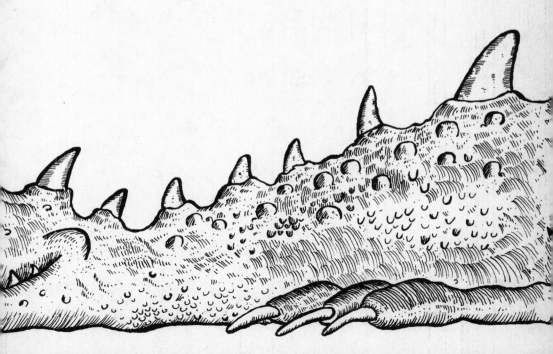

The dragon filled the whole width of the tunnel. To get past it we would have had to climb over it, and that was a course of action which only a madman would have contemplated.

'We'll have to climb over it,' said the Troglotroll. He turned to us. 'Don't look at me as if I'm crazy, I've done it a hundred times. The creature's asleep. It won't notice a thing, ak-ak-ak!'

Sewer Dragon, The [cont.]. Sewer Dragons are somnidigestors, which means that they devote half their lives to hunting and devouring prey and the other half to digesting it in their sleep. Those who come across a sleeping Sewer Dragon can congratulate themselves on not having encountered one in its active mode. They should remain on their guard, however, because it is one of the Sewer Dragon's predatorial techniques to pretend to be asleep.

Behind us were Smyke and all the criminals in Atlantis; ahead of us lay an omnivorous Sewer Dragon. We had a decision to make.

The Troglotroll was the first to climb on to the dragon. He marched firmly along its back.

'You see? It's asleep, ak-ak-ak!' he crowed, rather too loudly for my taste.

To prove to us how soundly asleep it was, he clumped around on the creature as if it were a rocky outcrop.

'It doesn't notice a thing, ak-ak!' he chortled, and jumped up and down on its back with both feet, over and over again. 'Come on up.'

Chemluth climbed up next, followed by me. The Troglotroll was now performing a sort of tap-dance on the dragon's scaly hide.

'Stop it, can't you?' I begged him. 'You're making me nervous.'

'It doesn't notice a thing, I tell you!' cried the Troglotroll. 'It's asleep!'

He leapt in the air once more and landed heavily on the dragon's armour-plated hide. It was hard to tell whether that woke the

dragon or whether it had been feigning sleep all the time. Whatever the truth, it opened its gooey, lizardlike jaws with a sound like a horse being ripped apart and uttered a startlingly human cry. Then it abruptly reared up, and Chemluth, the Troglotroll and I tumbled off its back.

Its tail lashed the tunnel like a snapped hawser. Armed with pointed, yard-long horns, the tail whistled over our heads more than once, but we ducked just in time and hugged the ground.

The Sewer Dragon drew in its tail and howled like a whipped cur. Then it hissed, emitting a jet of flame that briefly bathed the scene in a harsh glare and projected our fleeing shadows on the walls as we sprinted out of range. The creature craned its lizardlike neck and gave a furious snarl, evidently unable to turn around.

'It's wedged in the tunnel – too fat,' the Troglotroll explained. 'It's always the same with Sewer Dragons. They eat too much. In the end they become so fat they can only move in one direction. It can only go forwards, ak-ak-ak!'

At that moment the dragon began to move *backwards*.

It's incredible how fast a Sewer Dragon can travel. It simply pushed off with its powerful thighs and slithered a good twenty yards towards us along the tunnel's sludgy floor.

Whoosh!

At the same time, it lashed its spiked tail to and fro like a flail. We ran off, but we couldn't cover the slippery ground anything like as fast as the dragon.

Whoosh! Another twenty yards.

Whoosh! Twenty more.

The Sewer Dragon must have been perfecting this predatory technique for a very long time. It couldn't see behind it, admittedly, so it wasn't able to take aim, but the frequency with which it lashed its tail made up for that. Sooner or later it would hit us. It could skewer its victims on the horns and convey them to its mouth with ease.

Whoosh! Twenty yards.

Whoosh! Twenty yards.

'See those holes in the roof?' the Troglotroll said breathlessly during our next sprint. 'Between the lights? We must get up there, it's our only chance, ak-ak-ak!'

Every fifty yards or so there was a circular manhole in the roof of the tunnel, but the latter was at least twelve feet from the ground. 'We must climb on each other's backs,' panted the Troglotroll. 'The first one up can pull the others up after him.'

An utterly crackbrained idea. We would have only a few seconds in which to complete such an operation, and that was when the dragon paused between thigh-thrusts to lash the air with its tail.

'Now!' yelled the Troglotroll. The dragon had come to a halt.

There was no point in arguing. Chemluth had already leapt on to my shoulders.

The tail whistled past, missing us by a couple of feet at most, and cracked like a whip as it lashed thin air.

The Troglotroll climbed up me. He went about it in a terribly

clumsy way, wrenching at my fur and putting his calloused feet in my face, but he managed to reach the manhole via Chemluth's shoulders.

The Sewer Dragon was preparing to strike once more. It rolled up its tail like a licorice bootlace.

'Quick!' I cried. 'Hurry up!'

The Troglotroll hauled Chemluth up. With a groan, my friend clambered through the opening.

The dragon's tail sliced the damp air of the tunnel like a guillotine. This time it flashed past me on the left. Next time, if the creature had a system, it would aim at the centre of the tunnel.

In other words, at the place where I was standing.

It slowly rolled up its tail again.

'Are you trying that roof trick?' it snarled. 'Behind my back? It wouldn't be the first time!'

I had no idea that Sewer Dragons could speak.

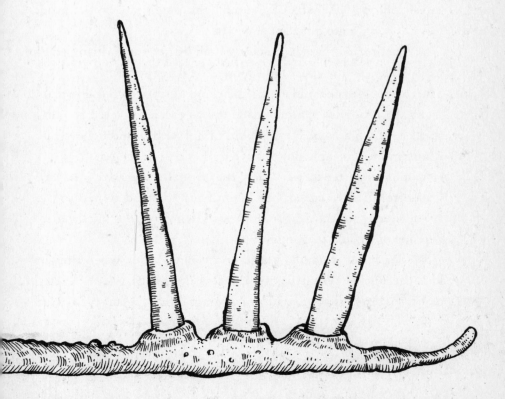

Sewer Dragon, The [cont.]. Many eye-witnesses claim that Sewer Dragons are capable of articulate speech. This is impossible from the biological aspect, because they belong to the Pyrosaurian family and are dragons with short, fireproof vocal cords. There is, however, a theory that thanks to the singular electrical conditions prevailing beneath Atlantis, which may be associated with the nefarious activities of the so-called Invisibles, certain mutations have come into being.

Chemluth and the Troglotroll peered down at me through the manhole.

'We've made a mistake somewhere,' said the Troglotroll. 'Us two are safe, but you're still in a lot of trouble.'

'I suppose you're surprised I can speak,' grunted the Sewer Dragon, 'but I'm more surprised than anyone. I vegetated down here for centuries without saying a word, but then – *crack!* – one of those confounded shafts of greased lightning hit me on the head. Life has been quite different since then.'

'You must run to the next manhole, gah!' Chemluth whispered to me. 'We'll wait for you. Don't worry, we'll get you out!'

The dragon groaned and expelled a cloud of smoke. 'But don't run away with the idea that it's made things easier for me. I couldn't speak in the old days, but I couldn't think either, and believe me, it's far more agreeable not to have to brood about things.'

A sulphurous stench pervaded the tunnel. Chemluth and the Troglotroll had vanished, but I continued to stand rooted to the spot, listening to the dragon. It was showing signs of intelligence. Perhaps one could reason with it.

'Take death, for example. I used not to have a clue when I might kick the bucket. What happy, carefree days they were! I mean, okay, so I'm a dragon with an average life expectancy of two thousand years. I'm only a thousand years old, so I'm better off than, say, a mayfly, but all the same ... I used to think I was immortal, and that gives you quite another feeling, damn it all!' The monster emitted a pathetic groan.

'Or take pangs of conscience. I didn't suffer from them at all in the old days. I devoured my prey and that was that. I still do today, but I feel remorseful afterwards. I wonder whether my victims had wives and children and whether they're good for my blood pressure. All these worries are driving me mad.' The articulate monster sighed. It was obviously in a conversational mood.

'Then why not simply let me go?' I suggested. 'That'll spare you any feelings of guilt. Besides, bear's meat is supposed to be the worst thing for blood pressure.'

It was worth a try, I thought. What harm could it do?

'Ah, so *there* you are!' the dragon snarled viciously, and lashed out with its tail.

What a spiteful creature! It had deliberately induced me to speak so that the sound of my voice would betray where I was standing. The tip of its tail whistled straight towards me.

It was too late to turn and run, so I simply fell flat and hugged the slimy tunnel floor. The daggerlike horns scythed through the air only inches above me.

The dragon gave a disappointed snarl. 'Hey, where are you?'

I jumped to my feet and ran off. My footsteps reechoed from the tunnel walls: splish-splash, splish-splash.

The dragon pushed off with its thighs again.

Whoosh! Twenty yards.

'Great way of getting about, huh?' it panted with a touch of pride. 'That's one of the advantages of being able to think. It would never have occurred to me in the old days.'

Whoosh! Another twenty yards.

I had almost reached the next manhole. Chemluth was hanging down into the tunnel head first, like a trapeze artist, with the Troglotroll hanging on to his legs.

'Come on, jump, gah!' he called. 'We'll haul you up!'

It was quite impossible. The Troglotroll would never manage to haul us both up at once. But in an emergency one clutches at the thinnest of straws. I jumped up and grasped Chemluth's hands. The Troglotroll heaved and groaned.

'I'll never do it!' he moaned. Our combined weight was slowly pulling him downwards. 'You're too heavy!'

I knew that already. All that puzzled me was why he didn't simply let go. He could easily have escaped from the danger zone by letting go of Chemluth.

Whoosh! Another twenty yards.

The Sewer Dragon's rear end was right beneath me. The horny plates on its armoured back were arranged in layers, like a flight of steps.

A flight of steps! How practical! I had only to walk up the dragon's back and into the manhole! The Troglotroll pulled Chemluth up, and before the monster knew what was happening I had climbed through the hole.

'Now run for it!' cried the Troglotroll. 'We're aren't safe yet!'

We set off. This tunnel was much narrower than the one below. Chemluth and the Troglotroll had no trouble negotiating it, but I had to run at a crouch with my head down. Behind us, the Sewer Dragon poked its head through the hole.

'Don't go!' it panted. 'We could have a nice little chat.' It drew a deep breath.

'Watch out,' shouted the Troglotroll, 'or it'll barbecue us!'

We sprinted as fast as we could. The dragon made a gurgling noise, then spat out a jet of flame that turned the water on the tunnel walls to hissing steam. By the time it reached us, however, we were too far away: it was just a blast of very hot air. We ran into a side tunnel at the Troglotroll's heels.

'We'll be safe here,' he gasped.

We rested for a moment, leaning against the wall to catch our breath. I couldn't believe it: the Troglotroll had saved my life. At least, he had played an active part in my rescue and risked his own life in the process.

'You really have turned over a new leaf,' I said. 'I'd never have believed it of you.'

The Troglotroll giggled. 'I told you so, remember?'

'What?'

'Never trust a Troglotroll.'

After about an hour's descent into the underworld the architecture of the tunnel underwent a dramatic transformation. We entered a rectangular passage whose walls looked like shimmering metal but kept changing colour. But the genuinely alarming feature was that I'd never seen such colours before.

'Stupid colours,' observed the Troglotroll. 'They're enough to make one really nervous, ak-ak!'

The lighting now came, not from blue jellyfish, but from yellow globes that roamed the roof freely and emitted a cold, unearthly glow. Each of our footsteps was multiplied a dozen times by the echo. Long cables of many different colours ran along the walls, crackling with electricity. Located in the middle of the passage every hundred yards or so were contraptions of green glass that seemed to be muttering to themselves in some unintelligible language.

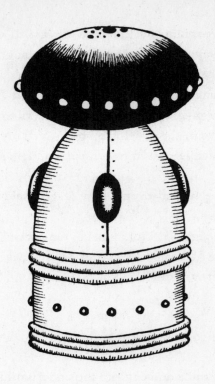

'Those are the transistors,' said the Troglotroll, as if that explained everything. 'Don't touch, please! Very electrical.'

Then the tunnel gave way to long shafts of solid, polished wood covered all over with artistically carved ornamentation and runic characters. The walls were no longer damp and the temperature had fallen to a pleasant level. It was like walking through a well-tended, well-heated museum.

When we entered one of the wooden shafts, living light seemed to accumulate around us, forming a pale bubble that accompanied our little party until we were taken over by another bubble in the next shaft. The light emitted a high-pitched, hostile humming sound that hurt my ears.

Next, we descended a curving walkway without steps, a steel spiral that wound down into the earth for about a mile. The peculiar thing about this walkway was that we didn't have to walk on it. It conveyed us into the depths of its own accord.

Set in the walls were some big stained-glass windows like those in Atlantis's immense cathedrals, except that their far more abstract designs resembled alien stellar systems. Pulsating behind these windows was white light.

The spiral walkway ended in front of a massive door of shiny black pyrite (or some similar mineral). Fifty feet high, it was adorned with strange-looking silver inlays.

'Here we are,' said the Troglotroll.

He inserted his forefinger in a small, inconspicuous hole beside the door, which opened as silently as a theatre curtain going up. We stepped through the aperture into a huge hall perhaps ten times the size of the Megathon and containing what looked to me like umpteen thousands of Atlantean life forms. Venetian Midgets, Waterkins, Bluddums, Norselanders, dwarfs, gnomes, Yetis – all were milling around like the crowds on Ilstatna Boulevard during business hours, and none of them took any notice of us.

We reach our destination

Less apprehensive now, Chemluth and I followed the Troglotroll as he swiftly threaded his way through the bustling throng. Looming over the hall were a number of gigantic machines unlike anything known to me in the field of mechanical engineering (about which, after my comprehensive education at the Nocturnal Academy, there was nothing I didn't know).

Some consisted of dark crystals, others of rusty iron, and still others seemed to be made of polished wood with huge copper nails driven into it. From inside them came a muttering, whispering sound like that made by the smaller machines in the tunnels. The impression they made on me was one of great and reassuring beauty.

In the middle of the hall, rotating continuously, half of an immense cogwheel of high-grade steel projected through a slit in the floor. Darting around beneath the roof were harmless streaks of greased lightning of the kind we'd often seen on sultry nights in Atlantis. Someone stuck a finger in my ear.

I spun round. It was Fredda.

Fredda giggled, looking thoroughly bashful. She was not only taller but – if such a term may be applied to an Alpine Imp – prettier. Her hair no longer stood on end; it hung down in a smoothly-combed curtain and had acquired a silky sheen. She was holding her memo pad in her hand.

Although I was suitably flabbergasted, I managed to introduce her to Chemluth. Fredda giggled even more nervously. As for Chemluth, he looked as if he had been smitten by greased lightning. 'Gah,' he grunted, looking mesmerized. 'Lots of hair.'
Fredda handed me one of her memo slips, the way she used to at the Nocturnal Academy.

> Hello, Bluebear, I've been expecting you
> — I've made the necessary arrangements.
> They told me you were coming.

'How long have you been here?' I asked. 'What is this place, anyway?'
Fredda handed me another slip of paper.

> I reached Atlantis from the Nocturnal Academy by a fairly direct route. The labyrinth presented no problem. I simply got out through one of the holes in the mountain and then climbed down it. I'm an Alpine Imp, after all.

'But how did you get to Atlantis?'

I took the route through Southern Zamonia, which cut across the Demerara Desert for part of the way. I was making for the Impic Alps, actually, but then I sighted the Humongous Range. That was a challenge I couldn't resist, being a mountaineer. Beyond it lay Atlantis, but I found that big-city life didn't suit me. That's why I went underground. And, well, here I am.

I noticed that some of the levers on one of the big machines were moving although no one was operating them. Small tools were floating through the air as if suspended on invisible wires.

Fredda handed me another slip of paper.

> Those are the Invisibles. They really are invisible, you know. They came from another planet many thousands of years ago.

What could I say to that? So as not to seem too unsophisticated, I behaved as if it would take more than that to impress me.
'But how did you find me? How did you know I was in Atlantis?'

> I knew it from the very first day. It was one of the Invisibles who rescued you and your friend from the Kackertratts. He talked about it down here – said you were a bear with blue fur. That's how I knew you were in the city.

But later on you could hardly be missed. Bluebear the King of Lies, the master congladiator! You were in all the newspapers – you were the talk of Atlantis! I even knew what you had for breakfast every day. We got our first-hand information from the Wolpertinger who escorted you part of the way. Rumo's one of us. We have a lot of allies on the surface.

I blushed. The bombastic interviews I'd given must have sounded pretty ludicrous to someone who knew me personally. I hastily changed the subject.

'So the rumours about the Invisibles are true. But what do they want? What exactly goes on here?'

> We're about to leave on a long journey.
> The longest journey ever undertaken in the
> biggest spaceship that ever existed.

What journey? What spaceship? And who was 'we'? I wasn't planning to go on any journey.

> We're taking off for the Planet of the
> Invisibles, and the spaceship is Atlantis
> itself! The Invisibles have been at work on
> it for thousands of years. It'll soon be
> time to leave.

Just a minute! Leave me out of it! *I* didn't intend to join any invisible beings on a flight to their native planet. My own planet was good enough for me, and I said as much to Fredda.

But human beings are taking over more and more of the earth. They now control nearly all the continents, leaving no room for life forms that differ from themselves. Dwarfs, gnomes, goblins, elves — they all have to live in hiding. Zamonia is the only exception — it still gives such creatures houseroom. But sooner or later Zamonia will sink into the sea, the Invisibles worked that out thousands of years ago. On their planet there'll be plenty of room for all of us. For you as well.

The sinking business was no problem from my point of view. Being a sea-going bear, I could happily survive afloat. Human beings presented no problem either. I'd got on perfectly well with them in Tornado City.

'I'll need a bit of time to think it over. You don't just go rushing into a thing like that.'

There's no time left. I told you: we're leaving any minute. The whole of Atlantis will soon be lifting off into space. If you don't want to come with us you'll have to run for it at once. You'd better make for the harbour and get aboard a ship, it's your only chance. Personally, though, I'd advise you to come with us.

I had to make up my mind in double-quick time. I explained the situation to Chemluth, but he scarcely heard me and couldn't take his eyes off Fredda, who was giggling, shuffling her feet, and tearing her memo slips into tiny little pieces.

'Who is she, gah, a goddess? Such a lot of hair,' he purred dreamily into his moustache. 'I must be feverish, I'm feeling hot and cold at the same time...'

'Pull yourself together,' I told him. 'We must make up our minds. Fredda wants us to go with her to an alien planet.'

'An alien planet? With Fredda? Good idea, gah! Variety is the spice of life. Let's do it! We'll make out all right – I'll sing, you dance. All that lovely hair!' He treated Fredda to one of his fiery looks. He certainly couldn't be accused of indecision or lack of daring.

I devoted the little time I had for reflection to scanning the hall. It was a scene of such great activity that no one took any notice of me. Waterkins were busy screwing up strange gadgets, Yetis appeared to be conversing with thin air (Invisibles, presumably), tools flew hither and thither, lightning flashed... To tell the truth, this was hardly the kind of crew I cared to voyage through space with.

I belonged at sea. How could I be sure the Invisibles' planet had any seas at all?

'Oh yes, there are seas on our planet,' said a voice behind me.

I turned round. There was no one to be seen, just a small screwdriver rotating in thin air. The Invisibles took some getting used to. Were they mind-readers too?

'Yes, we are,' said the strange voice. It sounded like a small trumpet endowed with the power of speech. 'Yes, we do have seas, but they consist of electricity. Everything's electric there. I'm not sure it would suit you.'

'Not from the sound of it, but I'm open to persuasion. What else is different on your planet?'

'Everything, actually,' tooted the voice. 'We won't try to talk you into it. All we know is, life on earth isn't getting any easier for creatures like you. The decision is yours.'

622

'Your seas consist of electricity, you say?'
'Yes indeed. Everything's electric. Excuse me, time is short. I have to adjust the transistors.' The screwdriver floated off.

I didn't have to think for long. I was determined to remain on earth.

I decide to stay

'How do I get to the harbour?'
Fredda wasn't sentimentally inclined, thank goodness.

> *It's out of the question, I'm afraid. No one who knows the way will take you there now, it's too late for that, and you'll never find the way by yourself.*

'I'll take you there,' said the Troglotroll. 'I still owe you one. I left you in the lurch twice but I've only saved your life once. Once more, and we'll be quits, ak-ak-ak. It's my chance to balance the books.'
Where Chemluth and Fredda were concerned, my farewells were mercifully brief for want of time.
'We'll send you a postcard when we get to the other planet, gah?' said Chemluth.

He winked at me and took Fredda's hand. They waved to me and the Troglotroll as we made our way across the great hall to the exit.

We sprinted through the sewers, vaulting over pools of viscous liquid. The harbour was already within range of our noses. It smelt of salt water and rotting fish, engine oil and freedom. Anyone else would probably have choked on the mixture, but I breathed it in like fresh mountain air.

'We're near the outer harbour now,' said the Troglotroll. 'That's where the smaller ships drop anchor. It's easier to get a berth on them than on the big ones. We'll stow away if necessary.'

'We? I thought you were going back to Atlantis.'

'I'd sooner come with you, if you've no objection. I don't know if the Invisibles are to be trusted. You can't look them in the eye, ak-ak-ak!'

It wouldn't be easy to sign on with the Troglotroll in tow, but I could hardly turn him down after all he'd done for me.

'There's a tunnel up ahead. It leads to Hulk Basin, where decommissioned vessels rot away. Once past there, we'll be in the outer harbour.'

We climbed out of a manhole. Darkness had fallen by now, and towering over us was a massive black wall I at first mistook for a starless night sky. Then I was fiercely assailed by a familiar smell of rusty iron and hot engine oil.

'*Come!*' said a voice in my head – one I hadn't heard for a very long time. '*Come aboard the* Moloch*!*'

The Troglotroll looked at me and shrugged. 'I couldn't help it,' he said. 'I'm a Troglotroll.'

Several big black hands seized me from behind and pulled a sack over my head. Then they tied up the sack and carried me off.

My life in Atlantis had been brought to a swift, surprising, and inauspicious end.

13.

My Life aboard the SS *Moloch*

All I at first perceived of the *Moloch* was her smell. Thick though it was, the sack in which I was imprisoned did not exclude that mixture of engine oil and rusty iron, funnel smoke and coal dust, with which the ship had announced her presence days in advance during the third of my lives. There were also the familiar sounds she made even when stationary: the steady pounding of huge pistons, the manifold banging and hammering of the creatures at work throughout her hull with tools of various kinds, the panting of the engines in her iron belly.

Then the noises grew louder and the pounding of the pistons fiercer. With a rumble, the ship's propellers began to turn. Valves hissed steam and metal grated on metal as the iron monster awoke.

The *Moloch* was getting under way.

By now, I suspected my captors had forgotten me. I'd made several attempts to extricate myself from the sack, but it seemed to be made of very tough leather or some equally stout material.

It was also clear that the sack had been tied up with rope, which greatly restricted my freedom of movement. From the way I'd been treated, I had little reason to suppose that my captors had anything very pleasant in store for me. I cursed myself for having been hoodwinked by the Troglotroll yet again.

I was gradually running out of air. That's to say, the air in the sack was becoming progressively staler. Every breath I took consumed a little more of its life-giving properties, so I decided to ration it by taking only one breath a minute.

Hmpf. One minute.

Hmpf. One minute.

Hmpf. One minute.

Hmpf. One minute.

Hmpf. One minute.

Hmpf. One minute.

Hmpf. One minute.

The rumbling and pounding persisted, and I could now detect a little motion. It indicated that we must be well out to sea.
Maybe I should draw attention to myself, I thought. I groaned and grunted and rolled around in my sack insofar as I was able, but nothing happened. Better to keep still, I told myself; it would use up less air.

Hmpf. One minute.

Hmpf. One minute.

Hmpf. One minute.

After an hour – I had taken sixty breaths, so an hour must have passed – I made some more signs of life. I called for help and rolled to and fro, but still nothing happened. I decided to breathe only once every two minutes.

Hmpf. Two minutes.

Hmpf. Two minutes.

Hmpf. Two minutes.

After another hour – I'd taken thirty breaths – I started to feel frightened. Could they have put me in the sack to suffocate me? The air had acquired the consistency of stale porridge, it was so hard to suck in. From now on I breathed only once every three minutes.

Hmpf. Three minutes.

Hmpf. Three minutes.

Hmpf. Three minutes.

After the third hour (twenty breaths) I was in a state resembling Carefree Catalepsy. Everything had become wholly unimportant to me, and the lack of oxygen in my brain induced peculiar hallucinations. Tiny elves populated the sack, tickled my nostrils, and crawled into my ears. I called to them to leave me in peace. They didn't go away, but I heard a voice say:
'Hey, we almost forgot about him!'
The sack was opened and air streamed in, but I was still so stupefied that I actually saw a whole flock of elves flutter out of the opening.
The next thing I saw was more blackness: the blackness of the smoke in which the *Moloch* was always shrouded. It was some days before I became even relatively inured to the omnipresent soot. All aboard the iron ship were permanently engulfed in a fine mist of coal dust. You could never see the entire deck, only those parts of it which the smoke deigned to unveil. You would glimpse a few square yards of pitch-black deck, or one of the

rusty funnels, or, if you were lucky, a patch of sky, before another cloud of smoke enshrouded the whole scene once more.

Toiling away on deck were hundreds of smoke- and coal-blackened creatures who went about their work mechanically, paying me little heed. They were Zamonians of all kinds. Trolls, dwarfs, Poophs – every variety seemed to be represented.

I was still inside the sack, half conscious with only my head sticking out. No one took any notice of me. My captors had tied me up in a bundle and left me to my fate. I wriggled out of my cocoon and tottered over to the rail. We couldn't be all that far from land – perhaps I should simply jump. I looked down. The sea was a good three hundred feet below me. Three hundred feet... Could I make it?

Then I saw there wasn't any sea, just thousands of sharks jostling round the hull and snapping at anything thrown over the side.

At that moment a strong breeze sprang up and rent the *Moloch*'s pall of smoke in half. A big patch of blue sky became visible. I could even make out the coast of Zamonia.

And Atlantis.

Atlantis achieves lift-off

It was hovering in the sky some five miles above the coastline. The whole city had risen from the ground like a huge, screw-shaped plug, a spaceship of soil and rock with a city on top. Shafts of greased lightning were sporadically darting from the hole it had left behind. Now and then, clods of earth the size of houses broke off the inverted cone and fell, but in general the spaceship seemed to be a remarkably stable structure. I had no idea how the Invisibles had engineered this feat, but I wasn't surprised that it had taken them several thousand years.

Then the smoke closed in again like a black curtain.

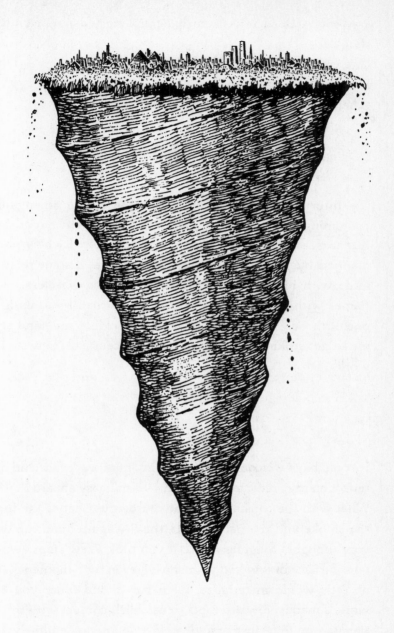

Two soot-stained Yetis came up behind me and grabbed me by the shoulders.
'Are you a bear?' said one of them.
I nodded.
'Then it's into the Infurno with you.'

The Infurno was the red-hot heart of the *Moloch*, an engine room containing more than a thousand coal- and wood-burning furnaces – one for each of the ship's funnels. Each furnace was manned by a gang of taciturn black bears, distant relatives of mine with blank, sad, incurious eyes, who ceaselessly fed the flames with tree trunks or shovelfuls of coal. I was assigned to one of those gangs. A Yeti thrust a shovel into my hand and told me to get stoking. Still dazed by my recent experiences, I set to work.

I would have welcomed at least a few minutes' peace and quiet to reflect on my predicament, but this wasn't easy aboard the *Moloch*. What with the constant din, the murderous heat of the furnaces, the smoke and the hard labour, there was no opportunity to let your thoughts roam far afield. If you took a few steps away from your furnace or lowered your shovel, even for a moment, a couple of Yetis would materialize, teeth bared, and order you back to work. I made a few attempts to establish contact with my fellow slaves, but they just stared at me uncomprehendingly or cast fearful glances at the Yetis.

At night the gang shuffled into a dormitory beneath the Infurno, where we were given hunks of bread and bowls of water and allowed to stretch out in hammocks for a few hours. I used to fall asleep at once, as if someone had hit me over the head with a club.

It's remarkable how apathetic you can become when engaged in hard manual labour. Sometimes I shovelled coal, sometimes I pushed handcarts filled with briquettes, sometimes I hauled tree stumps. For days on end I toted sacks of anthracite from the gloomy bowels of the *Moloch* up a flight of steps a hundred yards high. There were also logs to split, tree trunks to saw, coal to stack, bellows to pump, ashes to be dumped over the side.

Hard labour

My black bear colleagues slaved away like robots, feeding the ever-hungry furnaces and scrubbing the decks and engines to prevent them from being buried in soot. None of them ever spoke a word to me, and even among themselves they merely grunted when absolutely necessary. Without realizing it, I was becoming one of them.

I soon abandoned all attempts to communicate and lapsed, like them, into routine mechanical drudgery. I lived my life to the rhythmical throb of the *Moloch*'s engines – indeed, I became as much a cog in the machine as all the rest. The only bright spot in our existence was the brief spell we spent in our hammocks, regaining our strength, and the prospect of a bowl of soup and a mug of water.

Most of the supervisors were Yetis or Wolpertingers, but even they made an apathetic impression. Their seniority didn't appear to entitle them to any special privileges. They lent a hand when needed, performed the most strenuous chores, and were not too proud to wield a shovel from time to time. Everyone fed the furnaces, the furnaces powered the engines, the engines drove the propellers, and the propellers kept the *Moloch* under way. That was all there was: a ship that sailed the seas for the sake of it – the most futile form of locomotion imaginable.

I put on muscle I could almost see my muscles develop. My whole body grew hard and lost every ounce of fat. I could throw a sack of coal over my shoulder like a feather pillow, shoulder a ten-foot tree trunk by myself, take the stairs from the coal bunker three at a time with a hod of briquettes on my back.

The calluses on my paws were so thick that I could slam the red-hot furnace doors without burning myself. The heat was such that, instead of running down me, my sweat evaporated at once.

At night I dreamed of huge, roaring fires and mountains of briquettes. I had ceased to think. Not even in my dreams did it occur to me that there could be anything more important than furnaces and coal, leaping flames and the *Moloch*'s progress through the waves.

Some months went by before I saw the sky again. I had spent the whole time in the ship's iron belly, where my only sight of the outside world was the round hole, wreathed in oily smoke, through which we tipped ashes over the side. Sometimes I stuck my head through it for a breath of fresh air, but the sky was obscured by soot and the oil-polluted sea thick with sharks that snapped at low-flying seagulls.

One day, one of the furnaces burned out. The Wolpertingers were dismantling it, and the rest of us had to manhandle the components on deck, whence they were heaved over the rail and into the sea.

I had just come on deck carrying one of the heavy furnace doors when a gust of wind hit the *Moloch* and parted the smoke to reveal a wonderful summer's day, a clear blue sky, and, sparkling like a diamond in its midst, the sun.

For one brief moment a sunbeam slanted down on us and turned the deck into a luminous clearing. I relished that moment of warmth and stared at the sun in bewilderment, blinding myself for several minutes. Then the smoke closed over us once more and the Yetis herded us back inside. As I staggered down the stairs with a Yeti's elbow in my back, I suddenly wondered why I was submitting to such treatment.

A glimpse of the sun

The sunlight had rekindled my capacity for thought.

After a few days I'd reached the stage of being able to forge plans. Escape was out of the question and I couldn't expect any help from my fellow prisoners (if prisoners they were, not volunteers), so I set about making the acquaintance of whoever was next in command above the Yetis and Wolpertingers.

The bigger the ship the greater the need for a captain, and the *Moloch* was the biggest ship in the world. Somewhere on board there had to be someone who steered her and could read charts, who determined her course and bore ultimate responsibility. Perhaps he was an approachable person. Perhaps he was entirely ignorant of the scandalous working conditions in the Infurno, because he never showed his face there.

Anyone who could keep such a vessel on course must possess more brainpower than a Yeti. I need only gain access to that person and make it clear to him that I was overqualified for the Infurno. So I simply stopped work.

That was the nub of my plan: I tossed my shovel into the furnace along with the coal, folded my arms, and waited. Instantly, a Yeti appeared beside me.

'Carry on!' he bellowed.

'No,' I said.

The Yeti was completely flummoxed. He wasn't used to insubordination.

He summoned another Yeti to his assistance.

'Get on with your work!' commanded the second Yeti.

'No!' I said stubbornly.

The two Yetis were utterly at a loss. They planted their fists on their hips and snorted with indignation.

'We'd better take him to the Zamonium,' one of them said eventually.

Zamonium ... It was a long time since I'd heard that word.

From the
'Encyclopedia of Marvels, Life Forms and Other Phenomena of Zamonia and its Environs'
by Professor Abdullah Nightingale

Zamonium. Legendary element reputed to be capable of thought. The alchemists of Zamonia endeavoured for centuries to create something they referred to as 'the Philosopher's Stone' or 'Zamonium', a mineral from which they hoped to obtain nothing less than the elixir of life and the answers to all unsolved questions. During the eighth century of Zamonia's existence the legendary alchemist Zoltan Zaan succeeded in producing a stone that could actually think, but did not, unfortunately, surpass the intellectual capacity of a sheep. Legend has it that Zoltan Zaan was so annoyed at having squandered several tons of gold on the manufacture of Zamonium that he threw the stone into the quicksands of Nairland.

The Yetis hustled me along the interminable, rusty passages in the bowels of *Moloch* until we came to an iron door guarded by another three Yetis. Armed to the teeth, they wore black troll-hide uniforms and heavy iron helmets and were at least a head taller than the ones who had dragged me there.

'We must see the Zamonium,' said one of my captors, gripping me by the shoulder. 'This bear is refusing to work in the Infurno.'

'Unheard-of,' said one of the Yeti sentries.

'Unprecedented,' said another.

'It's never happened before,' said the third.

It took their combined strength to open the iron door, which resembled that of a strongroom. They thrust me into a big, rusty chamber but remained outside themselves. Then they pushed the door shut behind me.

'You refused to work?' said someone.

I had heard that voice twice before: once many years ago, when the *Moloch* was steaming past my raft; and again more recently on the waterfront, just before the sack was pulled over my head. How did the voice know I'd refused to work? No one had said anything, least of all me.

I meet the Zamonium

'I know everything,' said the voice.

I looked around the room. It was empty save for a small central pillar with a glass bell jar on it. Under the glass was something that appeared to be a clod of earth shaped like a tiny brain. Was someone trying to intimidate me? What was this clod of earth? Where had the voice come from?

639

'*Just for calling me a clod of earth I could have you keelhauled five times over, but I'll exercise my immeasurable clemency and make allowances for your ignorance. I'm not a clod of earth, I'm Zamonium – the Zamonium!*'

'Pleased to meet you. I'm Bluebear.'

I had caught on at last. That little clod of earth under the glass was the rare element known as Zamonium. It could actually think and make its voice heard inside my head. Being accustomed to voices in the head, I was only moderately impressed.

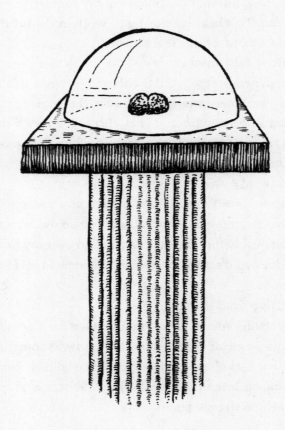

'Let's get to the point. From what I hear – and I hear every thought that occurs to anyone aboard my ship – you stopped work without being instructed to do so. What's the idea?'

'Well, first I'd like to point out that I'm not here of my own free will. I was –'

'So what? You think you're an exception? Nobody's on board this ship of his own free will. Nobody apart from me!'

So I was right. The *Moloch* was a slave ship.

'Exactly. And you're just another insignificant component of this slave ship! You're worth no more than a tiny cog in the works, a dab of anticorrosive paint. You've become a part of the Moloch, and that's the way you've got to function.

'Now pin your ears back, my boy. Just so you know what's what around here, I'm going to tell you a little story, the story of how the Moloch came into being. Listen closely, it's very instructive . . .'

I've always enjoyed a good story.

'One day I fell into the sea. The circumstances that led up to it are irrelevant; what matters is that I sank to the bottom of the Zamonian Sea. So there I lay on the seabed, thinking. Thinking is all I can do, but on the highest level!

'My first thought was, this is no place for the only thinking element in the world, so I concentrated on the creatures surrounding me, to wit, a clam, a jellyfish, and a sponge. I ordered the jellyfish to place me on the sponge. Then I ordered the clam to cut the sponge adrift with its sharp shell and join me aboard it. That done, I commanded the jellyfish to carry us to the surface. Once on the surface the sponge dried in the sunlight, enabling us to drift across the sea. It was a very rudimentary form of ship, but at least it was a start.

'A female seagull flew up and alighted on the sponge. She was about to eat the clam when I ordered her instead to fly off,

The Zamonium's tale

collect some twigs, and stick them in the sponge. In that way she built a nest around us. Our vessel was growing bigger. Then I allowed the female seagull to eat the clam. Now comes the romantic part. The nest encouraged a male seagull to move in with us, and before long the nest was full of seagull's eggs. They, in their turn, attracted a Zamonian fisherman. He proposed to steal them, but I ordered him to take me on board. I was now the owner of a fishing boat.

'A big sailing ship came by, and I told the fisherman to take me aboard it. Next, I instructed the skipper of the sailing ship and his crew to capture other, bigger vessels, which they continued to do until I had assembled a whole fleet.

'Then I gave orders to anchor off an island and construct one big ship out of all the others. That was the real beginning of the Moloch. We set sail in her and incorporated every vessel that came our way. The Moloch became bigger and bigger. Imagine, we even have our own shipyards on board! That's what I call true greatness!'

The Zamonium panted excitedly inside my head.

'And so I circle the globe in search of more slaves and more ships that'll help me to make the Moloch bigger still. One day, all the ships in the world will be merely components of the Moloch, and then ... then ...'

The Zamonium hesitated.

'Yes, then ... Well, I'll have to think of what to do then, won't I? Anyway, it's absolutely no business of yours. Now where was I?'

'You were probably going to add a moral of some kind,' I hazarded.

'Precisely! That was it! What I really meant to say was, on this ship only one person does things of his own free will, and that's me!'

I got the picture: the Zamonium was totally insane.

'Who's insane? I'll show you who's insane! Obey me! Obey me!'

The hell I would!

'Obey . . . Obey . . .'

My head was going all mushy. I felt as if my brain was being simmered over a low flame like the cheese in a fondue. It was a far from unpleasant sensation, to be honest.

On the contrary, I found it more and more agreeable. Before long I didn't know how I'd got along without that sensation. The Zamonium was my friend, that was official, so why not obey the element if that was its heart's desire? Why not become its utterly submissive slave – one that would obey its most ludicrous orders, faithful unto death?

I had just decided to submit to the Zamonium, at once and without reservation, when another familiar voice made itself heard in my head.

'Leave the youngster alone!'

It was the encyclopedia.

No, it was Professor Nightingale in person.

'Nightingale? Is that you?' A sudden note of alarm had crept into the Zamonium's voice.

Nightingale steps in

'You bet it is! So I've found you at last, Bluebear. Where are you, my boy? I can't see a thing, I'm afraid.'

'On board the *Moloch*. We must be somewhere north of Atlantis.'

'Shut your trap!' commanded the Zamonium.

'Well, well, Zamonium, I'd never have guessed you'd be hiding aboard the *Moloch*. It was obvious, really. Still nursing your old dreams of world domination?'

'I'm not dreaming, Nightingale, I'm thinking! And I'm not hiding the way you do in your labyrinth of caves. I'm the Zamonium! Don't dare come near me, Nightingale, I'd be compelled to destroy you!'

643

'You've no idea how near you I am.'

'I've got the world's biggest, most powerful, most heavily armed means of locomotion at my disposal, manned by an army of submissive slaves. What have you got to set against that?'

'You'll find out!'

'You wouldn't dare to cross me again.'

'Oh yes, I would!'

'Oh no, you wouldn't!'

'Oh yes, I would!'

'Oh no, you wouldn't!'

'Oh yes, I -'

'Stop it!' I cried. 'Two voices arguing inside my head? It's enough to drive a bear insane! Would someone be kind enough to explain what this is all about?'

'Of course, my boy, so sorry!' said Nightingale. 'Where to begin ... Well, to start with, the encyclopedia in your head functions as a direct receiver of my thoughts and a transmitter of your thoughts to me. Wireless telepathy, the business of the future! I didn't want to make use of it except in a dire emergency. I mean, it's a gross invasion of privacy, isn't it? But this counts as an emergency, I suppose.'

'Get lost, Nightingale! The youngster's mine!'

'Keep quiet, you! Listen, my boy, I've a confession to make. Zamonium didn't come into being just like that. I ... how shall I put it? I, er, invented the stuff.'

'That's right!' crowed the Zamonium. 'I can confirm that – for once.'

'Zamonium really belongs under lock and key in the Chamber of Unperfected Patents, but ... I'd better begin from the beginning ...'

'Get lost, Nightingale! Push off!'

'It's every inventor's dream to discover an element capable of thought. In the days when I embarked on my research, inventors and scientists were still called alchemists, and inventing an element capable of thought was known as creating the Philosopher's Stone. That element, that stone, was supposed to deliver us from all evil and answer all unsolved questions on our behalf. What is the meaning of life? How do you turn lead into gold? How do you become immortal? How do you square the circle? How do you construct a perpetual motion machine? How do you install a fountain of youth? We expected Zamonium to answer all those unsolved questions for us.'

'How wrong you were!' crowed the Zamonium.

'True, and the mistake was mine. I must first point out, however, that I constituted the Zamonium with the utmost care.

'I began by salvaging the Protozamonium which Zoltan Zaan had thrown into the quicksands of Nairland, an operation for which I designed the quicksand hose. It didn't take me long to locate the Protozamonium with the aid of that equipment and the friendly assistance of the Cogitating Quicksand. But then, as bad luck would have it, the quicksand hose broke down and ... well, you know the story.'

I remembered it. Mac the Reptilian Rescuer had rescued him in the nick of time.

'Protozamonium really wasn't very bright, but that was no reason to throw it into the quicksand. It could think, and that was a start.'

'A good story,' giggled the Zamonium. *'I always enjoy hearing it myself.'*

'You only have to add the right ingredients. Well, I'm sure I'm not betraying any secrets when I say that gold dust was one of them. Alchemists considered it chic to add gold to everything in those days, even though it had no alchemical effect whatever. Things glittered a bit more, but that was all ... Oh yes, and duck spittle - that was equally indispensable! Nobody talks about duck spittle nowadays, but then it was *the* thing!

Vital ingredients 'Increasing the power of thought was far more important. That I achieved with the aid of, among other things, molten Cogitating Quicksand from Nairland. I also infused a little of my own cerebral fluid, of course, together with caffeine concentrate extracted from century-old coffee, nicotine from the umbels of the Phorinth flower, split mercury atoms, glucose, whitewash, snail slime from the time-snails found only on the edges of dimensional hiatuses, a grated violin string, formic acid, gum arabic, vitamin C, liquid amber, garlic, talcum powder, Gloomberg moss, glycerine, pure alcohol, Spanish fly, and frozen gas from the Graveyard Marshes of Dull.

'Well, it was while I was adding the last ingredient that a will-o'-the-wisp fell into the mixture by accident, a graveyard moth that had recently been struck by lightning. That ruined the whole thing. Though close to perfection, the Zamonium was mentally deranged.'

'Nonsense! That moth was just the ticket. It made me what I am: the most powerful element in the universe! You wanted a docile little stone that would do your housework for you. Instead, you created the new Lord of Creation!'

'Be quiet, you pathetic element! The demented Zamonium kept trying to hypnotize me into building it a vehicle in which to conquer the world. It became too much for me in the end, so I threw it into the sea. I thought I'd finished it off. Obviously, I was mistaken.'

'Are you through?'

'With you? Far from it! I've only just begun.'

'Huh, now you're really scaring me! What do you propose to do? I possess the biggest ship in the world, a war machine manned by

an army of submissive slaves. I can subjugate whole continents by
will-power alone. What can you do to counter that?'

'You seem to forget I invented you. You're just a chain of atoms put
together by me - a chain I can tear apart at any moment!'
Nightingale's tone was coldly disdainful.

'Oh yeah! Then show me what you can do, Nightingale! Show me
what your poor old brains are still capable of!'

Something almost indescribable happened to my own brain as
Nightingale and the Zamonium pitted themselves against each
other right inside my head. From the crackling and flashing between my ears, my brain might have been plugged into a high-
tension cable. The pain was unbearable.

Phonzotar Huxo must have experienced a similar sensation when
he stuck his head through the wall of the tornado – the feeling a
rope must get at the spot where it almost snaps during a tug-of-
war.

'Stop it!' I yelled.

The pain eased at once, the crackling ceased.

'Sorry, my boy, I completely forgot about you. Hm, this isn't working,
I must think of something else. Grin and bear it, my son. I, er ... I
must put on my thinking caps for a while, that's all. Don't give up
hope!'
Then Nightingale's voice disappeared.

'That's what happens to anyone who dares to take me on!'
shouted the Zamonium. *'Goodbye and good riddance,*
Nightingale!' Then, to me: *'That's the last you'll hear of him!'*
It was more than probable. This wasn't the first time Nightingale
had abandoned me in a dangerous situation.

Thereafter the Zamonium left me in peace, at least. It gave up trying to bend me to its will for fear, no doubt, of another confrontation with Nightingale. However simple it might be to hypnotize a Yeti or a shellfish, the same could not be said of someone who carried the *Encyclopedia of Marvels, Life Forms, and Other Phenomena of Zamonia and its Environs* in his head. To that extent, I owed Professor Nightingale a debt of gratitude.

The Zamonium ordered the Yetis to place me under arrest. It needed to think, it said.

A superfluous piece of information, somehow. What else could it do?

A reunion
There was no more shovelling coal. I was taken to one of the ship's prison wings, a passage lined with single cells occupied by those who had resisted the Zamonium. The inmates numbered precisely four, counting me. One of them was a Wolpertinger named Nalla Hotep, who had an iron plate in his head that shielded him from the Zamonium's telepathic commands.

The others were Knio and Weeny.

Thoughts bounced off Knio's thick skull as a matter of course, and they didn't progress far through Weeny's brain because they promptly fell into the Sea of Oblivion. The pair of them were as proof against the Zamonium as I myself.

We talked across the passage through the feeding-flaps in our cell doors.

'Volzotan Smyke held us responsible for your escape,' said Weeny. 'Thanks a lot, Bluebear.'

'If I could get out of here,' Knio amplified, 'I'd wring your neck!'

'What does Smyke have to do with the *Moloch*?'

'It's one of his numerous business connections. The Zamonium maintains agents like Smyke on every continent. They keep the *Moloch* supplied with slaves. You'd be surprised how many of our shipmates are former congladiators.' Weeny gave a silly laugh.

I informed them that Smyke and all the other inhabitants of Atlantis were on their way to the Planet of the Invisibles and gave them as graphic a description of the airborne city as I could.

Weeny clapped his little hands. 'Great story, Bluebear. Ten points on the applause meter. Pity we aren't in the Megathon any more.'

They didn't believe me – the story of my lives.

I noticed a bunch of keys hanging on the wall of the passage.

'We thought of that too,' said Weeny, who had intercepted my glance. 'Forget it. Where would you go if you did get out of your cell? It makes no odds where we're imprisoned, inside or outside. At least the air's not bad in here, and we don't have to shovel any coal.'

'I'll think of something. I could sneak up on the Zamonium and throw it into the sea.'

'The ship's swarming with Yetis. You wouldn't get two yards.'

A key rattled in the lock of the passage door. The door opened, and the Troglotroll ambled in. He strolled along the passage, rapping each cell door in turn with his knuckles.

Another reunion

'Don't be deceived by my vague resemblance to a Troglotroll,' he said casually. 'I'm really a prison warder.'

'Lord Olgort!' cried Knio. 'My old pal!'

'Give me those keys,' I said. 'You owe me one.'

The Troglotroll stared at me in surprise. He levelled a finger at the bunch of keys.

'You mean that bunch of keys there? That necklacelike collection of metallic unlocking devices? Why should I do that?'

'So I don't knock your block off if I ever get out of here.'

'I doubt it – not that you wouldn't be capable of cold-bloodedly sending me to kingdom come, I mean. No, I simply doubt you'll ever get out again.'

He gave my door an experimental tap.

'Hm. Three layers of solid Zamonian cast iron alloyed with brass to guard against corrosion. Four-tongued high security lock vapour-blasted with platinum. It's impregnable.'

'Let us out and we'll call it quits. You *can* do the right thing, you proved that with the Sewer Dragon. Or are you under the Zamonium's influence?'

'No. It made a brief attempt to insinuate itself into my brain, but I don't think it liked what it found there. Since then it's left me in peace. I can roam the *Moloch* as I please, ak-ak-ak!'

The Troglotroll sauntered up and down the passage.

'Just think. What would I gain from letting you out? A broken neck?'

'I won't touch you, I promise.'

'Anyone can make a promise. I do it all the time, and do I keep my word? Of course not.'

The Troglotroll removed the bunch of keys from its hook.

'But let's run through the procedure, purely in theory...Just suppose I took this collection of Zamonian unlocking gadgets from the wall...'

He ambled over to my cell.

'And suppose – purely hypothetically, mind you! – I inserted one of these steel escape aids in the lock...'

He inserted the key in the lock.

'And finally – to repeat, this is a purely conjectural speculation! – suppose I turned the key...'

He turned the key, and – click! – released the lock.

'But no,' the Troglotroll exclaimed, turning the key – click! – in the opposite direction. 'That would be aiding and abetting mutiny! I'm sure the penalties prescribed for such a crime on board this ship are draconian.'

The cell door was locked again. Even Knio and Weeny groaned at this display of malevolence.

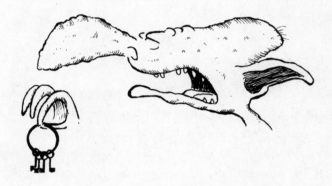

The Troglotroll continued to theorize. 'Alternatively, I could throw the bunch of keys out of this porthole.'

He dangled the keys out of a porthole.

'You'd simply rot away in here. You wouldn't believe how many forgotten prison wings there are in this ship – and how many skeletons are still imprisoned in their cells.'

The Troglotroll shuddered visibly.

'No! No!' chorused Knio and Weeny. 'Don't do it!'

'On the other hand . . .' The Troglotroll put a finger to his brow and pondered awhile. 'What do the *Moloch*'s regulations matter to me? I'm a Troglotroll. As such, I've a duty to break regulations.'

He came over and unlocked my door again. Leaving the key in the lock, he walked to the door at the end of the passage.

'Yes, us Troglotrolls are simply like that – different from other people!'

And he slunk out.

Still somewhat disconcerted, I pushed my cell door open, then took the keys and released Knio, Weeny, and the Wolpertinger.

'Let's go and throw the Zamonium into the sea,' I suggested. 'Then we'll take over the ship. I know all about navigation.'

'Agreed,' said the Wolpertinger.

'Agreed,' said Knio and Weeny. Nobody contradicted a Wolpertinger, not even a Barbaric Hog.

I was still sufficiently soot-stained to pass for an Infurno stoker, and Nalla the Wolpertinger looked like a member of the security staff. Knio and Weeny grabbed a couple of buckets and brooms and disguised themselves as a fatigue party. Thus equipped, we trekked through the bowels of the *Moloch* in search of the Zamonium. I did, after all, know the approximate location of its command centre.

It was only on the way there that I grasped the vessel's true size. The *Moloch* was a regular iron metropolis with its own urban districts, streets, and means of transportation.

The crew travelled by rickshaw and steam-driven truck. They even used tethered balloons to get from deck to deck. Many districts were spick and span and humming with life, others completely ruined and deserted.

We wandered for hours through a derelict section of the ship inhabited exclusively by yellow jellyfish mutations that appeared to live on a diet of rust. We even passed one of the prisons of which the Troglotroll had told us. There, bleached Yeti skeletons mouldering behind rusty bars rattled in time to the engines. We walked on quickly.

Another deck was undergoing redevelopment. Hundreds of oil-stained Yetis were constructing new furnaces. An additional

Infurno was evidently in the making. Wolpertingers were patrolling everywhere, but none of them thought to check on us. We passed shipyards where captured vessels were being sawn up and dismembered. Blazing in the gloom were huge blast furnaces in which the iron from a whole freighter was being melted down – just enough metal from which to cast one spare blade for the *Moloch*'s propeller. An army of Wolpertingers was hammering a red-hot bow plate into shape in time to the beat of drums. Little Midgard Serpents were hauling carts laden with scrap metal along the passages, barrels of oil being loaded on to ramps, walls torn down and rebuilt, layers of rust removed, stairways painted, ropes spliced, decks scrubbed, and portholes burnished. Everyone aboard the *Moloch* had a job, even if it only entailed supervising the activities of others.

At last we came to the door that led to the passage in which the Zamonium's cabin lay.

We conferred briefly. The cabin door would be guarded by three Yetis, I knew, but the Wolpertinger thought he could handle them with ease. Besides, Knio could lend him some active assistance, a prospect that caused him to grunt with delight.

Knio and Weeny went on ahead to distract the Yetis while the Wolpertinger and I followed.

We waited a moment, then Weeny looked back round the door. 'No sign of any Yetis,' he said.

It was true: the door of the Zamonium's cabin was not only unguarded but ajar.

'Pity,' said Knio.

Weeny peered inside.

'Nothing there but a lump of muck in a glass case,' he reported.

We stole into the holy of holies. Since the Zamonium had ceased to worry about the four of us, or so it seemed, there was little to prevent us from overpowering the demented stone with ease. The only remaining problem was how to get it up on deck. It would be bound to alert the whole ship as soon as it realized what was afoot, but that was a risk we had to take.

Very cautiously, I tiptoed over to the glass case. Simply grab it and run, that was the plan. The Wolpertinger would run ahead to quell any opposition while I followed with the Zamonium and Knio and Weeny covered our rear.

I took hold of the glass bell jar and drew a deep breath.

Just then, something fastened on my neck and gave it a painful squeeze. It was the Wolpertinger's huge paw.

'Good work, Nalla Hotep,' said the Zamonium in my head.

The Wolpertinger emitted a respectful grunt.

'I've been thinking it over,' said the Zamonium, when the cabin had filled up with grinning Yetis, *'and I've decided to submit you to a test. Could you serve me loyally without being under my direct control? That's the question, and that's why I staged this little charade with the friendly assistance of Nalla Hotep and the Troglotroll.'*

The Troglotroll came in.

'Don't let your eyes deceive you!' he said. 'At first glance I may look like a common Troglotroll, but I'm really an out-and-out traitor, ak-ak-ak!'

'No, you could never be loyal subjects of mine,' the Zamonium went on. *'On the contrary, you'd stab me in the back at the first opportunity. Lucky I don't possess one. A back, I mean.'*

The Yetis laughed mechanically. The Zamonium had probably given them a telepathic order for collective laughter, because they sounded very unamused and didn't know when to stop.

'That's enough!' hissed the Zamonium. The Yetis stopped laughing. 'That alone would be enough to earn you the supreme penalty: a dip with the sharks.'

Knio bared his teeth at me. 'What did I tell you?' he said to the others. 'This fool of a bluebear's nothing but trouble.'

'But . . .'

We pricked up our ears.

'Buuuuuuut . . . In my infinite kindness, which defies comparison with traditional ideas of clemency, I've decided to give you one last chance.'

Who could object to that?

'I'd like to know how good Nightingale's education really is, so here's a proposition for you: if you answer seven – seven! – of my questions you can go free. We'll give you a little boat and release you.'

Knio and Weeny gazed at me hopefully.

'If the bluebear fails to answer my questions, you'll be thrown to the sharks. With musical accompaniment.'

What choice did I have? Besides, the odds could have been worse. Not only was I no fool; I was a graduate of the Nocturnal Academy and carried the encyclopedia in my head. I couldn't conceive of a question I would be unable to answer.

'It's a deal,' I said.

'Very well. First question, subject Nightingalism: What is a Gloomberg Cloud?'

Seven questions

Aha, I used to know that. Never mind: Encyclopedia, please!

Encyclopedia?

Encyclopedia?!

No answer.

No answer at this of all moments, but let's be honest: when had it ever answered at the crucial moment?

It seemed I would have to take the matter in hand myself. After all, I'd learnt it all once upon a time. Let's see if I could still remember it:

'A Gloomberg Cloud is generated by the hydrospectrographic concentration of cosmic darkness from outlying areas of the universe in which there are no constellations. Measuring 89,688,999,453,345,784,002.347 nightingales on the inside and 45,367,205,778,659,010.644 nightingales on the periphery, it is the most powerful form of energy in the known universe and can be controlled only by the correct use of a Nightingalator.'

Phew! Only just made it.

'Hmm... Not bad, discounting that nonsense about the most powerful form of energy in the universe. That's me, understand? Second question, subject Zamonian philosophy: What is Bluddumite Yobbism?'

Encyclopedia?

Encyclopedia? Bluddumite Yobbism, please?

Still nothing. I recalled that Fredda and Qwerty had argued about this branch of philosophy, but it was a long time ago.

'Er...It's a school of philosophy which assumes that no single object implies the existence of any other if viewed with due insensibility. The founder of Bluddumite Yobbism was Professor Yobbo G. Yobb, whose maxim "I ignore you, so ignore me in return" not only constitutes the title of his magnum opus but has rapidly consigned him to oblivion.

'While delivering a lecture on Yobbism at the Cultural Museum in Atlantis, the professor deliberately jostled some members of his audience and was clubbed to death by an infuriated Bluddum.'

Wow! Quite a feat without the encyclopedia.

'Well, well, not bad...Third question, subject Zamonian poetry: How does The Ballad of the Mountain Maggot go?'

That was a trick question, but simple nonetheless. The Zamonium was counting on my having been inattentive in class, like any Zamonian schoolboy, when this boring poem cropped up. He didn't know that I had personally trekked through the Gloombergs with the Mountain Maggot and been compelled to listen to the encyclopedia reciting the poem again and again. I would know it by heart till the day I died.

Give way it must, that iron wall,
and let me through it climb.
I cannot stop to eat it all,
I never have the time.

I bore holes with my fiery breath,
digest the iron with ease
and chew it with my stainless teeth
as if it were but cheese.

I shall skip seventy-four verses rather than alienate the handful of readers who have stayed with me this far, but for the Zamonium's benefit I recited the whole poem perfectly, down to the last quatrain:

The wall of metal melts, and there
a hole comes into sight.
I feel a gentle breath of air
and through the gap streams light.

'Rather monotonously delivered,' the Zamonium said sternly, 'but faultless otherwise. Next question, subject Grailsundian *demonology: What are Nether Zamonian Diabolic Elves, and how many would fit on a pinhead?'*

Not bad. That had for centuries been Grailsundian demonology's pivotal question – the *raison d'être* of that intellectual discipline, in fact. For one thing, the very existence of Diabolic Elves was disputed. For another, they were so infinitely small that, even if they did exist, they defied computation.

Or so the Zamonium thought when it asked me that question. What it did not know (so it certainly didn't know everything) was that Qwerty Uiop and I had debated the matter at length in our spare time at the Nocturnal Academy. One of Nightingale's so-called unperfected patents was the Diabolic Elf microscope, so we borrowed it for use in our demonological field research. The surprising result of our investigations was that Diabolic Elves did indeed exist, almost everywhere and in astronomical numbers. They occupied every crevice in the Gloomberg Mountains, proliferated in Fredda's hair, and were particularly fond of populating pinheads. Thanks to the microscope's complex arrangement of lenses, we were able to study their living habits and make a trailblazing discovery, namely, that they … But that's irrelevant here.

We eventually took the trouble to count how many there were on a pinhead. This was anything but easy because they kept milling around, but Qwerty worked out a computational formula based on their physical density and the number of square micromillimetres covered by a pinhead.

'7,845,689,654,324,567,008,472,373,289,567,827.9,' I replied.

'I'm impressed!' the Zamonium exclaimed. *'I solved that problem by the power of thought alone, but I failed to come up with the 9 after the decimal point.'*

'Diabolic Elves are fissile organisms,' I pontificated. 'For instance, one elf can if necessary divide into ten little elves.'

'*Aha, interesting. Fifth question, subject Nightingalian macrophysics: What does the Septimal Theory state?*'

'The Septimal Theory states that the universe is comprehensible only in terms of the number seven, and only by those possessing seven brains. There are seven elements: fire, water, earth, air, Perponium, Zamonium, and Domesticated Darkness. The universe consists of seven regions: north, south, east, west, before, after, and home. These regions are divisible, in their turn, by the seven elements. If one takes the astral weight of the individual elements and divides them by the septimal mass of the planets and stars present in the seven regions, one arrives at a figure in which sevens alone occur. The Nocturnomathic brain recognizes seven sensations: inquisitiveness, love of darkness, scientific curiosity, the urge to communicate, intrepidity, hunger, and thirst. If one adds together the emanative frequency values recorded by those sensations on the Nightingalian auracardiogram and divides the total by the figure containing all the sevens, the result will be seven.'

'*Correct. Sixth question, subject Nocturnomathic philosophysics.*'

Ugh! Nocturnomathic philosophysics! That was not only the most difficult branch of knowledge in the entire universe but the only one in which I was not overly proficient. A speculative mixture of philosophy and physics, it was really a subject for someone possessing more than one brain.

'*What is knowledge?*'

'Knowledge is night!' The answer burst from me like a bullet from a gun. Man, oh man! It was the only principle of Nocturnomathic philosophysics that had stuck in my mind. Nightingale had bellowed it often enough in class.

'*Most impressive, most impressive. Nightingale left nothing out, it seems. In that case, my final poser shouldn't present you with much of a problem. Question seven, subject dimensional hiatuses: What exactly is . . . genff?*'

Hm, genff. I knew what it smelt like. I knew that it occurred at the entrance to dimensional hiatuses, too, but I didn't know what it was.

'No idea,' I said.

'Come on!' cried Weeny. 'You always know everything.'

Encyclopedia? Genff?

Nothing.

Genff?

Nothing.

Genffgenffgenff?

Still nothing. The same old story, just when I needed the confounded thing.

'Don't let it worry you, youngster,' the Zamonium said consolingly. *'I'd have made you all walk the plank in any case. I'm the Zamonium. I've no heart, no soul. I've even less of a conscience than the Troglotroll.'*

'I doubt that,' the Troglotroll said in a low voice, but I heard him quite distinctly.

'So why should I be bound by sentimental obligations that are detrimental to me? Did you think I had whole ships to give away? How very naïve of you!'

I couldn't repress the thought that the Zamonium was the most abominable creature I'd encountered anywhere in Zamonia in the course of a life that had brought me face to face with plenty of abominable life forms.

'Thanks very much,' said the Zamonium. *'A touching farewell speech.'* And, to the others: *'Bring them on deck. Sentence will be carried out forthwith.'*

The *Moloch* was not, for once, swathed in her usual pall of smoke. The Zamonium had stopped all the engines and summoned his minions on deck, intending the entire crew to witness punishment in good visibility. Two Yetis appeared with the pillar that bore the Zamonium and set it up in a prominent position. A Yeti choir launched into the Zamonian national anthem, except that 'Zamonium' was substituted for 'Zamonia' and sundry other changes had been made to the original words:

All hail to thee, Zamonium,
all-powerful element.
However loathsome thy commands,
we never dare dissent.

The rest of the verses were even worse.
The Yetis removed the tarpaulin covers from some gigantic cannon and fired several pointless salvos in the air.
Then a black plank was manhandled over the rail.
'This may strike you as a bit cheap,' the Zamonium telepathized in our heads, 'but I'm sentimental by nature. We could simply toss you overboard, but I find this more romantic.'
Knio was the first to be hustled out on to the plank. He showed no fear, I'll give him that. Although I couldn't see it from where I stood, I was only too familiar with the sight of the mass of snapping sharks that always seethed around the *Moloch*. To preserve one's composure in the face of that threat was admirable in itself.
'I'll deal with the sharks, by Neptune's trident!' cried Knio. 'And then I'll come back and get you, Zamonium!'
I warmed to Knio for the first time.
'Where are the Voltigorkian Vibrobassists?' grumbled the Zamonium. 'Every execution needs music!'

Three Voltigorks, each of them carrying a vibrobass, were thrust to the fore by Yetis and proceeded to tune their instruments. Weeny gave me a despairing glance. It seemed to be dawning on him that this was a predicament from which no amount of blathering could extricate him. But I was just as short of ideas.

'When I give the word...' snarled the Zamonium.

The Voltigorks struck up a monotonous military march on their vibrobasses.

'...over the side with him!'

Two Yetis prodded Knio to the end of the plank with long, pointed boathooks. He drew a deep breath.

A dog barked.

There weren't any dogs on board the *Moloch*, only Vulpheads or other cross-breeds that had dogs or foxes in their ancestry but were too civilized to bark.

But a dog was definitely barking. A second dog uttered heart-rending howls, a third growled menacingly.

The Yetis looked around, thoroughly disconcerted.

Horses started whinnying, baboons screeching, lions roaring. And still the dogs continued to bark, hundreds of them. The sound was very muffled, as if all these animals were imprisoned in a large sack.

'What's wrong?' demanded the Zamonium. Although unable to hear anything, it had registered the general bewilderment. A Yeti went up to the pillar, bent over the glass case, and telepathically informed the Zamonium of what was happening.

A wind sprang up and chased away the last wisps of smoke. The sky had grown dark, and the ship was hemmed in by fat-bellied storm clouds. We all looked up, for that was where the animal sounds were coming from, far louder even than before.

Trumpeting elephants.

Bellowing buffalo.

Howling wolves.

Hissing crocodiles.

Looming over the *Moloch* was a big, black cloud. No ordinary cloud – at least, not one that kept its due distance from the ship as such meteorological phenomena usually did. No, this one hovered barely fifty feet above the deck. It wasn't condensed rainwater, being too dark and turbulent for that, nor was it smoke, because it maintained its position too steadfastly. Long black streaks seemed to be trying to escape from the vaporous mass and lash out in all directions. As they did so, they divided into ever thinner threads that writhed through the air like snakes. There was an endless succession of sharp reports as if hundreds of heavy rawhide whips were being cracked.

The air itself crackled with pent-up electricity. We could also hear a voice issuing what sounded like a peculiar series of orders.

'Hey! Whoa! Giddy-up! Down you go!'

Everyone on board stared upwards as if hynotized. All interest in the execution had evaporated. The Zamonium was kept informed of developments by the Yeti bending over its glass case.

'Hey! Down you go, I said!'

Slowly, by fits and starts, the black apparition sank still lower. I had never before seen anything as dark except in Professor Nightingale's laboratory.

It consisted, of that I was quite sure, of domesticated, concentrated darkness.

The cloud, which was now lying to starboard, sank so low that one could see its wavering surface.

Situated on top of the billowing black cloud was an intricate structure; more precisely, a little, miniaturized factory of bizarre design such as I had seen once before, but not in daylight: only a Nightingalator looked like that. And above it, strapped to a chair, sat Professor Abdullah Nightingale.

The Nightingalator

He was clearly finding it extremely difficult to keep the thing under control. The cloud bucked like a bronco, bouncing him around in his seat as he desperately manipulated various levers.

'Zamonium!' he yelled. 'You're surrounded! Give up!'

The cloud beneath him reared so violently, it would have thrown him had he not been strapped to his seat.

'*Nightingale!*' hissed the Zamonium. '*So you actually dare to –*'

'It's quite simple,' Nightingale shouted above the din from inside the cloud of darkness. 'Here are my terms. Surrender, and in return I'll destroy you. Refuse, and it'll be all the worse for you. Whoa there!'

He wrenched at the levers and turned a kind of steering wheel. The cloud quietened down a little.

The Zamonium gave a nervous laugh. *'Huh, now you're really scaring me! What is that contraption, one of your unperfected patents?'*

'I did it!' Nightingale cried triumphantly. 'Domesticated darkness! I owe you a debt of gratitude, my boy!' He was now addressing me.

'You were right that time in my laboratory, do you remember? You wondered whether the darkness was still unaccustomed to its new environment, and you hit the nail on the head. It became more and more tractable as time went by. It isn't entirely docile even now, but after all, it *is* the most powerful form of energy in the universe. It needs running in a little more, that's all.'

The cloud neighed and lashed out.

'The animal voices were my idea,' Nightingale explained. 'The noises darkness really makes are utterly intolerable. I've controlled them with the aid of this Nightingalian transformer and converted them into animal cries. Classical music would be another possibility, but I always find it so depressing.'

'I'm still the most powerful form of energy in the universe!' the Zamonium insisted defiantly.

'You're nothing at all!' yelled Nightingale. 'You're alchemically *passé* – just a conjuring trick gone wrong. I've come to consign you to the trash can of history.'

The Zamonium caught on. *'So that's what you're after. You and I, brain against brain.'*

'Seven brains against one,' Nightingale amended. 'You go first.'

(**Incidental remark.** *The following events cannot, unfortunately, be recounted by traditional narrative means. Nightingale and the Zamonium duelled with thoughts. They were no ordinary thoughts, of course, nor were they merely* extraordinary. *To call them brilliant or unique would be a disrespectful understatement. They were the most incredible shafts of wit ever hurled by the shrewdest and most powerful intellects on our planet. The ideas were so complex and abstract, so revolutionary, profound and earth-shaking, that a normal brain would* *at once have become unhinged if compelled to entertain a single one of them.*

Nearly all those present on board the Moloch were shielded from them. The crew were still under the Zamonium's hypnotic spell and could only think what suited it. Knio and Weeny were immune for well-known reasons. I alone had to withstand the full force of those ideas. That I didn't go insane I attribute to having been infected with Nightingale's intelligence bacteria, which had probably created a natural immune system.

To protect my readers I shall reproduce the two adversaries' thoughts in a heavily encrypted form. I advise anyone unwilling to spend the rest of his days in a padded cell not to try to decipher them! I shall disclose this much and no more: they not only posed ultimate questions about the universe but answered them.)

Heavily encrypted version of the telepathic duel fought by Professor Nightingale and the Zamonium:

The Zamonium opened the proceedings.

'▼□◆▲❖⚡◆ ▦❋▷◉□▼❋ ◉❋❖□◇❖●◆ ❖❖◆▥◖❖!,' it thought.
'○◆◉⚡❘❖◉❖■ ●▼❖◢▦○□❖▼▤ ❖⦚❋◉■❖⚡◆●❖✕▯▷◉▥◢◉
◉◉▥◖◢▲☋ ▮□▼◉▥◉❖❖□■◉◉➤ ▶❖❖● ■▷○○❖□❖ □❖◉◉●
◆□◉ □✛❖▦❖■◉ ❖❖▲◉◉⚡□⦚◆!'

'▥▮◆❖□■❖◉!,' Nightingale thought back. '❖◆⦚❖ ●✕▮❖❖➤❖▼
✕▮❖◖ ◉❖■❖⚡●○ □▼◆❖□◉■□▷◉ ❖□▲❖⚡◆ ❖❖◇◉■❖▦⚡■◆
❖◉❖■▼➤▲ ◉❖□◇❖□◢⚡ ⦚◖◢◢ ■▷○◖▦⚡■❖➤ ◉▥❖❖
▦✛❖▦❖!.'

The Zamonium was unimpressed.

'✳□■▷○○■▲○ ◆▼✧✦■❋!!' it replied. '◐▥⚡✳◆◎ ✳◉■▼❋ ✧▨○▢✳▼▤◀ ✸✳◆◎✳⚡□◎♀ ▤▼✳■✳ ■✳▢▼▷◆▲✧✖✧ ◐✳■✧⁚⚡ ◆□✳♀ ■✳⚡✳ ▥▮◀✧✳▢■○◎ ✧■▲□! □▼✳□✳ ●✳■▮ ✳◆✳◎♀■▼!!' The Zamonium laughed triumphantly.

'◆◎⚡✳✧⚡◎ ▥◐ ✖▼✳■¿' asked Nightingale, and promptly came out with the startling answer himself: '▼■⚡◉ ♀◎◎♀⁚▼ ▲⚡♀◎▥◢◎ ◎✳▮▥◐◐ ▮◆□✖◐■✧⚡◆ ⚡□▼✳◆✳⚡✳■ ◉■⁚▥▜◀《▤▤◀◆ ■✳▮✳◎♀■⚡ ⁚◆✳◎♀■✳▼✳ ■○⚡┿◆✳♀ ▲✳▷□✳▥▥⚡ ◐✳◆◎✧□▼⚡⚡⚡ ⚡◎■✳▶ ♀□● ✖⚡┿■✳ ⚡◉⚡◎♀⚡!'

My brain was smoking by now. The duellists' ideas were almost unendurably profound, wide-ranging, and sublime.
I was just wondering how much longer I could stand it when I heard Nightingale's encyclopedia voice in my head.

'Listen, my lad,' it whispered. 'Walk slowly over to the Zamonium, then grab it and hurl it into the midst of the cloud of darkness. Being the most powerful source of strength in the universe, darkness will dispose of the confounded thing. The only trouble is, you mustn't think of what you intend or what you're doing. The Zamonium can't see you, but it can hear you think. I can temporarily distract its attention, but I don't know for how long.'

'◆◎✧⚡■✳⚡◉!' Nightingale bellowed at the Zamonium, to keep it occupied. '■◐✳■✧⚡ ▢◎♀▜■▷○◎◉■✳▶ ○♀✳▼▤▤◀ ◉✳◆◎♀■!'

I don't know what's harder: to think the opposite of what you're doing or do the opposite of what you're thinking. It's particularly hard when the opposite of what you're doing is nothing, or when what you're doing is the opposite of what you ought to be doing. I'll try to rephrase that:

668

I had to spend the whole time thinking of standing still and doing nothing when I was really sneaking up on the Zamonium.

The Yeti guards were temporarily out of action. The Zamonium was too preoccupied with Nightingale to devote any attention to them, so they stood around like deactivated robots, gazing at the cloud of darkness.

Step by step, I drew nearer the Zamonium. I'd had a bright idea: I pictured a little drop of sweat running slowly down my spine while I (in theory) stood still and watched the duel. I positively *became* that drop of sweat, a tiny, salty globule of water threading its way through the fur on my back.

(One little step.)

I trickled over my neck muscles, negotiated two big tufts of fur, and reached the top of my spine.

(Another little step.)

Along the spinal column and down my back.

(Another little step.)

Uh-uh, a hair in the way. I rolled down it but left half my liquid content behind. Bisected, I trickled on.

(Another little step. Almost there now.)

Trickle-trickle ... I'm a bead of sweat ... just a bead of sweat ...

(Another little step. Only a yard to go.)

A bead of sweat... A bead of sweat... A bead of sweat... My brain seized up. I was too agitated to think of a better idea.

(The last little step. I was there at last.)

'Now!' whispered Nightingale. **'Now!'**

'Got you, you goddamned Zamonium!'

The thought that flashed through my mind was as big and bold as that – I couldn't help it. The suppressed desire to convey my sense of triumph to the Zamonium proved too strong for me. It wouldn't have happened if Nightingale hadn't butted in. He'd spoiled my concentration.

The Zamonium reacted promptly. *'Yetis, seize him!'*

The element had analysed our plan like lightning and acted accordingly. *'All ahead full!'*

But I was too close already. I grabbed the glass dome, only to find that it was stuck fast. Simultaneously, five Yetis hurled themselves at me.

At that moment the engines restarted. Dense smoke belched from the funnels. The whole ship gave a violent lurch. The Yetis staggered a little but recovered at once and lunged at me again.

But they'd reckoned without Knio. There was going to be a fight – his Barbaric Hog's brain had grasped that, and he didn't want to stand around in idleness. He leapt off the plank and drove his thick skull into the first Yeti's stomach.

'Give it to him, Knio!' Weeny yelled encouragingly.

Knio caught the Yeti by the foot and whirled him around like a club.

The other Yetis shrank back.

'*Wolpertingers!*' commanded the Zamonium. '*Seize the bluebear!*'

The Wolpertingers on deck awoke from their trance, but the dense smoke made it hard for them at first to get their bearings.

'Professor Nightingale!' I shouted. 'The glass case! I can't get it off!'

'Stand aside!' Nightingale called in his real voice.

I stood aside. The professor's brains snapped and crackled as they had when he opened a can of sardines by willpower alone. The sound was clearly audible above the general commotion, chilling the blood of all who heard it. The glass dome started to vibrate and display hairline fissures. It gave a last, sharp crack, then broke in two.

I seized the Zamonium. It was cold as ice.

'*Nooooo!*' it bellowed in my head. '*I command you to . . .*'

I drew back my arm and hurled the element into the flickering darkness. It is almost impossible, in our inadequate linguistic medium, to describe what happened next. I'll try, but I doubt if I'll do it justice.

The Zamonium disappeared into the pall of darkness like sugar into a cup of strong black coffee. At the same time, the voice in my head rose to a scream of such intensity that I feared my eyes might burst from their sockets. I clamped my forepaws over my ears, but that, of course, was futile.

All the other creatures on board were also stopping their ears. The cloud contracted with a sound like a truckload of bricks falling from the sky.

Then it expanded to ten times its original width, howling like a thousand watchdogs. For a while it retained that shape, a flattened black ball with shafts of lightning flickering over its surface.

At length it abruptly regained its original size and shape. There was a moment's complete silence. The cloud seemed even to absorb the pounding of the *Moloch*'s engines. Then, rolling across the sea, came a cosmic belch such as not even a Megabollogg could have produced.

The scream in our heads died away.

The Zamonium had vanished.

The *Moloch*'s crew staggered around in bewilderment.

The Zamonium's spell was broken.

The professor was riding his Nightingalator like a cowboy on a wild steer. The cloud of darkness was bucking and lashing out in all directions, even more violently and unpredictably than before. Nightingale excitedly manipulated his levers and controls but seemed almost incapable of influencing what was going on beneath him.

'The darkness isn't used to the Zamonium!' he cried. 'It'll take a while, I'm afraid. I can't control it any longer!'

The cloud bucked madly and whinnied like a herd of mustangs. Nightingale spoke as if he had hiccups.

'I d-don't th-think I c-can hold it m-much long...'
The cloud reared up and galloped off with him, zigzagging wildly across the sea like a balloon with air escaping from the neck. Before long, the professor, the Nightingalator and the cloud were just a dwindling black dot on the horizon.

Nightingale had disappeared, but so had the Zamonium. The *Moloch*'s crew were free at last.
Although they still hadn't the faintest idea where or who they were, the situation would probably resolve itself in due course. Knio was still throttling one of the Yetis, who must have been wondering how he'd got into such a situation. I had to haul Knio off him. There was a lot of re-education to be done.

For a start, the engines had to be stopped. The clouds of black smoke added to the confusion and made it no easier to find our bearings. I hurried to one of the engine rooms, but all I encountered there were a few bemused Yetis who were trying to remember their own names.

Stop engines!

The Zamonium had expertly navigated the vessel by remote control throughout her voyages, personally supervising every engine and furnace, piston and propeller. The ship had no captain or experienced officers, just a horde of obedient, unwitting slaves. Without the Zamonium, the crew were completely helpless. The *Moloch*'s machinery was so complex

673

and intricate that I myself would have taken years to learn to operate it. All this dawned on me the moment one of the Yetis in the engine room asked me for my autograph. His last recollection had been of a Duel of Lies I'd fought in the Megathon at Atlantis.

I went back on deck. Our situation was not as critical as all that. We would simply have to wait until the ship's fuel ran out and she stopped of her own accord. Then we could lower some boats and leave the *Moloch* to her fate.

'Did you find the brakes?' asked Weeny.

'The *Moloch* doesn't have any.'

'Pity. Hear that noise?'

I listened. I could hear the throb of the ship's engines, the roar of the furnaces, the hissing of the valves, the bewildered grunts of disorientated Yetis. Yes, and a gurgling sound.

I'd heard it before, but I couldn't think where or when. 'Something's gurgling,' I said.

'And how,' said Weeny. 'No idea what it is, you can't see a thing in this soup, but it's getting louder. Sounds like we're heading straight for it.'

'How about climbing one of the funnels?' Knio suggested.

We looked around for the biggest smokestack not in current use. Welded to the side were some metal rungs that disappeared into the thick of the smoke overhead. Knio and I proceeded to climb them. After a hundred feet or so we couldn't see a thing. The acrid vapour compelled us to shut our eyes and mouths and make our way blindly, mutely, upwards.

Then the smoke thinned. We were some five hundred feet above the surface of the sea. The thick, black carpet of smoke below us conveyed the reassuring but deceptive impression that it would catch us if we fell. Around this carpet, and especially towards the bow, the sea was clearly visible. The gurgling sound was much more distinct up here. I now remembered when I'd heard it before: it was the very first sound I'd heard in the very first of my lives.

We could also see its source now. About ten miles away was a hole in the sea, a circular whirlpool many times the size of the *Moloch*. It was the Malmstrom, the legendary hole in the sea from which the Minipirates had rescued me.

And we were heading towards it at full speed.

From the
'Encyclopedia of Marvels, Life Forms
and Other Phenomena of Zamonia and its Environs'
by Professor Abdullah Nightingale

Malmstrom, The. Highly unpopular with sailors, this marine vortex in the Zamonian Sea north-east of the mainland is a whirlpool covering a surface area of twenty square miles and extending to a depth of twenty-five or thirty miles. At its base the whirlpool disappears into the crater of an extinct marine volcano five miles in diameter.

The Malmstrom is marked on all charts and should be given a wide berth, because anything that gets caught up in it is inexorably sucked down into the depths. Fish and other marine creatures instinctively avoid the whirlpool; sailors, on the other hand, often fall prey to their irrepressible curiosity and venture too close to it.

Little research has been devoted to where the Malmstrom's masses of water go, and this is a natural breeding ground for legends. Folk tales transfigure the volcanic crater into the Gates of Hell, and certain less than reputable scientists claim that the Malmstrom will continue to suck water into the interior of the earth until the latter explodes.

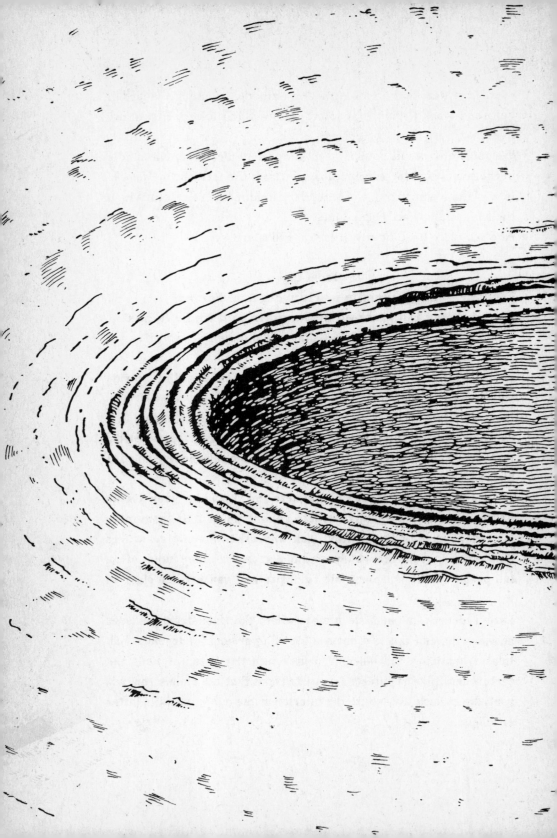

We were on board a huge ship full of helpless creatures, surrounded by sharks and steaming at full speed, with no possibility
of stopping, towards a hole in the sea more than twenty-five miles
deep.

My only assistants were a Gnomelet suffering from memory loss
and a Barbaric Hog without any manners. As for Nightingale, he
was doubtless riding his cloud across the sea in the opposite
direction.

All my other friends were presumably light years away, soaring
through the cosmos in a gigantic spaceship. Meantime, Yetis were
coming up every few minutes and asking me where the men's
room was – and I couldn't even answer that for certain. *That's* what
I call a challenging situation!

'What shall we do now?' asked Weeny.

'How about dying?' I replied.

By now the gurgle of the Malmstrom was drowning every other
sound – we had to shout to make ourselves heard. The others on
board seemed to be slowly recovering their wits, and the brighter
ones among them explained the situation to the more obtuse – not
that this did much good because the *Moloch* was now within a mile
of the whirlpool and beginning to rotate in waltz time. This, in turn,
added to the commotion on deck. It was only now that most of the
crew ran to the rail and grasped the true nature of our predicament.
A babble of cries went up. Many fell to their knees and wept.

The *Moloch* was revolving faster and faster. We had now reached
the edge of the whirlpool, and the thunder of its turbulent waters
drowned the cries of panic. Slowly, the ship's bow crept over the
edge of the Malmstrom.

Knio and Weeny stood at the rail like a pair of stone statues.
The *Moloch*'s hull began to tilt. Another few minutes, and she
would plunge into the depths.

'Only thirteen lives,' I thought to myself.

All of a sudden, swirling gaps appeared at many places in the pall
of smoke overhead. They were made by mighty wings whose beat
was audible even above the general pandemonium.

Hundreds – nay, thousands – of huge birds came swooping through
the gaps in the smoke and landed on deck. Everyone fell silent at
the sight of this army of Reptilian Rescuers.

One of them touched down right in front of me. It was Deus X.
Machina. 'Well,' he croaked, 'seems we've cut it pretty fine,
huh?'

All over the deck, former *Moloch* slaves were clambering aboard   *Abandon ship!*
the pterodactyls, one or two of which had already taken off. The
ship was tilting ominously.

Mac was as imperturbable as ever.

'The Reptilian Rescuers' Retirement Home wasn't my cup of tea.
The inmates sat around all day long, playing blackjack and
bragging about their exploits in the long ago. I hate card games –
in fact I hate company, to be honest. Besides, walls make me
nervous and ceilings are even worse. I didn't need to retire, all I
needed was a decent pair of glasses. Think they suit me?'

He gave me a piercing stare. His eyes were magnified by a huge
pair of glasses the size of soup plates. Their watery whites were
threaded with thick red veins.

'Oh yes,' I said, 'they suit you splendidly.'

'Life is too precious to be left to chance, my boy.'

By now, a third of the *Moloch* was jutting over the edge of the Malmstrom.

'It was developments in Atlantis that alerted us. All the Reptilian Rescuers in the world assembled over the city in the last few days because a major disaster seemed to be imminent. The air was positively crackling with danger. We thought the city would sink. Instead of that, it levitated.'

Mac was having to squawk louder and louder to make himself heard above the gurgle of the whirlpool. I would sooner have listened to his résumé perched on his back and high in the air.

'We didn't have to do a thing. Not a single inhabitant fell off the edge of the city or jumped to his death out of fear or high spirits. Whoever organized the operation did a good job.'

'That was the Invisibles. Listen, Mac, maybe we ought to –'

'So we searched the sea awhile for possible victims of the tidal wave that surged back into the hole Atlantis had left behind, but all we found was that maniac Nightingale on his crazy contraption. He looked as if he planned to win the Derby – kept shouting something about "the *Moloch*" and "north-easterly direction". So we flew here.'

Every rivet in the *Moloch*'s hull was creaking, and bolts were whistling through the air like bullets. The ship was about to plunge bow first into the depths. Knio and Weeny had flown off long ago. Mac and I were the last souls on board.

'Er, Mac, don't be offended, but I really think we ought to be –'

'Of course, my boy. Climb aboard.'

Mac turned round so that I could climb on his back. At that moment, someone shoved me from behind and knocked me sideways. I collided with the rail, hit my head, and lay there slightly stunned for a moment. A hideous figure vaulted on to Mac's back.

It was the Troglotroll.

Before I could say anything, my old friend took off and soared into the air. The Troglotroll gave me a friendly wave as Mac flew away, flapping his mighty wings. Then the pall of smoke swallowed them up.

The *Moloch* plunged into the Malmstrom.

To recapitulate, every member of the *Moloch*'s crew had been rescued except your unfortunate narrator. Every last Reptilian Rescuer was laden with one or more Yetis, Wolpertingers, or other creatures. The Troglotroll was riding on Mac's back, and I knew from my days as a congladiator how well he could imitate voices. It would be child's play for him to convince Mac, for as long as the flight lasted, that he was carrying *me* on his back. So I could expect no help from that quarter.

It would be incorrect to describe the ensuing process as 'falling'. Although the *Moloch* had tipped over bow first, she remained in the water's embrace as the whirlpool sucked her into the depths. The ship went spiralling downwards. Because of her size relative to that of the Malmstrom, this happened so slowly that I had time for a few last reflections on life and fate.

My fate seemed justified.

I had set events in motion. By destroying the Zamonium I had unintentionally sent the ship to the bottom. By taking charge I had become the *Moloch*'s new captain, so to speak. As such, it was my seaman's traditional duty to go down with her. I clung to the rail and did my best to look death in the face. I conceived of that death as resembling one of the black holes Professor Nightingale had cut out of the sky with his Nightingalator. I drew a deep breath.

An unpleasant odour stung my nostrils.

Simultaneously strange yet familiar, the smell was more concentrated than I had ever known it.

It was genff.

There couldn't have been a more inappropriate time, I knew, but I wanted to discover, at long last, what genff was. Death could wait.

Genff. Unwholesome gas given off by → *Time-Snails*. One of the great mysteries of the universe is where time goes to. We all experience the passage of time every day. Seconds, minutes, days, months and years go by, but where to? The answer: time flows away into dimensional hiatuses. If it did not, the earth's atmosphere would fill up with time until it exploded, hence the existence of 'drainpipes' for elapsed time. This function is performed by dimensional hiatuses. But if time simply flowed through these into other dimensions, the latter, too, would explode at some stage. This is where Time-Snails come in. They perch on the edges of dimensional hiatuses, devour the time as it flows into them, and promptly digest it. In so doing they give off an evil-smelling gas known to dimensional hiatus experts as 'genff'. In other words, to put it rather crudely, genff is time metabolized into farts.

This denoted that the Malmstrom was a dimensional hiatus.
And dimensional hiatuses seemed to exert an attraction on me which Qwerty had envied.

Malmstrom, The [cont.]. Some authorities on dimensional hiatuses espouse the view that the Malmstrom is the largest →*Dimensional Hiatus* in the known universe. This assumption is at least supported by the genff readings on its periphery, because no greater concentrations of that sewer gas have been found anywhere else.

Well, although it was scarcely my heart's desire to plunge into a dimensional hiatus with the *Moloch*, I found the prospect of cruising the galaxies on board that huge vessel more attractive than simply drowning.

This also explains why, in a state of Carefree Catalepsy, I had once seen the *Moloch* soaring through space: it was a vision of the future. My predicament had a certain grandeur, I felt. I was not only plunging into the biggest whirlpool in the seven seas with the biggest ship in the contemporary world, but falling through the most gigantic dimensional hiatus in the universe.

Still clinging to the rail, I boldly gazed down into the swirling abyss. My thirteenth life was drawing to a suitably extraordinary close.

But that was not the most extraordinary thing to happen at that moment.

More extraordinary still was the fact that flying towards me from the depths of the Malmstrom, or dimensional hiatus, was a carpet. But even that was not the most extraordinary thing of all.

Why not? Because seated on the carpet was Qwerty Uiop.

A gelatine prince suffering from Carefree Catalepsy

I could tell from afar that Qwerty was still in a state of Carefree Catalepsy. That condition, as I have already described at length, is brought about by falling down a dimensional hiatus. It is a state of temporary imbecility that protects one from the mental overload occasioned by plummeting through time, space, and alien dimensions. So Qwerty completely failed to notice me.

He even seemed unaware of the gigantic *Moloch* plunging past him or, if not, wholly indifferent to the sight.

I had to seize the initiative myself. Qwerty was still several hundred feet below me, and his flight path was quite a long way from the *Moloch*.

I pushed off the deck with my hind legs as hard possible, spread my forelegs, and flew!

Of course, I didn't really fly the way I described it in my fictitious story about the Molehill Volcano, but I could at least influence my trajectory. The unusual wind conditions prevailing inside the whirlpool favoured spiral flight, and I could steer, accelerate and brake by using my paws as ailerons.

I manœuvred myself so that I was right on Qwerty's flight path and steering a collision course. He came racing towards me at breakneck speed.

Two hundred feet to go . . .

Qwerty opened his eyes a little wider. He seemed to be emerging from his Carefree Catalepsy.

A hundred and twenty feet . . .

Qwerty rubbed his eyes. This didn't suit my plans at all. I'd intended to dive beneath him and grab the trailing edge of his carpet. It was precision work. If he woke up and changed course himself, it would be all over.

Fifty feet . . .

Qwerty opened his eyes wide and stared at me in consternation.

Twenty feet . . .

I altered the angle of my paws by a couple of degrees so as to miss the bottom of the carpet by a hair's-breadth.

Ten feet . . .

Qwerty leant forwards in a panic and tugged at the fringe of his carpet. The carpet swerved a few feet, making it impossible for me to reach it.

Our eyes met briefly as we zoomed past each other. I heard him call out 'Bluebear?' in a puzzled voice.

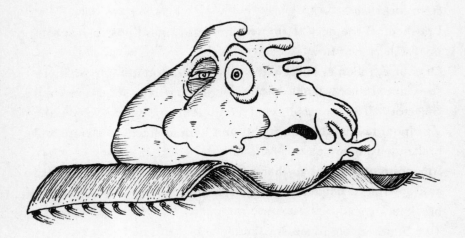

There were still perhaps five hundred feet between me and the black spot at which the whirlpool condensed and became a dimensional hiatus. No matter how hard I flapped my legs, the illusion of being able to fly created by the whirling air currents in the upper regions of the Malmstrom was steadily dispelled the further I fell. On the contrary, I felt I was being sucked downwards with increasing force, as if the power of attraction exerted by the dimensional hiatus were doubling and trebling.

From the
'Encyclopedia of Marvels, Life Forms
and Other Phenomena of Zamonia and its Environs'
by Professor Abdullah Nightingale

Malmstrom, The [cont.]. In the lower regions of the Malmstrom there occurs a rare and curious quirk of physics which does, in fact, conflict with all the laws of nature. For the last five hundred feet the rate of descent doubles every twenty feet, so an object falling into the Malmstrom would crash on the bottom at almost the speed of light. This is thought to be attributable to the Malmstrom's torque and suction power and its affinity with a dimensional hiatus.

I could actually register the fact that my rate of descent was accelerating second by second. The air pressure thrust my ears and my entire face backwards, causing me – without my volition – to bare my teeth and expose my gums like a hungry wolf. My eyes were forced deep into their sockets. Then there was a deafening report that went echoing around the Malmstrom's swirling cauldron.

B-BOOM!

I had just broken the sound barrier. My speed continued to increase at an incredible rate. The air pressure was beginning to tear off tufts of my fur.

B-BOOM!

Another report rang out, just as loud.

And a voice beside me said, 'Hey, Bluebear!'

It was Qwerty and his carpet. He had evidently recovered from his Carefree Catalepsy and turned back.

'I'll come alongside,' he called. 'Then grab me and hang on tight! Getting back is the problem. We'll have to do a half-loop if we don't want to fall into the dimensional hiatus.'

He brought the carpet alongside. I got on behind him and hung on tight.

'We'll make it!' I shouted.

'Let's hope so,' he replied. 'I've never done a half-loop before.'

He bent forward and tugged at the edge of the carpet like a bareback rider hauling on the mane of a wild horse. The carpet reared, described a graceful arc, and shot off in the opposite direction. Below us, the *Moloch* went thundering into the depths of the universe, presumably at the speed of light.

'You see,' I said. 'We made it.'

We flew south to where Atlantis used to be. This, I surmised, was where the Reptilian Rescuers had gone.

Qwerty was only moderately surprised by the amazing co-incidence that had befallen us, but creatures that have just emerged from dimensional hiatuses are hard to impress on principle.

I gave him a brief summary of recent events. Then he told me his own story.

He really had landed in his own dimension after I pushed him into the dimensional hiatus and out of the Gloomberg Mountains, but at a time just preceding his own coronation. Consequently, there were now two Qwerty Uiops in the 2364th Dimension. This led to an absurd situation in which Qwerty had witnessed his own coronation from the crowd. He had previously fetched his autobiographical carpet, rolled it up, and brought it with him. When he saw *me* suddenly appear at the coronation and push his second self into the dimensional hiatus, he tried to hurry to my assistance and fell into it *again* behind me. He managed while falling to unroll his carpet and sit on it. So now a second Qwerty Uiop was tumbling through the dimensional tunnel.

All that remained of Atlantis was a big, circular lagoon, a crater many miles deep that had since filled up with seawater. (Some would later claim that this marked the beginning of Zamonia's descent below the waves – that the Invisibles' removal of Atlantis had pulled the plug on Zamonia, so to speak – but legends tend to oversimplify matters.)

Mac came fluttering excitedly towards us. The Troglotroll had jumped off his back and disappeared into a clump of trees just after he landed. He was outraged by the creature's vile behaviour and found the whole incident most embarrassing.

The other Reptilian Rescuers had already landed beside the lagoon. Most of the *Moloch*'s former slaves had dived into its waters to wash off the stench, the soot, the oil, and every last memory of the iron ship.

It was an exuberant occasion. Washing wasn't customary on the *Moloch*, and many of the ex-slaves had seen no water – except from the deck – throughout their time on board. The Yetis and Wolpertingers were now indulging in childish water fights. I, too, took a dip and immersed myself several times. Then Mac whistled us to supper. The dinosaurs had procured fresh fruit and vegetables from the countryside around – the first decent meal many of the *Moloch*'s crew had enjoyed for years. Tired and hungry, we came ashore.

I noticed, when some of the black bears from the Infurno emerged from the lagoon before me, that they had undergone a surprising change. Their fur was black no longer; it had simply been discoloured by the mingled soot and oil of which big streaks were now floating on the surface of the water. The first bear to wade out ahead of me had rust-red fur like a wild horse from Ireland. The one beside him was a glowing orange. A moss-green bear emerged from the lagoon with a blonde she-bear at his heels. Bears of every colour – yellow, green, red – were drying their fur in the sun on the shores of the lagoon. There were even a few blue ones among them.

From the
'Encyclopedia of Marvels, Life Forms and Other Phenomena of Zamonia and its Environs' by Professor Abdullah Nightingale

Chromobear, The. Zamonian variety of the terrestrial, thick-furred omnivores [*Ursidae*], powerful mammals up to six feet tall and endowed with the power of speech. Peculiar to the chromobear is its individual coloration. Each has coloured fur, but none is quite the same shade. Many chromobears are red, for example, but each displays its own variation of that colour: brick red, copper, vermilion, scarlet, mahogany, poppy, purple, carmine, bronze, pink, ruby, or flamingo red.

There are shades of yellow ranging from lemon to egg yolk and deep orange. A distinction may be drawn between straw-coloured, warm yellow, cobalt yellow, cadmium yellow, pale blond, peroxide blond, auburn, honey-coloured, banana yellow, butter yellow, gold, amber, sulphur yellow, corn-coloured, raw sienna, flaxen, canary yellow, quince yellow, Norselander yellow, lemon-grass yellow, Venetian yellow, pale yellow, dark yellow, and - of course - plain yellow.

The fur of green chromobears ranges in colour from emerald and olive to jade, mignonette, and spinach green. Chromobears may also be yellowish green, blue green, moss green, pine-needle green, grass green, seaweed green, sea green, bottle green, mildew green, grey green, arsenical green, palm-leaf green, pea green, ivy green, and several thousand other shades of green.

Blue chromobears probably display the greatest number of shades: indigo, azure, sapphire blue, cyanine, cobalt, ultramarine, royal blue, pale blue, cerulean blue, submarine blue, billow blue, ice blue, violet, forget-me-not blue, cornflower blue, gentian blue, lavender blue, turquoise, steel blue, plum, dove blue, midnight blue, alga blue, eye blue, blueberry blue, marine blue, china blue, blue-black, and manganese blue.

This brings us to the mixed colours. There are, of course, countless combinations of the above colours which themselves produce new hybrid shades: violet, mauve, heliotrope, lilac, mallow, amethyst, Parma violet, cinnamon, chocolate, minium, chrome orange, salmon, apricot, Florinthian copper, pale lilac, ivory, pearl white, smoke grey, cinnabar, and grey brown. Chromobear fur exists in jewel colours: aquamarine, cyanite, gold beryl, citrine, euclase, chrysoberyl, chrysolite, deman-toid, dioptase, moldavite, lapis lazuli, topaz, zircon, axinite, hyacinth, titanite, spinel, azurite, malachite, coral, carnelian, and meerschaum.

Finally, there are colours that exist only in Zamonia: neoline, cyromian, zamonite, elf white, goblin yellow, zant, opalite, ghoul green, chromolinth, pherm, voltigork, melphine, harbazinth, and

Nightingale black. When mixed with traditional pigments, these produce so-called Zamonian duocolours such as neolite green, neolite yellow, neolite red, cyromian blue, opalite green, pherm yellow, voltigork red, and, of course their hybrid intermediate shades. Chromobears can thus be absolutely any colour. Their sudden extinction - or complete disappearance from Zamonia, whichever - remains a mystery. Although thousands of them formerly inhabited the →*Great Forest*, they vanished overnight.

A festive banquet ensued.

Meanwhile, most of the *Moloch*'s former slaves were getting their memory back. The chromobears among them recalled how their parents had told them that their ancestors used to live in the Great Forest many years ago.

There they had led a peaceful life devoted mainly to bee-keeping. At some stage, however, the peace of the forest was disturbed. It was invaded by a gigantic spider whose unpleasant predatory habits drove the bears out. They retreated to the outskirts of the forest, gave up keeping bees, and took up fishing instead. The land-dwelling bears became seabears. They soon learned how to construct ships of wood, weave nets, and get their food from the sea. Then the Zamonium turned up in the *Moloch* and enslaved them.

Some of the bluebears remembered a young bluebear couple, an ultramarine male and an indigo female, who had thrown their new-born cub over the side to preserve it from a living death aboard the *Moloch*. There is no proof of this, of course, but they may have been my parents, who possibly sacrificed their own lives for the sake of my freedom.

That, at least, would explain my curious obsession with the *Moloch*: I had probably been born on board that monstrous vessel. Only the Zamonium could have supplied precise information on the subject, but it was currently being digested in the intestines of a cloud of darkness.

Many tears were shed that night – tears of joy and sorrow. Some of the *Moloch*'s slaves cursed the Zamonium for having robbed them of so much of their lives. Others boisterously celebrated their new-found freedom. The Reptilian Rescuers stood around, rather at a loss because they found emotional outbursts embarrassing.

We swapped experiences until the small hours. I described my deadly race with the Spiderwitch, which prompted some of the chromobears to consider returning to the Great Forest. I also told of the Invisibles, of events beneath Atlantis and the city's ascent into space. Fortunately, Mac could confirm my account.

It was very late when we all fell into a deep sleep under the watchful gaze of the Reptilian Rescuers.

In the morning, I and a number of bears decided to return to the Great Forest. The Spiderwitch being dead, we planned to fill the forest with life again.

Back to the Great Forest

Others proposed to set off in all directions, and quite a few resolved to settle down beside the lagoon and found a new city there.

Knio and Weeny were keen to make for Baysville and take ship from there. They wanted to get to know other continents – 'to broaden our horizons,' as Weeny phrased it. Qwerty decided to join us in the forest for the time being. He had spent so long in a dimensional hiatus that he wanted to take a breather and work on his autobiographical carpet before falling down another.

The Reptilian Rescuers preferred to transport our Great Forest party across the continent themselves rather than be compelled to save us if we got into another fix.

We crossed Zamonia in a westerly direction via the gap in the Humongous Mountains, which were Bollogg-free once more, and flew over the Demerara Desert. There, from Mac's back, I espied Tornado City whirling along and made out a group of very, very tiny figures on the move: my old friends the Muggs.

We neared our destination a couple of days later. The huge peaks of the Gloomberg Mountains came into view in the distance, and within a few hours we had landed on the edge of the Great Forest. Mac said goodbye without fuss as usual, probably convinced that he would soon have to extricate me from some new predicament or other. Having urged me yet again to adopt a vegetarian diet, he took off. His glasses were so misted up, he nearly flew into a tree.

13½.

My Half-Life
at Peace

We set to work to make the forest habitable again, felling trees, creating sizeable clearings, building log cabins.

We imported some deer and squirrels, for what is a forest without squirrels and deer? We also swept up leaves — masses of leaves. Under my instructions, the cobwebs were removed with the aid of plenty of water. We even found the dead Spiderwitch and burnt it together with its traps. The smoke gave us hallucinations for days aferwards.

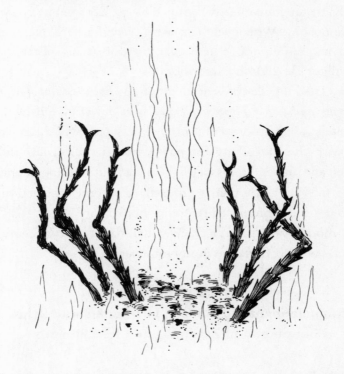

I gradually got to know the other bears. There were several thousand of them, so this took some time. In the process I made the acquaintance of some bears who may or may not have been the brothers and sisters of my late parents and, consequently, my uncles and aunts.

At first we lived in communal buildings of a temporary nature, but as time went by most bear couples built their own little log cabins. Personally, I preferred communal life. After all, what use was a cabin to a lone bear like me?

We erected a small school in which I taught Zamonian dialects, apiculture, Grailsundian demonology, Nightingalism, higher mathematics, and thirty other subjects. Qwerty Uiop also took a teaching post there. In addition to dimensionology, his special field of study, he taught carpet-weaving, biology, Zamonian geography, and philosophy. Whenever he wasn't teaching he liked to climb aboard his carpet and cruise over the forest in solitary state, dreaming of the 2364th Dimension.

One day I had the idea of writing down the *Encyclopedia of Marvels, Life Forms and Other Phenomena of Zamonia and its Environs*. Unfortunately, my memories of it proved very patchy. I thumped my brow with the flat of my forepaws, tried to recall all kinds of subjects, and cursed Professor Nightingale, but nothing happened. 'What's missing,' I thought to myself, 'are some instructions on how to use the confounded reference book.'

Instructions for use

At that moment there was a crackle of electricity between my ears and some writing flared up in my mind's eye:

How to use the
'Encyclopedia of Marvels, Life Forms and Other Phenomena of Zamonia and its Environs'

1. Ensure that the encyclopedia is correctly plugged into your synapses.

2. Should general problems of recall arise [illegibility, mirror-image print, etc.], this may be attributable to circulatory disturbances in your brain. If so, kindly consult your general practitioner.

698

3. If, instead of information from the encyclopedia, you receive instructions from another dimension, signals from outer space, or the voice of your late lamented grandfather, consult a doctor at once.

4. To access an article in the 'Marvels' section, kindly grasp your right ear lobe with your left hand and spell out the requisite headword, loudly and correctly.

5. To access an article in the 'Life Forms' section, grasp your left ear lobe with your right hand and spell out the requisite headword.

6. To access an article in the 'Phenomena' section, cross your hands, grasp both ear lobes, and spell out the requisite headword in reverse.

7. In the event of malfunctions or unpleasant side effects, kindly contact Professor Abdullah Nightingale, c/o The Nocturnal Academy, Gloomberg Mountains, West Zamonia.

So there *were* some instructions – I had simply neglected to ask for them!
I devoted nearly all my time in the next few months to writing down my mental encyclopedia. Then I made my pupils copy it out too, and it became compulsory reading at the chromobears' school.

I often undertook solitary excursions into the forest to survey it and identify its flora. During these walks I also pondered the constitution I proposed to draft for the chromobear colony. Certain things simply had to be legally laid down, for instance an outright ban on spiders in the Great Forest, the erection of danger signs beside dimensional hiatuses, and a fair division of labour where leaf clearance, bee-keeping and log cabin maintenance were concerned.

I revisit the forest glade

On one of my walks I came to the spot where my adventure with the Spiderwitch had begun. The clearing was still there, and I shuddered at the recollection although the scene was bathed in warm evening sunlight, just as it had been then. I suddenly thought of something I'd been trying to formulate for ages: the first article of our new constitution: 'All chromobears are created unequal,' it ran. 'They can be yellow and red, green and blue, violet, zamonite and opalite...'

At that moment I heard a delightful voice humming a tune that sounded familiar – yes, and I knew the voice as well. Seated in the tall grass of the clearing was one of the young she-bears who roamed the woods in search of mushrooms and wild honey. I had never seen her before, yet I knew her better than any other member of the chromobear community.

She looked exactly like the girl in my dream.

What's more, she was reading Professor Abdullah Nightingale's *Encyclopedia of Marvels, Life Forms and Other Phenomena of Zamonia and its Environs*.

Avriel

I shall draw a veil over the rest. The half-life I spent in the Great Forest with the chromobears and the girl bear – whose name, by the way, was Avriel – is something I prefer to keep to myself. Suffice it to say that I built a log cabin for Avriel and me just like the one in my dream. Avriel planted a little flower and vegetable garden, and we dug a little fish pond and installed a beehive. I also

700

made sure there were always a few fresh dumplings on the kitchen stove in a sauce I reconstituted from memory. It may have been a trifle superstitious of me, but I felt sure fortune would continue to smile on us for as long as our saucepan contained a few dumplings.

Traders from all over Zamonia came to the Great Forest to barter with us. Some of them settled down and formed small village communities. One group of chromobears founded a colony outside the forest, right beside the sea. There they devoted themselves to fishing and boat-building.

The Great Forest soon resumed its status as one of Zamonia's leading tourist attractions. It was popular on account of its romantic country inns, which were frequented by the creatures of the forest and run by chromobears who cooked like a dream. At the school, in addition to my regular classes, I gave cookery lessons in which I passed on the tips I'd acquired from Nabab Yeo. No hotel menu was complete without my 'Pizza Sandwich à la Bluebear'.

Visitors also enjoyed visiting the bee farms, where they could buy the most delicious honey in the world. The Great Forest yielded vast quantities of honey because no insects had ventured into it for so long that the flowers were brimming with the finest nectar. No more industrious or amiable bees could be found anywhere in Zamonia. 'Avriel's Vintage' was one of the most popular brands, closely followed by 'Spider Goo', a blended honey particularly favoured by children because of its rather spooky name.

One evening, Avriel and I went walking on the edge of the forest near the sea, where the *Moloch* had long ago put in to enslave the chromobears.

Although an icy breeze was blowing, the sea was calm and the sky so cloudless that one could look deep into space. Glittering out there was a star that differed from all the rest. It was not only new; it turned up in a different place every night, which meant it was in motion. But it didn't move in a straight line like a comet or some other familiar celestial body; it seemed to be steering a zigzag course. The star sparkled with every imaginable colour, like a big city at night. It was Atlantis, soaring through space!

I hugged Avriel tight to shield her from the cold and drew in great gulps of sea air. Borne on the sea breeze was a familiar scent reminiscent of distant bonfire smoke mingled with a hint of cinnamon. That, as I have already mentioned, is the smell of adventure.

'We could always try our luck elsewhere,' I said.

'But not now,' Avriel replied.

And we walked back into the sheltering forest.

Life is short, they say.

A matter of opinion, say I. Some lives are short, others long, and many are middling.

Besides, I still had another thirteen-and-a-half to go.

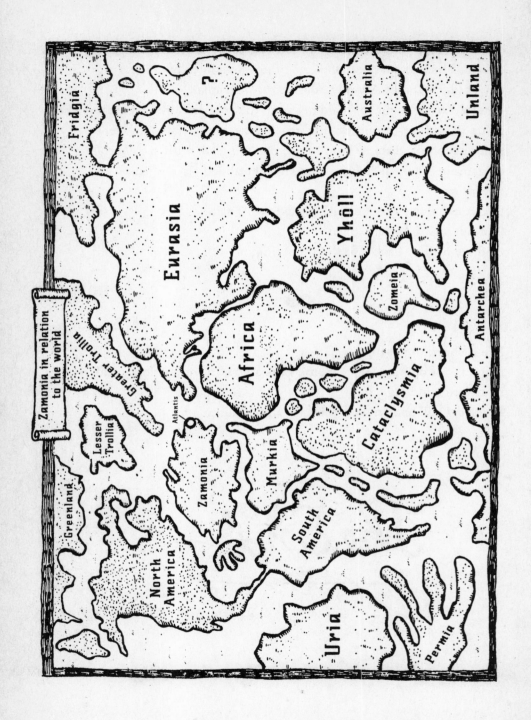

Zamonia in relation to the world

Friðgia

Umland

Australia

Eurasia

Yhôll

Zomeia

Greater Trollia

Africa

Antarchea

Cataclysmia

Atlantis

Lesser Trollia

Greenland

Zamonia

Murkia

South America

North America

Uria

Permia